No Place For A Woman

By the same author

Waiting in the Wings

Kiss & Tell

Such a Perfect Sister

Some Kind of Hero

Goodbye, Ruby Tuesday

No Place For A Woman

DONNA HAY

First published in Great Britain in 2006 by Orion,
an imprint of the Orion Publishing Group Ltd.

3 5 7 9 10 8 6 4 2

A CIP catalogue record for this book is available from the British Library.

ISBN-13 (hardback) 978 0 75285 998 9
ISBN-13 (trade paperback)) 978 0 75286 927 8
ISBN-10 (hardback) 0 75285 998 6
ISBN-10 (trade paperback) 0 75286 927 2

Typeset at The Spartan Press Ltd,
Lymington, Hants

Printed in Great Britain by
Clays Ltd, St Ives plc

The Orion Publishing Group's policy is to use papers that are natural, renewable and recyclable products and made from wood grown in sustainable forests. The logging and manufacturing processes are expected to conform to the environmental regulations of the country of origin.

The Orion Publishing Group Ltd
Orion House
5 Upper St Martin's Lane
London WC2H 9EA

www.orionbooks.co.uk

To June Smith-Sheppard
Always my friend and always there for me
no matter how many months go by.

Lots of people have given me help and advice on this book. I would particularly like to thank Women in Manual Trades for putting me in touch with several women builders, and Richard Fothergill, aka Dickie the Brickie, for his invaluable insight into life on a building site (and for explaining what a putlog hole was).

I would also like to thank Dr Andy Millman for his time and expertise. His medical advice was spot-on, and any mistakes are entirely mine. I realise I kept my 'patient' in hospital far longer than was medically necessary, but it was integral to the plot!

As ever, I must thank my agent Sarah Molloy and everyone at Orion for their help and encouragement. I am particularly grateful to Jane Wood for her excellent editorial guidance (even if we do differ in our definition of the word 'tweaking'), to Gaby Young for setting up the publicity, and to the whole sales team for being so enthusiastic and working so hard on my behalf. I would especially like to thank Meirion and Linda for a memorable two days in Guernsey. Sorry I didn't behave like a proper, grown-up author, but I don't get out much.

Finally, my love as always to my husband Ken and daughter Harriet. While everyone else only sees the finished result of a published book, they have to live through months of bad moods and domestic mayhem while it's being written. I don't know how they put up with me, but I'm glad they do.

Chapter 1

'What do you call this?' Joe Delaney looked down at his breakfast in disgust.

'Muesli. It's good for you.'

'Looks like budgie food to me. Hardly a proper breakfast for a working man, is it?'

'You know what the doctor said. No more fry-ups.'

'Flaming doctors! What do they know?' Joe picked up his spoon and prodded at the cereal.

'They know you've got angina. And they also know you'll have a heart attack before you're sixty if you don't start looking after yourself.'

'Rubbish, I'm as fit as I ever was.'

Finn looked at her father's broad-shouldered bulk. His face was lined and his hair had turned to grey a long time ago, but he was still the same big, dependable man she'd known for twenty-six years. And he refused to admit he couldn't go on for ever.

'All the same, it wouldn't hurt you to listen to someone's advice for once in your life.'

'That's good, coming from you. You're as pig-headed as anyone.'

'And we all know where I get it from, don't we?' Finn half-heartedly tackled her own cereal. Her dad was right; it *was* budgie food. Her stomach rumbled for bacon, eggs and a greasy helping of fried bread, but she didn't want to set a bad example. 'So what have you got planned for today?'

'Not a lot. Just a kitchen to finish, and a garden wall to do.

Ciaran can take care of that. I've asked him to stop off at the builders' merchants and pick up the bricks.'

You'll be lucky, Finn thought. 'What about the Stephensons' extension?'

'They've been having another think.' He rolled his eyes. Finn knew this job was becoming the bane of his life. Marcus Stephenson was an extremely picky client who kept changing his mind about what he wanted, depending on which architectural magazine he picked up. If the job hadn't been worth a lot of money, she had a feeling her father would have downed tools a long time ago.

'What is it now?'

'Oh, not much. They're only talking about making it *two* storeys now. They thought they might as well, while they're at it.'

'But you've already put the foundations in, haven't you?'

'Twice. And I spent nearly two days moving a drain to the other end of the garden, before they decided they wanted to turn the whole thing round, "so it catches the evening sun".' He shook his head.

'You're going to have to make them deeper,' Finn said. 'And that's not going to be so easy in that soil—'

'Well, it's got to go back to the planners first,' Joe interrupted. 'That'll take a few weeks. I daresay they'll have changed their minds again by then.' He looked at his watch. 'Where's Ciaran? He should be here with the van by now.'

Finn understood the unspoken message. Joe Delaney hated discussing work with her. 'Since when did Ciaran ever turn up on time for anything, unless there's something in it for him?'

'Now, Finnuala, don't talk about your brother like that.'

'But he's always letting you down. How often does he turn up late for work?'

'He can't help it. He's got a family, responsibilities—'

'That's a joke. You know as well as I do he spends more time with his mates than with Mel and the baby. God knows what they get up to.' In fact, she did know, but she didn't want to tell her father. That really would send Joe Delaney into an early grave.

'What do you want me to do, sack him?'

'That's what most people would do.'

'I can't run the business on my own, can I?'

'So take on someone else.'

'This is a family business. And since Ciaran's the only son I've got, it looks like I'm stuck with him, doesn't it?'

'He might be your only son but he isn't your only family.' Finn said quietly.

Joe sighed. 'Not again! We've already been through this a million times, Finnuala.'

'But it makes sense, doesn't it? You've always said you want the business to stay in the family. And I'm willing to do it, unlike Ciaran—'

'The building trade is no place for a woman, Finnuala. You don't know what it's like. It's dirty, heavy work. You're out in all weathers. And the lads on site use the kind of language I wouldn't want you to hear.'

'Don't you think I know all that? I practically grew up on a building site, remember?' Right until she'd started school, and all through every holiday she'd followed her father around as he worked. She had to, as he was a single parent and there was no one else to look after her, but she didn't mind. She'd play in the sand, or build with off-cut bricks. Sometimes Joe would push her around in the wheelbarrow, her legs swinging over the side. She'd wear a hard hat stuffed with newspapers to stop it slipping down over her ears.

At other times she would just watch him, fascinated by his skill and speed as he made a wall grow, every brick neat and level, or slicked plaster on to bare brickwork like pink icing, leaving it smooth and flat. As she got older he would occasionally allow her to help him mix mortar or check levels. By the time she was eleven she could accurately calculate how many bricks it would take to finish a wall, and knew what kind of timber should be used for different jobs.

And what was her big brother doing all this time? Out with his friends, getting drunk and stealing cigarettes from shops.

'You're better off where you are,' Joe said firmly. 'What's the matter, don't you like being a hairdresser?'

Finn looked down at her untouched bowl of cereal. 'Of course,' she muttered.

'There you are, then.' Seeing his daughter's sulky face, Joe relented and added, 'Look, if you really want to help me you can always type up some invoices.'

'I'm not a typist!'

'You're not a builder, either.'

Finn glared at him. *That's what you think.*

But there was no point arguing. Her father was right, they'd been through it a million times. And he always refused to budge. She picked up her mug and slurped her tea defiantly.

Joe frowned. 'Finnuala! Do you have to do that? When are you going to start acting like a lady?'

'Never,' Finn said. 'Sorry to disappoint you.'

She said it sarcastically, but deep down she meant it. Her father wanted nothing more than to see her wearing make-up and girly clothes. But instead he'd ended up with a stroppy twenty-six-year-old who kept her dark hair short and lived in jeans. Sometimes, when he looked at her, she could almost see him wondering where he'd gone wrong.

She hadn't even given any thought to being a girl until she was six years old, when she'd badly wanted a Tonka truck for her birthday. Her father had bought her a baby doll that wet itself and cried. It had lasted two days before Finn swapped it for an Action Man belonging to her friend's brother.

Joe finally gave up waiting for Ciaran and set off for work. Finn followed him to the door. 'What about your breakfast? You've hardly touched your muesli.'

'I'll get something on the way.'

He'd be stopping off at the café on the corner for a bacon sandwich, but she couldn't blame him: she fancied one herself.

She was rinsing their breakfast dishes under the tap when her mobile phone rang. It was Ciaran.

'Has he gone?' he asked.

'You've just missed him.'

'Thank God for that.'

'He was expecting you to pick him up. With that load of bricks you were supposed to get from the builders' merchants last night.' There was an ominous silence. 'You did remember, didn't you?'

'Damn. I knew there was something.'

'Ciaran!'

'Look, I had a lot on my mind, OK? I had some business to sort out.'

No prizes for guessing what kind of business it was. Shady, criminal business. 'You're so unreliable. You know Dad depends on you. Why do you keep letting him down?'

'I told you, I had to deal with something. Which is why I'm ringing. I don't suppose . . .'

Finn recognized the wheedling tone in his voice. Her hand tightened on the phone. 'What is it now?'

'The thing is, I had to pay this bloke back some money I owed him and it's left me a bit short—'

'How did I know that was coming?' Finn sighed.

'I just wondered if you could . . . you know.' In the background she could hear a radio playing, drowning out the sound of a wailing baby.

'Why should I keep bailing you out? You still owe me twenty from last week.'

'I know, and I wouldn't ask, but it's for the baby. We've run out of nappies and Mel doesn't get her child benefit until Monday.'

'You should have thought of that before you went off gambling with your mates, shouldn't you?'

'Who said anything about gambling?'

'Ciaran, it's *always* gambling.' He lost every penny he had to poker or the horses. He'd bet on anything. 'The trouble is, you're always losing.'

'I don't know why you're acting so high and mighty.' Ciaran's tone changed. 'You're not exactly whiter than white yourself, remember?'

'What's that supposed to mean?'

'I mean, maybe you'd better be a bit nicer to me if you don't want Dad to find out *your* little secret.'

Finn felt herself grow hot. 'Are you blackmailing me?'

'I need the money, sis.'

'So go ahead. Tell him. I don't care.'

'Are you sure about that? I don't suppose he'd be too pleased if he found out what his little girl was up to behind his back?'

There was a moment's silence. 'How much do you want?'

'Fifty quid should do it.'

'Fifty! You're joking, aren't you?' She heard the baby screaming louder and Ciaran's girlfriend Mel trying to shush him. 'I've only got thirty in my purse. You'll have to make do with that. I expect you can buy a packet of nappies with that, can't you?'

He sighed. 'I suppose it'll have to do. I'll come round and pick it up.'

'No, I'm going to work. I'll leave it under the stone by the front door. And I want it back the minute you get paid. I'm not made of money.'

'No,' Ciaran agreed seriously. 'I expect you need all your cash for all those beauty college courses you keep doing. What have you told him you're doing now?'

'Advanced nail techniques.'

'Nail techniques, eh?' Ciaran chuckled. 'I don't know how you think them up.'

'Lying must run in the family,' she snapped, and put the phone down.

It wasn't fair. Ciaran had all the chances she would have loved and he squandered them. He wasn't interested in following in their father's footsteps or taking on the family business. All he wanted was to make a fast buck from gambling or petty crime.

Sometimes she was tempted to tell her father exactly what his precious son got up to. But he'd only worry and his health couldn't take any more stress. Besides, Joe Delaney was no fool. He must know how little interest Ciaran had in the building trade. And yet he carried on, dragging him along behind him. Because anything was better than taking her on instead.

She glanced at the photo of her mother on the mantelpiece, one of the few her father put on show. Ciaran was a grinning toddler, sitting between his smiling parents on a family picnic. There were no pictures of Finn and her mother. Finnuala Delaney had died of a haemorrhage hours after giving birth to her. She was twenty-six, the same age her daughter was now. Finn couldn't look at that pretty, laughing face without feeling guilty.

She tugged at her short hair, so different from her mother's tumbling dark locks. Would she have turned out differently if her mother had lived? Maybe she wouldn't have ended up such a tomboy. But growing up in a house full of men, she didn't have much choice.

She drove her ageing Fiat to work. As she passed her father's yard she looked up at the painted sign over the gate: 'Delaney and Son'. No sign of the son, though. Finn caught a glimpse of her father loading timber on to their battered old pick-up and felt a stab of anger. Joe was in his late fifties now; he should be thinking about taking it easy, not doing all the donkey work. Especially with his angina. He'd tried to play down the last attack, but Finn still worried for him.

Perhaps it wouldn't be for much longer, she thought. Her father had recently bought a small plot of land from a farmer several miles outside the city. Once the planning permission came through, he was going to build a few houses and sell them on. He wouldn't make a fortune, but it would be enough for him to retire comfortably. Then Ciaran would take over the business. Not that there would be much of a business left after her brother got hold of it. He'd probably gamble it all away in six months.

She headed out of York and joined the motorway to Leeds, stopping off at a supermarket car park on the way. She grabbed her bag from the boot and headed for the toilets. Ten minutes later she emerged, transformed. She'd changed out of her neat skirt and blouse into jeans, fleece, high-visibility jacket and workboots. In one hand she held her bag of tools, in the other her hard hat.

She was ready for work.

She smiled, wondering what her father would make of it if he could see her now. He probably wouldn't believe she'd kept up this double life for so long, pretending to go to a salon when really she spent her days grafting on a building site. Just as he probably wouldn't believe that she'd actually managed to qualify in the trade as a bricklayer and joiner.

Sometimes she was tempted to tell him, particularly when he was sounding off about how the building trade was no place for a woman. But she was worried he'd be more furious than proud. Furious that she'd lied to him and gone behind his back – and that she hadn't turned into the lady he wanted her to be.

She'd tried, she really had. But after a couple of dead-end jobs she realized she wasn't cut out for being cooped up in an office. Building was in her blood and she could never settle for anything else, whether her father approved or not.

She'd gone to college to learn construction, although from her first day she already knew more than all the lads on her course, and almost as much as some of the tutors. She was keen to learn, and far more motivated than her fellow students, most of whom had drifted into the course after flunking their GCSEs. So it infuriated her when they were snapped up by local firms and she was left behind.

In the end one of the tutors on the course, George Dunn, gave her the chance she needed. He managed sites all over the county, and always took Finn with him in his regular gang of brickies and joiners. For the past two months they'd been working for a company called Tates, building a development of smart executive houses on the site of a former mill in the hills of West Yorkshire.

Just before she reached the site, she stopped at some traffic lights and glanced in the rear-view mirror, then reached into her pocket for a tissue and scrubbed off her lipstick. The men would have a field day if they caught her wearing it. It had taken her long enough to be accepted as one of the lads; the last thing she wanted to do was draw attention to the fact that she wasn't.

She passed through the metal gates, past the sign proclaiming 'Windmill Meadows – luxury homes coming soon', and past the Portakabin site office. There was no one around. Her car bumped over the deeply rutted ground, grooved with the tracks from the JCBs and lorries that ran in and out of the site.

She pulled up in the patch of ground that served as a car park, alongside a gleaming black Saab she'd never seen before. It was a cold November day, and the biting wind carried the smell of bonfires from last night's Guy Fawkes celebrations.

She zipped up her fleece and headed to where a bunch of the lads were gathered around one of the half-built houses, surrounded by ramparts of scaffolding. They stood in a grim-faced circle, grumbling into their steaming mugs of tea.

'What's this? A mother's meeting?' she grinned.

'Just checking out the new arrivals.' Rob, one of the other brickies, nodded towards the far side of the site, where another group of men stood huddled in the shelter of the workers' hut, another Portakabin.

'Has George taken on some new lads?'

'George has gone. He got his marching orders this morning.'

'Why?' Finn stared at Rob, shocked. George Dunn was a great site manager, very conscientious and good at his job. He knew what he was doing, and made sure everyone else did, too. There was never anyone standing idle on the site. And she had reason to be grateful to him personally, since he'd stuck his neck out and given her a job.

'We're not working fast enough, apparently. They want this place finished quickly so they've ditched him and brought in a new manager. And *he's* brought his A-team.' Rob nodded over at the other men. 'They look like a right bunch of cowboys to me.'

'C-cowboys,' Ivan agreed. He was a small, wiry man, with dark eyes that filled with tears whenever he talked about his wife and children back home in Romania. George had taken him on when he'd first arrived in England to find work, and now he laboured for Finn and Rob, mixing mortar and hefting around wheelbarrows of bricks. He was a little slow at understanding the others' broad Yorkshire accents, and embarrassed about his stammer and poor English, but he was a very hard worker, He'd also become very attached to Finn, once he'd got over his shock at seeing a woman on a building site.

'What about us?' Finn asked. George had taken them all on, so if he went, they might go, too. And with Christmas just a few weeks away, the last thing she needed was to be out of a job.

'They should keep us on. I reckon that lot will need all the help they can get.' Rob eyed them grimly.

They were interrupted by a stranger striding towards them. He was short and sandy-haired with a weightlifter's body and lowered brows.

'When you lot have finished your tea-break, the new boss would like a meeting.' His eyes skimmed the circle and landed on Finn. 'Who the hell are you?'

'My name's Finn Delaney. I work here.'

His brows lifted a fraction. 'You're having a laugh, aren't you?'

The others examined the mud on their boots. But Finn remained calm. 'Do I look as if I'm laughing?'

'Christ. No wonder the site's in such a mess.' The man walked off, shaking his head. Finn glanced around at the others, who all seemed embarrassed. They knew as well as she did that she'd had exactly the same reaction from them when she first started. It had taken her a long time to win them round and prove she could do the job; now she would have to start all over again.

'Who was that?'

'His name's Jason. He's the new ganger.' No wonder Rob looked put out. He'd been unofficial head man of their team. Now Jason had been brought in above him.

Their new boss was waiting for them outside the site office. Rob sucked in his breath through gritted teeth when he saw him. 'Bloody hell, now we're in trouble.'

'Do you know him?' Finn asked.

'Neil Tate. The gaffer's son, no less.'

Finn studied Neil from the back of the crowd. His sleek dark hair and immaculate suit stood out among the mud-spattered fleeces and woolly hats surrounding him. He seemed restless with energy, and his sharp gaze swept the group.

'I won't waste time,' he rapped out. 'This site is a shambles. The work is going too slowly and costing far too much.' There was a murmur of disagreement. 'I'm not here to argue with you, I'm here to tell you how it's going to be. The sales team will be here next month, and I want some houses for them to sell, OK?' His gaze slid past Finn, did a double-take and then moved on again. 'From now on, I want four houses finished a week.' Finn and Rob looked at each other. They were working flat out to build two a week. 'Don't worry, I'm not asking you lot to put yourselves out,' he went on. 'As you can see, I've brought in some extra help.'

'Where did he dig that lot up? Wakefield jail?' Rob muttered.

Finn studied the assembled crew of new men. With their motley collection of tattoos, baseball caps and body piercings, they looked like Ciaran's friends.

'How can we d-do this?' Ivan looked perplexed. The meeting had just ended.

'We can't,' Finn said. 'Not unless we start cutting corners.'

'I reckon that's what he wants,' Rob said. 'Just throw the houses up as cheap and quick as we can, then sell them. And never mind if they all start leaking in three months.'

Ivan shook his head. 'B-but they cost so much.'

'Just because Tates charge top whack for them doesn't mean they're worth it,' Rob said.

Finn was about to follow them back to work but Jason stopped her.

'Not you, Princess. I want you to work with some of the new lads. Show them the ropes, like.' His smile had a nasty edge.

Rob stepped in. 'She's on my team,' he said, but Jason shook his head.

'Not any more. Unless you want to take it up with Mr Tate?'

As the two men squared up to each other, Finn put her hand on Rob's arm. 'It's OK, I don't mind.' She smiled sweetly at Jason. 'I'm sure I can handle it.'

But she felt her courage failing when she approached her new workmates. She was used to rough-and-ready builders, but this lot looked downright mean.

'Meet your new brickie,' Jason said.

They all glared at her. Finn stood her ground and smiled back, although she wanted to run away.

'Are they taking the piss or what?' one of them grunted. 'We need someone to put up walls, not bloody curtains!'

The others laughed. Finn burned inwardly but kept quiet. They weren't saying anything she hadn't heard before. Let them have their fun and then she'd show them what she could do.

Squaring her shoulders, she said to Jason, 'What do you want me to do first?'

They all exchanged looks. 'Now there's a question,' one of them sniggered.

'Not sure you'd want me to answer that one, love,' said another, lazily scratching the expanse of walrus belly that gaped between his low-slung jeans and shrunken jumper.

Finn forced herself not to snap back the stinging retort that sprang to her mind. They were just schoolboys, she reminded herself. It wasn't worth losing her temper over such pathetic kids.

'You could go down to the caff and fetch the butties,' Jason suggested.

All eyes turned to her, waiting for her to protest.

She smiled. 'Fine. What does everyone want?'

Jason looked deflated. 'You don't mind?'

'No way. I could murder a bacon buttie myself.' She looked around. Her new workmates studied the ground with brow-furrowing concentration as they mumbled their orders. She'd obviously spoiled their fun. And she hadn't finished with them yet.

Bernie at the café on the corner grinned at her when she placed her order. 'Are you sure about this?' he said.

'Very sure.' Finn smiled back and held out her hand. 'Mustard, please.'

'But I've already put a load on, just like you said.'

'I think they could do with some more.'

He handed her the yellow plastic bottle. 'You do realize they won't be able to speak for a fortnight?'

'With any luck,' she said as she carefully unwrapped the sandwiches and covered each bacon rasher thickly in mustard. Then she wouldn't have to listen to their stupid, smutty comments.

It took precisely thirteen seconds for her protest to take effect.

'What the – Jesus!' Jason spat it out and reached for his Coke can. His face was puce, although whether that was because of rage or mustard Finn wasn't sure.

'Is there a problem?' She gazed at him wide-eyed. 'Mine seems to be fine.'

Jason tossed his sandwich away in disgust. Finn tried not to smile as she took a bite out of hers. That was the last time they would ever send her on the buttie run. Rob and the rest of the lads had tried the same thing when she first started work on the site. But after one of her bacon and mustard specials, they'd suddenly discovered they preferred to get their own.

She may have proved her point, but it didn't make her any friends. Unlike Rob and the others, her new workmates didn't seem to have a sense of humour. Unless it was a really crude one. Finn was used to Page Three calendars hung up in the site office, and usually managed to laugh off the sexist remarks. But Jason and his gang deliberately went out of their way to be offensive, cracking disgusting jokes and making vile remarks about women whenever she was in earshot.

By the time she got home her shoulders were aching from the tension of stopping herself from hitting someone. The traffic was bad all the way home and she was horrified to see her father's pick-up already parked in the drive. Finn pulled up next to it, panicking that she hadn't had time to change and was still in her work clothes. Her father might not be an expert, but even he wouldn't believe that spattered jeans and mud-caked boots were a new fashion look.

He was in the kitchen when she crept in. The door was ajar and she could see him at the table, bent over some paperwork. She pulled off her workboots and sneaked upstairs, carrying them in her hand.

'Is that you, Finnuala?' he called out when she was halfway up the stairs. She froze.

'Won't be a minute, Dad.' She ran up the stairs, hoping he wouldn't come into the hall. In her bedroom, she pulled off her clothes and changed back into the skirt and blouse she'd been wearing that morning. Then she dragged a brush through her hair to get rid of the cement dust and hurried downstairs again.

Joe Delaney looked tired as he sat at the table, sorting through the post.

'Anything interesting?' Finn asked, opening the fridge to see what they could have for dinner.

'You could say that. I've had an offer for the land.'

Finn looked over the fridge door at him. 'Who from?'

'Doesn't say. The letter's from some land agents. Acting for an unnamed buyer, it says here.'

'Sounds very mysterious.' Finn emerged from the fridge with a pack of pork chops and a bag of frozen mixed veg. She nudged the door closed with her foot. 'What makes them think you want to sell?'

'God knows. Maybe it's just something they do, putting in offers here and there.' Joe frowned down at the letter. 'Seems a bit odd, though.'

'You're not thinking of selling, are you?'

'I wasn't. But this is a very good offer. I could make quite a bit of money.' He looked thoughtful.

'You'll make even more if you build those houses like you'd planned,' Finn pointed out. 'That land's your retirement fund, don't forget.'

'Anyone home?' Her brother Ciaran stuck his head round the door. Tall and lanky, he towered over Finn. He had his parents' dark Irish colouring, a lopsided smile and an unshakeable belief that women found him irresistible. Which, for some reason, a lot of them did.

Strangely, his charm never worked on his sister. 'What do you want?' Finn said. Then, before he could reply, she added, 'You can't stay for dinner.'

'And why would I want to?' He looked at the packets in her hand. 'I don't know if anyone's ever told you this, but you're no Nigella Lawson.'

'Lucky you don't have to eat here, then.'

'Ah, but what about poor Ryan? He's desperate enough to eat anything, aren't you, Ryan?'

Finn looked up at the dark-haired man who lingered in the doorway. Ryan Hunter had once been Joe Delaney's apprentice. But even after knowing the family for thirteen years he always waited for an invitation to come in.

'In that case, I'm sure he'll be able to find a woman desperate enough to cook for him,' she replied.

'Take no notice of her, Ryan. Come in, lad.' Joe pushed back his chair, greeting him like the prodigal son. 'Long time no see. How's business?'

'Pretty busy.'

'With all the customers you stole from us,' Finn muttered, but no one listened to her.

Why did everyone make such a fuss of him? she wondered as she arranged the chops on the grill pan. Joe Delaney had given Ryan a chance. He'd taught him all he knew, then Ryan promptly dumped him and set up on his own in competition. As far as she was concerned, that made him a duplicitous snake.

There was a time when she'd felt differently, of course. When she was fourteen and they were doing *Wuthering Heights* at school, she'd convinced herself that the brooding eighteen-year-old Ryan was a cross between Heathcliff and James Dean. She'd developed a brief but monumental crush on him – which still embarrassed the hell out of her whenever she thought about it – until she'd found out the reason he was so quiet and troubled was because he'd spent time in jail for nearly killing an old man in a hit-and-run incident. She'd never felt quite the same about him after that.

'You'll stay for your dinner?' Joe said.

'There isn't enough to go round,' Finn said quickly.

'Thank God for small mercies,' Ciaran muttered.

Ryan grinned, which annoyed Finn even more. 'It's all right, I'm not staying.' He looked at his watch. 'I'm meeting someone in half an hour.'

'Now there's a surprise.' Finn upended the bag of vegetables into boiling water.

'Who is she? Anyone I know?' Ciaran asked.

'Wendy.'

'Wendy Grant? Still? That must be nearly three months you've been seeing her.'

'You'll be engaged next,' Finn said.

Ryan sent her a sharp look. It was a standing joke that his relationships usually fizzled out after six weeks.

'You'll stay for a drink, at least?' Joe said. 'We've a couple of beers in the fridge.'

Finn opened her mouth to remind him he was supposed to be cutting down on alcohol, then closed it again. What was the point? No one ever listened to her anyway.

'Besides, I wanted to have a chat to you,' Joe went on. 'What do you make of this?' He handed Ryan the letter.

Finn watched him reading it, feeling annoyed. Why did Joe have to discuss his business with Ryan, of all people? He hadn't let *her* read the letter.

'Bloody hell.' Ciaran whistled as he read over his friend's shoulder. 'Is that right? Is that really what they're offering?'

'It's a good price,' Ryan said, handing the letter back.

Ciaran snatched it out of his hand and read it again. 'It's an incredible price,' he said. 'Honest to God, Pa, you'd be mad to pass up that kind of cash.'

'It's meant to be an investment – sod it!' Finn cursed under her breath as she went to turn the chops and burned her fingers on the grill pan. Her father heard and tutted.

'But if you take this offer you'll make a packet anyway,' Ciaran pointed out. 'I'd call that a pretty good investment.'

'And you're such a financial whizz, aren't you?' Finn said.

Ciaran shot her a nasty look. 'You'd be surprised what kind of deals I've got going on.'

'Is that why you have to keep borrowing money from me?'

'Hush, you two.' Joe turned to Ryan. 'What do you think, lad?'

'I reckon you should stick to your plan and build those houses. You'll make more out of it in the long term.'

Joe nodded, satisfied. 'That's what I thought.'

'*I* said that!' Finn was outraged. But it was obviously different when Ryan said it. Her father took notice of *his* opinion.

They chatted for a while, then Ryan put his empty glass down on the table. 'I'd better get going. Thanks for the drink, Joe.'

'Any time, son. Will you see our guest out, Finnuala?' Joe said.

'What am I, the flipping domestic servant?' Finn said, clattering plates on the table.

'It's OK, I'll see myself out.' As he passed, Ryan leaned towards her and whispered, 'I think you should know you've got plaster dust in your eyebrows.'

Finn's hand shot up to cover her face, blushing. Ryan gave her a quick smile and left, Joe following.

As soon as they'd gone, she turned on Ciaran. 'Have you told Ryan about my job?'

'I might have,' Ciaran shrugged.

'Ciaran! It was supposed to be a secret.'

'Oh, keep your knickers on. He won't tell Dad.'

'I wouldn't bet on it.' Finn stared at the door. 'I wouldn't trust him further than I could throw him.'

'You've changed your tune. You were head over heels in love with him once.'

'I was not!'

'Come off it! You followed him round like a lovestruck puppy when he was working with Dad. It was embarrassing.'

'That was a long time ago. Before I grew up and realized what he was really like.'

They both shut up as Joe appeared. 'He's such a nice lad, that Ryan,' he said.

'He's a snake. I don't know how you can even have him in the house after what he did to you.'

'And what would that be?' Joe smiled.

'You know what he did. He learned everything from you, then set himself up in business and tried to take all your trade away.'

'He was my apprentice, Finnuala. And a good one, too. It was only a matter of time before he'd set up on his own. I knew it, and so did he. And as for taking away my trade – I reckon there's room for two builders in this town. Who knows, I might even need his help once I start building on my land?'

Chapter 2

It was a bitterly cold day. The mud cracked under her boots and her fingers froze through her gloves. Finn laid another brick in place and trimmed the mortar with the edge of her trowel. Not far away, Barry, her new team-mate, was doing the same, his hands a blur as he laid one brick after another, his right hand putting it in place, his left trimming the mortar in a swift, continuous movement.

He was fast, she thought. Too fast.

The walls were built in two layers, an inner skin of grey blocks, with the fascia bricks on the outside. Between them was a layer of insulating material. But the outer walls had to be attached to the inner one using special wall ties. The more ties they put in, the more secure the finished wall would be. But it meant cutting the insulation to fit around them, which was fiddly and time-consuming.

Barry had obviously decided it was too much trouble. He used hardly any ties, which meant he could slip whole sheets of insulation into the gap. It was quick, but hardly professional.

Finn wondered if she should say something, then decided against it. Barry wouldn't thank her for her advice. They'd hardly hit it off since they started working together two weeks ago. Brickies were supposed to work in pairs with a labourer between them, but Barry had made it very clear who was in charge. He was in his late thirties, with a broken nose and a head that seemed to grow straight out of his bullish shoulders. Unlike her last partner, Rob, who liked to chat as they worked, Barry treated her with silent contempt. He listened to his radio or joked with the other men. Finn knew he'd been teased by the others when he ended up with her, and that he resented her for it.

She wasn't even sure if he was a real bricklayer. She knew he got paid cash in hand and, like a lot of Jason's new team, slipped off to the benefits office to sign on. She kept telling herself it was none of her business and that she should just get on with her job, but it still troubled her.

She caught Ivan's eye. He smiled sympathetically. At least she had him for company now he'd joined her team as the labourer. Although he was so terrified of Barry the bully he'd virtually stopped speaking.

Her gaze strayed back to Barry. She bit her lip in an effort to stop herself speaking.

As if he sensed he was being watched, Barry suddenly looked up. 'What?'

'Nothing.' Finn ducked her head and laid another brick in place.

'Good.' Barry turned to Ivan. 'Oi, Dracula. Bit faster with those bricks, if you don't mind.'

Ivan stumbled over, hefting the wheelbarrow. Sweat poured down his face in spite of the cold November day. 'Y-you want m-me to b-bring some more?'

'If it's not t-too much t-t-trouble. Blimey, talk about being a few bricks short of a load,' he said to the others as Ivan started emptying the wheelbarrow. 'I don't know which is worse, being stuck with a woman or a moron.'

Finn's blood sang in her ears. 'You're the only moron around here.'

Barry turned to her. 'Did you say something?'

'You heard.' Finn met his gaze. 'Why do you have to pick on him all the time?'

'Finn, p-please,' Ivan begged, but Finn had had enough. It was one thing for Barry to have a go at her, but Ivan had done nothing wrong.

'Yeah, F-Finn, shut your f-fucking mouth,' Barry said. 'He shouldn't even be here, anyway. He's probably one of those asylum-seekers, sneaked over in the back of a lorry. I expect he's claiming all kinds of benefits.'

'You'd know all about that, wouldn't you?' Finn snapped. 'At least Ivan knows what he's doing, which is more than anyone can say for you!'

'What's that supposed to mean?'

'I've been watching you work. Have you ever actually done any bricklaying before, or are you just making it up as you go along?'

A mottled flush crept up Barry's face. He tested the weight of the brick in his hand as if he wanted to lob it at her head. 'That's none of your fucking business.'

'Is there a problem?' Jason came up behind them.

Barry jerked his head towards Finn. 'Just her, telling everyone how to do their job, as usual.'

'Only because you weren't doing it properly.'

Jason turned to her. 'I know you like to think you know everything but I'm the boss around here and I'm the one who gives the orders. Unless you reckon you can do my job, too?'

I probably could do it, and a lot better than you, Finn thought. The site was a shambles since George had gone. Jobs were left undone, there was mess everywhere and Jason seemed to spend most of his time playing cards in the site office instead of running the place.

But fired up as she was, even she could see it wouldn't be a good idea to tell Jason that.

'We shouldn't even be out here,' she said. 'It's way too cold.'

'Aw, what's wrong? Frightened you might get chilblains?'

'No. When the temperature drops below a certain level the concrete freezes rather than sets. You should know that, since you're supposed to be in charge?'

Jason and Barry looked at each other. 'She might have a point,' Jason said. 'Come on, lads. Everyone into the hut. Any excuse for a break. We might even get a couple of rounds of poker in.'

Finn sat on a pile of flagstones behind the workers' Portakabin, drinking her tea and fighting the urge to cry with sheer frustration. Inside she could hear the other men laughing and cracking jokes.

At her expense, no doubt. Two weeks ago she would have been in there with them, but the atmosphere on site had changed completely since Neil Tate took over. Now she hated coming to work. Her old gang used to tease her and make sexist comments, but she could handle that. There was nothing good-humoured about the way the new men on site tried to intimidate her. But they would never see how much they upset her. She wouldn't give them the satisfaction. She wrapped her frozen fingers around her mug, trying to warm them up.

'All right, love?' She looked up. Rob towered over her, mug in one hand, cigarette in the other. 'Not coming inside?'

Finn shook her head. 'I'm better off out here.'

Rob frowned down at her. 'They'll get used to you in time, you'll see.'

'I don't know if I'll get used to them.' Finn sipped her tea and stared into the distance to where they were putting up scaffolding on the far side of the site.

Rob squatted down beside her. 'This isn't like you. I remember when you first started here; you gave us all hell!'

'That was different. I knew you didn't really mean it.' Besides, if she stood up for herself now they'd probably all just laugh and say it was the wrong time of the month. 'Anyway, I can put up with the stupid jokes, I'm used to that. But I just hate the fact that the job isn't getting done properly. No one seems to care any more.'

'I know what you mean,' Rob agreed. 'You see that scaffolding they're putting up over there? It's dodgy, the lot of it. I reckon they must have got it dirt-cheap. Probably got thrown out by some other site.'

'But that could be a deathtrap!' Scaffolding had to be replaced after a few jobs as it wore out and became unsafe. Her father had been offered cheap stuff on many occasions, but he always turned it down.

'I told them it should be properly inspected, but our friend Jason said he'd get round to it later. I tell you, I'm not setting foot on it until the health and safety inspector's taken a look at it.'

'All he cares about is cutting corners, getting it done as quickly and cheaply as we can. Never mind that it's all rubbish.'

'These houses are palaces compared to some of the buildings Tates put up.' Rob took a long drag on his cigarette. 'There was this one place I worked on for them, down south. Converted tower block. Tates did a quick cosmetic job on it and let it out to tenants.' He shook his head. 'It wasn't just cheap, it was dangerous. Faulty wiring, missing joists, the lot. D'you know, some of the flats on the top floors didn't have proper running water?'

'Who'd want to rent a flat like that?' Finn asked.

'People with no choice. Asylum-seekers, mostly. The council are desperate for somewhere to house them. Tates buys up blocks of flats, does them up and lets them out. The local authority pays sky-high rents and everyone's happy.'

'Someone should do something about it.'

'Oh aye? And who's that, then?' Rob took another drag on his cigarette and watched the smoke curling up to the sky. 'You don't cross the Tates, Finn. Not twice, anyway.'

Finn gazed across at the site office. Neil Tate never ventured on site, preferring to stay behind closed doors on his rare visits. She only knew he was there today because she'd seen his Saab in the car park. 'I can't see what's so special about them. They're just people.'

'Very rich and powerful people,' Rob said. 'And they've got friends in high places. How do you think they get to build on sites like this?' He waved his hand around at the hills surrounding them. 'That old mill was supposed to have a preservation order on it, but Neil's dad Max chatted up a few of his mates on the council and suddenly it's OK to knock it all down.'

'Money talks.'

'Not just money, love. The Tates have got some dodgy connections, too. People you wouldn't want to meet in a dark alley, if you know what I mean.' He tapped the side of his nose. 'Max Tate never started off this rich. He made all his money as a slum landlord, buying up cheap houses with sitting tenants and then forcing them out so he could sell on for a profit. They say he still does it, although he claims to be strictly legit these days. And he covers his tracks so well with all these different companies he's got, you'd need to be Sherlock Holmes to find out. He's got fingers in a lot of pies, has Mr Tate. And not all of them are legal.'

'He sounds charming.'

'He's a brute in a Savile Row suit. And his sons are just as bad. Neil and James. He keeps them like a pair of half-starved Rottweilers, ready to tear someone's throat out whenever he gives the word.'

Finn gazed back towards the site office again. 'I wonder if he knows what kind of a mess his son's making of this place?'

'I don't suppose young Neil even knows himself. I get the impression he's not exactly experienced at this game.'

'Then maybe it's about time someone set him straight?'

Rob shrugged. 'You could try if it makes you feel better, but I wouldn't expect him to listen.'

There were raised voices coming from inside the site office as she approached.

'They can't do that!' Neil Tate was shouting. 'We've been through all this. How the hell are we supposed to sell high-end luxury houses with a bunch of peasants living at the end of the street?'

'If you remember, it was a condition of you being able to build here that you included a proportion of low-cost homes on the development,' another man's voice reasoned quietly. 'The local authority are only doing their job—'

'Screw them. This is our land and we're not handing it over to a bunch of fucking soap-dodgers. My father would go ballistic.'

Finn peered through the grimy, mesh-covered window of the Portakabin. Neil was leaning across the desk, confronting a nervous-looking man who held a plan in his hands.

'You tell the council if they want somewhere to put their peasants they can have one of our renovated blocks. Somewhere in the city so they won't have too far to go to the job centre. How about that?'

'I'm not sure.' The man looked sceptical. 'I suppose you would still be making provision for them, but I don't know if it's really in the spirit of the agreement—'

'Screw the agreement. You're our consultant, make it happen.' Neil sat back. The man hesitated, then, realizing he'd been dismissed, picked up his briefcase and headed for the door, bumping into Finn who was on her way in.

'Bloody consultants,' Neil grumbled aloud. 'You pay them a fucking fortune and all they do is tell you why you can't do something . . .' He looked up and saw Finn in the doorway. 'Hello. What can I do for you?'

His abrupt change of mood caught her unawares. Taking a deep breath, she said, 'My name's Finn Delaney, and—'

'I know who you are. I've been watching you. And I have to say I'm delighted we have a woman working on site.'

'Really?'

'Absolutely. It beats the hell out of looking at a bunch of hairy-arsed blokes all day.' He laughed.

Finn looked back at him, stony-faced. 'What a pity,' she said. 'For a moment I thought you might actually have a brain in your head and not in your trousers.'

She was surprised to see that Neil looked abashed. 'Sorry,' he said. 'I suppose you must get those kinds of remarks all the time.'

'Let's just say you aren't the first.'

'So, what can I do for you?'

'I want to talk to you about conditions on the site.'

'What about them?'

'I'm concerned about the standards out there. Some of the things we're being made to do are downright unsafe.'

He frowned. 'Such as?'

'I've made a list.' She took the piece of paper from her jeans pocket, unfolded it and handed it to him.

'You have been busy, haven't you?' He made a big show of smoothing it out. Finn cringed as he squinted to read her writing. Perhaps she should have taken some more time, typed it out properly instead of scribbling it down in her lunch-hour. But if she'd stopped that long to think about it she probably wouldn't be here now.

'Sub-standard equipment, building work being carried out too fast, and – what's this bit?' He showed her the paper.

'Foundations being laid on running sand,' Finn read out. 'They found some three days ago when they were digging out the foundations on plot twenty-three. It should have been seen by a building inspector to make sure it was OK to build on, but Jason told them to dump the concrete in anyway.'

There was a long silence as Neil scrutinized the rest of the list. 'You've made some very important points,' he said finally. 'I'll follow up on them immediately.'

Finn was taken aback. 'You will?'

'Of course. If what you say is true, then the situation is very serious. Thank you for bringing it to my attention.'

She regarded him suspiciously, sensing mockery behind his solemn expression. 'Are you winding me up?'

'Miss Delaney, I wouldn't dream—'

He didn't finish the sentence. From outside there was a scream and a crash, followed by the sound of shouting and running feet. Finn and Neil stared at each other for a second, then they both headed for the door.

Finn felt sick when she saw the figure lying face down among the fallen scaffolding.

'Ivan!' She pushed through the ring of men who stood around him, and knelt beside him. His face was blue-white and cold. 'Ivan, can you hear me?' There was no response.

'What happened?' Neil demanded.

'He was up there, filling in the putlog holes,' Jason pointed up a wall. 'He just fell.'

'Shit!' Neil pulled out his mobile phone.

'We've already rung for an ambulance.'

'I'm calling my father.' He headed back to the office.

Finn pulled off her gloves and groped around on Ivan's neck for a pulse, her own heart hammering until she felt the faint, steady beat under her fingers. 'Ivan? Can you hear me? It's Finn.' She frantically tried to remember the health and safety video they'd been shown at college. She felt helpless, but at least she was doing something. The others just watched her. Bloody heroes, the lot of them, she thought angrily.

Then, just as she was beginning to panic, Ivan groaned and his eyelids fluttered open.

'What happened?' he murmured.

'You had a fall. Don't try to move, we're getting help.' Finn looked around. 'Where's that ambulance?'

'It's on its way.' Jason loomed over her. 'Is he going to be all right?'

'I don't know.' She looked around, thinking she heard the ambulance pulling up. But it was just a forklift truck rumbling across the site.

Then she caught Jason's guilty look. Suddenly it clicked. 'He was standing on that forklift, wasn't he?'

'I couldn't say.' But he didn't have to say anything. They both knew that it was often a rushed job to fill in the putlog holes that were left when the scaffolding poles were removed. Sometimes, to save time and effort, labourers were told to stand on planks balanced across forklift trucks to do it. Most wouldn't risk it, but she knew Ivan might. Especially if he was bullied into it by Jason.

Neil hurried back, his phone still in his hand. 'How is he?'

'He's alive, if that's what you're worried about.'

'Thank Christ for that.' He turned away and muttered something into his phone.

Finn watched him with disgust.

Let's see if you're so pleased when he sues the pants off you, she thought.

Ivan escaped with a broken arm and a dislocated shoulder, although his concussion was so severe he was kept in hospital over the weekend for observation. Finn wasn't able to go and visit him until the Sunday afternoon, by which time he was back at home.

She was surprised to find Neil Tate at his bedsit, looking the picture of concern.

'What are you doing here?' she asked.

'Same as you. Checking on Ivan.'

No prizes for guessing why, she thought.

'Mr Tate has been very k-kind,' Ivan said, propping himself up against the cushions on the sofa.

'I'll bet he has.' Finn looked at Neil's blandly smiling face.

'L-look what he bring for me.' Ivan pointed to the laptop computer on his dining table. 'N-now I can send the emails t-to Anna and the ch-children.' He screwed up his face, trying to get the words out. 'And he s-say I can t-take as m-much time off as I n-need. With p-pay. He is very generous man.'

'And you're a very valued member of the team, Ivan my friend.' Neil leaned forward and patted his good arm.

'So valued you let him risk his life?' Finn turned to Ivan. 'You know why he's doing this, don't you? So you don't sue his company.'

'Now, Miss Delaney—'

Ivan looked perplexed. 'What is s-sue?'

'Take him to court. You know, to get compensation? He's trying to buy you, Ivan.'

'That's not true,' Neil said. 'We believe in looking after our employees, that's all.'

'Is that why you let him stand on a forklift truck to carry out that job?'

'I think you'll find I didn't let him do anything. If you remember, I was talking to you at the time.'

'That doesn't mean anything. You're supposed to be in charge of that site. That means you have a duty of care—'

'Please, please, I don't want to fight.' Ivan looked appealingly from one to the other.

'But don't you see, it's their fault you had that accident?'

He shook his head. 'I f-fell off, yes. But I d-do not know, perhaps it is my f-fault.'

Finn glanced at Neil's smug face. 'Perhaps we should talk about this in private?' she suggested to Ivan.

But even when Neil had left, Ivan was determined to stick to his story. As far as he was concerned, Tates had done nothing wrong. Neil had made all kinds of promises to him, including bringing his wife and children over for a visit. He was so looking forward to seeing them again that nothing else mattered. Certainly not bringing the Tates to justice.

Finn didn't have it in her heart to argue. She really couldn't blame him.

Neil was waiting for her outside, sitting behind the wheel of his black Saab. 'Well?' he said, getting out of the car. 'Do we have a lawsuit on our hands?'

Finn couldn't bring herself to look at him, afraid she might have to slap the self-satisfied look off his face. 'Apparently not.'

He sighed with relief. 'At least someone's got sense.'

'Only because you leaned on him.'

'Hardly. Look, I can understand your frustration but let's be practical about this. What good would it do to fight it through the courts? It would take months and your friend Ivan would just end up with the same result at the end of it. Maybe even less. My father has a pretty good team of lawyers.'

'I expect he needs them.'

'He does keep them fairly busy.' Neil reached an arm out towards her. 'I'm just being pragmatic. You can see that, can't you?'

Finn stepped back. 'Just because Ivan's let you off the hook, I don't suppose the health and safety inspectors will be so compliant.'

Neil's smile faded. 'What about them?'

'They'll need to carry out an investigation.' She stared at him. 'You *have* informed them?'

'I don't see any need to get them involved,' Neil shrugged. 'Look, we've made some mistakes, but we've learned our lesson, OK? We've cleaned up our act. The dodgy scaffolding's gone, and so have Jason and his gang.'

'You should never have taken them on in the first place.'

'Don't you think I know that now?' He moved to stand in her path as she headed for her car. 'I'll be honest with you. This is the first site I've managed, and I've made a mess of it. God knows, I've already had a bollocking from my father over it. But can't we just forget it? Move on?' He held up his hand. 'I solemnly promise to be a good boy and not screw up again, OK? Now why don't we have a drink and be friends?'

Finn almost relented. Then she remembered Ivan's apparently lifeless body lying there and how terrified she'd been. He might be happy enough, playing with his brand new laptop and looking forward to seeing his family again, but there was no way she could forget what had happened. And she didn't want the Tate family to forget, either.

'No thanks,' she said, shouldering past him.

Neil's eyes grew cold. 'I'm sorry you feel like that,' he said.

Her father was on the phone when she got home.

'Yes, Orla.' He lifted a hand in greeting, as Finn edged past and headed for the kitchen. 'No, I told you, we're all fine. Yes, of course we're eating properly. For heaven's sake, stop fussing, woman! I'm fifty-nine years old. I should know how to look after myself by now.'

Finn smiled as she filled the kettle. Auntie Orla often phoned to nag her father. She wasn't really related, but she'd been her mother's best friend since they were children and she'd known Joe since they were all teenagers growing up in the same village in the west of Ireland. Orla still lived there and worked as a nurse at the local hospital, although she occasionally ventured over to England for a visit.

Finn was taking the mugs out of the cupboard when her father appeared in the kitchen doorway. 'That was your Auntie Orla.'

'I guessed. So how are things in sunny Killmane?'

'Much the same as they've been for the past forty years. People being born, getting wed, falling out with each other, dropping dead. Nothing ever changes over there.'

'It sounds perfect.' She'd dealt with so many changes during the past couple of weeks, each worse than the last, that a bit of boring consistency sounded very appealing.

'Ah no, you'd hate it. You'd be climbing the walls in five minutes. I don't know how Orla's stood it for this long. She was always such a lively sort of woman.'

'She stayed for Uncle Donal, didn't she? He never wanted to leave Killmane.' Although why she was still there five years after her husband's death she didn't know.

'She sends her love, by the way,' Joe said. 'She wants to know if you're courting yet?'

'Chance would be a fine thing.'

The kettle boiled and she reached up to take two mugs out of the cupboard, then turned to find her father watching her thoughtfully. 'What is it?' She reached up, panicking for a moment that she might have another smudge of plaster dust on her nose.

Joe examined his fingernails. 'You don't – um – have a boyfriend or anything, do you?'

'You know I don't.'

'I don't know anything of the sort. That's the trouble.' He looked awkward. 'Your Auntie Orla seems to think we should sit down and have a talk about Life.'

'Dad! I'm twenty-six years old. I learned all that at school.' And not necessarily in the biology classroom, either. The graffiti in the girls' toilets was amazingly educational.

'That's not what I meant and you know it.' His ears were turning red with embarrassment as he stared down at his slippers. 'I know it can't be easy for you, not having a mother around. But I hope you know you can talk to me if you've got any – you know, problems.'

Finn filled the mugs, grinning. She could just imagine asking Joe Delaney's advice on her love-life. If she ever had one. 'Actually, there is something I'd like to ask you,' she said.

'There is?' Joe's head shot up, his face full of panic. 'I mean, that's great, love.' He gulped. 'Er – fire away.'

'What would you do if someone you worked with wasn't doing their job properly?'

He looked relieved. 'Is that it?' He thought about it for a moment. 'I suppose I'd try to have a word with them, sort it out that way.'

'And what if that didn't work?'

'Then I'd have a word with their boss.'

'That's what I thought.'

He frowned at her. 'Is someone not pulling their weight at that hairdressers?'

Finn dropped a teabag into each mug. 'Nothing I can't handle,' she said.

Chapter 3

Tates' head office was a low, modern building set in tree-lined grounds just outside York. Finn's palms were damp on the steering wheel as she parked her old Fiat in the car park. Making the appointment to see Max Tate had been an impulsive move, and she'd needed lots of confidence to get past his secretary. But two days later, some of her courage had escaped her. Maybe this wasn't such a good idea after all.

But it was too late to turn back. Here goes nothing, she thought as she pushed through the double doors into the sleek chrome and glass reception area.

The two women behind the desk looked sceptically at her when she told them she was there to see Max Tate. Finally, after making an endless show of taking down her name and details, one of them made the call to his office.

'He's in a meeting.' She replaced the receiver and looked Finn up and down, taking in her best Topshop jacket. 'Are you *sure* you have an appointment?'

Her superior attitude helped to restore some of Finn's boldness. 'I'm sure,' she said, through gritted teeth. 'I'll wait, shall I?'

'I'm not sure how long he'll be.'

'It doesn't matter.'

Finn sank into a squashy leather sofa, tugging her skirt over her knees and wishing she hadn't worn the 'work' uniform she used to fool her dad. She should have dressed in something that made her feel less self-conscious. She had a feeling she would need all the confidence she could muster when she met Max Tate.

After about twenty minutes the lift doors opened. Finn looked up hopefully, and was disappointed when a sleek blonde in a designer suit emerged and headed for the reception desk.

'I'm going out for lunch.' Her voice was soft but clear and well-spoken. 'If anyone needs me urgently they can reach me on my mobile.'

'Yes, Mrs Farrell.' The receptionist's deferential smile stayed in place for as long as it took for the blonde to get through the glass doors, then she turned to the other woman behind the desk. 'She didn't look too happy, did she?'

'I thought she was going to cry,' her friend agreed. 'I wonder who's upset her this time?'

The receptionist's smile switched off when she saw Finn standing at the desk. 'Oh. Are you still here?'

'Do you know if Max Tate is out of his meeting yet?'

'Miss Delaney?'

'Yes?' She spun round.

'Sorry to keep you waiting. I'm Max Tate.'

He held out his hand. Finn took it, and looked up at the man on the other end of the firm handshake. She wasn't quite sure what she'd been expecting, but it wasn't a tanned, fit fifty-something, with cropped, iron-grey curly hair, a broken nose and a surprisingly warm smile.

'I've booked us a table for lunch,' he said. 'I thought it might be easier for us to talk.'

'Oh, but there's no need. I just wanted to—'

'I insist.' His smile had a hint of steel. 'I much prefer to get out of the office if I can. Besides, it'll give us a chance to get to know each other.'

Finn glanced at the receptionists, who were both gawping, obviously wondering who this girl in her cheap chainstore outfit was, if she could bring the chairman of the company himself down from his executive offices. She was wondering the same thing herself.

'OK,' she said warily. This really wasn't going the way she'd expected.

'I'm very sorry I was late,' Max apologized again when they

were in his chauffeur-driven Jaguar. 'My last meeting ran over. A lot of people with too much time on their hands, I'm afraid.' His voice was deep and mesmerizing. Combined with the luxurious leather seats and the warmth of the car, Finn could have slipped into a trance if she hadn't been so tense about what lay ahead.

'I'm grateful to you for sparing the time to see me.'

'On the contrary, I was intrigued. It isn't often one of my employees pays me a visit. I don't get out on site nearly as much as I used to, as I'm tied to the office all the time. I like to know what's going on.'

'Actually, that's why I'm here. You see—'

Max held up his hand. 'Let's leave business until later, shall we? Why don't you tell me about yourself.'

'Why?'

'Because I like to know who I'm dealing with.'

Finn shrugged, embarrassed. 'There's nothing to tell.'

'Oh, come on. There can't be many young women like you. Why did you decide to become a builder? It's hardly what most girls dream of, is it?'

'I did,' Finn said firmly. 'My dad's in the trade. It was all I've ever wanted to do.'

'So why aren't you working with him?'

She hesitated. 'He wasn't very keen on the idea.'

'I don't blame him. I'm not sure I'd want my daughter working on a building site either. Although somehow I can't imagine her wanting to,' he added ruefully. 'She takes after her mother. Far more interested in shopping and beauty salons.'

'Doesn't she work?'

'If you can call it that. She's on my payroll, officially. Although whether she actually earns her living is debatable.'

'Lucky her. There must be some perks to being the boss's daughter.'

'Indeed. Ah, I think we're here.' He peered out of the window as the Jaguar stopped outside a little riverside country pub. 'I hope you like this place. It's very unpretentious.' He opened the door for her to get out. 'And they do a bloody good steak and kidney pie, too.'

Finn was relieved. She'd been expecting some horrendously over-priced posh place.

'I don't know about you, but I can't stand those awful, deathly silent places where you don't get enough to eat and you're terrified of spilling soup over the priceless damask,' Max went on, leading the way into the pub.

Finn glanced at him, startled. How did he know what she was thinking? There was something disarming about him, as if he could read her mind and stay one step ahead.

'Isn't this wonderful?' He looked out of the window at the swans swimming serenely. 'Now, what can I get you to drink? Shall we have a bottle of wine?'

'Half of lager, please,' she said, fighting to assert some independence. She felt as if Max was overwhelming her with his forceful personality. 'And I'm buying.'

'Just as you like.' Max looked amused. 'I'll have a whiskey. Irish, straight, no ice.'

She stole a look at him as she waited to pay for the drinks at the bar. He was less handsome than his son, yet there was something compelling about his battered prizefighter's face and intense dark eyes.

It was power, she decided. Max Tate oozed power and control. She could understand why he got his way so often, with that lethal combination of menace and charm. Not that either would work with her, she decided.

After they'd ordered their food, Finn was keen to get down to talking about the site, but Max kept asking her questions about herself. He seemed genuinely interested in finding out all about her, although Finn wondered how much he already knew. All the same, she couldn't help feeling flattered. She let her guard down and found herself telling him about her family, and how she'd defied her father to train as a builder.

She was still talking when their meal arrived.

'What about you?' she said, aware that she'd gone on far too long and had probably bored him to death.

'Oh, I daresay you've heard enough about me already. There's always someone ready to tell you a story or two.'

Finn blushed, remembering all the things Rob had told her. 'Are they true?'

'What do you think?'

She looked at him across the table, his flattened nose and hooded eyes at odds with his smartly tailored clothes. Under that veneer of sophistication, he looked like a tough streetfighter. A brute in a Savile Row suit, Rob had called him. And he was right. She could imagine a man like Max would think nothing of throwing off his jacket and giving someone a beating if they stepped out of line. Although these days he'd probably pay someone else to do it for him, she thought.

She left her meal half-finished and refused pudding. She wanted to get this meeting over with as quickly as possible. But Max seemed in no hurry as he ordered coffee for her and a brandy for himself.

'You know, you and I seem very much alike,' he said, as the waitress brought them over. 'We both know what we want, and we have the guts and determination to go for it no matter what anyone else says. I sometimes think my children have had it too easy. I wish they had the spirit to go out on their own instead of relying on me to pay their wages.'

'Maybe they feel they can't compete?' Finn suggested. 'After all, you must be a hard act to follow.'

'I wouldn't say that.' Max gave a self-deprecating laugh.

'Talking of which,' Finn said, seizing her chance, 'I wanted to talk to you about your son.'

'I hope he hasn't been making a nuisance of himself,' Max said. 'He told me about the accident on the Windmill Meadows site. Terrible, shocking business.'

'Exactly. That's why—'

'How is Mr Lupescu? Do you know?'

'He's getting better. But what I really wanted to say was—'

'Did he tell you we've arranged for his wife and kids to come over and visit? I thought it might help cheer him up.'

'I'm sure it will. But—'

'I've also told him if there's anything Tates can do for him, he only has to ask.'

'You could start by making sure your site isn't a bloody death-trap!' Finn blurted out, sick at being interrupted.

Max's brows rose. 'I take it you're not impressed with the way my son's been running the place?'

'He knows nothing about the construction business.'

'Do you think you could do better?'

She refused to be put off by his sarcasm. 'I couldn't do much worse.'

'So how would you run it?'

Finn thought for a moment. 'For one thing, I wouldn't treat health and safety like some big joke. And I'd stop taking on cheap, unskilled labour. And I'd make sure quality standards were maintained. There's no point in building houses quickly if no one wants to buy them because they're shoddy and badly finished.'

'I agree.'

She blinked at him. 'You do?'

'Of course. It would be commercial suicide to do anything else. So how would you make sure these issues were properly addressed?'

As Finn told him, Max watched her intently but she wasn't sure he was really listening. Maybe he was humouring her? Maybe, after she'd gone to all this effort, he'd just go back to the office and pat his son on the head anyway.

When she'd finished he sat back and said, 'Sounds good to me. How about you start tomorrow?'

Finn spluttered into her coffee. 'Are you being funny?'

'No, I'm being serious. How would you like to manage the site?'

She put her cup down. 'What about Neil?'

'As you say, he's clearly not up to the job. I made a mistake sending him there.'

Finn was dismayed. 'You're going to fire him?'

'Why should that bother you?'

'It doesn't.' But she was still shocked. If Max could dispose of his family so casually, what about his enemies?

Max broke into a grin. 'Don't look so alarmed, Finn. I'm not going to fire him. His mother would never forgive me, for one thing.' He sipped his brandy. 'No, I'm sure I can find something more suited to his abilities. Whatever they are.' He considered her. 'So what do you say? Do you want the job?'

Of course she wanted the job. But there was no way she could take it. 'There are loads of people on that site with far more experience than me.'

'Yes, but they're not here now, are they? They didn't have the guts to confront me face to face and tell me my own son had got it wrong.'

'That's not why I came here. I'm not after promotion.'

'I know that, but I'm offering it to you. What's wrong? Don't you think you can do it?'

Of course I can do it, she wanted to shout. It was the chance she'd been longing for, the opportunity to prove herself. She was on the verge of telling him she'd take the job when she suddenly caught the look in Max Tate's eyes and realization dawned.

He was trying to win her over, appealing to her vanity by offering her what she most wanted in the world. He was like the devil on her shoulder, whispering all the things she wanted to hear. And she'd almost fallen for it.

'I'm sorry, Mr Tate. I'm not for sale.'

His eyes flicked over her face for a second. Then he laughed. 'I really have under-estimated you, haven't I, Finn?'

'It doesn't take a genius to work out what your game is.' She was annoyed that she'd almost fallen for his flattery.

Max settled back in his seat. He looked as if he were really enjoying himself. 'Then let's cut to the chase. How much is this going to cost me?'

'I don't want your money.'

'You're the first person to say that to me. Certainly the first woman. So if you don't want a pay-off and you don't want promotion, what do you want?'

She gazed out of the window at the amber-gold drifts of fallen leaves on the river's edge. 'I just want to see things put right.'

'I've already done that.'

'I mean properly. Health and safety should be called in to investigate.'

'Why do we need them snooping around? The whole thing was a one-off. Probably caused by someone else's carelessness.'

'It was caused by your shoddy management, and you know it!'

'And will your workmates say that?' His eyes met hers over the rim of his brandy glass. 'I think you'll find no one even saw what happened. Even the poor sod who got injured can't remember. And if anyone asks him, he's ready to swear blind it was all his fault.' He leaned over and refilled her coffee cup. 'Look, Finn. I can handle the health and safety people. The thing is, I don't need the hassle at the moment. I've got too many other things going on.'

'You mean building unsafe flats for asylum-seekers?'

'You really shouldn't listen to all these rumours.' He smiled, unruffled. 'I just want this to go away. And if that costs me money – well, everything costs these days, doesn't it? God knows, this has already set me back enough. A whole bunch of first-class flights from Romania for one thing!' He chuckled. 'I think I've been reasonable about this. Everyone's happy.'

'Except me.'

'I'm sure we could come to some arrangement about that. Just tell me what you want.'

'I don't want anything from you.'

'Everyone has their price.'

'Not me.'

'Oh, I'm sure you have.'

Something about the way he looked at her sent a prickle down the back of her neck. She groped under the table for her bag. 'I'm obviously wasting my time here. I'm going home.'

'Fine. I'll finish my drink and we'll drop you back in town.'

'I'd rather walk.'

'Don't be ridiculous. It must be three miles.'

'I need the fresh air.' She stood up and hoisted her bag over her shoulder.

Max leaned back and looked up at her. 'You really are being very juvenile about this, Finn. I had hoped you'd see things my way.'

'Sorry about that.'

'So am I, believe me.' He sent her a long, leisurely look. 'I take it you won't be back on site tomorrow?'

'Definitely not. I quit.' There was no way she was setting foot on Tate land again. 'And don't think you've heard the last of this. I'll be taking it further.'

'Oh dear. What will you do? Write a stiff letter to someone?'

'You'll soon find out.' In fact, she had no idea what she could do, but she knew she had to do something.

Once outside, she thought about calling for a taxi then realized she'd spent her last tenner buying drinks in the pub. So much for being independent, she thought as she began the walk home. It was only a couple of miles but she'd over-estimated her ability to walk in heels. And it had started to rain. As she tottered along the roadside, Max Tate's Jaguar shot past her. She swore at the car as it sped away, but the figure in the back didn't even turn round.

She fumed all the way home. She wished she hadn't quit her job, but Max Tate had left her no choice. There was no way she could go on working for a crook who thought he could buy or bully his way out of trouble.

It took her an hour to get back to Tates' office where she'd left her car. As she reversed out of the parking space she didn't see the sporty silver Mazda heading towards her until it cut across her, filling her rear-view mirror. Finn slammed on the brakes, but not quick enough to avoid a sickening crunch and splinter of glass.

For a second she sat behind the wheel, too stunned to react. Then she leapt out of the car and went round to the back to check what had happened.

At the same moment a nervous-looking blonde woman stepped out of the Mazda. 'Is there much damage?'

Finn recognized her. It was the woman she'd seen earlier in Tates' reception.

'Not to you.' Finn inspected her own crumpled rear bumper and shattered brake-light. Typical; the silly cow who'd driven into her had escaped without a scratch.

'I'm so sorry,' the woman faltered.

'I should think so, too! What on earth were you thinking?'

'I didn't see you pulling out.'

'I'm not surprised, the speed you were doing.'

The woman reached into her bag. 'Let me give you my insurance details—'

'Great. Now I'll lose my no-claims discount.'

'Then I'll write you a cheque.' As she scribbled her signature, Finn noticed her hands were shaking. 'Will this cover it, do you think?' She tore out the cheque and held it out to her.

Finn looked at the noughts on the figure, then back at the woman. Her face was pale with shock. 'This is way too much.'

'It doesn't matter, really.' The woman stuffed her cheque book back into her bag, and Finn caught a discreet flash of her Cartier tank watch. She could certainly afford it. But all the same . . .

'Look, maybe it wasn't all your fault, OK? I wasn't exactly paying attention myself when I pulled out. Perhaps we should let the insurance companies take care of it after all.'

'No, no, it's fine, honestly.' She pressed the cheque into Finn's hand. 'Take it, please.'

She darted back to her car, head down. Finn watched as she pulled into a parking space then hurried towards Tates' offices, high heels clicking on the tarmac.

She looked down at the signature on the cheque: Gina Farrell.

Mrs Farrell had just given her more than she'd paid for the car in the first place.

Chapter 4

Gina Farrell sat in a cubicle in the ladies' toilets, clutching a sodden scrap of tissue to her eyes. For heaven's sake, stop crying, she told herself. Don't give those bitches the satisfaction. What if they walked in now and heard her? Wouldn't they love it if they knew they'd made the boss's daughter cry?

She felt as if she were thirteen and back at boarding school, snivelling in the girls' toilets because Sophie Harrington had made everyone send her to Coventry for letting in the winning goal in the hockey final.

And now, nearly twenty years later, she'd screwed up all over again.

She'd been so keen to make a good impression in her first week as sales and marketing manager. She knew there was bound to be some bad feeling at first; the senior marketing executive, Julie Palmer, had been in line for the job until her father had given it to her. But she was determined to prove she was up to it.

Unfortunately the other girls had been just as determined to see her fail. They were fiercely loyal to Julie and had gone out of their way to make life difficult for their new boss. Trish the secretary failed to pass on messages and left her letters languishing untyped at the bottom of her in-tray. Claire, the junior, insisted on reporting direct to Julie. And Julie was the worst of all. She undermined her wherever she could, ignoring her instructions and carrying on as if she, not Gina, were in charge of the department. The most humiliating moment was when she'd rewritten Gina's carefully crafted copy for the new sales brochure, telling her sweetly that it 'wasn't quite right' and insisting she was 'happy to show her how to do it properly'.

The tension between them had come to a head at that morning's meeting. Gina had gone in with high hopes and big plans, but, as usual, Julie had done her best to humiliate her. She'd interrupted her to take calls on her mobile, and questioned all her suggestions. Gina had bitten her lip as much as she could, not wanting to create a bad atmosphere. But when Julie had casually announced she had to leave the meeting early, she'd finally lost her cool.

'But we haven't finished.'

'I have another appointment.'

'Is it important?'

'I think so.'

They faced each other across the room. Gina had a feeling she knew exactly who Julie was meeting. She'd overheard her on the phone to the interior designers, discussing colour schemes for the new showhomes at Windmill Meadows. Julie knew very well Gina had asked to be included in their discussions.

By the time Gina found out about it, the designers would probably have ordered all the fabrics and furniture, and it would be too late to challenge Julie's decisions.

'Look,' she said, 'I know you think you should have had my job but I would still like to be consulted when you head off to meet people.'

'This is nothing to do with the job. It's personal.'

Gina stared at her, unsure whether to believe her or not. 'So what is it about?'

'I'd rather not tell you.'

Aware that the others were watching them expectantly like spectators at a tennis match, and determined not to lose another point to Julie, Gina said, 'In that case I'd rather you didn't go.'

Julie went red. 'Fine,' she snapped. 'If you must know, I have an appointment at the hospital to discuss infertility treatments. My husband and I are trying for a baby. Is that enough information for you?'

There was a deathly silence. 'Can I go now?' Julie said.

Gina nodded, feeling the weight of the others' eyes on her. The meeting limped on, but neither Trish nor Claire spoke to her, and Claire spent the whole time staring out of the window. Afterwards they both headed off to the local wine bar for lunch, obviously to bitch about her.

Gina had escaped from the office herself. She'd ended up sitting in a coffee shop in Parliament Street, nursing an espresso. She'd felt so humiliated she hadn't wanted to come back to the office, but she knew she had to face them or she would never return again.

Back at Tates, she emerged from a cubicle in the ladies loo and ran the tap. She was peering at her face in the mirror when the door opened and a young woman burst in.

'Bloody tights,' she muttered, hitching up her skirt. 'And they were my last decent pair.'

Gina turned to her. 'Sorry?'

'I've got a hole in my tights.' She pulled them off and dropped them in the bin. She was plump and curvy with messy auburn hair escaping from a pink scrunchy. Gina couldn't remember seeing her in the office before.

'I've got a spare pair in my bag if that will help?'

'Really? Wow, you're so organized.' The girl looked impressed. 'I never have anything useful like that. My handbag is full of crayons and plastic toys from McDonald's. Belonging to my kids, not me,' she grinned.

She looked too young to have children. Gina guessed she was in her twenties, but with her freckled snub nose and wide hazel eyes she could have been a teenager.

She rooted in her bag and took out the tights. The girl went to take them then snatched her hand back. 'I can't take those! They cost about twenty quid a pair.'

'It's fine, honestly.' Gina handed them to her.

'Are you sure? Thanks a lot.' She was already ripping open the packet. 'I'll buy you some more. As long as you don't mind Tesco's best?'

'You don't have to.'

'No, I will. As soon as I get paid. I'm Molly, by the way,' she said, balancing on one leg and struggling into the tights. 'I'm temping here.'

'Gina Farrell.'

'That's better.' Molly smoothed down her skirt. 'Thanks so much, you're a real lifesaver.' She turned back to the mirror and adjusted her ponytail. Gina noticed her scrunchy had a glittery Barbie on it. 'The only one I could find this morning,' she explained, catching her eye. 'It's bedlam in our house first thing.' She smoothed her hair back and it promptly escaped again. 'Oh God, it'll have to do. If Mr Tate doesn't like it, that's his problem.'

'Mr Tate?'

Molly nodded. 'James Tate. I'm standing in while his PA's on holiday. Do you know him? Actually, I'll be glad when this week's over,' she rushed on, not waiting for an answer. 'Between you and me, he's a right slave-driver. Never says please and thank you, just barks orders at me like I'm some kind of bloody robot. If I didn't need the money for Christmas I'd tell him where to stuff his rotten job.' She made a few more adjustments to her hair, then smiled in the mirror at Gina. 'Anyway, I'd better get back. I expect he'll have another mountain of stuff for me to do. Thanks again for your help.'

'No problem.' She watched Molly go, her curvy hips undulating under her cheap navy-blue skirt. She smiled to herself, wondering what her big brother made of his new temp. Not a lot, if she knew James.

She went back to the office. Claire and Trish were back from the wine bar, all flushed and giggly. But the laughter stopped as soon as she walked in.

Julie was there, too, looking the picture of injured innocence as she pounded away at her keyboard. Gina hesitated, aware that the others were watching her. 'Could I have a word, Julie?'

'Can it wait? I'm busy.' She didn't look up.

'It's about what happened earlier.'

'Forget it.'

'I just wanted to say, I'm sorry if I embarrassed you—'

'Like I said, forget it. It's over, OK?'

Gina shot a quick look at the others, then scuttled into her office and closed the door. She sank down at her desk, pushed her hair back off her face and let out a deep sigh. She couldn't do right for doing wrong.

It wasn't fair. All she wanted was a chance to fit in. She hadn't asked to take Julie's job. She'd begged to be allowed to take a more junior position, but no one would hear of it. She was Max Tate's daughter, and there was no way she was going to make tea.

It had been the same story when she'd worked in the Finance department. She'd been put in at a senior level and she'd been hopelessly out of her depth. But no one would help because they all resented her so much. In the end she'd had to leave.

She started at the little ping from her computer. An envelope symbol and the words 'You Have Mail' popped up on her screen.

It was an email from her daughter, Vicky, with a funny photo of her taken on her school field trip the previous weekend. She was swamped by a huge, dripping-wet dark-green cagoule, and only her cheeky little face poked out from the enormous hood. Her nose was smeared with mud. Attached were the words 'Love from Vicky' and a smiley face.

Gina felt tears pricking the backs of her eyes. Just looking at her daughter's toothy grin made her heart ache. She missed Vicky so much. Everyone said Heath Manor was a great school, with brilliant results and every facility under the sun. But it was still a boarding school, and Gina remembered how lonely and miserable she'd been when she was sent away. Vicky might be more confident and outgoing than she'd been at her age, but she was still only just eleven years old. She made up her mind to discuss it with Stephen again, see if they couldn't send her somewhere more local when she started secondary school in September.

She saved the message and turned her attention back to the Post-it 'to do' messages arrayed like bunting around her computer screen. There were a few calls to be made, advertising copy to be checked and proofs to read. And there was a call from the sales office on the Sunny Brook site, querying a price.

Sunny Brook. Every time Gina saw the name she had to smile. It conjured up pictures of lambs frolicking in green, daisy-flecked pastures beside a babbling stream under a cloudless sky. In fact, it was a rather dreary collection of shoebox-sized starter homes clustered around an overflow outlet. It had certainly given the interior designers a challenge, making the tiny show houses look spacious.

She dealt with all her calls, then turned her attention to the proofs for the Windmill Meadows brochure that Julie had so thoughtfully rewritten for her. She had to admit, it did sound much better than her version, waxing lyrical about its 'village atmosphere' and 'semi-rural feel', alongside lots of pretty pictures of rolling countryside and artist's impressions of what looked like mansions.

Her father had put a lot of money into the development, and he needed the houses to sell fast at premium prices to get a decent return on his investment. The brochure would help, as would advertising in the local press. But what they really needed was something big to catch people's attention. Gina was determined to make a success of the campaign. If only to show Julie and the others that she wasn't entirely useless, just because she was the boss's daughter.

She was still pondering this when another email envelope popped up on her screen.

'*Come and see me NOW – N*,' it said. Typical Nicole, Gina thought. No please or thank you. Not even a full name. As far as Nicole was concerned, everyone knew who she was. Or they damn well should.

She found her sister-in-law in the middle of the personnel department, giving a cowering young man a public dressing-down.

'And when I say I want something done now, I don't mean tomorrow or the next day, do you understand?' Her voice slipped into her old Grimsby accent, the way it always did when her temper rose. It was completely at odds with her stylish black Dolce and Gabbana suit and Manolo heels.

She slapped a file down on the unfortunate boy's desk, then turned and stalked into her office. Gina followed.

'What did he do to deserve that?' she asked, closing the door behind her. Trust Nicole to have secured a prime corner space, with floor-to-ceiling windows and designer furniture. A metal plate bearing the name 'Nicole Tate, Human Resources Manager' was stuck to the door. Unlike Gina, Nicole never liked anyone to forget who she was.

'He kept me waiting.'

'Did you have to embarrass him like that?'

'He deserved it.' Nicole slid behind her desk. Tall and strikingly attractive, she looked like a sexy Bond villain in her leather chair, with her black hair and eyes. The deep V of her jacket revealed a hint of cleavage edged with plum-coloured La Perla lace. 'Anyway, lady, you shouldn't be giving me lectures on dealing with staff. I've had a complaint about you.'

'Julie.' That hadn't taken long. 'Look, it was a misunderstanding. I tried to apologize but she wouldn't listen.'

'Gina, you're family. You don't have to apologize or explain.' Nicole consulted her notes. 'So what's this girl's problem?'

'She thinks I took her job.'

'You did, didn't you?'

'Yes. But I wish I hadn't.'

'So she's jealous. You can't blame her for that, can you? I'd be putting cyanide in your coffee if it was me.' Nicole closed her file. 'You've got to learn to fight back, show them who's boss.'

'That's the trouble. They know who's boss and they don't like it.'

'Who cares? That's their problem, not yours. So they give you a hard time – so what?' She leaned forward. 'You know what your trouble is, Gina? You want everyone to like you. You're like a Labrador, running around wagging your tail and trying to please everyone.'

There was no danger of that with Nicole, Gina thought. She didn't give a damn what anyone thought of her, which was how she'd managed to claw her way out of the typing pool and into her own executive office within five years. She was so ambitious Gina thought she would have made it even if she hadn't made the inspired career move of marrying the boss's son. And she hadn't finished yet. Nicole made it clear she wouldn't rest until she'd joined her husband Neil in the company's boardroom.

'Look, you're the boss's daughter. Of course everyone's going to resent you,' Nicole went on. 'No matter how brilliant you are, they're still going to think you've got the job because of that. Or they'll pretend to be your best friend to see what they can get out of you.'

'Maybe it would be better if I moved on.' Gina knew Nicole was right. She'd tried lots of other departments in the company; it had always been the same story.

'Are you mad? Why would you want to pass up a job like this? You've got it made here, far better than you'd get anywhere else. And let's face it, you're not exactly over-qualified, are you?'

'Thanks a lot. I do have four A-levels, you know. And lots of office skills.'

'Big deal. So you might end up as someone's secretary. Running around picking up some bloke's dry-cleaning and making tea at his meetings if you're really lucky. What a great job.'

'At least I'd be doing it on my own merits.'

'Oh, spare me!' Nicole lifted her eyes heavenwards. 'Look, Gina, take it from me. Life's tough out there. And if I was in your place, with all the opportunities you've got, I certainly wouldn't be thinking about giving it all up just because a couple of jealous bitches wanted to see me fail.'

'I suppose you're right,' Gina agreed.

'I know I am.' Nicole leaned back in her seat. 'So if I were you I'd go back to that department and start kicking some butt. Show them you can do the job and you're not going anywhere.' She pointed the tip of her Mont Blanc pen at her. 'You're a Tate, Gina. Start acting like one.'

That was the trouble, Gina thought as she walked back to her office. She didn't know how to be a Tate. She wasn't confident like her brothers. She didn't have her mother's glamour or her father's killer charisma. Sometimes she wondered if there had been a mix-up at the hospital. Even Nicole was more of a Tate than she was, and she'd only married into the family.

She went back to the office. Her sister-in-law was right, it was about time she took some control.

'I'm calling a meeting,' she announced.

'Another one?' Julie muttered, not looking up from her keyboard.

'Another one.' Gina gazed back at her, refusing to be daunted. 'And I want some ideas about the Windmill Meadows launch.'

'But we've already dealt with that,' Julie pointed out. 'Don't you remember?' She wasn't even attempting to hide her hostility now, as if the incident earlier gave her the right to be rude.

'I know, but I want something more than the usual sales material. A different approach.'

'But we always do it like that,' Claire said.

'Which could be why sales have been so disappointing on the other sites, do you think?' Gina looked at Julie when she said it. She might think she knew everything about marketing, but her sales figures told a different story.

By the time she got home three hours later she was exhausted. She'd hoped that giving her staff the chance to exercise their creative powers might energize them. But it was like trying to reanimate a corpse. All through the meeting, Claire had stared at her blankly, Trish had chewed her way through two biros, while Julie had done nothing but shake her head in slow disbelief at all Gina's suggestions.

Now all she wanted to do was kick off her shoes and relax on the sofa in front of *EastEnders*. So it was a surprise to see her husband Stephen's car parked outside the house.

He was in the drawing room, staring out of the French windows into the garden, a glass of whisky in his hand. For a moment Gina stood and gazed at him in silent adoration. He looked so handsome, framed by the swathe of cream curtains, his fair hair brushed back from his face, showing off his aristocratic cheekbones and full, slightly sulky mouth. No wonder the tabloids called him 'the heart-throb of the House of Commons'.

And he was hers. She felt a familiar surge of disbelief that out of all the women he could have had, Stephen Farrell MP had chosen her.

'Stephen? This is a lovely surprise. I didn't think you were back until the weekend?'

'Don't you remember, it's the constituency get-together

tonight?' He gave a sigh. 'Darling! You've forgotten, haven't you?'

'I don't think you ever told me.'

'Of course I told you. I showed you the invitation weeks ago, remember? Honestly, Gina, some political wife you are!'

He planted an affectionate kiss on the top of her head. Gina smiled up at him distractedly, but she was puzzled. She was sure she would have remembered the party. But she shrugged. Stephen was right; she was forever forgetting to write things down in her diary.

But after the day she'd had, the last thing she felt like doing was nibbling dried-up canapés and making small talk with the local Tory worthies.

'You don't have to come if you don't want to.' Stephen must have noticed the exhaustion on her face. 'I can easily go on my own.'

'No, no, of course I'll come.' She dredged up a smile. 'I'll just go and get ready.'

As she ran up the stairs, Stephen's voice followed her. 'Don't be long, we're due there in half an hour. And wear your blue dress.'

There was no time for a bath or even a shower. And she would have to think of a quick way to rescue her limp hair. She wished she'd taken the time to blow-dry it properly that morning, instead of spending an extra ten minutes in bed and then rushing out with it half-damp. Her mother would have despaired of her. Rose Tate never left the house unless she was perfectly coiffed and as well groomed as if she were attending a royal garden party.

She made some quick repairs to her face, outlining her green eyes with bronze pencil and adding more lipstick. Then she rifled through her wardrobe and pulled out the dress Stephen had suggested.

She felt depressed just looking at it. Stephen had bought it for her last birthday from a designer shop in London. It was frighteningly expensive and might have looked gorgeous on anyone else. But the royal-blue colour always made her pale skin look washed-out, however much make-up she slapped on. And the floaty fabric only emphasised her too-slender figure.

She went to put it back in the wardrobe but hesitated. On the other hand, Stephen *did* adore it . . .

'Ready, darling?' He came in as she was pinning up her hair. His smile dropped when he saw her. 'Oh. I thought you were wearing your blue dress?'

'I thought it might be a bit too dressy. And this colour suits me better, don't you think?' She certainly felt a lot more confident in the cinnamon wrap-dress.

Stephen frowned. 'Don't you like the dress I bought you?'

'It's not that. I just thought—'

'It's fine, you don't have to explain yourself to me.' His lower lip jutted as he fiddled with his cufflinks.

Gina eyed him warily. 'I could get changed?'

'I told you, it's fine.' He looked at his watch. 'Hurry up, will you? We should have left ten minutes ago.'

He was sulking, she realized with a heavy heart as she listened to him stomp downstairs. Now he would hardly speak to her all evening and the whole thing would be even more of a nightmare, unless she did something about it.

Stephen looked pleased when she followed him to the car five minutes later, wearing the blue dress. 'That's better.' He smiled his approval and leaned over to kiss her cool cheek. 'You look gorgeous, darling.'

She didn't feel it. She pulled her pashmina around her exposed shoulders and tried not to mind that Stephen had got his way again. It was his evening after all, she told herself. And it was just a silly dress. No big deal. Hardly worth getting stressed about, anyway.

She stole a sideways glance at him. He looked immaculate as ever in a dark Paul Smith suit and a stripy shirt, not modern enough to frighten the Tory matrons but not too stuffy either. Perfect, just like him. OK, so he could be a little over-bearing at times. But he was also kind, generous and caring.

And as her mother constantly reminded her, she was lucky to find someone like him – especially with her chequered past.

She was eighteen and in her first year at university when she got pregnant by an anthropology Ph.D. student called Tom. Her parents were appalled and wanted her to have an abortion. But Gina was determined to go ahead with the pregnancy. At least she had Tom's support. Until he suddenly acquired a large research grant to study the pygmy tribes of the Amazon basin, and took off without telling her, never to be heard of again.

Her parents tried again to talk her out of it, insisting she should give the baby up for adoption as soon as it was born. But Gina was determined to prove she could go it alone.

Cut adrift from the security of her family, she struggled through the rest of her pregnancy living in a bedsit and doing part-time bar jobs to make ends meet.

Things became even worse after Vicky was born. Gina thought she would be overwhelmed with love and that everything would come naturally to her. Instead she was swamped with feelings of misery and not being able to cope. She had no money, and no one to turn to for help and advice. All she had were endless days in a grubby flat with a baby who seemed to cry non-stop, as if she sensed what a useless mother she was stuck with.

Gina felt as if she'd reached rock-bottom. She'd failed herself, her family and, most of all, her innocent baby. In the long, dark, soul-destroying hours of the night, she got it into her head that her daughter would be better off without her.

So one evening she waited until she'd given Vicky her last feed and put her down for the night. At 2 a.m., she put a note through her neighbour's letterbox for her to find in the morning, took a handful of the sleeping pills the doctor had prescribed for her when she was stressed during her first-year exams, and washed them down with a bottle of vodka.

She woke up in hospital. Her neighbour had come home in the early hours from a party, found the note and called the police. They'd broken in and discovered Gina unconscious.

Her parents had acted immediately. Gina and Vicky were brought home, back into the protection of her family. She was grateful for their kindness, even after she'd let them down so badly. But the experience had taken away her self-confidence and made her doubt her ability to cope on her own.

Then, five years later, she met Stephen Farrell, a promising young lawyer with political ambitions. Within a few months they were engaged and for once Gina felt as if she'd finally done something right. Her father splashed out on a big society wedding and Gina basked in the warmth of her family's approval.

But she came down to earth with a bump when, just before he walked her down the aisle, her father turned to her and said, 'Try not to screw this up, won't you?'

And that's what she'd been doing for the past five years. Trying not to screw up.

Chapter 5

As they drove to the constituency party, Stephen gave her the usual rundown on who was who, including who she had to be especially nice to.

'. . . Now, make sure you ask about Pauline's husband, he's recently been in hospital. God knows why, but I expect she'll bore you about it. And please be nice to Alan, the chairman. He's a lecherous old goat, but you should be able to handle him. But watch what you say to his appalling wife, Liz, because any gossip goes straight back to him. Better still, don't talk to her at all.'

'Talk to Alan, don't talk to Liz. Got it.'

He went on, listing the other party guests and their faults and foibles. Gina tried to concentrate but gradually tuned out, thinking about the day she'd had at work. She would have liked to tell Stephen about it, but she didn't feel she could burden him with her petty troubles.

Stephen swung the car into the car park and parked up beside all the Volvos and 4x4s. 'If in doubt, just smile, look beautiful and keep your mouth shut. You can do that, can't you?'

'All three at the same time? Gosh, I don't know,' Gina muttered, but Stephen was already halfway across the car park, shaking someone's hand, his politician's smile firmly in place.

The party was being held in the local constituency office meeting room. As they ascended the narrow flight of stairs, Gina could hear the sound of laughter and the clink of glasses coming from above.

A waiter stood at the door with a tray of wine. 'Go easy on

that,' Stephen warned as she reached for a glass. 'Don't want you getting plastered, do we? Hugo, hello.' He beamed as a man and woman approached them. 'And Belinda, too. Looking as gorgeous as ever.'

There was soon a small crowd gathered around him, all wanting to meet and greet their glamorous local MP. Especially the women. Gina was almost swamped in the crush of polyester and pearls.

She couldn't help but admire the way he flirted and flattered his way around the room, offering a kiss here, a compliment there. He was born to be in politics, she decided. She could almost imagine him taking the top job one day, though she could never for a moment imagine herself as the Prime Minister's wife. She'd be counting the hours until she could escape and put her feet up back at Number Ten.

'It's Stephen's wife, isn't it?' Gina swung round and found herself at eye level with the massive, pink, crepe-covered bosom of a large woman with teeth like a racehorse. She pumped Gina's hand enthusiastically. 'Pamela Walton-Hedges.'

Gina focused on the hairy mole on the woman's upper lip and tried to think. Now was this the lesbian who bred spaniels, or the woman she wasn't supposed to speak to?

Pamela's smile became steely. 'Stephen must have mentioned me. I'm a governor at Woodcote Lodge school?'

'Oh, right. Of course.' She still had no idea who she was.

'Actually, I'm also an old girl,' Pamela confided. 'And I must say I had a very jolly time at Woodcote. Hard work, you know, and lots of discipline, but the results speak for themselves.'

'They do, don't they?' Gina gazed at Pamela's wobbling chins.

'Anyway, I'm sure your daughter will thrive there. If she gets in, of course. Competition for places is extremely fierce and even I don't have that much influence.' She gave a snort of laughter.

Gina stared perplexed at Pamela. 'I'm sorry, you've lost me. What's this about my daughter?'

Before she could answer, they were interrupted by Mark Warren, Stephen's political agent. 'Pamela! How wonderful to see you. And Gina, too. Hello, darling.' He kissed her on both cheeks, then turned back to Pamela. 'So how's life in the spaniel-breeding business these days?'

Gina was relieved Mark had taken the pressure off her. But she was still puzzled about what Pamela had said.

She'd heard of Woodcote Lodge school, of course. It was always at the top of the exam league tables. It also had a reputation for old-fashioned discipline, high standards and a regime that made the army look relaxed.

She'd certainly never thought of sending Vicky there. So where had Pamela got that idea from?

She found out a few minutes later when Stephen joined them. Pamela had already barged off across the room to greet an old friend.

'It was meant to be a surprise.' He looked disappointed. 'I've managed to sweet-talk Pam into getting Vicky an interview. Isn't that marvellous? Usually the waiting list is years long. You practically have to put your name down when the kid's an embryo.'

'I wish you'd told me.'

'Like I said, it was supposed to be a surprise.' He studied her face. 'I thought you'd be pleased?'

'I am, but—'

'Woodcote Lodge is a fantastic school. Its reputation is absolutely first class. Don't you want to have a chance like that?'

Gina glanced at Mark. She would have preferred to talk about it in private. 'I just wish you'd discussed it with me first.'

'What's to discuss? I've only got her an interview. She still might not get in.' Stephen's mouth turned down. 'I thought you'd be pleased I was taking an interest. I had to pull a lot of strings to get this far.'

'I know. And I'm grateful, really.'

'Although obviously it's *your* decision where we send her,' Stephen went on. 'As I'm constantly reminded, she's your daughter, not mine.'

Mark coughed. He looked as uncomfortable as Gina felt.

'That's not true, I've never said—'

'Look, if it's going to cause this much hassle I'll just tell Pam to forget it.'

'No! Don't do that. I'm grateful, Stephen, honestly. It wouldn't hurt to look around, would it?'

'That's what I thought.' Stephen looked satisfied. 'Now, if you'll excuse me, I should go and have a word with Alan.' He shouldered his way back through the crowd.

'Take no notice.' Mark read her expression. 'He's just a bit uptight at the moment. There's talk of an election in the late spring, and this is hardly a safe seat.'

'Do you think Stephen could lose?'

'*He* thinks he could. That's why he's got to be so careful.'

Gina felt herself relax. She liked Mark. He was easy company and managed to stop Stephen from getting too pompous. He wasn't just his agent, he was his best friend. They'd known each other since boarding school, and had been through law college together. But they couldn't have been more different. Stephen was tall, fair and slightly uptight; Mark was dark, stocky and so laidback he was almost horizontal.

Mark glanced around. 'Look, I'd better go and talk to a few people. Do you want to come with me?'

'I'll be fine. You go and schmooze.' Gina smiled back at him. She knew he had a job to do, just like Stephen.

Once alone, she gulped her warm wine and looked around for someone to talk to, but everyone had already gathered into unfriendly little groups, their backs turned to her.

She put her empty glass down on the table and slipped off to the loo to touch up her make-up. As usual, her eyes immediately went to her faults. Her fine, floppy blonde hair, her wide mouth, her long nose. People often said she was beautiful, but that wasn't what she saw when she looked in the mirror. She hitched up the straps of her dress, trying to conceal her lack of cleavage. A dress like this needed curves, and lots of them. She was as flat as an ironing board.

Her mother would be proud of her, she thought. A former model, Rose Tate regarded slenderness as the Holy Grail of beauty. When Gina had first shown signs of a blossoming teenage figure, Rose had immediately dragged her to a 'marvellous' doctor she knew, who'd prescribed tablets that made her jittery and unable to sleep, but also made her puppy fat melt away. Unlike her mother, however, slenderness didn't seem to suit her. While Rose still looked lithe and fabulous, as if she'd just stepped off the catwalk, Gina just looked gaunt.

When she returned to the party, they were marshalling people to either side of the room, clearing a space in the middle for the speeches, and Gina ended up being pushed to the sidelines. Alan the chairman took to the podium, thanking everyone for coming and cracking some jokes that made everyone laugh politely. Then he announced they were showing a sneak preview of a new party political. They all did their best to make excited noises. Gina looked around for Stephen, but there was no sign of him.

Then just as the lights dimmed and the plasma screen went on, she saw him on the far side of the room, at the back of the crowd. He was with a young woman she hadn't seen before. Gina caught a glimpse of her just as the room went dark.

'. . . Vote Conservative. For a better future.' As the final words echoed around the room, the lights went up again and there was a polite ripple of applause. Gina looked around. Stephen and the young woman were deep in conversation.

She found Mark. 'Who's that girl?'

'Lucy?' Mark shrugged. 'She's Stephen's new researcher.'

'What happened to the old one?'

'He left a couple of months ago.'

'Stephen never told me.' Gina watched them, their heads close together. There was something about the way Lucy looked up at him that sent an immediate warning prickle over her skin.

Just then Stephen looked up and saw her watching them. He gave her a self-conscious wave and moved through the throng towards her. Lucy followed.

'There you are. I thought you'd got lost.' He put his arm around her. 'Gina, I want you to meet Lucy Archer, my new researcher.'

'Hello.' Lucy held out her hand. She was very young and pretty in an earnest way. She wore flat shoes, a sensible knee-length navy skirt and a stripy shirt with the collar turned up. Her straight fair hair was held back with an Alice band. 'Stephen's told me so much about you.' Her accent was straight out of a Home Counties boarding school.

'Really? He's told me nothing about you.'

Lucy turned pink. 'I'm not surprised. I'm only a very lowly researcher.'

'For now,' Stephen put in. 'But I predict great things for this young lady. She'll soon be going places.'

'Oh!' Her round blue eyes shone behind her granny spectacles. 'Stephen's teaching me everything he knows.'

Gina didn't know why Lucy bothered her. She was so young and wholesome, but there was something too adoring about the way she gazed at Stephen. Of course she was bound to fancy him. He was her mentor, and everyone said power was an aphrodisiac, didn't they? And even without the power, Stephen was a very attractive man.

Like probing an aching tooth, she couldn't stop asking questions about her as they drove home She found out Lucy Archer had been working for Stephen for a month, after coming down from Oxford with a double first in politics and economics.

'She's incredibly bright,' Stephen told her. 'And absolutely passionate about politics.'

Unlike me, Gina thought glumly. 'She's got a huge crush on you.'

'Do you think so?'

'You'd have to be blind not to see it. And she's very pretty.'

'I hadn't really noticed.' He glanced at her. 'What's all this about? You don't think I fancy her, do you?'

'I wouldn't blame you if you did.' Gina stared straight ahead. 'Like I said, she's an attractive girl.'

'So are you.' Then, just as she was beginning to feel slightly reassured, he added, 'Besides, I'd have to be suicidal to go near her. The press would crucify me.'

Chapter 6

Finn dragged her bag out of the boot of her car, glad another week was over. Her old boss George Dunn had started running a site down in Lincoln and, for the past three weeks, she'd been working for him, staying overnight at the local B&B and coming home at weekends. She'd told her father she'd been transferred temporarily to another salon.

It wasn't ideal but it was better than sitting at home twiddling her thumbs. She'd applied for a few local jobs but the construction trade was a small world and she was wary of meeting someone who knew her father. And the fact that she was a woman didn't help. Once or twice she'd got as far as turning up on site, only to find that the vacancy had been miraculously filled.

'Dad?' she called out, then remembered her father was at the council meeting. His planning application was due to be rubber-stamped before the committee this evening, and he wanted to be there. He wasn't due home until eight, and it was only six now.

So she was surprised to hear a key in the door just as she was getting changed. She went downstairs and met Ciaran in the hallway.

He jumped when he saw her. 'You nearly gave me a heart attack! I didn't think anyone was home.'

'Why are you here, then?' He didn't answer. 'Ciaran?'

He looked shifty. 'It's just a bit of business, OK?'

'What kind of business?' She folded her arms across her chest.

Ciaran didn't meet her eye. 'I've just got some stuff I need to leave here for a few days.'

'And this stuff is stolen, I suppose? How many times have I told you, you're not keeping stolen goods in this house? Dad would have a fit if he found out.'

'Dad's not going to find out if you keep your mouth shut, is he? Go on, Finn, it's only for a couple of days. It'll be gone before you know it. And I've got nowhere else to stash it.'

'Why can't you keep it at your place?'

'Mel would go mad. And you know how tiny our flat is. She'd find it in no time. She's like a bloodhound.'

'You should have thought about that before you stole it.'

'I didn't steal it. I'm just looking after it for a friend.'

'Then take it back and tell him he's got to keep it.'

'He can't. The police are sniffing round his gaff already. Look, there's a hundred quid in it for me if I can keep it safe until the heat's off. And Mel and I need the cash. It's not cheap, looking after a kid, you know. It needs nappies, clothes—'

'I know. I'm always giving you the money to pay for them, remember?'

Finn was sickened. Here she was, travelling miles up and down the motorway and working her backside off, and all Ciaran could do was get himself into trouble.

'I wouldn't have to ask you again if you let me keep this stuff at the house for a while.'

'Forget it.'

'It's not your house, anyway. It's Dad's.'

They heard the sound of a car pulling up outside. 'That sounds like him now,' Finn said. 'Why don't you ask him if he minds?'

But they stopped arguing when they saw their father's sombre face. Ryan was with him.

'You're back early,' Finn said.

'There didn't seem much point in stopping. I was first on the list.'

'So how did it go?'

'They turned it down.' Joe sounded dazed, as if he couldn't quite believe it himself. 'They're not going to let me build on the land.'

'But why?' Finn and Ciaran looked at each other. 'Did they give any reason?'

'Not much. Just a lot of nonsense about preserving the green belt, and traffic flows, and all that. I don't understand it.' He shook his head.

'But the architect said it was just a formality.'

'Seems he was wrong. We all were.'

Joe went into the sitting room and sank down on the sofa. He looked grey-faced and defeated. The others followed him, none of them quite knowing what to say.

It was Ciaran who spoke first. 'I said you should have taken that money.'

'Oh, shut up, Ciaran!' Finn went to sit beside her father. 'Surely there's some way we can fight this?'

'We could appeal, I suppose.'

'Then let's do it. There's no way that land should have been refused planning permission.'

'Finn's right,' Ryan said. 'You've got to take this to appeal, Joe.'

'Appeals take time and money,' Joe said. 'I've already invested everything I had to buy this land. I can't afford to lose any more.'

Finn looked at her father. She hated to see the crushed look in his eyes. She felt like marching down to that town hall now and knocking the blocks off those smug councillors who'd destroyed his hopes and dreams with a flick of their pens.

'Then we'd better start straight away.' She stood up and reached for her jacket.

Joe looked up at her. 'Where do you think you're going?'

'Down to that meeting. I want that lot to know we're not taking this lying down.'

'Sit down, Finnuala,' Joe said. 'I'm not having you marching down there shouting the odds.'

'Your dad's right,' Ryan said quietly. 'It wouldn't help.'

'It would make me feel a lot better.' Finn directed her frustration at Ryan. What was *he* doing here, anyway? 'We've got to do something.'

'True,' Ryan agreed. 'But storming down to the town hall isn't going to help your dad, is it?'

Finn glanced at her father. She could see Ryan was right, which just made her even more furious. 'So what do you suggest we do?'

Ryan was about to answer when the phone rang. Ciaran got to it first. He listened, then handed it to Joe. 'It's for you.'

Joe took the phone. 'Hello? Yes, this is Joe Delaney.' He listened intently for a few minutes, his face expressionless. 'How much did you say? Can I think about that? I see. Well, thank you for calling.' He put the phone down and looked around at their expectant faces. 'That was the land agents – you know, the ones that wrote to me before? They've made another offer.'

'Well, that's it, then. Problem solved.' Ciaran rubbed his hands together. 'They can take it off our hands.'

'They've offered half what they did before.'

'What?' Finn snatched up the phone and hit 1471. 'They can't do that. I'll tell them where they can stick their offer—'

'No, Finnuala.' Joe took the receiver out of her hand. 'If the worst comes to the worst we might have to consider it.'

'But the land is worth more than that.'

'Not without planning permission it isn't.' Joe shook his head. 'I can't imagine anyone would want it if they can't build on it. We'll be lucky to get anything back on it at all.'

'We should build the houses anyway. Let the council tear them down if they dare!'

'And how would you sell them?' Ryan reasoned. 'Do you seriously think anyone would buy a house knowing it could get demolished at any time?'

Finn glared back at him. 'I don't see you lot coming up with any better plans.'

'That's because we're still thinking about it.'

'And while you're still thinking we're losing money.' Finn looked at her father, willing him to fight. This wasn't the way he'd brought them up, to accept defeat without a murmur. But it seemed as if all the energy had gone out of him. 'Anyway, if the land's so useless why do those agents want it so badly?'

'God knows,' Joe said. 'Perhaps they know something we don't.'

Finn frowned. 'Come to think of it, they were a bit quick off the mark, weren't they? How did they know it had been turned down for planning permission?'

'Maybe they were at the meeting.' Joe looked wearily at her. 'Why don't you put the kettle on, Finnuala? I could murder a brew.'

Put the kettle on, Finnuala. Finn stomped around the kitchen, filling the kettle and dropping teabags into the pot, feeling aggrieved as she listened to Joe, Ciaran and Ryan talking in low voices in the other room. Holding a council of war while she was banished to the kitchen to make the tea. Why could he discuss business with Ryan and not his own daughter?

And yet she was the only one coming up with any ideas, if anyone bothered to listen.

That call from the land agents still troubled her. Why would they bother to get in contact so quickly? They had to be desperate to get their hands on the land, which meant it couldn't be that useless. And how did they know their planning permission had been turned down? Maybe her father was right, and they had been at the meeting. Or maybe they already knew what the outcome would be?

She splashed tea into the mugs, feeling agitated. Let the men talk and feel sorry for themselves. If they didn't want her to be involved, fine. She was going to sort this out on her own.

On Monday morning Finn called to tell George she'd had a family crisis. Then she drove into Leeds to visit the Land Registry offices. The woman behind the counter helped her find the right plans for the area.

Finn had seen these plans a hundred times before when they were spread out on the kitchen table. There was her father's field – a tiny, insignificant blob edged with a red line. It was bordered on one side by the road and on the others by surrounding farmland.

Then she spotted another, slightly larger strip of land behind her father's. That was also bordered in a red line, meaning it belonged to someone else.

She picked up the plans and went back to the desk. 'How can I find out who this land belongs to?'

'You can't,' the woman said. 'We don't give out that kind of information here. All we can tell you is when the land was registered.'

'What does that mean?'

'Land has had to be formally registered for the last twenty years or so. So if it was bought or sold since then it will show up on our records.'

'Could you look for me, please?'

The woman went away. Finn drummed her fingertips on the desk and waited.

Finally the woman returned. 'This is the date that piece of land was registered.'

Finn looked down at the slip of paper. The land had been bought six months before her father bought his. 'And you can't tell me who owns it?'

'Sorry, no.' Then, as Finn turned to walk away, she added, 'But you could try the rates office; they'd be able to tell you who's paying rates for that land.'

'Thanks.' Finn paid her money to buy a copy of the plans, rolled them up and took them back to her car.

She headed to the council rates office, but everyone was at lunch. Finn sat down to wait and studied the plans again, looking for clues. The mystery piece of land was locked in behind her father's. Finn wondered why anyone had bothered to buy it when the only access to the road was straight through Joe's land.

That was it. She leapt to her feet, stuffed the plans back into her bag and went back to the reception desk. The receptionist eyed her wearily, then went back to her magazine. 'They're not back yet,' she said, not looking up.

'I've changed my mind. Is there anyone in the planning department I could speak to?'

Thankfully, the young planning assistant was keen to help. 'There don't seem to be any plans lodged for that area,' she said.

'But I remember there were some pre-planning discussions. That means the developer approached us to find out what they needed in order to be sure of planning permission.'

'And what did you tell them?' Finn asked.

'Well, obviously they would need access to the main road. They couldn't develop it otherwise.'

'So they'd need this piece of land here?' Finn pointed to her father's field.

'That would be the best route. Unless they bought this lot and built a road all the way round.' She indicated a curve through the surrounding farm's fields. 'But that would be very expensive, and a lot more work.'

'And do you know who owns this land?'

'I've got the file here.' The girl flicked through a few pages. 'Ah, yes. A company called Grantwich Holdings. Is that any help?'

'Not at the moment,' Finn said. 'But it's a start.'

She drove back through the country, intending to speak to the farmer who'd sold her father the land. He'd be able to tell her who to contact at Grantwich Holdings.

As she turned the corner before Joe's field at Whitecroft Farm, she almost crashed into a black Saab parked on the blind bend.

She cursed as she swerved to avoid it. Then she saw Neil Tate standing at the gate, looking over her father's field.

She parked her car on the verge further up the road then came back. 'What are you doing here?'

He turned to look at her. 'Finn Delaney. Fancy seeing you here. Or are you stalking me?'

'I asked you a question. What are you doing on our land?'

His brows lifted. 'Your land?'

She pointed over the gate. 'That field belongs to my father.'

'Does it? I was told it might be on the market soon.'

'Who told you that?'

'My brother James.' He gazed back across the field, squinting at the horizon. 'He told me to come and look at it. Said the owner might be wanting to get rid of it now their planning permission has been turned down.'

'And why would you want it, without planning—' Realization hit her like a slap in the face. 'You're Grantwich Holdings, aren't you?'

His face was blank. 'I have no idea what you're talking about.'

'Don't give me that. You own that land over there. And you can't build on it without access through ours.'

'You might well be right, but you'd have to talk to my brother about that. James handles all the acquisitions. I'm just a humble foot soldier in the great Tate army.'

Finn looked him up and down, from his designer overcoat to his handmade shoes. 'Humble? You?'

'OK, so I'm an arrogant, self-satisfied shit of a foot soldier. Blame my upbringing.' He shrugged.

She tried hard not to smile. 'So you don't know anything about Grantwich Holdings?'

He shook his head. 'My family never tells me anything. Between you and me, I'm sort of the black sheep. But it wouldn't surprise me if my brother was behind it. I can see why they'd need your land.' He glanced sideways at her. 'Are you sure you wouldn't want to sell?'

'No way.'

'Oh well, it was worth a try.' He pulled up the collar of his coat against the drizzle. 'But I'm warning you, my family doesn't give up easily. What have you got against us, anyway?'

'I think you're crooks. You use your money and your power to trample over anyone who gets in your way.'

'I can't argue with that,' Neil agreed affably. 'My father certainly likes to win. So does my brother.'

'And you're nothing like them, I suppose?'

'I wouldn't say that. But they don't quite know what to do with me. James is my father's right hand man. He's terribly serious, never puts a foot wrong. He went to university and got a first. I went to university and got kicked out for sleeping with the vice chancellor's daughter.'

Finn stared. 'Can you get kicked out for that?'

'No. But I did sleep with his wife too.'

'Sounds like you're more of a wolf in black sheep's clothing.'

'You could be right. At least, I'm not very good at doing as I'm told. Big problem with authority. I suppose that's what comes of having an overbearing father. I'm actually quite damaged.'

His dark eyes were looking straight at her now, teasing her. She wasn't used to men looking at her like that. She knew she wasn't exactly ugly, but she'd become used to playing down her looks and being treated like one of the lads on site. She dragged her gaze away, not wanting him to see how much he'd unsettled her.

'So why do you want to hang on to this land, anyway?' he said. 'It's no use to you without planning permission.'

We can get it on appeal.'

'You won't win.'

He said it with such quiet confidence, Finn felt a stab of unease. 'What makes you so sure?'

'If my father wants that land, he's going to have it. Why do you think you didn't get that planning permission?'

'He *bribed* them?'

'You said it yourself: we use our money and power to trample over anyone who gets in our way. And, thanks to my father's friends in high places, you probably won't be allowed to build so much as a garden shed on that land.'

'Until you get hold of it, and suddenly everything will be fine,' Finn said.

'I don't know about that. Like I said, I don't deal with that side of things. But I'm sure we can come to some arrangement that will suit our friends on the council.'

'I bet you can.' Finn felt suddenly, overwhelmingly depressed. But there was one thing she couldn't work out. 'Why are you telling me this?'

'Because I think you've had a rough deal.' He leaned towards her. There were amber flecks in his dark brown eyes, she noticed. 'And I'm hoping that one day you might forget I'm a Tate and learn to trust me.'

Before she could reply, her phone rang. Finn jumped and turned away to answer it.

'Finn?'

'Ryan?' Hearing his voice snapped her out of her trance.

'Look, I don't want you to panic,' as soon as he said it her heart started pounding, 'but you need to get to the hospital as soon as you can. It's your dad . . .'

Chapter 7

Ryan was waiting in the corridor outside the Intensive Care Unit when Finn rushed in twenty minutes later.

'How is he?'

OK, I think. They won't tell me much, but I gather they've managed to stabilize him.'

'Oh, thank God.' Finn put her hand to her trembling mouth, fighting back the emotion. The adrenaline rush that had brought her flying to the hospital ebbed away, leaving her weak. 'Where is he? I have to see him.'

'I'll tell them you're here. But take a minute to calm down first.'

'How can I calm down? My dad's just had a heart attack!' Then she saw the pallor in his face and realized he was just as scared as she was. 'Sorry,' she mumbled.

'Don't worry about it.'

'Where's Ciaran?'

'I don't know. I've tried ringing him at home but there's no one there. And his mobile's switched off.'

'Typical. Why wasn't he with Dad when this happened? He was supposed to be doing a roofing job with him today.'

'He couldn't make it, so Joe asked me to help him instead.'

'It's not right, Ciaran should have been there. What if this had happened when he was on his own? What if he'd fallen . . .' Hot tears stung her eyes as the enormity of the situation hit her.

'Shh, it's OK.' She felt a scrap of tissue pushed into her hand. 'I'll go and find that doctor.'

She sank on to a plastic bench and waited. The fluorescent strip lights were festooned with limp tinsel and paper chains in an attempt to make the place look festive. The determined cheeriness only made her feel worse.

Ryan returned a moment later with some tea. 'They've sedated him, but they say you can go in in a minute. Look, try not to worry. He's going to be fine. He's tough, your dad.'

'That's what I thought.' Her hand shook as she took the cup from him. She'd always thought her father was strong, invincible. She remembered all the times she'd turned a blind eye to the sneaky cigarettes and fry-ups. 'I warned him this would happen. I told him he had to take care of himself. Why didn't he listen to me?'

'You can't make Joe Delaney do anything he doesn't want to do. He's stubborn.'

She smiled slightly at that. Her father *was* stubborn. Maybe he'd be too stubborn to let a stupid old heart attack get the better of him.

She looked around. 'Maybe I should give Ciaran another call.'

'I left another message, while I was looking for the doctor.'

'Thanks.' Finn was grateful for his calm, reassuring presence. 'Do you think it was my fault?' she asked. 'I've been giving him such a hard time, trying to get him to fight that planning permission—'

'You can't blame yourself.'

'But I should have been looking after him, not nagging him into an early grave.'

'He's a grown man, you can't watch him twenty-four hours a day.'

'All the same, I should have been there.'

'I was with him, remember?'

'That's different. You're not . . .' Not family, she wanted to say, but stopped herself when she saw the hurt look in his eyes.

At that moment a doctor rounded the corner. 'Miss Delaney?'

Finn jumped up. 'Have you seen my dad? Is he going to be all right?'

'He's doing well. I'll take you to see him, shall I?'

The cardiac ward was dark and silent apart from the bleeping of the machines. It took all her courage not to cry out when she saw her father with wires coming out of him, attached to various monitors. He looked so frail against the pillows, nothing like the strong man she'd lived with and fought with and looked up to for so long. It suddenly occurred to her that she wouldn't know what to do if she lost him.

He turned his head to look at her. 'Flaming hospitals,' he grumbled. 'I don't know what I'm doing here. It was only a funny turn.'

Finn sagged with relief. 'It was a bit more than that, Dad.'

'Lot of fuss over nothing,' Joe went on. 'I've a good mind to discharge myself. Let them give the bed to someone who really needs it.'

'Not just yet, Mr Delaney.' The doctor smiled. 'Luckily the paramedics were able to administer the necessary drugs in time, so there was minimal damage to the heart muscle,' he told Finn. 'It's fortunate your friend Mr Hunter was with him, or it might have been a lot worse.'

Finn looked around for Ryan. She thought he'd followed her in, but there was no sign of him. 'So he'll be OK?'

'If he's sensible with his health.'

'I am still here,' Joe interrupted them, looking irritable. 'It's my heart that went wrong, not my hearing!'

'We'll need to carry out some tests to find out what caused the heart attack,' the doctor went on. 'Depending on the results, we may have to carry out an operation to open up the blood vessels and prevent another attack.'

'But I need to go back to work,' Joe protested. 'I've got a business to run.'

'I'm afraid it will be some time before you're fit to work again, Mr Delaney. You could be in hospital for a couple of weeks, and then you'll have to undergo several weeks of coronary care.'

'Don't worry, we'll take care of the business,' Finn reassured him.

'Doesn't look like I've got much choice, does it?' Joe looked grim at the prospect. 'Where's Ciaran?'

He's on his way.' Finn crossed her fingers. She hoped Ryan had managed to track him down.

She talked to her father for a few more minutes and made sure he had everything he needed. Then, as the sedative kicked in and his eyelids began to droop, she went back outside.

Ryan, who was slumped on the bench, shot to his feet when he saw her. 'How is he?'

'Almost his old self, would you believe. I never thought I'd be glad to hear him moaning!'

'Didn't I tell you? It'll take more than a heart attack to keep Joe Delaney down.'

'Worse luck. He's already fretting about the business. Why didn't you come in with me?'

'I thought you might prefer to be alone with him.'

Finn felt a stab of guilt. 'I'm sorry I said that – about you not being family.'

'You're right, I'm not,' Ryan said. 'But Joe's been good to me. And I've always thought of him as sort of like a dad. Especially since I never knew mine.'

He rarely talked about his background, but Finn knew he'd had a rough start. His father had walked out on them when Ryan was barely a toddler. He'd grown up looking after his mum and his younger brother Tony. But as a teenager he'd gone off the rails, ending up in a young offenders' institution as a result of the hit-and-run. When he came out, he'd found it hard to settle and find a job, until Joe took him on and taught him the trade.

'And I know he's always thought of you as a son.' Even though it annoyed her at times, she knew it was true.

'Thanks. That means a lot to me.'

'At least you're here, which is more than I can say for his real son. I don't suppose you've managed to get hold of Ciaran?'

'I spoke to him ten minutes ago. He's on his way.'

'Thank God for that. Shall we go outside and meet him?' As they headed down the corridor she said, 'I'm still furious about him dumping on Dad like that. I expect he was skiving as usual.'

'Don't be too hard on him. Your brother's not cut out to be a builder.'

'Then why doesn't he just tell Dad that, instead of leaving him in the lurch all the time?'

'Maybe he doesn't want to hurt his feelings. You know how Joe feels about his son following in his footsteps.'

Finn was silent. There she was, desperate to do just that, and her father wouldn't give her the chance. 'It's not fair,' she said.

'It's hardly your dad's fault. He doesn't know his daughter's a qualified builder, does he?'

'Only because he'd go mad if he did.'

'So what made you decide to do it?'

'I never wanted to do anything else,' she shrugged.

'It must be in your blood.'

'Try telling my dad that.'

'I can't imagine you working on a building site.'

Finn bristled. 'Don't you think I can cope?'

'I reckon you'd cope just fine. It's the other lads I feel sorry for.'

'Don't worry, I'm gentle with them.'

They ended up in the brightly lit reception area. It was early evening, and the place milled with visitors buying flowers and cards in the gift shop, while others anxiously scanned the signposts to the various wards.

'So do you think the stress of all this land business might have caused him to get ill?' Finn asked, as they loitered.

'I daresay it didn't help.'

'I hope Max Tate's pleased with himself.'

'What's he got to do with anything?'

Finn told him what she'd found out.

'And why's his son telling you all this?' Ryan wanted to know.

'He just wants the truth to come out, I suppose.' She tried to avoid Ryan's sceptical gaze. 'Anyway, it seems Tates are desperate to get their hands on Dad's land.'

'Perhaps it might be better if he sold it to them?'

Finn stared at him, aghast. 'You've changed your tune. What's brought this on?' Something in his expression made her look again. 'Ryan? Is there something you're not telling me?' He looked hesitant. 'Look, if you know something, I want to hear about it.'

Ryan sighed, then said, 'Your dad didn't just use most of his savings to buy that land. He borrowed from the bank.'

'How much?'

'Enough to cause him to worry about making the repayments. It gets more difficult with every month that goes by.'

Finn shook her head. 'No, you've got it wrong. Dad would never do that.' He'd always said that she should never buy anything she couldn't pay for, and never, ever borrow over her head. And how many lectures had he given her on the evils of credit cards?

'He thought it would be OK. Everyone kept telling him what a safe bet that land was. As soon as those houses were built he could pay off the loan easily, and make a decent sum on top to see him through his old age. He didn't think he could lose.'

She still couldn't believe it. Ciaran was the gambler, not her father. He would certainly never risk the business.

'So why didn't he tell me?'

'He didn't want to worry you.'

'When is he going to realise I don't need protecting!'

Just then Ciaran came hurtling through the automatic doors.

'Where the hell have you been?' Finn immediately took out all her frustration on her brother. 'Why was your phone switched off? Our dad could have been dying in there . . .' Then she saw Ciaran's pale, tearful face and some of her anger melted away. She reached for him, hugging him close. 'He's OK.' Her voice was muffled against his leather jacket. He smelled of stale beer and cigarettes. 'He's had a scare but they're pretty sure he'll pull through.'

'Can I see him?'

She nodded. 'He's been asking for you.' She pointed towards the doorway leading to the wards.

Ciaran hesitated, then turned back to her. 'Will you come with me?'

Finn was about to make a caustic comment about him standing on his own two feet, then she caught Ryan's eye. 'Of course,' she said. 'We'll all go.'

Ciaran gripped her hand when he saw his father in the bed, his eyes closed, his skin ashen.

'Holy Mother of God,' he whispered, crossing himself.

'I'm not dead, if that's what you're thinking.' Joe's eyes snapped open. 'And there's no need to whisper, you're not at a funeral!' His gaze fixed on Ciaran. 'Where have you been?'

'I had some business to sort out.'

'Oh aye? And what kind of business would that be?'

'Security.' He scratched his neck, a sure sign he was lying. 'Someone offered me a bit of extra cash, looking after a site. I thought the money would come in handy for Mel and the baby.'

'You should have been with Dad,' Finn said.

'It's all right, Finnuala, it's done now.' Joe lifted his hand and let it drop heavily back on to the bedclothes. 'But you're going to need to put all your energy into the business from now on,' he said. 'It looks like I'm going to be laid up for a few weeks and I want you to look after things until I'm back on my feet.'

'And how long do you think that'll be?'

'Does it matter?' Finn cut in.

'Finnuala!' Joe shot her a warning look, then turned back to Ciaran. 'I don't know. A month, maybe a bit more.' He smiled reassuringly. 'Don't worry, lad. You should be able to keep things ticking over until then.'

'Yeah, well, you see it's not that simple—' Ciaran began, but Finn cut him off.

'It'll be fine,' she said, glaring at her brother. The last thing she wanted was Joe worrying. 'You just concentrate on getting better, Dad. I can look after the business if Ciaran can't manage it.'

'Well, I suppose you could help out with the invoices and the banking. But only if it doesn't interfere with your hairdressing.'

Hairdressing! Finn was beginning to wish she'd never made up that stupid story. She was tempted to tell her father the truth right then but realized he didn't need any more shocks.

'And I can always lend a hand, too,' Ryan said. He'd been standing so quietly at the end of Joe's bed she'd almost forgotten he was there.

'Thanks, lad. I appreciate it.' Finn saw the warm look that passed between them, and fought down a surge of jealousy.

She listened as Joe told Ciaran all about the work they had coming up, and instructed him on how to price up any other jobs if they came in. Ciaran, to her annoyance, hardly seemed to be paying attention. He glanced at his watch a couple of times when he thought his father wasn't looking.

When they came out of the ward, Ciaran said, 'He seems on top form, doesn't he?'

'Has it ever occurred to you he might just be doing that to make us feel better?' Ciaran might not have noticed the anxiety in their father's eyes, but she had.

'He'll be fine.' Ciaran glanced at his watch again. 'Look, I've got to shoot off, OK?'

'But they should have the results of the tests soon.' Finn followed him down the corridor. Ryan came after her. 'Don't you want to stay and find out if Dad needs an operation?'

'I would, but I promised I'd be somewhere. Which reminds me, can I borrow your car?'

'Where's yours?'

'Failed its MOT. I had to get a taxi here.'

'Then you can get a taxi home, can't you?'

'I could if you lent me a tenner?'

Finn sighed, reached into her pocket and pulled out her car keys. 'I want it back outside our house by tomorrow morning, OK? No later. Ciaran, are you listening?'

'Yeah, yeah, I'm listening. Thanks, sis, you're a star.' He planted a quick kiss on her cheek.

'I'm a mug, that's what I am,' Finn muttered, as he sauntered across the car park.

She and Ryan stood outside the hospital, sheltering from the cold December air beside a lopsided Christmas tree. Light spilled out from the doorway behind them.

'What are you going to do now?' Ryan asked.

'I'm going to wait around and see the doctor, then I'll to sit with Dad for a while.'

'Do you want me to hang around and give you a lift home?'

Before she could open her mouth to reply, a voice shouted, 'Ryan? Ry-an!'

They turned. A redheaded woman was hurrying across the car park towards them, huddled in a fake-fur jacket, her handbag swinging. Finn thought she heard Ryan sigh, but when she looked at him he was smiling.

'Wendy. What are you doing here?'

'I got your text, so I came straight away.' The woman's wide eyes were filled with concern. 'Are you OK? You said you'd had to go to hospital—'

'I'm fine. It's Finn's dad who was taken ill.'

'Oh, I'm sorry.' Wendy's gaze skimmed over Finn then went straight back to Ryan. 'God, you had me so worried! I thought you'd had an accident, or something really awful.'

'No, it's nothing really awful,' Finn said. 'Just my dad in intensive care.' But Wendy didn't seem to hear.

'You didn't have to come,' Ryan said. 'I texted to say I couldn't see you.'

'And what was I supposed to do, sit at home worrying? Anyway, I'm here now. So we might as well go for a drink or something.'

Ryan glanced at Finn, 'I was going to stay . . .'

'No, it's fine. You go. I don't want to spoil your evening.'

'If you're sure?'

But Wendy already had her arm tucked firmly through his, leading him away.

'You'll let me know if there's any news?' Ryan called back over his shoulder.

Finn watched them go. From the look on Ryan's face she had the feeling Wendy wouldn't last much longer. Ryan hated clingy women.

On the way back to the ward she bought herself a plastic, pre-packed ham and salad sandwich and ate it alone in the empty canteen. It was past visiting time and everyone had gone home. The catering staff were piling chairs on tables around her, to the accompaniment of piped Christmas carols played on a tinny sound system. She suddenly felt very lonely.

Later that night, after she'd made sure her father had everything he needed, she went home. As she headed towards the main gates a figure stepped out of the shadows in front of her. Finn let out a cry before she recognized who it was. Neil Tate.

'Bloody hell!' She put her hand to her fluttering chest. 'What are you doing here?'

'Waiting for you.'

'Until this time?' She looked at her watch. It was past nine o'clock.

'I was going to come in but I didn't want to intrude. How's your dad?'

'Why do you want to know? He's not going to die and leave you that land in his will if that's what you're thinking.'

Neil suppressed a sigh. 'Believe it or not, I was concerned.'

She wasn't sure if she did believe him. 'Sorry.' She rubbed her eyes. 'It's been a long day.'

'I'll bet it has. Do you want to go somewhere? We could get something to eat?'

'The only place I want to go is home.' She felt suddenly, overwhelmingly tired, as if all the emotions of the day had suddenly caught up with her. 'Besides, I've got to call Dad's family back in Ireland, let them know what's going on. But you could give me a lift home?' she added, remembering Ciaran had taken her car.

'Are you sure it's not too much trouble?' she said as they drove. The warm leather interior of Neil's Saab was so comfortable, she could have fallen asleep there and then.

'I've just spent two hours sitting in a freezing car park. I'm not going to object to giving you a lift home, am I?'

'It was very kind of you.'

'Haven't you heard? I'm all heart.'

As they turned down a shabby terrace of tall Victorian houses, Finn noticed through half-closed eyes a large hoarding illuminated in the moonlight. 'Bought for re-development by Tate Associates.'

'Your family gets everywhere, doesn't it?' she said.

'That's Paradise Road. My father's pet project. He plans to

knock the whole lot of those houses down and develop the entire area.'

'Seems a shame. They're lovely houses.'

'It's a dump.'

Finn looked up at the houses as they passed. Most of them had a dead look, with boarded-up windows and overgrown front gardens. But lights still blazed in the upstairs windows of one of the houses, right in the middle of the terrace. 'Are people still living there?'

'For now,' Neil said. 'They'll be moving on soon. Once they've sold to my father.'

'What if they don't want to sell?'

'They will if they've got any sense.' There was something about the way he smiled that made her uneasy. Until he added, 'I mean, look at the place. Would you want to live in a street full of derelict houses? The place is a magnet for druggies and troublemakers.'

They drove on. Finn was silent, preoccupied by what Ryan had told her about her father. She couldn't believe Joe had taken out that loan.

'You're very quiet. Thinking about your dad? Don't worry, he'll be fine. People recover from heart attacks all the time these days.'

'I hope you're right.'

'Perhaps I could talk to my father? Get him to ease off for a while?'

She looked across at him. 'Do you think he would?'

'I don't know. But I could give it a try.' He reached over and patted her hand. 'Look, my father's a businessman, but he's not a monster. I'm sure he'll take the pressure off your dad if I talk to him.'

'Thanks. That would be really kind.'

'I told you, I'm all heart.'

By the time they reached her house, Finn had already planned her excuses in case he tried to wangle an invitation to come in. She was almost disappointed when he said, 'I won't come in for coffee.'

'I wasn't going to ask you.'

Neil smiled. He leaned across towards her, and, for a moment, Finn panicked, thinking he was moving in for a kiss. But all he did was peck her cheek and unclick her seat-belt for her.

He must have read the confusion in her face. There was a teasing glint in his eyes as he said, 'Maybe next time.'

Did he mean the coffee or the kiss? Finn wondered as she scrambled out of the car.

Chapter 8

Woodcote Lodge was a grim Gothic building, all mullioned windows and ivy-covered walls. It sat in a gloomy valley, surrounded by looming Northumbrian hills and dark, bare trees.

'I'm sure it looks much better when the weather's nice,' Gina said as they hurried through the grey, drizzling rain. Vicky didn't reply. She hadn't uttered a word all the way up in the car. But her silence spoke volumes.

Stephen, however, was in raptures once they were inside. 'Look at this place, it's so full of history,' he said as they passed along hushed oak-panelled corridors hung with paintings of former teachers and famous pupils.

That's true, Gina thought. Woodcote Lodge was like a museum. The library was lined with dusty leather volumes that looked as if they hadn't been touched for years, some behind glass cases. The classrooms were gloomy and musty-smelling. And the science lab looked so antiquated she could almost imagine Louis Pasteur developing his germ theory in there. They should rechristen this place Dotheboys Hall, she decided.

The headteacher, Mrs Hardwick, would have made Wackford Squeers look positively liberal. She was a tall, austere woman with stiff, frosted grey hair and no make-up apart from a slash of fuchsia lipstick on her narrow mouth. A set of keys hung ominously on a chain, resting on her fearsome shelf of a bosom.

'Of course, I believe my girls thrive on discipline,' she said as she led the way past the sports hall. 'We have a very strict routine here at Woodcote. Early rising, plenty of physical exercise and lots of—' cold showers, Gina expected her to say, '—hard work. I hope you like hard work, Victoria?' She eyed Vicky severely.

'She prefers to be called Vicky,' Gina said. 'You like drama and art, don't you, darling?' She nudged her daughter, willing her to look keen for Stephen's sake. 'Her teachers say she has real talent.'

'Hmm.' Mrs Hardwick's mouth compressed in a 'we'll soon beat that out of her' way. 'We do place more emphasis on the academic subjects here.'

'Quite right, too.' Stephen glared at Gina as they followed Mrs Hardwick to inspect the dormitories.

'Do I really have to come here?' Vicky whispered to Gina.

Over my dead body. It was too depressingly like her old boarding school. 'Of course not, darling. I told you, we're just taking a look around.'

'Stephen seems to like it.'

'He does, doesn't he?' Gina was rather worried. He seemed to be sold on the idea already. He and Mrs Hardwick were practically holding hands by the end of the visit. She seemed utterly charmed with him, too. Any minute now she'd be organizing a public flogging for his entertainment.

'You could have been more enthusiastic,' Stephen accused when they were in the car heading home. 'And what was all that about Vicky being artistic?'

'She is.'

'There's no need to tell them that, is there. You know that's not what Woodcote is about.'

'Then maybe it's not the right school for Vicky.' Gina glanced at her daughter. She was moodily chewing her thumbnail in the back seat.

'Of course it's the right school for her. You liked it, didn't you Vicky?'

'No.'

'That's not the point, anyway,' Stephen said. 'No one likes boarding school unless they're Harry Potter. You want her to have the best education she can, don't you?'

'Of course, but—'

'So that's settled, then. Anyway, I've already talked Mrs Hardwick into letting her sit the entrance exam in January,' he added.

They drove the rest of the way in sullen silence. Stephen was sulking again, Gina realized. This became obvious when he announced he was taking Vicky straight back to school.

'But I thought we were all spending the weekend together?' Gina protested.

'Sorry, I can't. I've got some urgent work to do back in London. Anyway, Vicky's going to have to get her head down into those books if she's going to pass that entrance exam. Aren't you, sweetheart?' He winked at her in the rear-view mirror.

Gina could feel her daughter's reproachful glare on her all the way home. She knew Vicky was as disappointed as she was that she wasn't coming home for the weekend, and she knew she should have argued with Stephen about it. But she couldn't face another row.

But whatever happened, she was determined to stand up for her daughter when it came to Woodcote Lodge. There was no way Vicky was going there.

The following evening Gina went down to her parents' home near Wetherby for their annual Christmas bash.

Every year, on a Sunday in December, her mother opened up Lytton Grange for a big village party. She did it partly to raise money for the local hospice, but mainly to placate the locals, most of whom her husband had upset by closing off public footpaths across his land or blasting the cherished wildlife with his shotgun.

Those whom Rose Tate considered to be the hoi polloi were confined to the conservatory with mulled wine, mince pies and the local primary school choir, while the local VIPs were entertained more lavishly in the library. The room was garlanded with fresh greenery from the grounds, and twinkled with candlelight.

Gina stood beside the crackling fire, listening to the local magistrate drone on and trying to dodge the spraying crumbs from the vol au vent he'd just stuffed into his mouth. She smiled and nodded, but her mind was elsewhere.

She hadn't been able to concentrate on anything since earlier that day when she'd called Stephen's London flat and Lucy Archer answered. She'd sounded breezily confident as she told Gina that Stephen was having lunch with a trade delegation and offered to take a message.

At the time, Gina had been so taken aback she hadn't even found the voice to ask Lucy what she was doing alone at Stephen's flat on a Sunday. It was only when Stephen rang back that she'd pulled herself together enough to demand answers.

'She was just finishing a report for me, that's all. She's very keen,' Stephen had said.

I bet she is, Gina thought. 'Why couldn't she have taken it home with her?'

'Because all the material was at my place. Look, what's all this about?'

She took a deep breath. 'Are you having an affair with her?' Stephen laughed. 'I'm serious.'

The laughter stopped. 'Think about it, Gina. How could we be at it when she's alone at my flat and I'm with a bunch of shopkeepers from Sarajevo?'

He always tried to belittle her when they had a row. 'So how many other times has she been to your flat?'

'How should I know? She works for me.'

'She fancies you.'

His reply was a second too slow. 'I very much doubt that. I'm a married man.'

'Other married men have affairs.'

'Oh, for God's sake, Gina! I'll talk to you when you're less paranoid.'

He'd hung up. She'd waited for him to ring back but he still hadn't called. He was waiting for *her* to apologize, she realized.

'Will you excuse me for a moment?' Gina interrupted the magistrate as he launched into another tirade, and escaped to get another drink.

Nicole drifted up beside her, looking bored. 'God, this is dull, isn't it?' She took a glass of champagne from the waiter. She wore a black and white shift dress that emphasized her lean, elongated body. 'Max must hate it. He loathes people coming to Lytton.'

'He does it for my mother,' Gina said stoutly.

'Hmm.' Nicole looked at Rose, who was chatting to the mayor. 'She obviously enjoys it. I suppose it's her only chance to show off and play lady of the manor, isn't it? I bet she loves that.'

'Where's Neil?' Gina changed the subject.

'In a meeting with Max.' Nicole sipped her champagne. 'They've been locked away since we got here. God knows what they're talking about.' Gina guessed she'd like to be there, too, where all the important stuff was going on, instead of out here making polite conversation with people she couldn't be bothered with. Nicole wasn't the type to be left out of anything. 'I wish they'd hurry up and finish.'

'I expect my mother feels the same,' Gina said. 'Everyone keeps asking where Daddy is.'

'Whatever he's doing, I'm sure that it's more important than glad-handing some local busybody. He's got a business to manage; he can't fit that around your mother's social engagements. Where does she think the money comes from to pay for all this? *She* doesn't earn it, that's for sure.'

'That's not fair,' Gina protested. 'She and Daddy are a team.'

That was how she'd always seen them. Her father might be a powerful, dynamic man, but he couldn't have reached the heights he had without his calm, elegant wife by his side. She organized his life, and gave him a solid base from which to run his empire. Gina only wished she could be more like her.

'Well, if that's what you want to think – oh, hello. What's this?' Nicole turned her attention to the far end of the room.

Gina turned around. There, in the doorway, was her brother James. With him, looking decidedly nervous, was a young woman Gina vaguely recognised.

'It seems your brother's got himself a new lady friend,' Nicole remarked. 'Funny, she doesn't look like his type somehow.'

Gina had to agree. James, bespectacled and serious, only ever dated sophisticated, successful types like himself. This young woman had a pleasant, pretty face, framed by tendrils of auburn hair escaping from her thick plait. She wore a black chainstore dress, hardly any make-up and the diamonds that glittered around her throat were definitely not real. Gina thought she was a definite improvement on the norm.

The young woman looked over, caught her staring and smiled. She nudged James, who glanced over at Gina, frowning. Then they began to thread their way across the room towards them.

'They're coming over,' Nicole hissed. 'This should be interesting. James! How wonderful to see you.' She air-kissed her brother-in-law's cheek. 'And who's this?'

'This is Molly Burton. Molly, this is my sister-in-law, Nicole, and this is my sister, Gina.'

'We've met.' Molly grinned at her. 'I still owe you for the tights, remember?'

'Oh yes, of course.' Gina suddenly realized who she was. 'I thought I recognized you.'

'We met at work,' Molly explained to James. 'Your sister came to my rescue.'

Nicole stared at Molly. 'You work for Tates?'

'I did, for two weeks. That's where we met, isn't it?' She smiled up at James, who looked vaguely embarrassed.

'So what happened to Rachel?' Nicole asked James.

'We're not seeing each other any more,' he said shortly. He turned to Molly. 'Shall we get a drink?'

'She's common,' Nicole commented, as they watched James and Molly walk away.

And you're not? Gina felt like saying. Nicole had clawed her way so far up the social ladder she sometimes forgot how far down she'd started.

'Wait until Neil hears about this,' she said. There was intense rivalry between the two brothers, and Nicole, like Lady Macbeth, was determined her husband was going to come out on top. 'He'll have a fit. Who'd have thought it of James? He must be desperate.'

'I know what you mean,' Gina agreed. 'Imagine, dating one of the staff. It's so downmarket.'

Her barb hit its mark. Nicole shot her a look and stalked off. Her sister-in-law deserved it. How could she criticize Molly when she'd been barely more than a secretary herself when she married Neil?

She glanced across at Molly and James. They were laughing at some shared joke, his dark head bent close to hers, looking into her eyes. Common or not, anyone who could bring such a smile to her brother's face had to be special.

She refilled her glass and went outside for some fresh air. The terrace was lit up by strings of lights, and more sparkled in the shrubbery like fireflies. A huge Christmas tree had been installed beside the french windows.

The terrace stretched all along the back of the house. Her father had built Lytton Grange after he and Rose moved up from London thirty years earlier. It was his own personal palace, spacious, luxurious and full of light. But Max also jealously guarded his privacy. He'd surrounded his dream home with high walls and electronically operated gates, and dotted the grounds with CCTV cameras and security lights. As the neighbouring landowners died or sold up, he bought more land and built stables, tennis courts and a pool house. But even though he had no qualms about building houses in other people's backyards, he refused to develop the land around his own home. Lytton Grange stood in an oasis of solitude.

'Gina?' Her mother stood at the french doors. Rose Tate looked as slim and chic as ever in a pale-grey silk Dior dress and beaded jacket, her ash-blonde hair in a stylish bob. 'What are you doing skulking about out here? Why aren't you talking to people?'

'Just coming,' said Gina. 'You look lovely, Mummy, by the way.'

'Do you think so? This dress is terribly old.' Rose smoothed the silk. She'd been a top model back in the 1960s until she'd married Max, and she still regarded looking good as a full-time job. She'd tried to make her daughter do the same. Good grooming had been drummed into Gina from the moment she was old enough to put on her own shoes. Unfortunately, in her case, it never seemed to work. There was always something – a missing belt, a scarf tied wrong, hair needing a trim – that stopped her looking as perfect as her mother.

'I need you,' Rose said, as Gina followed her back inside. 'James has brought some new girl with him and now he's disappeared into a meeting with your father and left me to entertain her.'

'She seems rather nice to me.'

'Hardly suitable for James.'

No need to ask why. Her mother might be the perfect wife and hostess but she was also a crashing snob.

'There are more important things in life than wearing the right shoes,' Gina said.

'I'm well aware of that, Gina. I'm also aware that someone in James's position needs a partner who'll be an asset to him. Speaking of which, where's Stephen?'

'In London.'

'I thought he was coming home this weekend?'

'He had to go back to work.'

'He's so dedicated,' Rose sighed.

Gina took a deep breath. She had to confide in someone or she'd go mad. And if she couldn't tell her mother, who could she tell? 'I think he's having an affair.'

Her mother stared at her blankly for a moment. 'He told you?'

'No, he denies it.'

'Well, then. You've got nothing to worry about, have you?'

'But what if he's lying?'

'Gina, if Stephen says there's nothing going on, you should believe him,' Rose said firmly.

Turn a blind eye, in other words. Gina knew she shouldn't have been surprised by her mother's advice. Rose had been doing it for years.

She could still remember the first time she'd found out her father was unfaithful. She was fifteen and at boarding school. A newspaper diary columnist had printed a snide piece about Max Tate and his 'constant companion', an upmarket lawyer called Elizabeth Mann. They'd managed to snatch a photo of the two of them leaving a London hotel together.

'You know what that means, don't you?' Sophie Harrington had gleefully pointed out. 'They're having an affair.'

'That's not true!' Gina fought back. But as the days went by, and more stories appeared, even she had to admit the awful truth.

She felt betrayed. She'd always adored her father and it was a devastating blow to find out he was less than perfect. She was convinced it was the end of her life as she knew it. She couldn't eat or sleep because she felt so sick with anxiety, just waiting for her mother to call with the news that she'd left her father and moved out of Lytton Grange.

But she'd heard nothing. And when she finally managed to get home on weekend leave, she was stunned to find nothing had changed, except her mother was sporting a new diamond the size of a duck egg. It was as if the affair had never happened.

Until the next time. Now the whole family had learned to follow her mother's example and ignore their father's indiscretions. Even Gina had finally accepted that they were just another part of his fascinating but flawed character. Max, for his part, kept his adventures discreet for his wife's sake. They were brief, rarely serious, and never threatened their rock-solid marriage. It was a compromise that everyone lived with.

'Look, all marriages go through bad patches. You'll come out the other side eventually,' Rose said. 'Just try not to get over-emotional about it. You know what you're like. You blow everything out of proportion.'

Maybe she was right, Gina thought. After what had happened to her when Vicky was born, she hardly trusted her own judgement.

'There's that girl, over by the drinks table. Getting steadily plastered, I shouldn't wonder.' Rose gave Gina a little shove. 'Go and talk to her.'

Molly was making small-talk with the wine waiter. She beamed with relief when she saw Gina.

'Thanks heavens, a friendly face. James has gone off to discuss business with your dad and no one seems to want to talk to me.' Molly gazed around mournfully. 'I suppose they know I'm not important enough.'

'Another drink?' Gina offered.

'Better not. I don't want to get drunk, then I'd really embarrass myself. Talking of which, I think I owe you an apology. I remember saying some awful things about James when we first met. I had no idea he was your brother.'

'That's OK,' Gina replied. 'Anyway, you were right. He can be a bit uptight sometimes.'

'I know. I thought he was a bit stand-offish at first, but that's just a front really.'

'Is it?'

'Oh yes,' Molly nodded earnestly. 'He's actually quite shy.'

Gina thought of all the times she'd heard her brother negotiating a land deal, nailing the seller to the floor with his tough bargaining. 'Really?'

'And he's gorgeous, obviously. In a kind of cool, Colin Firth way.'

'If you say so.' But somehow she couldn't picture her big brother as a romantic hero. 'So how did you two get together?' She knew Molly was dying to tell her.

'Well, it was quite funny really . . .' As Molly rattled on, telling the story of how James had been rude and abrupt to her once too often and how she'd thrown his typing in his face and walked out, Gina was amazed that her taciturn brother was attracted to such a chatty girl. James used words like they were £50 notes; Molly barely paused for breath. Opposites did attract, obviously.

'. . . And so he sent me flowers to apologize and I thought no way, so I sent them back, and then the next thing I knew he turned up on my doorstep and asked me out.' Molly grinned. 'Sorry, am I talking too much? I always gabble on when I'm nervous. And believe me, your family makes me very nervous.'

'They make me nervous, too.' On second thoughts, she could see what her brother saw in Molly. She was open, charming and honest.

She hoped it would last, but she had her doubts. Molly might be a lovely girl, but she looked as if she could be quite feisty. And the Tate men were used to getting their own way.

Max Tate stood at the window of his study, listening to the sound of the school choir drifting up from the conservatory below. All those people. Milling around his home, gawping at everything.

He loathed the so-called VIPs most. There they were, knocking back his champagne and pretending they were all great friends when forty years ago they wouldn't have given him the time of day.

Max's hand tightened around his heavy crystal tumbler of whisky. At the same time, part of him enjoyed the thought of them looking around, admiring his art and his antiques, envying his lifestyle and wondering how much it must have cost.

Not bad for a boy from the back streets of Leeds, he thought with satisfaction. A boy whose father had walked out and whose alcoholic mother had put him into care, then taken his brothers and sisters back and left him behind. A boy who'd been sent to Borstal for petty theft and told by the magistrates that he was on a one-way ticket to prison. He hadn't come by his fortune easily, or even honestly. He'd had to do some fairly despicable things in his time. But looking around at what he had now, he realized it was worth it.

'O come let us adore Him . . .' The kids' voices rose from below, straining on the high notes.

He blamed Rose for this. She was in her element, wandering around downstairs in her designer dress, playing Lady Bountiful to all the locals. At least she hadn't tried to suggest he should dress up as Santa and hand out gifts to the local kiddies as she had one year.

'But it's for charity, Max,' she always said when he complained.

'So? We'll write them an obscenely big cheque. Then we can tell them all to fuck off.'

Rose had winced. Even after all these years, he still shocked her with his rough attitude. Unlike him, she had breeding. Minor aristocracy, no less. That was partly what attracted him to her.

Back in the 1960s, after he'd made his fortune back in Leeds, he'd moved down to London to try his luck. His gritty northern personality and wads of cash had made him popular on the London scene and he was soon mixing in the most fashionable circles.

From the moment he'd laid eyes on Rose at a party he'd made up his mind that she was the woman he wanted. No, make that *deserved*. It still made him smile to think how he'd swept her off her feet from under the noses of all those chinless wonders. Her father hadn't approved – at first. Max might be rich, but he was also trade, and rough trade at that. But new money was better than no money, and he hadn't complained when Max paid the heating bill on his crumbling family pile. It was amazing how people stopped noticing which knife and fork you used when you were rich.

They'd been married for nearly thirty-five years, and Rose was as beautiful as ever. Max still got a kick out of the way other men looked at her. He loved owning beautiful, desirable things. And he owned Rose just as he owned his vintage Jag and collection of first editions, But for how much longer?

He put the glass down and sat at his antique rosewood desk to study the figures his accountant had given him. Poor sod, he'd been trembling when he gave Max the bad news. As if Max didn't know his financial position to the last penny. He didn't get where he was by letting other people take control of his cash.

But seeing it all there, laid out in black and white, still brought it home to him. He'd taken a few risks over the past year or so. He'd borrowed heavily to buy land, speculating on what he could make. Usually it wasn't a problem. Max had got rich by making big gestures, sweeping in where others feared to tread. He was a gambler. And these gambles should have paid off, too. But property prices hadn't soared, and there had been endless problems and hassles and delays, which meant he couldn't make the money fast enough. Now the bank wanted their money back. For once, the money wasn't there to pay them.

The situation wasn't a disaster. Yet. The banks trusted him and were keen to stay friends, so they were willing to give him some leeway. But he needed some of his investments to start paying off – and soon.

He reviewed the figures again. The latest luxury development, Windmill Meadows, should have started selling by now, but construction was behind schedule. And it had already cost him a packet after that accident on site.

Then there was Paradise Road. He stood to make a killing on it, if all went well. But it was a painfully slow business. Most of the residents had given in to his generous financial inducements in the end, but there was one stubborn old couple who refused to budge.

Max drummed his fingers on the polished wood. He'd been patient long enough. If they didn't sell up soon he was going to have to persuade them in some other way. He smiled. It was a long time since he'd used those kind of tactics.

His gaze moved down the column of figures and came to rest on the final entry: Whitecroft Farm. That was the one that irritated him the most, because it had been such a monumental cock-up. He'd borrowed from the bank to buy the land, but thanks to James not looking over the deeds properly, it turned out he'd only bought half of it. He needed the other half, or his would be useless. Unfortunately, the farmer was a wily old bastard, and while Tates were still negotiating he'd gone and sold it to this Joe Delaney character. Now *he* was refusing to sell it.

At this very moment his sons were blaming each other for the catalogue of errors.

'You're supposed to be in charge of land acquisitions,' Neil accused James. 'You should have had that deal sewn up.'

'I would have if you hadn't gone in throwing your weight around,' James reminded him. 'That guy only sold it to someone else because you got all heavy-handed and pissed him off.'

'I had to do something,' Neil shot back. 'You weren't getting anywhere.'

Max listened to them bickering, both vying to be top dog. He didn't mind; it pleased him to hear them arguing. Divide and rule, that was his motto. It stopped them getting too comfortable and turning on him. This way he could control both of them.

'So what are you going to do about it?' he asked.

'It's all under control,' Neil said confidently.

'And would you like to tell us how?'

'Old man Delaney's been whipped into hospital with a heart attack. They reckon it's all down to stress. Apparently he's having a few money troubles.'

I know how he feels, Max thought. Not that he'd ever confide in his sons. Fortunately he managed to hide his financial dealings with such a complex network of different business names and offshore holdings his own accountant could barely keep track of them all.

'I'm sorry to hear that. So you think he might be forced to sell?'

'I'm certain of it.'

'And what makes you think he'd sell to us?' James said, clearly put out that his brother was getting all the attention.

'Because his daughter is a very special friend of mine.'

James's lip curled. 'Does she know you've got a wife?'

'I see no reason to disappoint her. Yet.'

'You're despicable, do you know that?'

'Maybe, but I get results. I reckon by the end of the month we'll have that land. And I'll have Finn Delaney.' He smiled at the prospect.

Max looked up sharply. 'Did you say Finn Delaney? The girl who used to work for us and tried to cause all that trouble?'

'That's the one. Pretty little thing, isn't she?'

'She's a tiger.' He didn't blame Neil for wanting her. He wouldn't have minded taking her to bed himself, if he hadn't already been preoccupied with his latest, extremely demanding mistress.

Max caught the look of disdain James was giving them both. He was like his mother, cool and sophisticated. Neil was more of a streetfighter like himself.

'Don't look so dismayed, James. At least your brother's showing some initiative.'

'That's what I'm afraid of.' James took off his glasses and polished them. 'When Neil starts showing initiative is usually when it all starts going pear-shaped.'

'Then it's just as well I've got a Plan B, isn't it?' Neil said.

'Which is?'

'Joe Delaney's son. Bit of a petty criminal, not too bright,' he explained to Max. 'He's looking after the business while his dad's laid up.'

'Don't tell me you're planning to sleep with him, too?' James said.

Max laughed.

'We have some mutual friends,' Neil glared at his brother.

'He's getting himself into trouble with them. Owes them big time.'

'Your thugs are going to put the frighteners on him, you mean?'

'Wait and see. While you're still firing off begging letters through your land agents, they might actually get us somewhere.'

'In jail, probably.'

Max looked from one to the other as if he were watching a tennis match. Yes, Neil was definitely the impulsive one, the risk-taker. James was more measured and calculating. He was the one Max had to watch out for, he decided.

'Look, I don't care how you deal with it – just deal with it,' he said bluntly. The choir had launched into 'Ding Dong Merrily On High' and it was giving him a headache. 'I want this business sorted. And I want it sorted now.'

Chapter 9

It was nine o'clock in the morning when Finn hammered on the door of the Bargeman's Arms, Ciaran's local. The pub had a dead look, its shutters pulled down against the weak morning sunlight that tried to push its way through the mist hanging over the path. A dank smell rose from the canal.

She knocked again, shoving her hands into the pockets of her fleece and stamping her boots on the frosty ground.

Finally she heard a grumpy voice inside saying, 'All right, keep your hair on, I'm coming.' There was the sound of bolts being drawn, then the door was opened a fraction and a stubble-chinned face appeared in the narrow gap. 'What do you want?'

'Is Ciaran here?'

'Who wants to know?'

'I'm his sister. Is he here or not?' Finn craned her neck to peer into the darkness behind him.

He stuck his head back in and called out, 'Ciaran? Someone to see you. Says she's your sister.'

The door closed in her face. Finn had raised her hand to knock again when it re-opened and her brother stumbled out, bleary with sleep, his dark hair sticking up.

'What are you doing here?'

'I could ask you the same question.' She fanned away his stale alcohol breath. 'Why aren't you at work?'

'I had something to do.'

'I've had Marcus Stephenson on the phone, threatening all kinds. You should have been there an hour ago.'

'Oh, him.' Ciaran rolled his eyes. 'He's an old moaner, that one.'

'He's got a right to be. According to him, you haven't been there for three days. And when you have turned up it's been a disaster. What are you playing at?'

He winced and held his head. 'Keep it down, will you? You don't have to shout.'

'I'll do more than shout if you don't get yourself over there and sort things out. We can't afford to lose that job.'

'We won't lose it.'

'That's not what Mr Stephenson said. He's threatening to sack us if we don't get our act together.'

'Like I said, he's an old moaner. It won't hurt to keep him waiting a couple of days.'

'A couple of days? A couple of days?' Finn yelled. Ciaran shrank back. 'Go home and get cleaned up. I want you at the Stephensons' place in an hour. And you'd better be ready to grovel.'

'Now just a minute. Who's in charge of this business?' Ciaran straightened his shoulders.

'You are, God help us.'

'Exactly. So don't come round here giving your orders, OK?'

Finn recognized that stubborn expression. He was the same when they were children. The more she tried to push him, the more he dug his heels in.

'Fine,' she snapped. 'But I just hope you've got a good explanation when Dad asks why his best customer has dumped us!'

Her boss George had given her a new job in Leeds, but all day she was preoccupied with worry that Ciaran wouldn't turn up at the Stephensons'. She kept looking at her mobile phone, terrified in case Marcus Stephenson rang to say he'd decided to get someone else to finish the job.

She couldn't have blamed him if he had. From what he'd told her on the phone, Ciaran had made a right mess of the job. She was just glad her father wasn't there to see it.

After work she hurried home to get changed, then headed for

the hospital to catch the last of visiting hour. She felt guilty that she couldn't have got there sooner, but she needn't have worried; Joe wasn't alone. At first Finn didn't recognize the dark-haired woman at his bedside. But as she got closer she realized who it was.

'Auntie Orla!' Her hand flew to her mouth. She'd completely forgotten that she'd called a few days before to say she was coming over to see Joe. 'Oh Lord, I thought it was Thursday you were coming?'

'It *is* Thursday, Finnuala,' her father said.

'Is it?' She was so busy the days just seemed to pass in a blur. She glanced at Orla. Damn. She'd been planning to spend the evening tidying up the house before she arrived.

Orla seemed to read her thoughts. 'Are you sure it's still convenient for me to stay?' she said in her soft Irish accent. 'I can always book into a B&B?'

'No, no, it's fine. I'm glad you could come.' And so was her father, judging by the smile on his face. 'So, how are things back home?'

'Orla's just been filling me in on the gossip,' Joe said.

'It didn't take long.' Orla grinned. In her early fifties, she was a few years younger than Joe. Her dark hair was threaded with grey and lines fanned from the corners of her blue eyes, but she was still a lovely woman.

She listened to Orla and her father chuckling together over the latest outrageous goings-on in the village, and felt pleased. It seemed such a long time since she'd heard him laugh like that. And he was so distracted by Orla that he forgot to ask how Ciaran was getting on, so that was a blessing.

'Are you sure you don't mind me landing on you like this?' Orla asked as Finn drove her home half an hour later.

'Not at all. I'll be glad of the company. And I know Dad likes having you here.'

'Do you think so?'

'He's been looking forward to it.'

Orla smiled. 'I've been looking forward to seeing him, too. I was so worried when you rang and said he'd been taken ill. I would have dropped everything and come there and then if I could.'

'You're a good friend.'

'We go back a long way.' Orla looked thoughtful. 'So, how is he? Really?'

'Getting stronger every day. Driving all the nurses mad asking when he can come home, so I suppose that's a good sign. How long are you planning to stay, by the way? You didn't say on the phone.'

Orla's blue eyes twinkled. 'Trying to get rid of me already, are you?'

'I didn't mean it like that.'

'I know, I was only teasing.' She twisted her wedding ring around on her finger. 'I was hoping to stay around at least until Joe gets out of hospital. And then maybe for a couple of weeks after that, just so I can make sure he's back on his feet. If that's OK with you?' She looked across at Finn. 'Say if it's not convenient; I realize you might not want me around for that long.'

'That's fine. We've got plenty of room.' Finn pulled the car into the drive beside the van. 'And you can keep an eye on him when he comes out, stop him overdoing it.'

'That's what I thought,' Orla nodded. 'I hoped it might take the pressure off you. It can't be easy, working full-time and looking after the house.'

'Ah, yes. About that.' Finn pulled a face as she hauled Orla's cases out of the boot. 'I'm afraid the place isn't exactly spotless. I was going to tidy round before you came, but I just haven't had time.' She led the way into the house, conscious of the shoes and boots abandoned in the hallway and the pile of post on the hall table she hadn't had time to look at.

'It's OK, I wasn't expecting a showhome.'

'You probably weren't expecting a hovel, either.' She led the way into the kitchen, shoving the washing basket out of the way with her foot.

'I've seen much worse than this, I assure you.' Orla put her bags down. 'Now, why don't you put the kettle on while I unpack? Then I'll make a start on this place.'

'Oh no, you don't have to.'

'I want to. I might as well make myself useful since I'm going to be here for a while. Anyway, you know I hate sitting around.'

Finn made the tea and took it up to Orla, then sat on the bed and watched as she unpacked her cases. Orla moved around the little guest bedroom with purpose and energy, fitting her carefully folded clothes into drawers and searching out hangers. Finn could imagine her moving around the wards of the little cottage hospital in Killmane, her presence soothing but efficient.

'So how are you?' Orla asked as she shook the creases out of a blouse and hung it up. 'How's work?'

'Fine.'

'Your dad tells me you're doing well at that hairdressing salon of yours?' Orla frowned. 'Funny, it's not a job I would have imagined you doing.'

'Oh, you know. I've always been very – um – creative.' Finn felt herself blushing.

'I don't remember that. But I do remember you hacking all the hair off your Barbie doll when you were six.'

'You see? I was talented even then.'

'Hmm, I don't know if I'd call it talent.' Orla folded up a jumper and placed it in a drawer. 'What about your brother? How's he getting on?'

'He's OK.'

'Then someone must have been sending up a few prayers to St Jude, the patron saint of lost causes.'

Finn saw the look in Orla's shrewd blue eyes and knew she'd seen right through her. 'I am a bit worried about him,' she admitted. 'He's supposed to be running the business but the way he's going he'll run it into the ground by the time Dad's better.'

'And I don't suppose you've told your father any of this?'

Finn shook her head. 'It would only worry him and I want him to concentrate on getting better. You won't say anything to him, will you?'

'Not if you don't want me to. Although it's about time someone put him straight. Joseph's always had a blind spot where his son's concerned. And his daughter.'

There was something about the way she looked at her that made Finn wary. Did she suspect something? But there was no way she could know, could she? Finn hoped she hadn't noticed her workboots abandoned in the hall, or the toolbag hidden under a tartan rug in the boot of the car.

Fortunately Orla changed the subject. 'So are you courting?'

Finn laughed. 'Are you?'

'In Killmane? There's not a decent man within twenty miles. Besides, in my job most of the men I get to meet are over eighty and incontinent.'

'That's an improvement on the men around here.' Finn sat back on the bed and tucked her knees under her chin. 'Would you like to meet someone?'

'I don't know. Maybe after all those years of marriage I'm better off on my own.'

Finn wondered if she meant she wouldn't find anyone good enough to take her husband's place, or if she didn't want to go through the experience again. Orla rarely talked about her late husband, and Finn had never been able to work out if their marriage had been happy or not. They'd always been complete opposites in character; Orla was lively and sociable, while Donal had been quiet and serious, with no time for frivolities. But they'd stayed together for twenty years, so they couldn't have hated each other.

'Anyway, don't change the subject.' Orla scolded her. 'I asked you first.'

'Actually, there is someone.'

'Oh yes?' Orla sat down next to her on the bed. 'Who is he? No, don't tell me, let me guess. That nice friend of your brother's. The one who used to work for your father?'

'You mean Ryan?' Finn laughed. 'No chance.'

'Really? He always struck me as a nice lad.'

'I'm not sure about that. Anyway, there's nothing going on there. No, this one's called Neil.'

She felt shy just saying his name out loud. They'd only been out for a couple of drinks, but he did seem pretty keen. He'd even sent her flowers afterwards, which had thrown her into total confusion.

She still wasn't sure if she could totally trust him, but at least her father hadn't had any more hassle from the land agents, so she supposed he must have kept his word about that. And he didn't seem like a Tate. He was funny and caring, always asking about her father. Finn was still wary, but her defences were beginning to break down.

It was all a new feeling for her, this romance business. She'd had boyfriends in the past, of course, but she'd always been too intent on pursuing her career and getting men to take her seriously to think about relationships. And growing up in a house full of men hadn't given her much practice in all the girly stuff like flirting. She knew she wasn't bad-looking, but she'd always assumed men wouldn't be interested in a tomboy like her. But Neil seemed interested. More than interested, in fact.

'I hope I get to meet him while I'm here,' Orla said.

'Oh, I don't know about that. It's not that serious.' Finn dismissed the idea, embarrassed. 'You won't tell Dad, will you?'

'I don't see why you can't tell him yourself. He's hardly going to put his foot down and stop you seeing him, is he? You're twenty-six, not sixteen!' Orla patted her arm. 'Don't worry, your secret's safe with me. Although it seems to me there's a lot you're not telling your dad at the moment.'

Luckily, before she had a chance to say any more, the phone rang. Finn rushed downstairs to answer it.

At first there was a long silence. Then a muffled voice said, 'Is Ciaran there?'

'No, he isn't. Who is this?'

Another pause. Then the voice said, 'Never mind that. Just tell him we're watching him.'

'If you were watching him that well then you'd know he wasn't here, wouldn't you?'

Finn slammed the phone down. Moron. It was probably just one of her brother's idiot friends messing about.

But she couldn't help feeling relieved Orla was there to keep her company as she switched on the lamps and drew the living-room curtains, shutting out the darkness.

Chapter 10

Gina Farrell sat in her marble-lined bathroom and stared at the little white plastic rod in her hand. However hard she looked, the blue line was still there.

She still couldn't believe it. How could she be pregnant? She and Stephen hardly ever slept in the same bed any more, as he spent so much of his time in Westminster.

She wasn't sure what he'd make of it. They'd talked about starting a family, but Stephen had always insisted it wasn't the right time. They had to plan for these things, he'd said. Then, when she'd raised the subject again a few months later, he'd said, 'Should we really be thinking about children anyway? When we have kids I want to be a real dad, not away in London while they're growing up.'

But Gina had never got round to going back on the pill because it gave her headaches, and sex happened so rarely it was hardly worth it.

She looked back at the rod with a mixture of fear and excitement. She was terrified of what he was going to say, but at the same time part of her was thrilled at the idea of having a new life growing inside her. She really wanted a baby with Stephen; although he was great with her daughter Vicky, she felt a baby of their own would make their family complete.

And it might stop him running off with someone else. She pushed the unworthy thought from her mind.

She'd tried not to let the thought of Lucy haunt her, although everywhere she looked there seemed to be more clues. Stephen was always too busy to come home these days. He'd also bought a new mobile phone, but wouldn't give her the number – 'It's just for work emergencies,' he'd told her. And whenever Stephen's photo appeared in the paper, Lucy's earnest little face was always lurking somewhere in the background. Gina had become used to hearing her voice on the end of the line when she rang Stephen at work or at his apartment.

She put her hand over her flat stomach. She wished she could tell Stephen about the baby straight away. But he'd flown to Brussels late last night to discuss EU subsidies. He wasn't due home until late Sunday evening.

Gina tried not to think about whether he'd gone alone, but somehow she doubted it.

'Mum? Are you OK in there?' Vicky tapped gently on the door, rousing Gina from her troubled thoughts.

She slipped the plastic rod into her dressing-gown pocket, threw the packaging away and opened the door.

'I thought you were sick or something.' Vicky's face was anxious. She'd come home from school for the Christmas holidays the day before.

'I'm fine.' In fact, she suddenly felt elated. Her darling Vicky was home, and, although this baby might not have been planned, she couldn't help being excited about it.

'So what are we going do today?' Vicky asked. 'Could we go shopping?'

'We certainly need to. You're growing out of all your clothes.' She could hardly believe how Vicky had shot up in the last few months. At this rate she would be as tall as her in a year or two. 'But I thought we could take a quick trip to look around a new school first.'

'Another one? But it's the holidays.' Vicky pulled a face.

'I know, but it's their last day of term today and this is the only chance we might get.'

'So where is it? Miles away, I suppose?' she said sulkily.

'Actually, it's the local comp.'

Vicky's expression brightened. 'Really? Are you serious? But I thought Stephen said I wasn't to go there.'

'It wouldn't hurt us to look, would it?' That was all they were doing, she told herself. Anyway, it wasn't as if she'd gone behind his back to arrange it. St Luke's was having a carol concert and, as the local MP's wife, she was expected to attend. And if she and Vicky just happened to take a look around afterwards, maybe talk to one or two teachers – well, she was only showing an interest, wasn't she?

'Then later maybe we could have a takeaway and watch a DVD?' she suggested.

Vicky's nose wrinkled. 'What kind of DVD?'

'A nice slushy romantic one?'

'Mum! Yuk! How about a horror film?'

Now it was Gina's turn to wrinkle her nose. 'We'll discuss the details later, shall we?'

She'd got dressed and was just searching for her car keys when Vicky said, 'I forgot. Grandad's secretary called. Can you ring him back as soon as possible?'

'When did he ring?'

'While you were in the bathroom.'

Gina glanced at her watch. That was nearly an hour ago. Her father hated to be kept waiting.

Vicky must have noticed her expression because she said, 'Sorry. Have I done something wrong?'

'It doesn't matter.' Gina stroked her daughter's hair. 'You carry on looking for my keys while I give him a quick ring.'

'Your father's been trying to get hold of you all morning. He wants to see you.' Janice, her father's PA, didn't sound impressed.

'Did he say why?'

'No idea. He just said to tell you to come in and see him as soon as possible.'

Gina glanced at Vicky, waiting by the door with the car keys in her hand. 'I'm on my way.'

'Change of plan,' she said as they got into the car. 'We've got to make a quick detour to Grandad's office.' At least, she hoped it would be quick. The carol concert was due to start in an hour.

Her father was in a meeting when they arrived. 'Will he be long?' she asked Janice.

'He didn't say. You can wait in his office, if you like?'

Gina gave Vicky a pound coin and sent her to explore the vending machine on the next floor while she waited. Her father's office always made her feel slightly uneasy. In contrast to its modern, minimalist surroundings, it looked like a nineteenth-century gentleman's study, full of heavy antique furniture and lined with shelves of old leather-bound books. A leather winged armchair and Chesterfield sofa were ranged around a coffee table. On the table was one of her father's beloved chess sets. Max might not have read any of the books on the shelves, but he played chess obsessively. And he always won.

She went over to the window and looked out over the car park, watching the office staff scurrying out of the building on their way to lunch. She checked her watch again. She wished her father would hurry up. At this rate, she and Vicky would barely make it to St Luke's.

She decided to write him a note to let him know she had to leave. She sat down at his desk and opened a drawer to look for a pen and a piece of paper. As she did, she noticed a letter lying on top. She recognized the bank's headed notepaper. Without thinking she reached in to move it, when –

'Don't touch that!'

She jumped. 'I'm sorry. I was just looking for a pen. I wanted to write you a note.'

Max reached past her and slammed the drawer. And then, suddenly, he smiled. 'For pity's sake, don't look so terrified! Anyone would think I was going to beat you.'

He laughed, and so did Gina, uneasily. After thirty years, her father's quickfire changes of mood still left her feeling unsure of herself.

'So why aren't you at work today?' he asked. 'Don't tell me – Christmas shopping?' He rolled his eyes. 'Your mother's been at it for months now. Or so it seems from the credit card bills.'

'Something like that.' She looked at her watch. 'Why do you need to see me?'

'I just wanted to know what this was about.' He picked a file from the desk and flicked through it. 'I've got a whole bunch of invoices here, for florists and caterers and marquee hire. And I'm told they all come from you. What's going on?'

Gina looked at the file. 'Where did you get those?'

'Never mind where I got them. What's it all about?'

Gina fumed quietly. She could only guess someone in her office had sneaked behind her back to her father. Most probably Julie. She was just waiting for her chance to stick the knife in. 'It was supposed to be a surprise.'

'You know I don't like surprises, Gina.'

'If you must know, I'm organizing a big launch for the Windmill Meadows site. It's an important development, so I thought I'd try to raise its profile. I've arranged for the mayor to open it officially,' she added, hoping to impress her father.

'And you reckon a few flowers and some pompous old git cutting a bit of ribbon is going to shift more houses, do you?'

Gina faltered. 'It will make it more of a media event. The local press are going to be there.'

'The less that lot know about me and my business, the better.' He regarded her sternly. 'You do realize you've cut into the site's profits by organizing this shindig? Now we're going to have to sell even more houses to pay for it. We've already had to lower our projections because the market's flattened.'

'I'm sorry. I thought it might help.'

Max sighed. 'Go on, then. Organize your party, if you think it's worth it. It's probably too late to cancel, anyway.' He tossed the invoices back into the in-tray. 'But in future, don't use your initiative, OK? I am trying to run a business here.'

Just at that moment the office door opened. Her father swung round, ready to snarl at the interruption, but his expression changed when he saw Vicky in the doorway. 'Sweetheart, when did you get home? Your mother didn't tell me you were here.' His eyes met Gina's accusingly over the top of Vicky's head as he pulled her into his arms.

Gina suppressed a twinge of jealousy as she watched him sweep his granddaughter around. He'd never been that pleased to see her.

★

They made it to St Luke's just in time for the end of the concert. The headteacher Mr Lloyd was very understanding about it and invited them for tea and mince pies in the staffroom afterwards. He was delighted when Vicky showed an interest in the school, and immediately arranged for one of the senior prefects to show them around.

'Although I'm afraid it's not terribly grand,' he said.

He was right, it wasn't nearly as grand as Woodcote Lodge or even Vicky's prep school. But it was light, airy and very welcoming. The pupils' art decorated the corridors instead of portraits of worthy old girls, and the library was inviting, with computers instead of dusty old first editions.

Vicky was especially impressed with the school's new drama studio. 'It's got a real stage and lighting and everything,' she enthused. 'Oh, Mummy, please can I come here next year?'

'We'll see.' Gina had already made her mind up she loved the place, too. Now all she had to do was convince Stephen.

On the way home they stopped off at the video shop to choose a DVD, then at the Chinese takeaway where Gina let Vicky select all her favourites from the menu.

When they got home, they changed into their pyjamas and ate cross-legged in front of the TV in the cosy family room, their plates on their laps, watching the movie. Or rather, Vicky watched. Gina kept her face averted as the psycho maniac stalked across the screen, picking off annoying teenagers by increasingly violent means.

'I don't know how you can watch this stuff,' she complained.

'It's great.' Vicky didn't take her eyes off the screen. 'Anyway, they deserve it. I mean, who'd be stupid enough to go down to that cellar on their own?'

'True.' Gina rubbed at a grease spot on the carpet where she'd dropped her spring roll. It felt deliciously naughty. Stephen hated anyone eating in the sitting room, even if it was just the two of them.

She felt guilty, but in a way she was glad he wasn't home. She enjoyed having Vicky to herself. And even though Stephen tried hard, somehow it was much harder for them to relax when he was around.

She kept stealing glances across at her daughter. Vicky's face was losing its childlike softness, starting to show glimpses of the young woman she would become. Her fair hair was darkening at the roots. By her age, Gina's mother was already hauling her off to the salon to get some highlights. But Gina preferred her daughter's hair natural.

It made her sad, too. Not so long ago all Vicky was interested in were pets, ponies and wearing pink. Now she'd changed, and Gina hadn't even been there to see it.

She missed her so much when she was away at boarding school. They phoned and texted each other all the time, but it wasn't the same as having her there. She wondered whether now might be a good time to approach the subject with Stephen of her going to a local school. With the baby on the way, it might be better if they were all together. She didn't want Vicky to feel left out.

The baby. The thought hit her again. She'd been thinking about it all day but it still didn't seem real.

After the film they cuddled up on the sofa together. Gina put her arms around Vicky's skinny frame and buried her face in her daughter's hair, breathing in the fresh shampoo smell.

'There's something I wanted to talk to you about,' she said.

Vicky snapped round to look at her. 'You and Stephen are getting divorced?'

'No!' Gina was taken aback. 'What gave you that idea?'

'No reason,' Vicky mumbled, settling back into her arms. 'It's just what people usually say when they've got something to tell their kids, that all.'

'No, this is good news. I hope. I'm going to have a baby.' Vicky went very still. 'Well, say something,' Gina laughed nervously.

'When?' Vicky asked.

'I'm not sure. Sometime in the summer. I haven't worked out my dates yet.' Gina moved her head to look at Vicky's profile. Her expression gave nothing away.

She wondered if she'd done the right thing, telling her like this. She didn't want to ruin her holiday. Having a pregnant mum was probably a major embarrassment to an eleven-year-old. 'I know it's a shock,' she said quickly. 'But it'll all be fine, I promise.'

Vicky thought about it for a moment. 'Does this mean I can go to St Luke's? Then I could be here when you have the baby.'

'I suppose it would make sense.' She was already worried about Vicky feeling left out. 'But I'd have to talk to Stephen about it.'

'Talk to me about what?' said a voice from the doorway.

Chapter 11

'Welcome home, Vicky darling.' He looked at the foil containers on the coffee table. 'Have you been having a party?'

'It was only a takeaway.' Gina felt herself tense and realized her daughter was doing the same. 'What are you doing here? I thought you weren't coming home until Sunday.'

'You're not the only one who can do things on the spur of the moment, sweetheart.' His smile was forced. 'You've been complaining we don't spend enough time together, so I thought I'd sneak away early. Besides, I wanted to see my little girl.' He put his arms out to Vicky. After a moment's hesitation, she got up and hugged him.

'And what's this you've been watching?' He picked up the DVD case. '*Death Grip III*, eh? Sounds a bit menacing. Are you sure this is really suitable for an eleven-year-old, Gina?'

'Vicky chose it.'

'I daresay she did. But we don't want to give her nightmares, do we?' He tightened his arm around Vicky.

'I think I'll go to bed,' Vicky said.

'Not just yet, young lady. Haven't you got something to show me first? This term's report?' he prompted when Vicky looked puzzled.

Gina saw her daughter's shoulders slump. 'Couldn't we leave it until the morning?' she pleaded.

'I'd rather see it now, if you don't mind?'

Vicky glanced at Gina, who nodded for her to fetch it. They both steeled themselves as he sat down to read.

'Not much of an improvement on last term,' he frowned. 'And what's happened to your maths?'

'I hate maths.'

'Everyone hates maths, sweetheart, but that doesn't mean you don't have to try.' He folded up the report and stuffed it back in its envelope. 'You'll never get into Woodcote Lodge if those grades don't improve.'

'I'm not going to Woodcote Lodge. Mummy says I can go to St Luke's. Isn't that right, Mummy?'

Stephen looked at Gina, his brows rising. 'Is that right, Mummy?'

'Why don't you go up to bed, Vicky?' Gina smiled tensely. 'I'll come up and say goodnight in five minutes, OK?'

'Stephen's not angry, is he?' Vicky asked as she lay in bed, the duvet pulled up to her chin.

'Of course not, darling. Why should he be?'

'Maybe I shouldn't have said anything about St Luke's.'

'I'll talk to him.' Gina hugged her daughter. She smelt of freshly laundered pyjamas and toothpaste.

'Are you going to tell him about the baby?'

'I don't know.' She wanted to, but she wasn't sure it was the right time. Even though she tried to reassure Vicky, she could tell Stephen's mood could go either way. 'He's rather tired. Perhaps I'll leave it.'

Vicky nodded. As Gina got up to leave she said, 'I am pleased about it. If you are.'

Gina smiled. 'I'm glad.'

She just hoped her husband felt the same.

Downstairs, Stephen was in the kitchen, throwing away the takeaway cartons. 'There's fried rice on the carpet,' he said, not looking at her.

'Sorry. I'll clean it up.'

'I already have.' He let the pedal-bin lid slam shut.

Gina eyed him warily. 'You're angry, aren't you?'

'I'm not angry at all. Just disappointed, that's all.'

'Nothing's been decided yet.'

'Really? I got the impression you and Vicky had it all sorted.' He threw open the fridge and took out an opened bottle of wine. 'How do you expect me to be a father to her when you're constantly undermining me?'

'I don't.'

'Oh, you do. You never include me in these kind of decisions. And you encourage Vicky not to show me any respect.' He poured the wine into a glass.

'That's not true!'

'Every time I try to help, you shut me out.'

'Look, there's a reason I want her to go to the local school.'

'And that's all that counts, isn't it? What you want? Never mind me or my opinions.'

'Stephen, please. I'm trying to talk to you.'

'Why bother talking to me about anything?' He drained his glass and refilled it. 'You know, sometimes I just feel like an outsider in my own home.'

She took a deep breath. 'Maybe you wouldn't feel like that if we had a child of our own.'

'Maybe.' He refilled his glass. 'But that's not going to happen, is it?'

She raised her eyes to look at him. 'Maybe it already has.'

He stared at her so blankly at first she wasn't sure if he'd even heard her. 'What?'

'I'm pregnant.' Her smile faltered.

He took a gulp of his drink. 'How the hell did that happen?'

Gina laughed nervously. 'Oh, you know. The usual way. Boy meets girl, they fall in love . . .' Then she saw his thunderous face. 'Look, I know we didn't plan it, but we always said we'd have a baby one day, didn't we? Stephen?'

He put his glass down. 'I'm going out.'

'Don't go. We have to talk about—'

But it was too late. The front door had already banged shut.

She sat up until midnight, waiting for him to come home, her emotions veering wildly from anger to fear to panic and back again. One minute she was furious that he'd walked out on her. The next, she'd convinced herself he'd had a terrible accident and was lying dead in a ditch. His mobile was switched off, but that didn't stop her ringing it every ten minutes.

Finally she rang Mark. There was music playing softly and voices in the background as he answered.

'Gina! This is a lovely surprise. What can I do for you?'

'Sorry to interrupt your evening, but have you seen Stephen?'

'Isn't he in Brussels?'

'He came home early.' She fought to stop her voice trembling, but Mark heard it.

'Gina, what's happened? Have you two had a row?'

'A bit,' she admitted. 'He went out a couple of hours ago and I haven't seen him since. I just wondered if he was with you.'

'He hasn't turned up here. Do you want me to come over?'

The voices in the background got louder. Gina heard a woman laughing. 'No, it's fine. I can hear you've got company. But you will let me know if you hear from him, won't you?'

'Don't worry, I'll tell him to come straight home and stop playing silly buggers.'

Gina smiled and dashed away a tear. 'Thanks, Mark.'

'No problem, love. Try to get some sleep and don't worry about him. If I know Stephen he's probably in a bar somewhere, drowning his sorrows.'

Gina put the phone down. She wished she could believe that, but she had a feeling she knew where Stephen was – heading straight back to London and Lucy.

And she'd driven him away. She buried her head in her hands, drumming her temples with her knuckles. How could she have been so stupid? It was a bad time to tell Stephen about the baby, just after a row, when he'd been working all day and was obviously under stress. He'd been spoiling for a fight, looking for an excuse to run away, and she'd handed it to him on a plate.

She fell asleep on the sofa and woke before dawn. It took her a moment to realize where she was. As soon as she did, misery swamped her. She ran to the window, but Stephen's car wasn't there. It was five in the morning. He'd been out all night. If he'd done it deliberately to punish her he couldn't have made her feel more wretched.

She tried his mobile. It was still switched off. She thought about calling Mark again, but her pride wouldn't allow it. She knew Stephen wouldn't be there. She also knew that however sweet Mark was to her, his first loyalty was to Stephen.

She knew she wouldn't sleep, but she crawled into bed. She didn't want Vicky to find her in a dishevelled heap on the sofa. She had to keep everything normal, for her sake.

But Vicky was shrewder than she'd given her credit for. She saw straight through Gina's determinedly upbeat mood and the industrial quanties of concealer covering the shadows around her eyes.

'You've had a row, haven't you?' she said.

'Of course not, darling. I told you, Stephen had to go to work.'

'On a Saturday?'

'He had some constituency business to finish for tomorrow.' Gina couldn't meet her daughter's eye as she pulled the crust off her dry toast. It was all she could face this morning. 'He'll be home soon, you'll see.'

Vicky looked troubled as she stirred her spoon around her untouched cereal bowl. 'Can I go and see Chloe today?' she asked.

Gina looked up. Chloe was a friend of Vicky's from prep school who lived nearby. 'But we were going to spend the day together. I thought we could decorate the tree?'

'We could do it another time, couldn't we? I texted Chloe last night and her family are going to the Bahamas for Christmas. I won't get to see her otherwise. Please?'

They looked at each other across the table. Gina was about to argue, then changed her mind.

'If that's what you want.'

Perhaps it was for the best if Vicky wasn't around when Stephen came home. If he came home.

He still hadn't turned up by the time she'd dropped Vicky at Chloe's house. Unable to face staying in an empty house, she called her mother.

Rose was surprised to hear from her. 'You want to meet up? Today? I thought you were spending time with Vicky?'

'She's with a friend. I thought we could go shopping in York.'

'On a Saturday before Christmas? Are you mad?'

'We could go for tea at Betty's? Please, Mummy?'

'Oh, very well.' She heard her mother's sigh down the line. 'Although I'm warning you, the traffic will be appalling.'

She was right, of course. Gina had to fight her way through the teeming streets of Christmas shoppers to join the queue waiting outside Betty's.

Her mother arrived twenty minutes later, just as Gina was being shown to a table.

'Heavens, you look glum.' Rose leaned over to brush her cheek with her lips, giving her a waft of Arpège. She looked elegant as ever in beige trousers and a matching cotton sweater, a rust-coloured print scarf draped artfully around her shoulders. 'If you keep frowning like that you'll be able to park a bicycle in the lines between your eyebrows.'

'Sorry.' Gina forced a smile.

'What's so urgent that you had to see me today?' her mother asked after they'd ordered and swapped the usual chit-chat about how hellishly busy it was and what a nightmare it was to park.

Gina gazed out across St Helen's Square, watching the shoppers hurry past the window. There was so much she'd wanted to tell her, but now she was here she found her upper lip stiffening. 'Do I need a reason to see my own mother?'

'No, but you sounded as if you were going to burst into tears on the phone. So what is it this time?'

Gina watched a man playing a violin, the open case at his feet. 'Stephen and I have had a bit of a row,' she admitted.

'I knew it. I suppose it's all over this silly affair business?' Rose lifted her perfectly plucked brows. 'Honestly, Gina, you don't know when to give up, do you? If you're not careful you'll drive him away. And then where will you be?'

Gina was taken aback. She'd been about to tell her all about the baby, but now she didn't know what to say. 'Maybe I'm better off without him,' she said.

'Now, we both know that's not true.' Rose looked reproving. 'You're not strong emotionally, Gina. You don't cope well on your own, do you? Look how you fell to pieces after Vicky was born.'

'I was very young, then.'

'Marrying Stephen was the best move you could have made,' Rose went on, ignoring her. 'He's been good to you, Gina. And to Vicky, too. There aren't many men who would have taken on a single mother, especially not one as fragile as you. And he's a good man. You'd be making a terrible mistake if you gave him up.'

'I think he's giving me up.'

'Then it's up to you to make sure he doesn't.' Rose's eyes flashed. 'Tell me about this woman. Who is she?'

Gina was still explaining as their food arrived. Rose looked from her salad to Gina's plate of pasta, her mouth tightening in silent disapproval. She needn't have worried. Gina felt too queasy to do more than pick at her food.

'What do you think?' Gina asked when she'd finished talking. 'Is he having an affair, do you think?'

'Possibly,' Rose shrugged. 'But it doesn't sound too serious.'

'Not too serious? My husband is sleeping with someone else and you don't think it's serious?'

'Shh! Keep your voice down, for heaven's sake!' Rose glanced around the restaurant, her fork poised halfway to her mouth. 'Look, all men have affairs, Gina. It's the way you deal with it that matters.'

'And how should I deal with it?'

'If you've got any sense you'll keep quiet and let it all blow over.' Rose's voice was soft but steely.

'You don't think I should confront him?' Gina said.

'Not unless you want to lose him.' She regarded her daughter pityingly. 'If you say nothing, it will probably be over in a few months. Maybe less. But if you start trying to force the issue . . .' She shook her head. 'Men don't like drama queens, Gina. They find them incredibly tiresome. Leave all the histrionics to the other woman. You'll see, sooner or later she'll overplay her hand, start making all kinds of demands on him. Then he'll come running back to you.'

I don't know if I want him back, Gina thought. Then she

realized her mother could be right. What if she couldn't cope without Stephen? Especially now she had a baby on the way. She might end up in the same mess she'd been in with Vicky. 'And what if he doesn't come back?'

'Of course he'll come back, darling.' Then, just as she was feeling reassured, her mother added, 'There's probably a general election coming up in the spring, isn't there? He wouldn't want to rock the boat before then.'

At least Rose was right about one thing; Stephen was waiting for her when she got home. Gina saw his car parked in the drive and felt a mixture of hope and fear.

He was in the kitchen, fiddling with the complex espresso-maker Gina had never quite got the hang of. 'Cappuccino?' he said, holding up a cup.

'Please.' It was a peace-making gesture, she registered with relief. Perhaps everything was going to be all right after all.

'Where's Vicky?'

'At Chloe's. She rang earlier to ask if she could stay the night.'

'Probably a good idea. We should talk,' he said, over the hiss of steam from the machine.

'Yes.' But she'd already made her mind up to listen rather than speak. She wanted to hear what Stephen had to say, to try to understand things from his point of view. Perhaps all he needed was time to get used to the idea.

He put the cup down in front of her, then sat down opposite. 'I've been thinking,' he said, 'and I really don't think you should have this baby.'

Gina reeled back in her seat as if he'd slapped her. 'What?'

'I'm not ready to be a father.'

'You're already a father. To Vicky.'

'That's different. Vicky's older, she can take care of herself. This baby would be too big a responsibility.' He stirred his coffee. 'We've talked about this already, haven't we? I told you I wanted to be there for you and our kids, not traipsing backwards and forwards to Westminster, and missing them grow up.'

'So give up politics,' she said. 'Other people do it.'

Stephen looked incredulous. 'After all the years I've spent getting this far? Don't you think you're being a bit selfish?'

'No more selfish than you are, telling me to get rid of our baby because it interferes with your career.'

'I'm thinking of you, too.' Stephen's voice was suddenly soft and persuasive. 'I admit I'm not ready to be a father. But I don't think you're ready to be a mother again, either.'

'What do you mean?' she asked, knowing perfectly well what he was insinuating.

'You know what happened last time. What if you get ill again? I won't be here all the time to look after you. What if you harm yourself, or our baby?'

'I won't.' Why did people keep saying that, acting as if she couldn't be trusted?

'I wish I was as sure as you.' Stephen reached across the table for her hand, his face sorrowful. 'I don't mean to upset you, but I'm only saying this for your sake. I reckon you should think very carefully about whether you want to go through with this. You wouldn't want anything bad to happen again, would you?'

'And what if I don't want an abortion?'

Stephen's hand slid away from hers. 'Then I suppose we'd have to reconsider our future,' he said stiffly.

'You mean you'd walk out on me?'

'I hope it wouldn't come to that.'

'So do I. Because it wouldn't look very good, would it? I can just see the headlines now: "MP walks out on pregnant wife". It wouldn't do much for your re-election chances, would it?'

Stephen's eyes were icy. 'The election will be over long before this baby comes along.' He pushed away his coffee cup and stood up. 'Don't even think about trying to trap me like that, Gina. Because you'll end up the loser.'

Gina sat at the table for a long time after he'd gone. He was right, she shouldn't have challenged him like that. What if he called her bluff and walked out? He might not leave her before the election, but there was nothing to stop him going afterwards.

The thought suddenly terrified her. She'd always thought she'd got stronger over the years, put her mental illness in the past. But was that just because she had Stephen's support? What if he took that away from her? What if everyone was right and she couldn't cope without him?

Chapter 12

It was Christmas Eve on the men's cardiac ward. The nurses bustled around wearing tinsel strung around their necks like feather boas. The porter pushing the tea trolley wore a jaunty Santa hat.

Joe Delaney was sitting up in bed reading a letter when Finn arrived.

'Good news?' she asked, dumping the magazines and treats she'd brought with her on the bed.

'Oh, aye.' Joe stuffed the envelope into his bedside cabinet. 'I've been here that long I'm on the consultant's flaming Christmas card list!'

'It won't be for much longer.'

'I'll still be stuck in here over Christmas, though.'

'What are you complaining about?' Finn teased him. 'You usually only spend Christmas Day lying on the sofa watching telly and being waited on hand and foot. I can't see it'll be much different, really.'

'Very funny.'

'Seriously, we'll all be here to help you celebrate. Me and Auntie Orla. And Ciaran, Mel and the baby,' she added, although she was less sure of that. Ciaran had been avoiding her lately. 'Orla and I wondered if you'd like the priest to come and say a special mass for you, as a treat?' she added, her tongue firmly wedged in her cheek.

'That's all I need. People praying for my immortal soul like I'm already half dead and buried!' Joe grimaced. 'Where is Orla, by the way? I thought she might have come with you.'

'She'll be in later. She had to do a last-minute shop at the supermarket.'

'She's a good woman.'

'She's great.' It had been a huge help having her around. She'd cleaned the house, including the bits Finn usually missed or ignored, and filled the freezer. It was wonderful to come home to a cooked meal every night instead of having to fend for herself. She raised Joe's spirits, too. He always seemed much brighter after her visits. 'I'm glad she's staying for Christmas,' she added. She hadn't been looking forward to spending the day on her own.

'Anyway, I thought these might cheer you up.' She handed over the bag of treats. 'The latest copy of *Construction News* is in there. And I managed to get your favourite sweets this time.'

'It'll take more than a bag of mint humbugs to make my day,' Joe said, helping himself to one anyway. As he rifled through the various bags of goodies, Finn thought about the letter he'd been reading. Where had it come from? Neither she nor Orla had brought him any post, so it must have been delivered direct to the hospital.

'So how's your brother?' Her father asked the inevitable question.

'He's fine. I think. I haven't seen him for a while.'

'I expect he's busy working.'

I wish he was, Finn thought. She'd got tired of answering calls from disgruntled customers when Ciaran hadn't bothered to show up. Mr Stephenson was on the phone practically every day with another complaint.

'If he's that busy, perhaps I could help him?' she suggested, but her father was already shaking his head.

'You stick to hairdressing,' he said. 'Ciaran can look after the business.'

'But—'

'Finnuala, the building trade is a man's game. Let's leave it at that, shall we?'

'No, we won't leave it at that.' Usually she wouldn't argue, but his dismissive attitude irritated her. 'Why are you so against the idea of a woman working on a building site?'

'Because they don't belong there, that's why.'

'God, you're so old-fashioned! For your information – Dad?' She saw the sheen of perspiration on his brow. 'Dad, are you all right?'

'My – chest . . .' He gestured for her to ring the bell beside his bed, his face grey. 'Get a nurse.'

Finn dived for the bell. Almost immediately, a nurse appeared. 'What's the problem?'

'I think he's having some kind of attack.'

The nurse took one look at him fighting for breath, and summoned a doctor. Finn was ushered away as the screens were whipped around, shutting her out. Moments later, two porters appeared, wheeling a trolley between them.

'He's going to be OK, isn't he?' she pleaded, but no one heard her. She tried to follow the trolley as it was whisked down a corridor, but it disappeared through a set of double doors, leaving her behind.

She sat on a chair outside the doors to wait. And wait. By the time the consultant appeared again she'd managed to convince herself the worst had happened.

'Is he . . . ?' she whispered, too afraid to say the words.

The consultant shook his head. 'Your father's stable. I'm afraid he's suffered something called ventricular tachycardia – it's an irregularity of the heartbeat, quite common after a heart attack. We've given him drugs to stabilize him.'

'Is he going to be all right?'

'We're going to have to see how he responds to the drugs we've given him. If they don't work, he might need an operation. But there's no reason why he shouldn't make a full recovery. Don't worry, Miss Delaney. Your father's a fighter.'

Finn went back to the ward, still shaking. What if she'd brought on this attack, arguing with her father about the business? Why couldn't she just learn to keep her mouth shut?

She tidied up his tray, trying to make herself useful while she waited for news. As she was putting the humbugs away in his bedside locker she spotted the letter.

She recognized the printing on the envelope. It was from the land agents.

She took it out, stealing guilty looks over her shoulder, half expecting him to come in at any moment and tell her off for snooping.

She read it, then wished she hadn't. The agents had made another offer for the land, but it was even less than their last offer. They must think he was desperate.

Rage burned through her. No wonder he'd been taken ill, if it did the same to his blood pressure as it was doing to hers. How could they do it? she thought. How could they send a letter like that to a sick man in hospital? More to the point, how could Neil do it to her? He'd said he would make sure her father was left alone, and he'd let her down.

Furious, she rushed outside and called his mobile from the car park. It was switched off. She dialled his office number.

A tipsy-sounding woman answered the phone. 'I'm afraid Mr Tate isn't here,' she slurred down the phone. In the background Finn could hear the sound of an office party, music mingling with the sound of laughter.

'Can I leave a message? It's very important I speak to him today.'

'I'm sorry, Mr and Mrs Tate have gone away for Christmas. They flew to Antigua this morning.'

'Did you say *Mrs* Tate?' Finn felt light-headed.

'That's right. They'll be back after New Year if you'd like to call back then.'

Orla did her best to be reassuring when Finn got home and told her the news.

'It's a setback, but it's not the end of the world.' She immediately adopted her brisk nurse's voice. 'The worst that could happen is your dad might need an operation. But he's been through worse than this. He'll make it.'

'That's what they said at the hospital.'

'There you are, then. They should know.' Orla regarded her shrewdly. 'So why do you still look as if you've got the weight of the world on your shoulders?'

'It's nothing.'

'It doesn't seem like it to me.' Orla wiped her hands on a tea towel and sat down. 'What's happened?'

Reluctantly, Finn told her about the letter and the phone call she'd made to Neil. As she told her about what the secretary had said, rage and humiliation came flooding in, and she found herself choking back tears of anger.

'Oh, Finn, I'm so sorry.' Orla reached for her hand. 'You really liked him, didn't you?'

'It's not just that.' She didn't know how she felt about him any more, apart from incredibly angry. 'I just feel so stupid. How could I have not known something like that?'

'How were you supposed to know? Some men are very good liars.'

That was Neil Tate, all right. He'd lied to her and let her down in every way. She'd trusted him, and he'd betrayed her.

And she'd let him do it. She cringed to think how silly and naive she'd been, allowing herself to respond to him when all along he was probably laughing at her. Well, he wasn't going to be laughing by the time she'd finished with him.

'The best thing you can do is put it down to experience and forget all about him,' Orla said.

'Oh, I will,' Finn agreed.

After she'd got even with him.

Chapter 13

Gina nervously checked the glossy sales brochures, counting them for the fourth time. They were stacked in a neat pile, all ready to hand out to the press and local dignitaries. She hoped she'd ordered enough for all the guests. She thought she'd added the numbers up correctly, but there seemed to be an awful lot of people streaming into the marquee.

At least the weather seemed to be on her side. After a grey, drizzly Christmas and New Year, January had started out crisp and clear. The sky was a bright, cold blue and a chilly breeze whipped through the filigree of bare trees surrounding the Windmill Meadows site. Gina was glad she'd had the good sense to put heaters in the marquee. Perhaps she should have ordered hot mulled wine instead of chilled champagne?

Oh well, it was too late to worry about that now. She checked her watch again, and glanced anxiously towards the gates. Her father was late. She should have expected it. Even though Max Tate detested unpunctuality in other people, he made a point of keeping others waiting, simply because he could.

She consulted her clipboard again, mentally ticking off her list. She couldn't believe she'd managed to remember everything. It was going suspiciously smoothly. The guests had all arrived, and they seemed to be enjoying the champagne and canapés in the marquee. The showhomes were finished and looking their best, sitting among the manicured gardens with their tinkling fountains and beds of winter flowering shrubs. Who would have believed the gardeners had been there at dawn, planting them?

It all looked perfect, just as she'd hoped. She was desperate to make a good job of this, to show her family that she really could do something right.

'How's it going?' She turned around, still clutching her clipboard like a lifeline. Molly stood behind her with James. It still gave Gina a shock to see them together, even though they'd been dating for several weeks now.

'Fine – I think.'

'You think? You'd better be sure. You know how Dad hates anything going wrong.'

James' tone alarmed her. She'd already had several sleepless nights over this. And when she did doze off, she was usually woken up by an anxiety dream where some disaster happened. A couple of times she'd been close to cancelling the whole thing.

'Stop bullying your sister, James. I'm sure everything will be brilliant.' Molly smiled warmly at Gina. 'You've done a fantastic job. It all looks wonderful.'

'Thanks.' Gina looked at James. 'Do you think he'll like it?'

James gazed around for a moment, then back at her. To her surprise, he smiled. It was like watching the sun coming out from behind a cloud. 'I'm sure he'll be very impressed,' he said. 'Well done, Gina. You've worked very hard.' To her amazement he leaned forward and gave her a kiss on the cheek. A rather formal peck, but still a kiss.

She watched them heading off to the champagne tent. What was it with those two? Logically they really shouldn't be together, yet they seemed to work. It was as if Molly knocked off her brother's sharper edges, made him more human somehow.

If only Neil had married someone like Molly, she thought, as Nicole bore down on her. She was swathed in a bright scarlet coat that looked striking against her dramatic dark colouring.

'No sign of them yet?'

'Not yet.'

'They'd better hurry up, everyone's getting half-cut in the beer tent.'

'It's a marquee,' Gina corrected her.

'Whatever. They'd still better get a move on. Although I suppose your mother's still trying to decide what hat to wear.'

Gina excused herself and headed to the marquee to warn the wine waiters not to be too hasty to refill the guests' glasses. She would have liked a glass of wine herself, but she knew she had to be careful. Besides, she already felt queasy with nerves. Or was it the dreaded morning sickness again? She seemed to have it all the time now. Far worse than she ever had with Vicky.

As she went in to give the show homes a last-minute once-over, she caught Julie and Claire gossiping in the kitchen of the four-bedroom detached. Despite doing nothing to help organize the day, they'd insisted on coming along to enjoy the champagne and get away from the office. And they weren't going to miss the chance to see her fall flat on her face either. Seeing them made her even more determined to make the day a success.

'When you two have finished, perhaps you'd like to hand out some promotional literature to our guests?' she said.

'Don't know why we're bothering,' she heard Julie mutter to Claire as they stomped past her. 'Most of them are only here for the free champagne anyway.'

Gina ignored them. She wasn't going to let anyone spoil her day. Desperate for something to take her mind off her father's late arrival, she headed back to the marquee with an armful of sales brochures. As she threaded her way through the crowd, handing them out and chatting to the guests, she noticed a woman striding purposefully across the grass.

She dumped the rest of the brochures into Claire's arms and went out to meet her. 'Hello? Can I help you?'

The woman stared back at her. She was younger than Gina and a few inches shorter, with cropped dark hair around a pointed elfin face that seemed too pretty for the tough leather jacket she wore. She also looked familiar, although Gina couldn't remember where they'd met. 'I'm looking for Neil Tate.'

She scanned her guest list. 'And you are?'

'My name's Finn. And there's no point looking on your list, you won't find me. Is Neil here?'

'He's in the VIP tent. But wait, you can't go—' But the woman had already slipped past her.

Gina was about to follow when one of the security guards called out, 'Mr Tate's here, Mrs Farrell.'

'Oh, right. Thanks.' Gina glanced back at the tent, hesitating for a moment. Then she turned and went to greet her father.

Whatever the woman wanted, she was sure her brother could deal with it.

Finn headed straight for the drinks and determinedly downed a glass of champagne. Her nerve, which had carried her here, was now failing as she tried to avoid the curious glances of the well-dressed people around here. Perhaps she shouldn't have come after all.

But at the same time she knew this would be a good chance to confront that lying rat Neil and let him know what she thought of him. Not just for hurting her, but for using her to get at her father over the piece of land. He'd been avoiding her calls since he got back and she wanted to see him face to face.

When she spotted him on the far side of the tent, laughing and joking with a group of men, she was just about ready for him. Grabbing another glass of champagne, she pushed her way through the crowd towards him.

'Hello, Neil.'

He didn't even flinch. 'Finn. This is a pleasant surprise.'

'Isn't it?' She smiled. 'You're very tanned. Did you have a good time in Antigua?'

'Yes, thank you.' He excused himself from the group of men and steered her away into a corner. 'So what are you doing here?'

'Oh, I just thought I'd pop in and take a look around, as I used to work here. It all looks very nice, by the way.'

'Thanks.' Neil's smile was beginning to grow uneasy.

'I suppose you're planning to do something similar at White-croft Farm once you've got your hands on our land?' She raised her voice just enough for a few people close to them to turn around.

Neil's grip tightened on her arm. 'Why don't we talk about this outside?'

'Why? Are you afraid your wife might see us? Where is she, by the way?' She scanned the crowd. 'I'd love to meet her.'

'Some other time.' Neil's smile was fixed as he tried to manoeuvre her towards the doorway.

'You're not denying you're married, then?'

'Why should I?'

'Does your wife know about us?'

'There is no us, Finn. We went out for a couple of drinks together, that's all. Or did you think there was more to it than that?' he said patronizingly.

Finn felt herself blushing and changed the subject abruptly. 'You promised to leave my dad alone.'

'Sorry,' he shrugged. 'But like I said, when the Tates want something, we usually get it.'

'It's we now, is it? I thought it was your brother pulling all the strings?'

'Don't underestimate me, Finn. I can pull a few strings if I need to.'

Something about the way he said it made realization dawn. 'That's why you did it, isn't it? You thought you could persuade me to sell you the land.' He was silent. 'You conniving little—'

'Neil?' Before Finn could say anything else, they were joined by a tall, glamorous woman in a red coat.

Finn looked at her full, sulky mouth and disdainful eyes. 'You must be *Mrs* Tate,' she said. She and Neil looked as if they belonged together.

'And you are?'

'She's just leaving.' Neil steered her towards the doorway and out into the bright January sunshine. 'And in case you're thinking of saying anything to Nicole, I'd advise you not to bother,' he added in an undertone. 'She wouldn't believe you.'

'I couldn't give a stuff about Nicole. I just came here to tell you to lay off my dad.'

'Sorry, sweetheart, no can do.'

'Then I'll go to the press and tell them what you're doing.'

'Do you seriously think that would scare my father? Darling, he plays golf with the editors of most of the nationals. And as for the local press – forget it. All it takes is a phone call from Max Tate and they'll back off faster than you can say, "Hold the front page." ' He sent her a patronizing look. 'If you really want to help your dear old dad, the best thing you can do is run off home and persuade him to sell to us.'

Gina found herself holding her breath as the driver opened the car door to let her parents out. Rose emerged first, looking elegant in a fuchsia pink coat and dress, her ash-blonde hair swept up inside a matching pill-box hat. Her father followed, immaculate in a dark suit. There was such an air of power and authority about him, it was all Gina could do not to drop a curtsey. She had to keep reminding herself this was her own father.

'Welcome to Windmill Meadows. If you'll come this way?' She led them proudly up the curving path towards the marquee, where a podium had been set up outside the show house. 'We thought we'd start with your speech, then declare the site open and move on to organized tours of the site.'

'And the press?'

'I've got packs ready with all the information about the houses, and I've arranged a photocall with you and the local councillors after your speech.' Her words came out in a breathless rush, tumbling over themselves, eager to win a word or a smile.

Max gazed around. 'It all seems like a lot of fuss over nothing to me,' he said. 'But since we're here, I suppose we'd better get on with it.' He strode off towards the marquee, leaving Gina feeling deflated. What had she expected? Lavish praise, maybe a hug for her efforts? That wasn't her father's style at all. At least he hadn't derided her, and that was something.

'You could have dressed up,' Rose hissed out of the corner of her mouth as they followed Max. 'You look as if you've come straight from the office.'

'I have come straight from the office.' Gina looked down at her serviceable cranberry skirt-suit. She was tempted to point out that not everyone had the luxury of being able to spend all day in the beauty salon, but she couldn't be bothered to argue.

Her stomach flipped and she felt queasy again. She hadn't been able to face anything for breakfast. Whether it was nerves or morning sickness, she was sure she wouldn't be able to make it to the podium to deliver her opening speech.

She went to find James. He was chatting to one of the councillors on the planning committee and didn't look as if he would welcome being disturbed. But luckily Molly was nearby, shovelling down handfuls of canapés out of sheer boredom.

'Hi.' Her smile turned to concern when she saw Gina's pale face. 'Are you OK?'

'Not really. Can you ask James if he'll give the opening speech and introduce my father?'

'Of course, if I can get a word in edgeways. He's been talking to that councillor for ages. But don't you want your moment of glory?'

'No, honestly. I don't feel too good.'

Molly smiled sympathetically. 'Don't tell me – stage fright?'

'Something like that.' Gina managed a weak smile.

She didn't wait to hear her brother's speech. She didn't even get as far as the loo. She just made it to the back of the marquee before she was violently sick in one of the ornamental flowerbeds.

Oh God, she thought as she squatted on her hands and knees among the dwarf conifers, was it always going to be like this? This little one had made its presence felt right from the word go.

She stood up, wiping her mouth and brushing the damp grass off her skirt. She had to get back to the party. Her father's speech would be over, and they'd be looking for her.

She headed back around to the other side of the marquee – and walked straight into pandemonium. Around her, the crowd was pushing and jostling, people were jeering and laughing, flashbulbs were popping. In the middle of it all, her father stood on the podium, slowly wiping his chin with a handkerchief.

James pushed his way past her. 'Where the hell have you been?' he yelled at Gina. 'Some maniac's just attacked Dad.'

She didn't have a chance to answer before he'd disappeared, forcing his way into the crowd.

'She threw something,' Molly explained breathlessly, catching up with her. 'I didn't see what it was, but it was a direct hit.'

'Oh, no.' Gina elbowed to the front of the crowd in time to see her brothers bundling the dark-haired girl away towards the gates. The press photographers pursued them, flashbulbs still popping.

Gina looked at her father. He surveyed the crowd, unsmiling.

Finally he leaned towards the microphone. 'Well,' he said, 'I suppose that's one person who won't be putting her name down for one of our houses.'

The crowd laughed. Her father made a few more off-the-cuff jokes and then went back to his speech, outwardly so cool it was as if the moment had never happened. But underneath his mask of good humour, Gina could sense the seething fury.

And she knew exactly who was going to get the blame for it.

'What were you thinking? What the fuck were you thinking?'

Gina shrank down in the low-slung leather chair as her father paced the office, towering over her. Her brothers sat side by side on the sofa, silent and sombre.

'How the hell did she get in? Why weren't you checking invitations on the gate?'

'I didn't have time. I was busy doing everything else.' Gina glanced at her brothers. Neil didn't look at her, but she saw sympathy in James's eyes.

'Someone should have been doing it. You were supposed to be managing a team, weren't you? Or don't you have any management skills at all?'

'I thought—' she began to explain, but Max held up his hand.

'No excuses. It's not good enough, Gina. I said it was a waste of time and money, but I didn't think even you could turn it into a fucking fiasco! I take it you've seen this?' He thrust that evening's paper in front of her. Gina nodded dumbly. Every time she closed her eyes she saw that photo of her stony-faced father, wiping his chin. Below it the headline screamed out, 'TATE THAT!'

'It's not all Gina's fault,' James said.

'Yes, it is!' He shook the paper at Gina again. 'So what have you got to say for yourself?'

'I know I made a mistake—'

'Mistake? It was a monumental fuck-up. And the Tates don't do that.'

Gina stared down at her hands. Her father had been humiliated and he needed to blame someone. The best thing she could do was quietly take it until his anger ran out of steam.

'I'm sorry,' she said. 'It won't happen again.'

'Too bloody right. You're fired.'

'What?' James and Gina said together.

'I don't think you're ready to be marketing manager. You can stay in the department, but I'm giving Julie Palmer your job.'

'You can't do that!'

'Can't I? I think you'll find that as it's my company I can do as I like.'

'But I can't work for Julie.' A few weeks ago she wouldn't have minded going in at ground level, but now she didn't think she could face the others' smug faces. She stuck out her chin. 'If you make me do that, then I'd rather resign.'

'Fine, if that's what you want.'

'That's not fair,' James said.

Max turned on him. 'Who asked for your opinion?'

Gina looked at her father, then at her brothers. Neil still refused to meet her eye. James shook his head.

She stood up. 'I'll go and clear out my desk, shall I?'

She waited, but her father still didn't move. He was staring down at his chess board, studying the pieces. She'd been dismissed.

She went back up to her office. Claire and Julie were perched on Trish's desk, gossiping. They sprang up when she walked in.

Julie followed her as she walked into what was her office. It already seemed strangely empty and unfamiliar. Two boxes sat on the desk.

'I've already packed your things up. I hope you don't mind? Only I needed to move my stuff in,' she said sweetly. 'I suppose you'll be having my old desk now, won't you?'

'Not necessarily,' Gina said, picking up one of the boxes. 'I'm leaving.'

'Another new department?' Julie smirked.

'No.'

She headed for the door, leaving them open-mouthed behind her. It wasn't until she'd reached the car park that it finally sank in what she'd done.

It wasn't losing her job that hurt. It was the way her father had looked at her. As if he really didn't care.

'Did you have to do that?' James asked, when Gina had gone.

'She's got to learn.' Max stared down at his chessboard. He'd left his black pieces in a sticky situation earlier on, and he still hadn't worked out what his next move should be.

Perhaps he had been too harsh with Gina. She couldn't help being a lightweight, he shouldn't have expected any more from her. But raging at her was the only way he could get rid of some of the anger he felt for that bitch Finn Delaney.

Max Tate wasn't used to being humiliated, especially by a little nobody like her. Not only that, she was proving to be a real thorn in his side. And that was the last thing Tates needed at a time like this.

'Looking on the bright side, at least Windmill Meadows made the front page,' Neil said.

Max glared at his son. 'Is that supposed to be funny?' He focused intently on the chessboard, trying to think. All the bad publicity wasn't going to help his upmarket development sell quickly. Plus the remaining house on Paradise Road was bound to be coming up for sale soon, and he needed the cash to snap it up before anyone else did. And the repayments on the Whitecroft Farm land were beginning to stack up with nothing to show for it. He needed to start building before all their potential profits were eaten away.

He needed the Delaneys' land. That was what it all came down to.

'Tell me about the Delaneys,' he said.

'They're in a bit of trouble at the moment,' Neil said, eager to show off his knowledge. 'As you know, the father's been in hospital with a heart attack. He's due to be discharged any day now, but he'll be out of action for a few weeks yet. The son's supposed to be running the business, but frankly he's a cretin. He couldn't run a bath let alone a business.'

'So they'll end up in trouble eventually?' Max said. 'Suppose we hasten things along a little? If they were short of cash they might need to get rid of a few of their assets to stay in the game.'

'So they might have to sell the land?'

'What's wrong with waiting?' James said. 'You've said yourself the business will run into trouble eventually.'

'Because I don't like waiting.' Max's voice was menacingly soft. That girl needed to be taught a lesson in manners.

He reached across and made a decisive move with his black rook, locking his opponent in with nowhere to go. 'The gloves are off. I think it's time we declared war on the Delaneys.'

'Let me get this straight,' Orla said. 'You threw a canapé at this man?'

'A mushroom vol au vent.' Finn examined the bruises on her arm where she'd been manhandled off the premises. 'And he's lucky I didn't throw the whole plate at him.'

'You're lucky he didn't press charges,' Orla said.

'I might, though.' Finn winced. 'Do you think I could do them for assault?'

'I think you're better off doing nothing.' Orla shook her head. 'What do you think your father would have made of his daughter ending up in jail?'

'I didn't think of that,' Finn admitted. She'd meant to leave after the row with Neil, but she'd been so furious that when she'd seen Max Tate up on that stage, looking so smug and spouting off about how fantastic the Tates were, she'd thought about her poor dad lying in hospital and her temper had taken over.

'Maybe you should start thinking,' Orla warned her. 'And we'd better not let your dad see this, either. It would give him another coronary for sure.' She looked at the photo on the front page of the newspaper. 'Although it might also give him the best laugh he's had for ages.' Her mouth twitched. 'I know I shouldn't say it, but it sounds like that eejit deserved it. Look at his face!'

Finn looked. Behind the handkerchief, Max's eyes were furious.

A shiver ran over her skin. She was suddenly worried she might have made a bad situation a whole lot worse.

Chapter 14

'You're lucky I don't call the police,' Marcus Stephenson said.

Finn stood in the middle of the site, looking around her with a terrible feeling of déjà vu. She didn't blame him for being angry. Despite all her warnings, Ciaran had been up to his old tricks again. Worst of all, he'd been fiddling the books.

'I wouldn't have known about it if my architect hadn't happened to check the dockets,' Mr Stephenson said. 'Apparently your brother's charged us for enough materials to build the Taj Mahal. And we've yet to *see* half the stuff he's ordered. So where is it?'

'I'm sure there's a good explanation.' Although the only one she could think of was that her brother had been doing the old builder's trick of over-ordering for materials, then keeping them for himself or selling them on and pocketing the cash.

It looked as if Marcus Stephenson had come to the same conclusion. 'Perhaps it's best if we just call it a day?'

'No! I'll make sure you get your money back. Every single penny.' Even if she had to turn Ciaran upside-down and shake him until his fillings dropped out.

'It's not just the money. Your brother's work hasn't been up to standard. The building inspector's due at the end of the week. He'll probably condemn the lot.'

And Delaneys would get the blame, Finn thought. Not just her brother Ciaran, but her dad, too. Bad news spread fast, and it could seriously affect their business.

'We could try to put it right, if you'll give us a chance,' she said.

'Oh no.' He shook his head. 'I've given your company too many chances, and look where it's left me. Weeks gone and half a useless extension. No, I'm going to have to call in some real builders, see if they can salvage anything from this mess.'

'Please don't,' Finn begged. 'Just give us another day. Twenty-four hours, and then you can throw us off the site.'

'It's a bit hard to throw someone off the site if there's no one on it.'

'Please. We've been going through some problems at the moment, with my dad being in hospital. But I promise we can sort this out for you.'

'Do you seriously think I'd want your brother anywhere near this place, after the way he cheated me?'

'My brother won't be involved, I promise you. I'll do the work myself.'

'You?'

'I'm a fully trained bricklayer and joiner. I can show you my qualifications, if you like?'

Mr Stephenson looked dubious. 'I'm not sure . . .'

'Twenty-four hours, that's all I'm asking for. If you don't agree I can make some progress on the job in that time then I'll walk away. And we'll refund all the money you've paid us so far,' she added rashly, then wished she hadn't when she saw the gleam in his eye.

'You're on,' he said. 'And I'll want a discount on the remaining work. For all the inconvenience. Say – ten per cent?'

Finn did some quick calculations in her head. They were barely making money on the deal already, with her having to correct so many of Ciaran's expensive mistakes. With another ten per cent knocked off they'd be lucky if they broke even. Maybe they should cut their losses and walk away?

Then she weighed it up against the bad publicity they'd receive. Mr Stephenson knew a lot of people in this leafy suburb. If they did a good job, his neighbours might start wanting their houses extended, too. But if he gave them a bad name, mud would stick. They'd be lucky if they worked in this area again.

She took a deep breath. 'It's a deal.'

As soon as Mr Stephenson had gone, Finn looked around the site and wondered what the hell she'd let herself in for. This mess would take twenty-four hours to get straight, before she could get any more work done.

But she had to do it. She blew on her hands and stamped her feet on the hard ground to warm herself up as she thought about what to tackle first. She had to get some of the old rubbish moved, and pick up some new bricks. The last lot Ciaran ordered didn't match the existing brickwork at all.

And as if she didn't have enough on her plate, the van had been vandalized last night. It was probably just kids, but it was still a nuisance. It would make the job a lot more difficult.

She rang the builders' merchants. Luckily they had the bricks she needed. But they couldn't deliver them for three days. If she wanted them, she would have to come and collect them herself.

Finn thought about her trashed van. 'But I can't get there today,' she said. 'Can't you deliver them? Just this once?'

'Sorry, no can do,' the voice on the other end of the line was gruff. 'If you want them, you're going to have to pick them up. But we could lend you a trailer, if that's any help?'

Finn thanked him, and hung up. At least it was something, a small chink of sunshine in her gloomy day. She kicked at a brick, wishing it was her brother Ciaran's backside. This was all his fault. While she was fretting, he was probably sleeping off a hangover after a night playing poker with his low-life mates.

She took her car to the builders' merchants, and on the way she made a detour to Ciaran's flat. Mel opened the door on the chain and peered out.

'Oh, it's you.' She unclipped the chain and let Finn in. She was still wearing her dressing gown, baby Joseph clamped under her arm. She looked as if she hadn't slept for days. Her unwashed blonde hair hung limply around her pale face.

'If you're looking for your brother, I haven't seen him.' She padded back down the narrow hallway towards the kitchen, her slippers shuffling. Finn closed the door and followed her. She watched as Mel hoisted the baby back into his high chair and continued spooning mashed-up rusk into his mouth.

'Didn't he come home last night?'

'I just said that, didn't I?' She pointed a spoon at Finn. 'And if you see him, you can tell him I'm getting sick of being here on my own, hiding from his dodgy mates.'

'What dodgy mates?' Finn pulled out a chair and sat down.

'Some blokes he met at the pub. Real flashy types, throwing their money around, telling him about all the deals they've done, promising to cut him in on the action. Ciaran was dead impressed.'

'I can imagine.' Her brother was always falling for get-rich-quick schemes, which probably explained why he was always broke.

'He kept telling me how he was going to make a packet and get us out of this place. Somewhere with a garden for the baby.' She scooped up some rusk that had dribbled down Joseph's chin and put it back into his mouth. 'Only it didn't happen, as usual.'

'Do you know why?'

'He fell out with them.' Mel pushed her hair out of her eyes. 'Knowing Ciaran, he probably owed them money. Anyway, they've started ringing here at all hours, and one turned up on the doorstep last night, looking for him. Ciaran is saying he's not scared, but I know he is. And I don't blame him. I wouldn't like to get on the wrong side of them, either. That's why I'm keeping the chain on the door, just in case.'

'Why don't you go to the police?'

'Ciaran would never let me do it. Besides, they haven't actually threatened me or anything.'

'But they've threatened Ciaran?'

'I don't know. He won't tell me what's going on, just keeps saying he's dealing with it. But I think it's got too much for him, which is why he's gone into hiding.' She wiped the baby's chin with a cloth. 'I'm a bit worried what they might do if they can't get their hands on him. What if they take it out on me or Joseph?'

Finn felt a wave of disgust and anger for her brother, leaving his girlfriend and baby son to the mercy of dangerous thugs. 'You can't stay here. You and Joseph have got to get away. There isn't much room at our place at the moment, but you're welcome there.'

Mel shook her head. 'Thanks, but I'm moving to my mum's today. It's Ciaran I'm worried about. What if they find him?'

It'll serve him right if they do, Finn thought. Maybe a beating might knock some sense into him. It was no less than she wanted to do herself. Then again, he was her brother. Even if he was a hopeless idiot at times.

'I'm sure Ciaran can look after himself,' she said.

On the way to the builders' merchants, she thought about the nuisance phone calls she'd been getting. Two or three times a week, sometimes asking for Ciaran, sometimes just an ominous silence. And then there was her van. She'd told herself it was just kids. But what if Ciaran's friends had paid her a visit?

She returned from the builders' merchants with a trailer load of new bricks a couple of hours later to find a familiar blue pick-up parked across the Stephensons' driveway, blocking her out. She didn't have to see the white letters printed on the side to know who it belonged to.

Furious, she shot out of her car, slammed the door and marched up the drive. She found Ryan in the back garden, examining the mess. He turned as she approached, a wary edge to his smile.

'Finn? What are you doing here?'

'You're unbelievable, do you know that?' She confronted him, hands on her hips. 'My father's ill in hospital and you're trying to poach our business.'

'What?' He looked around. 'You mean, this is *your* job?'

'As if you didn't know! Don't tell me, you just happened to be passing and decided to drop in and tell the owners how you could do it much better?'

'I couldn't do much worse.' Finn burned with humiliation as Ryan looked around. The last thing she wanted was for their rival to see what a mess Ciaran had made. 'Look, I didn't know you were working here. All I know is we got a call from the owner of the house asking us to give him a price for finishing a job because he didn't think his builders were up to it.'

'What? The snake! He promised me he'd give us another chance. Twenty-four hours, he said.'

'It'll take more than twenty-four hours to put this straight.'

'That's all I've got, isn't it? Otherwise I expect you and your boys will be here bright and early the following day to take over.'

'I already said. I didn't know it was you.'

'I don't suppose it would have made much difference, would it? What is it you always say? All's fair in love and war?'

'Actually, it's your dad who always says that, not me,' Ryan pointed out quietly.

'And you're determined to put him out of business, aren't you?' Finn ignored him. 'Don't you have any conscience at all? After all he did for you—'

'Now, hang on a minute!' Ryan turned on her. 'Don't you dare tell me how much I owe your dad. I know that better than you ever will. And as for putting him out of business, I reckon your brother's managing that all by himself. This is a shit job and you know it.' He jabbed an angry finger at her. 'You can have a go at me if it makes you feel better. But it's Ciaran you should be talking to.'

'Don't you think I would, if I could find him?' Finn shot back. 'I'd wring the little swine's neck if he hadn't disappeared off the face of the earth.'

Ryan frowned. 'Where is he?'

'How should I know? According to Mel, he's got himself into trouble with some local gangsters and done a runner. As if I didn't have enough to deal with.'

She buried her face in her hands, feeling tired and defeated. She sensed Ryan moving towards her and tensed, wondering if he was going to put his arm around her. Suddenly she wouldn't have minded resting her head on that solid shoulder, just for a moment.

But he didn't. 'Maybe it's time your dad found out what's going on.'

'No.' Although it might serve him right to see what kind of a mess his golden boy had made, she didn't want to give her father any more stress. 'I'll sort this out somehow.'

'On your own? I don't see how.'

'I've got to try.' She faced him. 'Promise you won't tell Dad? He'd be so upset, I don't know what it would do to him.'

Their eyes met, just as Mr Stephenson emerged from the house. 'Well, what do you think – oh, it's you.' His smile disappeared when he saw Finn. 'I wasn't sure you'd be back after this morning.'

'Oh, I'm back, all right,' Finn said firmly. 'A deal's a deal and I'm not about to squirm out of it.'

Mr Stephenson had the grace to look embarrassed. 'Yes, well, I've been having second thoughts about that.' His glance slid away to Ryan. 'What do you say? Do you want to finish the job?'

'I'd be happy to finish it,' Ryan said. Then, as Finn drew breath to protest, he added, 'But if you've made a deal with Miss Delaney here, I think it's only fair you should honour it. Give her the chance to put things right. I mean, it's only twenty-four hours,' he added, as Mr Stephenson looked unconvinced. 'We wouldn't be able to start by then anyway. Hopefully the least she can do is clear up a bit before we move in.'

Finn seethed quietly as she watched the knowing, matey smile that passed between them. All boys together. Let the little girl think she was in with a chance, but they knew who was really in control.

'If that's what you think is best,' Mr Stephenson agreed. 'And you'll give me a price on the job?'

'I'll get it faxed over to you later today.'

They shook hands on it. Finn couldn't bear to watch so she picked up the wheelbarrow and stomped back to the front of the house to start unloading the bricks.

She was still piling up the wheelbarrow when Ryan came out five minutes later.

'I hope you're pleased with yourself?' she snapped.

'Don't start that again.' He nodded towards the trailer. 'Why have you got that?'

'The van got trashed. So did you and your new best friend work out a good deal?'

'Not bad.'

'And meantime we lose out.'

'You were going to lose out anyway. At least I've got you your twenty-four hours. Not that I think you're going to get much done in that time.'

'Not if I waste my time talking to you.' She picked up the barrow and steered it down the drive, narrowly missing his shins. 'Now if you'll excuse me . . .'

'Would you like some help?' Ryan called after her.

'I think you've been helpful enough, don't you?'

'At least let me lend you a couple of my lads, just for the rest of the day?'

Finn hesitated. She was sorely tempted. Hefting bricks about was not only back-breaking, it was also time-consuming. It would have made far more sense if she had a couple of labourers to do the fetching and carrying for her while she got on with the job.

But she didn't want Ryan muscling in, thinking she wasn't up to it. 'No thanks,' she said stiffly.

Ryan swore under his breath. 'Christ, you really are stubborn, aren't you? I'll see you tomorrow.'

Over my dead body, Finn thought as she watched him drive away. And after a few hours working on this site, it probably would be.

She hadn't expected Orla to be at home when she got back later that evening. As Finn staggered in, still in her scruffy work clothes, she was shocked when Orla came out of the kitchen to greet her.

'I thought you were going to the hospital?'

'I did, but your dad was tired so I thought I'd come home early and get on with some ironing.' She looked Finn up and down, taking in the filthy jeans and her dirt-streaked face. 'Tough day at the salon, was it?'

'I—'

'It's OK, Finn, you don't have to make up any more stories. I think I'm old enough to work out what's really going on.' She smiled. 'You gave yourself away when I spotted the toolbag in the boot of your car. So how long has this been going on?'

'A few years.' It was a relief to tell her. Finn hated lying, and it was getting more and more difficult to creep out of the house every morning with her work clothes in her bag.

Auntie Orla listened sympathetically as she told her the whole story. 'So why have you never told your father any of this?' she asked.

'You know what he's like. He wants me to be a lady.' She pulled a face.

'I'm sure he just wants you to be happy.'

'Then why doesn't he let me help out with the business? He'd rather hand it over to a loser like Ciaran. That says a lot, doesn't it?'

'He's probably trying to protect you. You know what men are like with their little girls.'

'Or maybe he just doesn't want me around?'

Orla looked surprised. 'Now, why on earth would that be?'

'Because I remind him too much of Mum.' She looked down at her fingernails, ingrained with brick dust. 'I know he blames me for her dying. And the fact that I look so much like her just makes it even worse for him. Every time he looks at me he remembers what he lost.'

'That's just silly,' Orla said. 'Your father loves you very much, I know that for a fact.'

'Maybe he does. But he loved Mum more.' And she would never be able to replace her, however hard she tried. 'Maybe it would have been easier if I'd been a boy. But when he looks at me he always seems so – disappointed.'

'Is that why you became a builder?'

Finn shrugged. 'Not the only reason. Building's all I've ever wanted to do. But I suppose I did want him to notice me. I wanted to show him he could still be proud of me, even if I wasn't like my mother.' She looked rueful. 'The stupid thing is, I've never been able to get up the courage to tell him. Ironic, isn't it?'

'Oh, sweetheart.' Orla hugged her. 'If anyone's let your dad down it's that brother of yours. He's the one who should be making up to Joe, not you. I've a good mind to put your father straight on a few things myself.'

'Please don't do that.' Finn pulled away from her. 'He'd only worry if he knew what was going on.' And he might try to stop her, which she really didn't want.

'But you can't manage on your own. You'll kill yourself.'

'I'll be fine. Anyway, I'm enjoying it.' Although her aching muscles told a different story.

'How can you enjoy breaking your back on a building site in freezing weather like this?'

'It's a hell of a lot better than being cooped up in a stuffy office.'

Orla shook her head. 'You really are your father's daughter, aren't you?'

Finn showered and changed into a clean pair of jeans. As she returned to the kitchen the doorbell rang.

'I'll get it. You go and eat your supper, it's on the table.' Orla bustled past her, heading for the front door.

'If it's Ciaran, tell him I want a word with him.'

But it wasn't Ciaran. 'Your friend's here to see you.' Orla came back in, fluffing up her hair and looking surprisingly flustered.

'Who – oh, it's you.' Her voice flattened as she saw Ryan in the doorway.

Orla, on the other hand, fluttered around him, offering him cups of tea and slices of homemade cake. Finn had to hold on to her supper in case she snatched it away and offered him that, too.

'Really, I can't stay,' he declined politely. 'I just came to give these to Finn.' He dropped a leather keyring on to the table beside her plate.

Finn looked down at it, then back up at him. 'What is it?'

'It's a key to one of my vans. I thought you might like to borrow it until yours is fixed.'

'Oh, isn't that kind?' Orla said.

'Hmm.' For a split second she was grateful. Then suspicion overwhelmed her. 'You mean so I can drive around advertising your business all over town?'

'I mean so you don't have to struggle with that daft little car of yours,' he shot back. 'But if you'd rather do it your way . . .'

'No.' As he went to take back the keys Finn reached out for them and beat him to it. 'Thanks,' she muttered. 'I appreciate it.'

'Any time. No news of your brother?'

Finn shook her head. 'I'll try calling him again later on.'

'Do you want me to look for him? I know some of the places he hangs out.'

'Would you? Tell him I'm going to kill him when I get my hands on him.'

'I expect that will bring him running.'

'Are you sure you wouldn't like a cup of tea, Ryan?' Orla offered.

'No thanks, Mrs O'Brien. I'd better get going.'

'Got a date, have you?'

'Auntie Orla!' Finn glared at her.

'Only with a paintbrush,' Ryan said. 'I'm renovating my house.'

'Are you now?' There was a glint in Orla's eyes that Finn didn't quite trust. 'So you're thinking of settling down, are you? Got anyone in mind?'

'For heaven's sake.' Finn let her knife and fork drop with a clatter. 'If you're trying to ask him if he's got a girlfriend then the answer's yes.'

'Actually, I haven't,' Ryan said. 'Wendy and I have split up.'

'That's interesting,' Orla said. 'Finn recently split up with her boyfriend, too.'

'He wasn't my boyfriend. And even if he was, I'm not looking for another one.' Finn shot her a warning look. 'From now on I want to stay single.'

'I didn't know you had a boyfriend?' Ryan said.

'His name was Neil,' Orla supplied helpfully. 'Neil Tate.'

'Oh, him.' Ryan looked thoughtful. 'Didn't you throw an egg at his father?'

'It was a mushroom vol au vent,' Finn mumbled.

'And he deserved it,' Orla added.

'Perhaps you should have thrown it at his son, if he dumped you.' Ryan stood up. 'Anyway, I should be going. I'll let you know if I catch up with Ciaran.'

'Thanks. And thanks for the loan of the van.'

'No problem.' He gave her a quick smile and then he was gone.

The front door had barely closed before Orla rushed back in

and plonked herself down at the kitchen table. 'Ooh, Finn, he's changed a bit since I last saw him.'

'Has he?'

'How could you not notice? He was always a nice-looking lad, but now!' She fanned herself with a teatowel. 'I'm telling you, if I was thirty years younger . . .'

'You'd be welcome to him.' Finn speared a green bean with her fork. Her supper had gone cold while Ryan had been hanging around. 'He's not my type.'

'He's certainly interested in you.'

Finn laughed. 'Auntie Orla, have you been at the cooking sherry? This is Ryan Hunter we're talking about.

'He came all the way over here to bring you his van. That must mean something.'

'It means we're practically family, and he feels he should help out. He's doing it for Dad, not me. Anyway, he's too much of a love 'em and leave 'em type.'

'Maybe that's because he hasn't met the right girl?'

'And maybe you've been reading too many romantic novels?' Her mobile rang and she reached into her pocket for it. 'Hello?'

'Sis?'

'Ciaran! Where the hell have you been? I've been looking for you all day. The Stephensons—'

'Never mind them,' Ciaran cut her off. 'Finn, you've got to help me.'

The desperation in his voice turned her cold. 'What's wrong?'

There was a brief silence. 'I'm in a bit of trouble.' She heard him gulp. 'The thing is, I've been arrested . . .'

Chapter 15

'I'm telling you, I didn't nick anything.' Ciaran shredded a beermat between his fingers, not looking at her. They'd just come from the police station, where Finn had spent hours going through all the paperwork, listening to what the duty solicitor had to say, arranging a court date and signing the forms to pledge his bail money, even though she begrudged every penny.

Not that Ciaran was grateful. He was as silent as a sulky teenager until they left the police station, when he insisted on going straight to the nearest pub for a pint 'to get his head straight'.

'So I suppose all those stolen DVD players just magicked themselves into your lock-up, did they?'

'I didn't know they were there, all right?'

'You're saying you were framed?' He shrugged. 'Come on, I'm not that daft. It was your lock-up, you were the only one with a key. And you've handled stolen goods before.'

Guilty colour crept up his neck. 'OK, so I was looking after them for a friend.'

'Some friend!' Finn's pent-up anger exploded. 'How could you do it, Ciaran? You know all the stress this family's been under. How could you be so stupid?'

'You don't understand,' he said quietly.

'Oh, I understand, all right. Some mate of yours goes on the rob and then asks you to stash his stuff for him until he can get rid of it. Then the police raid your place, find it and charge you with possession of stolen goods. And you won't even give them his name to save yourself.'

'I can't.'

'Honour among thieves, is that it? You'd rather go to jail than grass up a so-called friend?' She glared at him as he sat, his hands locked together, staring into his pint in shame. 'Well, I just hope he made it worth your while because, according to that solicitor you could go down for this.'

'It won't come to that.'

'With your record? The judge isn't going to slap your wrists this time.' She wanted to hit him she was so frustrated.

'I had no choice, OK?'

'Of course you had a choice. You could have said no. You could have done the right thing for once. But no, someone flashes a handful of tenners under your nose and as usual—'

'Look, it wasn't like that. I had to do what they wanted, or—'

The flash of desperation in his face made her wary. 'Or what, Ciaran?' He was obstinately silent. 'Tell me!' A thought struck her. 'Is this anything to do with those men you owe money to?'

He glanced up sharply. 'How do you know about them?'

'Mel told me.'

His mouth compressed into a stubborn line. 'She shouldn't have said anything. I said I'd sort it.'

'Oh, and you've really done that, haven't you?' She ran her hand through her hair. 'What the hell have you got yourself into, Ciaran?'

He couldn't look at her as he spoke. 'They said they'd hurt Mel – and the baby.' He spoke so softly she had to lean closer to hear what he was saying. 'I didn't know what else to do. I tried giving them back the money I owed them, but they said it wasn't enough.'

'So why didn't you go to the police?'

He laughed harshly. 'You don't know what they're like. Anyway, why would the police care? I owed them, remember?'

'But they were threatening you.' She wasn't even sure she believed his story yet. All she knew was she'd never seen her brother looking so scared.

'How could I prove it?' He downed his pint and put the empty glass back on to the table, his hand shaking. 'They said they were going to give me another chance to clear my debt. I just had to do a job for them, they said. Then we'd be even.'

'They wanted you to hide their stolen property?'

'Not just that.' He took a deep breath. 'They wanted me to torch a house.'

'What?' Finn sat back in her chair. This was beginning to sound like a bad gangster movie.

'For the insurance, they said. I was going to do it at first. I thought, it's just bricks and mortar, they'll collect their insurance money and we'll all be happy. But when I got to the place, Paradise Road, I found out there were people still living there. An old couple.' He looked up at her. 'They didn't care. They wanted me to burn the house with them still in it. Make it look more like an accident, they said.'

Finn put her hand over her mouth. Suddenly she felt very sick. 'They wanted you to *kill* people?'

Ciaran shook his head. 'They said it'd be safe, that they'd get out in time. But I didn't know that for sure, did I? I mean, what if they didn't? What if someone ended up dead because of me?' His eyes were bleak, dark hollows. Finn knew her brother was a rogue, but there was no way he had it in him to hurt anyone.

'What did you do?'

'I backed out, told them I couldn't do it. They seemed fine about it, said they'd get someone else to do the job. A couple of days later they called to say they wanted their stuff back from the lock-up, but when I got there the police were waiting.'

'So they set you up?'

'I reckon they must have done. It could have been worse, I suppose.' He tried, and failed, to smile.

'Jesus, Ciaran.' Finn sighed. She didn't know whether to hug her brother or hit him. 'Who the hell are these people?'

His gaze dropped back to his half-empty glass. 'I can't tell you that.'

'But you've got to tell the police.'

'I can't! If I grass them up they'll come after the rest of the family. They've already said they would. I've got to protect you lot.' Finn thought about her trashed van and the silent phone calls, and wondered if it wasn't too late for that. 'And I wouldn't even be safe in jail. They say they've got mates who can make life tough for me inside.' He sank his head into his hands. 'This is such a mess.'

'You're telling me.'

Something niggled in the back of her mind. Paradise Road, Ciaran had said. Now where had she heard that name before?

'So what do I do?' Ciaran said.

'Surely they'll leave you alone now they've taught you a lesson?'

'I'm not sure. Maybe this will be the end of it.' His hunted look said he wasn't convinced. 'All the same, I reckon I should lay low for a while.'

'You've got to come home,' she said finally. 'You'll be safe there. You can sleep on the sofa—'

'Then you wouldn't be safe, either. You don't understand what these people are like. I wouldn't want to put you and Orla in danger.' Shame you didn't think about that sooner, Finn thought. But he looked so desperate, she couldn't find it in her heart to be angry with him. 'No, I'm better off on my own.'

'But where will you stay?'

'I'll find somewhere to crash, don't worry. It'll be safer for everyone that way. Just keep an eye on Mel and the baby for me?'

'Of course. But are you sure you'll be all right?'

He managed a rueful grin, more like the old Ciaran. 'Don't you worry about me. I'm a survivor. Although I could use some cash?'

Sighing, she fished in her back pocket for her purse and slid a couple of £5 notes out of it. 'That's all I've got,' she said, pushing them across the table.

'Cheers. I owe you.'

The next day she tried to bury her concerns about Ciaran by concentrating on her work. She was at the Stephensons' site early and worked for hours without a break. She carted bricks from the front of the house to the back, mixed mortar, built walls, checked and re-checked levels without stopping. Her back ached, but at least it helped keep her anxieties about her brother at bay.

But whenever she took a break, she couldn't help thinking about that house in Paradise Road. There was something familiar about that name, but she couldn't remember where she'd heard it before. It was like an annoying tickle in the back of her brain.

Thankfully she was alone for the most of the day, since Mr and Mrs Stephenson were out at work. By the time Mr Stephenson returned later that afternoon, she had met her 24 hour deadline. She'd managed to undo all Ciaran's bad work and made more progress than she'd hoped for.

'You see?' she said as she proudly showed Mr Stephenson around the site. 'I would have done more, but you can't build walls too high in one go. You have to wait for the mortar to go off, otherwise it could bow.'

'I'm impressed.' He didn't sound it. Finn looked at his sombre face.

'Is something wrong?' she asked. 'Like I said, I would have done more, but—'

'It isn't your work.' He pulled a piece of paper out of his pocket and handed it to her. 'This was waiting for me when I got back.'

Finn read the note, her anger growing. It was 'from a concerned friend' warning that Ciaran had been arrested and asking Mr Stephenson if he really wanted a thief working for him.

'Is it true?' Mr Stephenson asked, as Finn gave it back to him.

'My brother isn't a thief.'

'But he was arrested?'

'He was set up,' she said, but she could see from his face that he didn't believe her. 'And besides, even if he did do it, he's not working here any more. I am.' She faced him boldly. She knew he was going to kick her out, but she was determined not to go without a fight. 'I don't have a criminal record, Mr Stephenson. You can check with the police if you don't believe me.'

'I'm sure that's not necessary—'

'And you've said yourself my work is up to standard.'

'Well, it is, but—'

'But you want to get rid of me anyway? Well, I can't blame you for that.' She began gathering up her tools.

'Now, hang on a minute,' he said. 'Who said anything about getting rid of you?'

She looked up at him, unsure about what she was hearing. 'But I thought—'

'That I'd throw you out because of something your brother did?' His brows lifted. 'As you said, Miss Delaney, that would hardly be fair. And besides, a person is innocent until proven guilty in the eyes of the British justice system.'

'Yes, but—'

'Look, I know you think I'm a fussy old stick, but I'm actually not a bad guy.' He smiled ruefully. 'All I want is to get this extension built and finished, preferably before the next millennium. And looking at what you've done today, I reckon you might just be able to do it.'

'Definitely,' Finn nodded.

'So that's settled, then. You'll finish the job?'

She smiled back. 'I'd love to.'

She went home to shower and change out of her work clothes, then headed to the hospital to see her father, taking Orla with her. He was in a good mood because the consultant had told him he could come home by the end of the week.

'I'll be glad to be out of this place,' he said. 'Back in the land of the living.'

'I expect they'll be glad to get rid of you.' Finn tried to look pleased about the news but her mind was reeling, wondering how she was going to keep all the family dramas from him. It was a lot easier when he was safely tucked away in hospital.

'Where's your brother?' Joe said. 'I haven't seen him for a few days.'

Finn glanced at Orla. 'He's been – um – a bit tied up.'

'I expect he's been busy on the Stephensons' site. How's he getting on, do you know?'

'It's coming on fine,' Finn said, glad to be able to tell the truth for once.

'You see? I knew the lad would come good if he was given the chance.' Joe Delaney smiled with satisfaction. 'And you said he wouldn't be able to cope. Just goes to show, doesn't it?'

'Doesn't it just?'

'Why didn't you tell him Ciaran had been arrested?' Orla asked, as they left the hospital and darted across the car park to escape the icy rain.

'The same reason I haven't told him how useless he is.' Finn fumbled in her pocket for her car key. 'You saw how happy he was. How could I ruin that?'

'You'll have to tell him sometime. What if Ciaran's sent down?'

'I'm praying it won't come to that.'

She'd become so used to making the drive home from the hospital, at first she barely noticed the sign at the end of the road. She read the words as usual, but it wasn't until she'd reached the next junction that their significance finally sank in. She braked and swung a u-turn, earning herself a chorus of disapproving beeps and expressive hand gestures from the other drivers.

'What are you doing?' Orla gasped, loosening herself from the seatbelt that had snapped taut across her throat.

'I just need to look at something.'

She pulled right down the turning to look at the sign: 'Bought for re-development by Tate Associates.' Below it, nearly falling off its wooden post, was the street nameplate.

Paradise Road.

She suddenly remembered passing the same street with Neil. How he'd told her about his father's big plans for the place.

'What's so special about this street?' Orla peered through the rain streaming down the window. 'It seems pretty rundown to me.'

'Hmm.' Finn pulled up and turned off the engine. 'You wait here. I'm going to take a look.'

She got out of the car, pulling the collar of her jacket up to protect herself from the rain, and walked down the street. Paradise Road was a terrace of unloved Victorian houses, the picture of faded elegance. Once they might have been genteel homes, but now most of them were empty and boarded up.

The facts stirred around in her mind, colliding and then

bouncing off each other. What had Neil said about them? His father needed all the houses to redevelop the street. But there was one couple who refused to budge. *They'll sell if they've got any sense.* He'd sounded so confident. And now her brother had been blackmailed to torch a house there. Surely that had to be more than coincidence?

She was soaked with rain by the time they got home. 'I'd better check the answer-machine, just in case anyone's called with work.'

'I'll do it. You get changed out of those wet clothes before you catch your death,' Orla ordered. 'Then I'll make us something to eat.'

Finn was halfway up the stairs when she heard the splintering crash. For a split second she froze, then she hurtled back to the sitting room.

Orla stood in the middle of the room, pale with shock, surrounded by a shower of broken glass. Half a broken brick lay on the sofa, inches from where she stood. Wind blew through the shattered window, fluttering the curtains.

'Are you OK?' Finn was surprised at how calm she sounded, even though her heart was crashing against her ribs and adrenaline had flooded through her body, turning her legs to jelly.

'I think so. I was just reaching down to press the button on the answer-machine, and – that came through the window.' She pointed shakily at the brick. 'If it had been a few seconds later . . .'

'Don't.' Finn shuddered.

She moved to pick up the brick but Orla stopped her. 'No, don't touch it. The police will want it for forensics, or something.'

'We can't call the police.'

'Are you serious? Someone pitches a brick through the window and you don't want to call the police?'

'It was probably just kids.'

'The same kids who trashed your van, I suppose?' Orla confronted her, hands on her hips. 'Is there something you're not telling me?'

'I can handle it, OK?'

As she went to leave the room, Orla called after her, 'And what if that brick had hit me? Could you have handled that?'

Finn was up a stepladder nailing a sheet of plywood over the broken pane with icy rain running down inside her collar when Ryan turned up half an hour later. She stopped, her hammer poised, when his van drew up and he jumped out.

'Orla phoned me. She said you'd been having some trouble.' He squinted up at her, shielding his face from the rain. 'She wasn't kidding, was she?'

Finn turned back to hammer in another nail. 'She shouldn't have called you.'

'No, you're right, she shouldn't. *You* should have.'

'Why?'

'Because I want to help you.'

'There's no need. As you can see, I'm sorting it.' She scrabbled in her tool-belt for another nail. Her fingers were so cold it took her a while to get a grip on one.

'Have you called the glazier?' Ryan asked.

Finn pulled a face. 'Dur, now why didn't I think of that? Of course I called. Several, in fact.'

'And?'

'None of them can come until first thing.'

'That's not good enough. Let me make a few calls.' He pulled out his mobile and began punching buttons.

'I told you, they can't make it until the morning.'

'We'll see about that.' He went into the house, already talking to someone on the other end of the line. Why did Orla have to ask him to interfere? She was doing fine on her own.

Five minutes later he came out again. 'It's all sorted,' he said. 'They'll be here in an hour.'

'And I suppose they'll charge an extortionate call-out fee?' Finn wondered why she couldn't bring herself to be grateful.

'They're doing it as a favour to me. Don't fall off your ladder thanking me, will you?' He strode back into the house before she could answer.

She found him in the kitchen with Orla. She was still pale and her hands shook as she wrapped them around a glass of brandy. Seeing her so upset made Finn feel guilty. Maybe she should have called the police after all.

Orla looked up. 'Look at you. You still haven't got out of those wet clothes.'

'I'll do it later. I'm going to get rid of that broken glass in the sitting room first.'

At least rooting around under the sink for a dustpan and brush gave her something to do. She had the feeling that if she stopped moving even for a second she would collapse into a heap and she didn't want to do that, certainly not in front of Ryan.

'How are you feeling, Auntie Orla?'

'A bit shaken-up, love.'

'Orla tells me you don't want to call the police?' Ryan said.

'What could they do? It was just kids.' She glanced around and saw the look that passed between them. 'I'm telling you, it was – ow!' She came up too quickly and banged her head on the sink waste.

'Let me help you . . .' Ryan made a move towards her, but Finn shook him off.

'I'm fine,' she insisted.

'For God's sake, woman, why do you have to be so bloody independent all the time? Why can't you let someone help you?'

'Because I don't need it.' She picked up the dustpan and headed for the sitting room.

The brutality of the wrecked room made her feel sick. Finn looked at the brick, still on the sofa. She couldn't bring herself to touch it. As she steeled herself to reach out for it, a hand came from over her shoulder and took it away.

She looked up, startled, and found herself staring into Ryan's eyes. He looked so concerned that she had to force herself not to cry.

'Why don't you tell me what's really going on?' he said.

'I told you, it's just—'

'Kids. So you keep saying.' He turned her to face him. 'This is me you're talking to, Finn. I already know Ciaran was arrested.

And I know the kind of people he's mixed up with. So why don't you tell me the truth?'

Suddenly she was too tired and upset to go on lying to everyone. 'I think the Tates are behind it.'

'The Tates?' Ryan whistled. 'Bloody hell, you must have really upset young Neil.'

'This isn't funny, Ryan. Anyway, it's Ciaran who's upset them, not me.'

She told him everything her brother had told her, and all the bits she'd managed to piece together herself.

'The stupid bastard!' Ryan swore softly under his breath when she'd finished talking.

'That's more or less what I said.' Finn managed a wry smile.

'How could he put you all in danger like that? And after everything Joe's been through already . . .'

'Don't.' That was what worried her. The possibility that they wouldn't stop, and would somehow find a way of hurting her father. They'd proved they were capable of anything. 'But it's not just Ciaran, is it? Tates want Dad's land. And it looks like they'll do anything to get it.' She ran her hand through her damp hair. 'I wish he'd never bought it.'

'So do I.' Ryan thought for a moment. 'I want you and Orla to pack a bag. You're coming home with me.'

'I'm not going anywhere. What if they come back and torch this place?'

'All the more reason for you not to be here.'

They looked at each other for a moment. 'Orla can go with you,' Finn said at last. 'But this is my home and I'm not going to be forced out of it.'

'Then I'll stay here with you.'

'There's no need, honestly.'

'But I promised your dad I'd take care of you.'

'I can look after myself.'

'That doesn't stop me worrying about you.'

His mobile rang before she could reply. Ryan glanced at the caller display screen, then switched it off and stuck it in his pocket.

'Who was that?' she asked.

'Wendy.'

'I thought you weren't seeing her any more?'

'I'm not.'

'But she won't take the hint?'

'Something like that.' He turned to face her. 'So are you coming with me?'

Part of her wanted to say yes. But then she reminded herself this really wasn't his problem. 'I told you, I'll be fine. But I think Orla might feel better if she was away from here.'

But she was wrong. 'I'm not going anywhere,' Orla declared firmly. 'If Finn's staying, then so am I. And there's no need for you to hang around, Ryan. I'm sure Finn was right, and that it was just kids messing about. They won't be back.'

Finn caught Ryan's look and felt guilty. 'You've got my mobile number in case there are any problems?' he said. 'Phone me if you need anything, day or night.'

But once she'd closed the door on him, she began to wish she'd taken up his offer to stay the night after all. The bravado she'd felt while he was in the house deserted her once he'd gone.

Chapter 16

Two days later, her father was finally ready to come home. Just her luck, it happened to be the same day Ciaran was due before the magistrates. Finn left Orla fussing over the house in preparation for Joe's return, and headed off to court.

She was surprised to see Ryan waiting in the street outside the court. It was strange to see him in a smart suit instead of his usual workshirt and jeans.

'Before you say anything, I'm not here because I think you need help.' He held up his hand as she opened her mouth to speak. 'I'm here because I'm Ciaran's friend.'

'I was going to say I'm glad you're here.'

'Are you?' Ryan looked taken aback.

'I'm sure Ciaran will appreciate your support.' She squinted down the road. 'Any sign of him yet?'

'Not yet.'

'I hope he's not going to be late. That won't go down well with the magistrates.'

'Relax, he'll be here. He's got ten minutes yet. Shall we wait for him inside?'

They sat side by side on a bench in the wood-panelled waiting area. Finn stared at the posters on the walls offering victim support counselling.

Ryan seemed ill at ease, she noticed. He shuffled his feet and kept his eyes fixed on the tiled floor.

'Does this feel strange to you?' she asked.

Ryan lifted his head. 'What do you mean?'

'You've been here before, haven't you? Except then you were in the dock.'

She saw his expression darken and realized it was a tactless thing to say.

'That was a long time ago,' he said.

'I know. I'm sorry, I shouldn't have mentioned it.' She knew Ryan never talked about it. 'Take no notice of me, it's just nerves. What if they send Ciaran to jail?'

'It won't come to that. He'll probably just get off with a fine or community service.'

'I hope so. I don't know how I'm going to explain it to Dad if he doesn't.'

'You still haven't told him about Ciaran?'

'No, and I'm not going to. Here comes Mel.' She changed the subject as Ciaran's harassed-looking girlfriend hurried down the corridor towards them, baby Joseph in her arms. She stopped short when she saw Ryan and Finn.

'I didn't know you were both going to be here.'

'Where else would we be? Let me help you with that.' Finn went over to her as she struggled to loop the baby's changing bag over her shoulder. 'How are you feeling?'

'Fine,' she said, but she didn't look it. Her eyes were red-rimmed.

'It'll be OK,' Finn tried to reassure her. 'You know my brother. He can talk his way out of anything.'

'Not this time.'

'What do you mean?'

Before she could answer, Ciaran's solicitor came out of a side room. 'Is Mr Delaney here?' he asked. 'They're just about to start proceedings.'

'Not yet,' Finn said. 'He's probably just stuck in traffic—'

'He's not coming,' Mel blurted out. They all turned to look at her. 'He came to see me last night, said he couldn't face going to jail. He told me he was going to do a runner.'

'Do you know where he's gone?' Ryan asked.

Mel shook her head. 'He didn't say. He just gave me some cash, and told me he'd call me.'

Finn could feel her temper rising and fought to control it. 'Why didn't you tell us this last night?'

'I wanted him to get away. I love him.' She sniffed and wiped her nose on Joseph's babygro.

The solicitor looked sombre. 'I'll go and have a word with the police. You do know what this means, don't you?' he said to Finn.

She nodded. 'He's violated his bail conditions.'

'What does that mean?' Mel asked.

'I'm going to have to pay up the money I pledged for his bail.'

'Will it be a lot?'

'A lot more than I can afford.' She ran her hand through her hair. 'Jesus, what a mess.'

'I – I'm sorry.' Mel's eyes filled with tears. 'I didn't think. I only wanted to help Ciaran.'

'Oh, you've really helped him, haven't you?' Finn snapped. 'Now when they catch him they probably *will* lock him up and throw away the key!'

'I'll look for him,' Ryan offered.

'Do you have any idea where he might be?'

'No, but I could ask around.' He waited for her to argue, but Finn had run out of ideas.

'You'd probably be better at finding him than me,' she agreed. 'And I have to go and pick Dad up from hospital.'

'Leave it to me.'

Finn went to see the solicitor about Ciaran's disappearance, and handed over a cheque for the bail money, hating every moment. After she'd finished all the paperwork, she came out of the court and walked straight into Neil Tate. He was waiting outside, leaning casually against his black Saab as if he didn't have a care in the world.

'I hear your brother's bolted,' he said.

'What are you doing here?'

'I'm a concerned citizen, here to see justice being done and all that.' He shook his head slowly. 'Poor Finnuala, what's he done to you? First he gets you into trouble with a load of thugs, then he skips bail and leaves you to pick up the bill. That's going to leave a hell of a hole in your finances, isn't it? Perhaps you should think about selling something?'

'Perhaps you should think about getting lost?' Her hands balled into fists at her sides and she fought the urge to punch the smug look off his face. 'I know it was your friends who set him up. And I know it's you who's been threatening us. But it won't work.'

Neil leaned closer. 'Then why do you look so frightened?'

'Just leave me and my family alone.' She went to move past him but he reached out to grasp her wrist. 'Get off me.'

'You heard what she said.' A shadow fell over Neil as Ryan stepped between them.

Finn caught a flash of fear in Neil's eyes before his confidence reasserted itself. 'And what are you going to do about it? Hit me?' He released Finn's arm. 'Even a meathead like you wouldn't be stupid enough to commit assault outside a courthouse.'

'Maybe not.' Ryan's voice was low and threatening. 'But there are plenty of dark alleys around here. I wouldn't go wandering down any if I were you.'

'I don't respond well to threats.'

Ryan thrust his face closer. 'Then why do you look so frightened?' he mocked.

'I'm not the one who should be frightened, believe me.' Neil stepped away from Ryan and brushed an imaginary speck of dust from the lapels of his jacket. 'Wish your father well from me, won't you?' he called to Finn. 'He comes out of hospital today, doesn't he?'

'You didn't have to leap in and rescue me,' she said to Ryan as Neil drove off.

'It wasn't you I was rescuing, it was him. You looked as if you were about to hit him.'

'I was.' She watched Neil's car turn the corner. How did he know her father was due out of hospital, unless he was planning to make more trouble?

It touched Finn to see her father sitting in the plastic armchair beside his bed, his small suitcase packed and ready to go. He looked fitter than he had a month ago, but he still wasn't the big, powerful man she'd always known.

'He's been ready since first thing this morning,' the nurse on duty confided with a grin. 'He can't wait to see the back of us!'

'Where's your brother? Isn't he with you?' were Joe's first words the moment he saw her.

'No, he isn't.' She couldn't even be bothered to make up excuses for him any more.

'I suppose he's still working?' Joe nodded his approval.

'I'm sure he's busy, wherever he is.' Finn picked up her father's bag. 'Shall we go?'

Back at home, Orla had done them proud. The house was gleaming and spotless, fragrant with furniture polish. She'd made a chocolate cake as a celebration.

'Welcome home, Joe.' She hugged him warmly. 'It's so good to see you.'

'Now, don't make such a fuss. The way you two are carrying on anyone would think I'd been at death's door.' Joe tried not to look pleased at all the attention. 'Maybe I should go into hospital more often if the house gets a spring-clean like this?' he added, gazing around.

'Don't you dare.' Orla threaded her arm through his and led him to his favourite armchair. 'So what can I get you? A nice cup of tea? Piece of cake?'

'I'd like to take a look at the books, if you don't mind?'

'Oh no, you don't,' Orla stepped in, as Finn looked dismayed. 'You're not doing any work today, Joe Delaney.'

'But—'

'You've got to rest. Doctors' orders.'

'If you bothered to listen to the doctors as much as I have you'd know rest is the last thing I should be doing,' Joe replied. 'Most people who have heart attacks end up dying because their well-meaning relatives keep them sitting on their backsides wrapped in cotton wool afterwards. No, I need to be up and about. That's the best medicine for me. And I'll start by looking at the books,' he repeated to Finn.

'I – oh look, here's Ryan.' For the first time ever Finn was relieved to see his van pull up outside.

'Thank God for that,' Joe grumbled. 'It'll make a change from you two clucking over me like flaming hens!'

Finn was so anxious for news of Ciaran she didn't even mind that Ryan got a far warmer greeting from her father than she had.

'It's great to see you, Joe. You're looking well.' As he shook her father's hand, Ryan looked up, caught her eye and shook his head. The briefest movement, but it was enough to send her heart plunging into her shoes.

What the hell was she going to do now? She knew she'd have to explain to her father about Ciaran going AWOL, she just didn't know how.

After an agonizingly long tea and cake session, finally Orla managed to bully Joe upstairs to have a nap, leaving her alone with Ryan.

'Well?' she asked, as her father's protesting voice faded upstairs.

'No sign of him. I tried all his usual haunts, asked anyone who might know. It's a complete blank. I'm sorry.'

'You're not the one who should be sorry.' All Finn's anger was directed at her useless brother.

'What about the bail money?'

'I'll just have to say goodbye to it.' Although Neil was right; it had made a big hole in their finances, which were already feeling the pinch from the repayments on her father's loan.

'I could lend you some, if it would help?'

'It's kind of you, but we can manage.'

He sighed in exasperation. 'Finn, this is me you're talking to. Not your dad. You don't have to pretend everything's rosy when we both know it isn't.'

She let out a deep breath. It was so tempting to take his help, to stop fighting. But she just couldn't do it. 'We'll be fine.'

'Suit yourself. But there's no crime in being vulnerable, you know. I realize you're out to prove something to your dad but that doesn't mean you have to be all-powerful.'

That's a joke, Finn thought after he'd gone. With everything collapsing around her, the last thing she felt was powerful.

*

The following morning it was a relief to escape to work before her father had time to ask her any more awkward questions about her brother.

Thankfully Mr Stephenson had gone off with the architect to nag the people who were supposed to be making the roof sections, so she was able to lose herself in her work for a few precious hours, with just the drone of the radio for company.

At lunchtime she headed off to the builders' merchants to pick up some more materials. She was on her way back when her mobile rang.

'Finn?' She heard the breathless panic in Orla's voice and her heart began to race.

'What is it? Is it Dad?'

'It's OK, he's fine. I just wanted to warn you, he's had a letter.'

'Not those land agents again?'

'This one's anonymous. And it's about you.' Orla paused. 'He knows everything. Your job, Ciaran, the business. The whole lot.'

'Oh God.' No need to ask who'd sent the letter, anonymous or not. It might as well have had Neil Tate's name all over it. She bit her lip. 'Is he angry?'

'Put it this way, he isn't very pleased.' There was another pause. Finn thought she heard her father's voice in the background. 'Look, I think you'd better come home,' Orla said in a rush, then the phone went dead.

Finn stuffed her mobile back into the pocket of her jeans and tried to think. She decided to stop off at the Stephenson place on her way home to warn her client she was finishing for the day and to give herself some time to come up with a way of explaining her story to her father. Preferably a way that didn't involve admitting she'd lied to him for the past few years.

But when she got to the Stephensons', she was shocked to see her father's old BMW parked in the drive. Her first instinct was to run away and hide, but she forced herself to pull in beside it. She had to face the music sometime.

'As you can see, things are going very well. I'm really pleased,' she heard Mr Stephenson say as she rounded the corner of the house.

Her father grunted. 'And exactly how much of this is my daughter's work?'

'She did it all. To be honest, after your son let me down so badly – oh, hi, Finn. We were just talking about you.' He gave her a little wave. Finn barely smiled back. Her eyes were fixed on her father's face. Orla stood behind him, looking worried.

'I tried to stop him,' she mouthed. 'But he insisted on coming.'

'Dad?' Finn prompted.

Joe turned to Orla. 'Take me home,' he said.

Finn followed them to the car. 'Dad, please, listen. I can explain—'

He turned to her, his face rigid. 'We'll talk about this at home, Finnuala.'

Chapter 17

Joe was waiting for her. As she let herself in, Finn heard him talking to Orla in hushed tones. But as soon as she walked into the room Orla beat a tactful retreat. Finn caught the sympathetic look she gave her as she hurried past.

She regarded her father warily as he sat in his old armchair, tapping out a rapid rhythm on the worn arms. Joe looked old and tired, not nearly as fit as he had when he came out of hospital. Was it really only yesterday?

'Dad, I'm sorry,' she plunged in. 'But I can explain—'

'No need.' Her father held up his hand to silence her. 'I've called Ryan. He's told me everything.'

She was so annoyed she forgot to be contrite. 'You could have asked me.'

'I didn't know if I'd get the truth from you.'

'How could I tell you what was really going on? You were ill, the doctors said you didn't need any stress—'

'I'm getting plenty of it now, aren't I?'

'I couldn't tell you Ciaran was making a mess of the business.' He probably wouldn't have believed her anyway.

'Or that he'd been arrested? Or gone on the run?'

Finn looked down at her hands. Typical, she thought. Ciaran did the crime and somehow she ended up taking the flak for it. 'I didn't want to worry you.'

'Don't you think I have the right to know what's going on in my own family?' Joe rarely got angry, which made his temper all the more fearsome. 'I am still head of this house, aren't I? Or have you taken over that, too?'

'That's not fair.'

'Anyway,' Joe went on, ignoring her, 'I suppose it's nothing to you to tell me lies, is it? Apparently you've been doing it for years.'

'Look, I'm sorry I lied to you. The only reason I didn't tell you is because I didn't think you'd understand.'

'All these years you've been taking me for a fool.' Joe shook his head. 'All this time I thought you were doing so well—'

'I *am* doing well.'

'No, you're not.' Joe turned on her. 'You're a labourer, Finnuala. Do you think that's what I wanted for you? Do you think I wanted to see my daughter with hands like these?' He held up his calloused palms to her. 'I told you over and over again that I didn't want you working on site. It was the only thing I ever asked of you, and you ignored me.'

'Because it's all I've ever wanted to do. And I'm good at it, too. You've seen my work. You know I can do it.'

'That's not the point. It's not what I want for you. It's not what your mother would have wanted for you, either.'

'You can't tell me what to do, Dad. I'm twenty-six years old. What are you going to do, lock me in my bedroom?'

'I don't know what to do with you any more.'

The defeated look in his eyes hurt her. 'Look, I'm sorry I lied to you,' she said, 'and I'm sorry you had to find out like that, but I can't apologize for who I am. And I don't see why I should.' She crouched down so her face was level with his, and reached for his hand. 'All right, so I don't work in some fancy hair salon. But I've worked hard, and I kept this business afloat when Ciaran let you down. All I've ever wanted is for you to be proud of me.'

'Proud? I hardly know you any more.'

His words were like a slap in the face. Finn let go of his hand and straightened up. 'I've got news for you, Dad. You never knew me. Why do you think I lied to you all that time? I spent years trying to be the daughter you wanted me to be, the daughter I thought I ought to be. But I'm not and I never will be.'

'Believe me, I know that.'

'I'm sorry I've been such a letdown to you.' Her voice was choked, but she wouldn't allow herself to cry. 'Perhaps I should be more like Ciaran. Then maybe you might be proud of me.'

'Leave your brother out of this.'

'Why? He's the one who nearly ruined us. He's the one who broke the law and then went on the run. He's the one who dragged our name through the mud. And you're giving me a hard time just because I went behind your back and got a few qualifications.'

'I know what your brother's like, you don't have to tell me.' Joe glared at her from under lowered brows. 'Don't you think I've lain awake enough nights, worrying about him? But at least I knew I'd never have those kind of worries with you. You were my good girl, my hard-working daughter. The only one I could trust. But now I find out you've let me down, too. You're as bad as Ciaran.' He turned away from her to stare out of the window. 'Lord knows what your mother would make of all this if she was here.'

'But she's not here, is she? I know she was a paragon of virtue but I'm not going to spend the rest of my life trying to live up to someone I never even knew.'

'That's enough. I won't have you talking about her like that.'

'I'm not allowed to talk about her at all, am I? The only time you ever mention her is when you're telling me what a disappointment I'd be to her.'

'I said that's enough!'

'You know, you're right,' Finn said. 'I've had enough of trying to please you, lying to everyone to try to be the kind of person you want me to be. From now on, I'm just going to be myself. And if you don't like it – tough!'

It wasn't until she got to the safety of her bedroom that she allowed her tears to flow. She was still weeping silently into her pillow when Orla crept in a few minutes later.

'I've brought you a cup of tea.' She set it down on the bedside table. Finn waited for her to leave, but after a moment or two she sat down on the edge of the bed and put her hand on Finn's shoulder. 'You mustn't take too much notice of your father,' she said. 'He's upset. It's been a lot for him to take in. He didn't mean what he said.'

'Yes, he did. He hates me.' She wiped her tears away on the corner of the pillowcase. 'He's never wanted me around. He blames me because my mum died. He lost her and got me instead.'

For as long as she could remember, she'd felt guilty about her mother's death. Right from an early age she'd understood it was her fault that she'd died. If she hadn't given birth to her, her mother would never have suffered that brain haemorrhage and died. Her father would still have his wife if she didn't exist, it was as simple as that.

So she'd grown up trying to be as invisible as possible, thinking that if her father couldn't see her then he couldn't hate or blame her. While Ciaran skipped school and caused all kinds of trouble, she kept her head down and made herself as useful to Joe as she could.

But even that stopped working after a while. As he got older, the distance between them grew wider. As Finn turned from a girl into a young woman, the more she grew like her mother, the more her father turned away from her.

'Finn, listen to me. Your father loves you. He's just confused at the moment, that's all. He'll come round to the idea.'

'I don't care any more.' Finn reached for a tissue from her bedside drawer and blew her nose. 'If he wants me out of the business, fine. He can handle it all himself.'

But in spite of her defiance, she still felt a slight pang of guilt as she headed over to her father's yard to collect her tools the following morning. She didn't know how Joe was going to cope with the Stephensons' extension. It was physically demanding work, and they still had a long job ahead of them.

It wasn't her problem any more, she told herself. But she soon found out whose problem it was when she turned into the yard and almost crashed into the back of Ryan's blue pick-up truck.

She found him in the Portakabin office, going through the books.

'What are you doing?'

'Checking things over. Your dad asked me to keep an eye on the place.'

'And did he tell you to snoop through the accounts, too?' Finn reached across the desk and snatched the file from his hands.

'As a matter of fact, he did. And it's just as well. You're seriously behind on the VAT returns.'

Finn was too stunned to respond. 'You mean he's got you running this place?'

He eyed her warily. 'He said he'd told you about it?'

'Why should he tell me anything? I'm only his daughter.'

'I'm sorry,' Ryan said. 'I had no idea. Joe called me yesterday afternoon and asked me to take over this place while he's laid up.'

'And it didn't occur to you to ask why I wasn't doing it?'

'I don't want to get involved, OK? That's between you two. I assumed he'd spoken to you.'

That was a laugh. Her father could barely bring himself to look at her that morning.

'Well, that's great, isn't it? He'd rather have you running this place than his own daughter. That says a lot, doesn't it?'

'Like I said, it's nothing to do with me.' He went back to looking through the files.

Finn watched him, her irritation growing. 'I suppose this is perfect for you,' she said.

'Meaning?'

'This is your chance to run our business into the ground and get rid of the competition. Or just gently persuade Dad that he'd be better off going into partnership with you.'

'Now, just a minute—'

'Either way, it's going to be your name over that door before long, isn't it?'

She flinched as Ryan banged the file shut. 'Your dad gave me a chance when no one else would. Do you really think I'd do anything to hurt him?'

'Business is business.'

'Maybe to you. But Joe's been like a father to me. Now he's asked me to help him and that's what I plan to do. And if you don't like it, you know where the door is.'

She trembled slightly in the face of his anger. 'You'd love that, wouldn't you? If I was out of the way you could really take over the place.' She folded her arms. All her intentions to walk away had suddenly disappeared. 'Well, if you think I'm going to let that happen you're wrong. I'm staying right here where I can keep an eye on you.'

'Whatever,' Ryan sighed. 'But if you're staying around you might as well make yourself useful.' He picked up the files and dumped them into her arms.

'What's this?'

'VAT returns. The accountant needs them by tomorrow morning.'

'Why can't you do them?'

'And have you accuse me of snooping into your dad's business?' Ryan shook his head. 'Have fun, won't you?'

Two hours later she was drowning in paperwork and feeling absolutely furious.

Meanwhile, Ryan was out on the Stephensons' site, doing her job. She should be there now, not him. She'd worked hard on it, and he was probably taking all the credit for *her* work. The thought made her even more annoyed. So annoyed that she lost count of the row of figures she was adding up and had to start all over again.

And the phone kept ringing. Some of the callers mistook her for the secretary, which irritated her still further. But most of the calls were from Ryan's former girlfriend, Wendy.

'No, I don't know what time he'll be back,' she told her for the fourth time. 'Try his flipping mobile.' She banged the phone down. It was bad enough being stuck in the office, without having to fend off Ryan Hunter's ex-girlfriends.

Chapter 18

Gina sat in her car and checked her make-up in the rear-view mirror. Then she looked at the big blue gates, her heart fluttering. This was a big mistake, she should never have come. Why did she think she could get this job, anyway? She'd already had several other interviews and failed them. Even if she managed to keep control of her nerves, once a potential employer found out she was pregnant they didn't want to know.

That was why this job was so perfect. It was a temporary, three-month contract to sort out a backlog of paperwork at a builders' yard. Just what she needed.

'I don't even know why you're bothering,' Stephen had said. 'I expect Daddy will increase your allowance now you're about to produce another grandchild for him.'

But Gina needed a job. She wanted to prove to herself that she could do something without her father's help.

Besides, she wasn't quite sure what the next few months would bring. Stephen had put on a good show of being thrilled about the baby when the local paper found out and wanted to do a good news piece on them. But in private he didn't hide his resentment. Gina had the uneasy feeling he might dump her after the election.

She took a deep breath, picked up her bag, checked her lipstick again and forced herself to get out of the car. Even if she didn't get the job it would be good interview experience.

There was no one in the yard. At the far end was a Portakabin, which she assumed was the office. Nothing remotely scary so far, she thought. But her knees were still shaking under her skirt as she knocked on the door.

'Hello?' No answer. She opened the door and looked inside. 'Is anyone here?'

The phone on the desk rang, making her jump. She hesitated, waiting for someone to answer it, then realized there was only her around.

'Hello? Er – Delaney and Son?' she said, glancing down at the headed notepaper on the desk. 'I'm sorry, he's not in at the moment. Would you like to leave a message?' She reached across the untidy desk, pushing coffee cups aside to find a pen. 'Yes, I've got that.' She scribbled the message down. 'Thank you for calling. Goodbye.'

'Mrs Farrell?' She almost dropped the pen. In the doorway stood a tall, broad-shouldered man in paint-spattered jeans. His dark, curly hair almost touched the collar of his flannel shirt. His face was rugged rather than handsome. He smiled at her. 'I'm Ryan.' He nodded towards the desk. 'I see you've already made yourself at home.'

'I'm sorry, I didn't mean to interfere. But the phone was ringing, so I took a message.' She handed him the piece of paper.

'It's a good thing you were here.' He glanced down at the message. 'Do you mind if I give this guy a quick call back before I forget? Help yourself to tea or coffee, the stuff's out the back.'

This was turning into the strangest interview she'd ever had, Gina decided as she stood in the narrow galley kitchen waiting for the kettle to boil. But it was a lot more relaxed than having questions fired at her across a desk.

And they certainly needed someone, she thought as she looked back through the kitchen doorway at the office. It wasn't much – just a shabby desk, an ageing computer and a couple of filing cabinets. The desk was littered with paperwork, which also formed a teetering pile in the in-tray and on the floor.

Ryan came back as she was putting the soggy teabags into the bin. 'I made you one,' she said. 'I wasn't sure if you wanted it?'

‘Have you ever known a builder turn down a cup of tea?’ Ryan grinned. He had a nice smile, Gina decided. ‘But I’ll have to be quick. I’ve got to go out.’

‘Oh.’ She was disappointed. ‘Would you like me to come back another time?’

‘That depends on you. When can you start?’

She blinked. ‘You’re offering me the job?’

‘If you think you can bear it?’

‘I’d love it. But don’t you want to ask me any questions? My employment history, that kind of thing?’

‘It’s all on your CV, isn’t it?’

‘Well, yes, but—’

‘So if I need to know anything I’ll look it up.’ Ryan put down his cup. ‘Look, it’s only a temporary job and, as you can see, we’re pretty desperate. And I should have been fixing a guttering in Selby twenty minutes ago, so—’

‘I’ll start on Monday, shall I?’

‘That would be great.’ He was already heading for the door when Gina called after him, ‘You should know that I’m pregnant.’

He glanced down at her still-flat stomach. ‘Are you planning to have it in the next three months?’

‘No.’

‘Then I don’t see there’s a problem, do you? I’ll see you on Monday.’

She couldn’t wait to go home and tell Stephen the good news. He was back from Westminster en route for a meeting in Scotland.

Mark was with him. They were in the kitchen, surrounded by piles of letters. Gina felt slightly cheated that even on a rare day off she couldn’t have her husband to herself.

‘I got the job,’ she announced.

‘What job?’ Stephen didn’t look up.

‘The one in the builders’ yard. It’s only temporary, three to four months to reorganize their office.’

‘Wow, that’s fantastic. Well done, you.’ Mark got up and hugged her. Gina glanced over his shoulder at Stephen. ‘Isn’t that great news, Steve?’ Mark prompted.

'What? Oh yes. Terrific.' Stephen glanced up absently, then went back to reading his post.

'You'll have to forgive Stephen, Gina. He's in a bad mood because I'm making him do his homework. He's having to deal with a big backlog of mail about blocked drains and badly parked cars.'

'It's all bloody mind-numbing and trivial, isn't it?' Stephen threw down a letter in disgust.

'It's what you're there for, Steve, to represent your constituents in Parliament. It's not all cocktail parties and jollies to bonny Scotland, you know.'

'I won't be going anywhere if I don't get this lot finished.'

'I could help, if you like?' Gina offered. 'I'm not doing anything tonight.'

'Would you?' Stephen's mood brightened instantly.

'Hang on,' Mark said. 'It's hardly fair to ask Gina to give up her free time. You're the MP.'

'She offered, didn't she? She wants to help, don't you, darling?' Gina nodded. 'There you are, then. I can hand all this over to her and go away with a clear conscience, can't I?'

'If you say so,' Mark said. A look passed between them which Gina couldn't understand. 'Tell you what, Gina, I'll stay and give you a hand. How about that?'

'I honestly don't mind,' she insisted. She wanted to be helpful, to prove to Stephen that she was interested in his career. Perhaps then he wouldn't be so sulky and put out about the baby.

But her optimism disappeared when she went upstairs to finish Stephen's packing for him. His neatly ironed clothes were spread out all over the bed. As she folded up a shirt and went to put it in his overnight bag she noticed something sticking out of one of the pockets. She took it out and saw it was a train ticket to Edinburgh.

She smiled. No doubt Stephen would be rampaging around the house looking for that later on. She opened his briefcase to slip it in when she noticed there was already a ticket there.

Gina looked at the ticket in her hand and back at the one lying in his briefcase. No prizes for guessing who the extra ticket was meant for.

She heard him coming up the stairs and quickly stuffed the first ticket back into its hiding place, just as he came into the room.

He glanced at the open overnight bag and back at her. 'What are you doing?'

'I thought I'd help you pack.'

'You don't have to do that.' He zipped up the case. 'You've already been fantastic, tackling all that paperwork for me.' He dropped a kiss on her temple. 'You're an angel.'

Stephen left an hour later. Gina tried to forget about the ticket, and concentrated on sorting out the rest of the constituents' mail with Mark.

It was easy to forget her own problems once she saw what other people had to deal with. Old folk living in fear from teenage vandals, divorced fathers who weren't allowed to see their children, decent people trying to live their lives next to nightmare neighbours. She didn't know if it was her hormones making her emotional, but each successive letter moved her closer to tears.

'Surely there must be something else we can say, apart from "Thank you for your letter, we'll get back to you"?' she said as they worked their way through the pile.

'What do you suggest?'

'We could actually try doing something constructive.'

'Stephen does all he can,' Mark said.

Does he? Gina wondered. She didn't mean to be disloyal, but from what she could make out, her husband seemed more interested in furthering his Westminster career than representing the people who put him there. 'I'm sure he does, but these poor people need practical help, not just platitudes.'

Mark looked at her consideringly. 'Maybe *you* should stand at the next election?'

Gina blushed. 'Don't make fun of me.'

'I'm serious. You're bright, conscientious and you obviously care. You and Stephen could be a serious political force.'

'Oh, he'd love that, wouldn't he?' Gina laughed. 'But at least I could keep an eye on him.'

She regretted it the moment she saw the look in Mark's eyes. 'What makes you say that?'

'No reason.' She stood up. 'You must be hungry. Shall I make us some supper?'

They ate pasta at the kitchen table. Mark opened a bottle of red wine.

Gina eyed the bottle warily. It was one of Stephen's special bottles; he was bound to go mad. 'I'm not sure I should, in my condition.'

'One won't hurt you.' He filled up her glass. 'How's the morning sickness, by the way?'

'Don't you mean morning, noon and night sickness? Nearly over now, thank goodness. Although I still get the odd queasy feeling now and then.'

'If it's any consolation, it's often a sign of a healthy pregnancy. It's a reaction to the amount of hormones released, apparently.'

Gina gazed at him in amazement. 'I never realized you were such an expert.'

He shrugged. 'My sister's just had a baby. Believe me, what I don't know about childbirth – well, it's more than any single man should know, frankly.'

'It's probably more than most married men know,' Gina said. Stephen certainly hadn't taken an interest so far.

Mark seemed to guess her thoughts. 'He still hasn't come round to the idea?'

'He never talks about it. He prefers to pretend it isn't happening.'

'Maybe he's just taking time to get used to it. It must have come as a shock to him.'

'It came as a shock to me, too,' Gina said. 'I didn't set out to get pregnant. Although I didn't think Stephen would hate the idea quite so much.' She broke off, seeing Mark's awkward expression. 'I'm sorry, I shouldn't be talking to you like this. I know you're Stephen's friend. It's unfair to bring you into it.'

'I hope I'm your friend, too?' Mark smiled at her. 'Look, just give Stephen some time, OK? This fatherhood thing is all new to him. He'll come round to it in the end, you'll see.'

'I hope you're right.' She sipped her wine. After several weeks of abstinence it went straight to her head, making her feel warm and happy. Why couldn't she be like this with Stephen, laughing and chatting instead of always being on the verge of a row?

It helped that Mark was such good company. It made her wonder why he hadn't been snapped up by a woman years ago.

'So how come you've never married?' she asked.

'No one would have me.'

'Oh, come on. You're a great catch.'

'You make me sound like a prize cod.'

'I'm serious. You're funny, caring, very good-looking—'

'Mrs Farrell, please. You're making me blush.'

Gina looked at him and found she was blushing, too. For a moment their eyes met. Then Mark looked away. 'Maybe we should crack on with those letters?' he said.

The following morning Gina woke up flushed with mortification. It must have been the wine, she decided. Why else would she have been flirting with her husband's best friend?

Poor Mark had been so embarrassed. He'd laughed it off, but Gina could tell he couldn't wait to escape. He was probably terrified she was going to try to seduce him or something. Feeling guilty, she called Stephen. She was surprised when he wasn't at the hotel.

'He should have checked in last night. Could you have another look?' she asked.

'I'm sorry, madam, but there's no one of that name registered at this hotel,' the receptionist said in her soft Scottish accent.

Gina hung up, puzzled, then dialled Stephen's mobile. After several rings, he finally answered it. 'What is it?' he hissed. 'I'm in a meeting.'

'Why aren't you booked in at the hotel?'

His exaggerated sigh echoed down the line. 'You've called me out of an important meeting to ask me that? There was a mix-up with the bookings, so they had to move me somewhere else. OK?'

'Why didn't you tell me?'

'I was going to, but by the time I'd got it all sorted out it was too late last night. And I've been in meetings since first thing.'

There was an irritable pause. 'Why? Are you checking up on me?'

'Of course not.' She was glad he couldn't see the guilty flush creeping up her face. 'So where are you staying?' There was a crackle on the line. 'Stephen?'

'Sorry, you're breaking up. I'm going to have to go.'

'But—'

'I'll call you later, OK?' And he was gone.

'So, who is she?' Finn asked.

'Just someone I've taken on to help in the office for a couple of months. Don't worry, I talked to your dad about it.'

Shame you didn't talk to me, Finn thought. But why should he? As far as her father was concerned, Ryan made all the decisions these days.

She glanced out of the office window. There, as if to prove it, was his pick-up parked in her father's space.

There was no use complaining to her father about it. He was still barely speaking to her. He'd grudgingly given in when Ryan persuaded him he needed Finn at the yard, as long as she stuck to doing the paperwork. A rule which Finn planned to ignore as soon as she was free of the office.

'I thought you'd be pleased,' Ryan said. 'You're always complaining about being stuck in here.'

She was pleased, but she didn't want to let Ryan know that. 'It's a matter of principle,' she insisted. 'I would have liked to be consulted.'

Ryan muttered something under his breath which she didn't quite hear. 'Call it an executive decision,' he said. 'Besides, I need you on site. Marcus Stephenson's been playing up again. He seems to think Kev and Andy aren't nearly as good as you.'

'Really?' Finn's eyes lit up.

'I wouldn't say it if it wasn't true, would I? Believe me, the last thing I need is for you to get any more big-headed.'

She aimed a file at him as his mobile rang. Finn watched him answer it and heard the weary way he spoke to the caller.

'Let me guess – your ex again?' she said when he hung up. She'd got tired of taking calls from Wendy.

'Hmm.'

'Maybe your wonderful new secretary can get rid of her. When does she start, by the way?'

'First thing Monday morning.'

The first thing Finn heard when she arrived at the yard on Monday morning was the sound of laughter drifting across from the office. She headed towards it and peered through the window. Ryan was there with a blonde. He was leaning over her as she sat at the computer, pointing out something on the screen. Watching them laughing together, she felt even more like an outsider. And this was supposed to be her family's yard!

Suddenly Ryan looked up and caught her staring. He gestured for her to come in.

'Come and meet our new secretary. Gina Farrell, this is Finnuala Delaney.'

'Finn,' she said automatically, even more annoyed because he knew how much she hated being called by her full name. 'Only my dad calls me Finnuala.' She sized up the woman behind the desk. Gina was slender, attractive in a nervous kind of way and smartly dressed. Finn knew that suit must have cost more than a secretary's wages.

Then she remembered the woman who'd handed her that huge cheque in Tates' car park.

'We've met before, haven't we?' she asked.

'You could say that,' Gina replied coolly. 'I lost my job because of you.'

'I'm sorry?'

'The Windmill Meadows launch?'

'Oh God, of course.' Suddenly the penny dropped. 'You were there, too, weren't you?'

'You mean you saw her throw that egg?' Ryan said.

'How many times do I have to tell you, it was a mushroom vol au vent?' Finn turned back to Gina. 'Don't tell me they sacked you because of that?' She nodded. 'But it wasn't your fault.'

'I organized the event, so I got the blame.'

'I can't believe it.' Finn looked outraged. 'If you ask me, you're better off out of there, if that's the way they treat people.'

'Actually, I quite enjoyed my job.'

'How could anyone enjoy working for that bunch of crooks?'

'Some of them were nice.'

'You obviously don't know them.'

'I think I know them better than you.'

Something about the way she said it made Finn hot with indignation. 'Let me just tell you something—' she began, but Ryan stepped in.

'Shouldn't we be loading up the van? You know Marcus Stephenson gets twitchy if you're late.'

'I don't think your friend likes me,' Finn said, as they stepped out into the pale February sunshine.

'I'm not surprised. First you lob food at her boss and get her fired. Then you start attacking her within five minutes. It was hardly friendly.'

'She wasn't exactly friendly to me, either.' She glanced back at the office. She didn't like the disdainful way Gina looked at her, as if she was something she'd scraped off her designer slingbacks.

Gina watched Finn and Ryan loading up the van. Her jaw muscles ached from the sheer effort of keeping a fixed smile on her face when all she wanted to do was leap across the desk and grab Finn by the throat.

She'd nearly died when she saw her walk into the office. Until that moment she hadn't made the connection with the name.

She felt sick at her own stupidity. She'd been so optimistic as she got ready this morning, so determined to make a go of this new job. Now she couldn't believe her bad luck.

She couldn't possibly go on working here, that was for sure. How could she? She still had nightmares about that awful day at Windmill Meadows. She'd lie awake, going over and over it in her mind, wondering how she could have handled it better.

Her father would be furious if he knew she was here. Her whole family would probably disown her. But then, none of them had bothered to contact her since she'd left Tates. Not even James had phoned to check if she was OK. It was out of sight, out of mind as far as they were all concerned.

She stared at the invoices in front of her. She did need a job. She hadn't had any other offers, and Ryan seemed so nice. So nice she wondered how the hell he put up with someone like Finn Delaney.

She decided to stick it out. It wouldn't be for very long, after all. But in the meantime, perhaps it would be better if no one knew she was a Tate. The last thing she needed was more hassle from Finn.

Chapter 19

Finn was up a ladder fitting the window frames into the Stephensons' extension when Mel turned up, bumping little Joseph over the rough ground in his buggy. She was laden down with bags and dragging a baby car seat behind her.

'What are you doing here?' Finn hurried down the ladder. 'Has something happened?'

'I've had a call from Ciaran, if that's what you mean. He's fine.'

'Thank God for that.' In spite of all the trouble he'd caused, he was still her brother and she had been worried about him. 'I don't suppose he gave any clue where he was?'

Mel shook her head. Even if he had she probably wouldn't tell, Finn thought.

'Thanks for letting me know, anyway.'

She started back up the ladder. Mel stood at the bottom watching her.

'Can you take care of Joseph for me?' she asked.

'Sure. Just let me know when and I'll sort it out.'

'I need you to take him now. I've got a job interview.'

'What?' Finn stared down at her in disbelief. 'I can't!'

'But you said you'd help whenever I needed you.'

'I know, but, as you can see, it's not exactly convenient at the moment.' She glanced around, silently thankful that Mr Stephenson had gone off for a couple of hours. He wouldn't have taken kindly to her family turning up on site. 'Can't someone else do it?'

Mel shook her head. 'My mum's gone to Leeds with my auntie. I tried calling your house but there's no answer.'

'My dad's gone to the cardiac clinic. I expect Orla's gone with him. But if you could hang on for a bit, I'm sure they'd love to look after Joseph.'

'I can't, my interview's in half an hour. I wouldn't ask if I wasn't desperate.'

'Well—'

'It won't be for long, honest. I'll be back before you know it,' Mel went on, sensing weakness. 'I've packed all his nappies and a spare set of clothes in this bag. I'll just leave it here, shall I?' She dumped a blue elephant-patterned changing bag at the foot of the ladder. 'I've just given him a feed so he probably won't be hungry. But in case he is, there's an extra bottle in the bag. Just heat it up.'

'Now, hang on—'

'Got a bus to catch, sorry.'

'Mel!' But she was already gone, picking her way between the cement sacks in her high heels.

Finn stared down at the baby. He stared back, his face poking out from a grubby blue anorak, slate-grey eyes meeting hers in silent accusation.

'Well,' she said bracingly, 'looks like it's just the two of us, kid.' At which point the tiny face crumpled and Joseph began to howl at the top of his lungs.

It was amazing how quickly you got used to the noise, Finn reflected ten minutes later as she fixed the next piece of window frame into place. Having faffed around making sure he didn't need his nappy changing and knowing he didn't need another bottle, she'd finally concluded that baby Joseph was just as ticked off at being lumbered as she was. So she'd parked his buggy on the far side of the site and got on with her work, leaving him to yell his lungs out.

It seemed to work – for a while. After screaming himself red in the face, Joseph had gradually got fed up with the sound of his own voice and become absorbed in watching her instead. To keep him amused, Finn kept up a running commentary about what she was doing. He seemed to be listening intently, taking it all in with an expression of utmost concentration. He had a far longer attention span than his father, Finn decided. Perhaps the building gene had skipped a generation.

But then he got bored and started crying again. And this time he didn't stop. The sound was so loud and piercing, it seemed to drill straight through her skull until she felt like screaming, too. He was yelling so loudly she didn't hear the car pull up until a voice from the bottom of the ladder said, 'What the hell is going on here?'

She turned around so quickly she nearly lost her balance. Far below her stood Mr Stephenson. With him was a squat, balding man she recognized as Mr Warren, the local council building inspector.

Oh, sugar. She'd forgotten he was supposed to be visiting today to check up on what she'd done so far.

And of course it had to be Alan Warren, the sourest, most pedantic jobsworth of a man ever to grace a council office. A man who could reduce the toughest builder to tears of frustration.

'I didn't realize you'd taken on an apprentice, Miss Delaney?' He smiled thinly. 'Or have you opened a crêche?'

She hurried down the ladder, already babbling apologies. 'I'm so sorry, my brother's girlfriend turned up and she had a job interview and she said it wouldn't be for long and—'

'I would hardly have said it was the most appropriate place for a child.'

'No, well, of course not.' God, what did he think she was, some kind of idiot? Did he think she was going to give Joseph a chisel to amuse himself with, or something? 'Like I said, she wasn't supposed to be gone long.'

'Any amount of time is a compromise of site safety.' Mr Warren raised his voice to compete with Joseph's screaming. 'You do realize I could close you down for this?'

Finn glanced at Mr Stephenson, who was looking both murderous and panic-stricken. What a nightmare, she'd really let him down. And after she'd worked so hard to redeem herself and her dad's business in his eyes.

'I'll take him home.'

'I think you should, Miss Delaney.' Mr Warren's eyes were as small and cold as marbles. 'And in the meantime I'll take a good look at what you've done so far.'

And no doubt he'd find a million things to complain about, Finn thought as she struggled to clip Joseph's car seat into the back of her car. Alan Warren was nit-pickingly thorough and enjoyed finding fault with other people's work. But after the baby incident he would have it in for her even more. Not that she really thought she had anything to fear – her work was good and she knew it. But if only she could have been there to go round with them and hear what he had to say, she might have been able to defend herself. Instead she was stuck holding the baby. And Joseph's relentless screaming seemed even more piercing and shrill inside the close confines of her Fiat.

Ryan was in the Portakabin office when she got back to her father's yard. He sat on the edge of Gina's desk, going through the post as she typed. He seemed to spend a lot of time in the office these days, she noticed. How he managed to run her father's business and his own she had no idea.

Ryan's apprentice Kev was also in there, making himself a cup of tea. He was a slight, spotty teenager who wore a woolly hat permanently pulled down to the bridge of his nose.

They all looked up as Finn struggled in, screaming baby under one arm, baby paraphernalia in the other.

'What have you got there?' Ryan asked.

'A nuclear missile, what does it look like?' She dumped Joseph on the floor, where he immediately crawled off towards the filing cabinets while she untangled herself from the changing bag.

'I mean, why have you got him?'

'Mel dumped him on me. And you can stop smirking, or I'll make you change his nappy,' she warned Kev. She retrieved Joseph, who was investigating the wiring in the corner, and scooped him under her arm. Furious at being captured, he started to scream again.

'So what are you planning to do with him?'

'Heaven knows. I can't go back to Stephensons with him, and I was hoping to finish those windows today.'

'I could look after him,' Gina said.

Finn looked hopeful. 'Really? Are you sure?'

'I've finished the invoices and brought the books up to date. I've got nothing urgent to do for the rest of the afternoon. And I could use some baby practice.' She put her hand over her still-flat stomach.

'Thanks, that would be great.' Finn handed him over gratefully. Whether it was the novelty of a new face or confidence that he was in the arms of someone who knew what they were doing, Joseph stopped crying almost immediately. His crimson face subsided to a more normal pinkish baby colour, and he gave Gina a beaming smile.

'Look at that,' Ryan said. 'You're obviously a natural, Gina.'

'Either that or he's just exhausted himself screaming at me for the past hour,' Finn said.

She couldn't help feeling annoyed. There was no reason for it; in the two weeks she'd been working there Gina had streamlined their haphazard systems and got the office running so smoothly Finn hardly knew her way around any more. She always looked so well-groomed, and now she was a wonderful mother, too. Was there no end to her talents? Finn felt inadequate just being in the same room as her.

She'd tried to be friendly, but Gina was always so cool. She only ever seemed to smile when Ryan was around. Finn couldn't work out what she'd said or done to upset her so badly. Unless she still had it in for her over that silly business with the Tates?

'I think this little one might need changing,' Gina said.

'Is there anything I can do?' Ryan offered.

'You could heat up a bottle, if there is one?'

'It's in the bag.' Finn felt cross. Ryan hadn't offered to help *her* when she was so obviously struggling. 'But he was only fed a couple of hours ago,' she added, remembering what Mel had told her.

'I'll heat it up anyway. He might be hungry.' Finn wondered why Ryan was so keen to help Gina. Did he fancy her, she wondered? They certainly seemed to get on well together.

They headed off to the kitchen, leaving Finn alone with Kev.

She flicked through the post for several minutes before she realized he was still there, watching her. 'Can I help you?' she asked.

His eyes darted from side to side under his woolly hat. 'I just wondered – if you'd like to come out with me on Thursday? It's my birthday, and I thought we could have a night out at that new club in Leeds . . .' The words tumbled over themselves in a rush to escape.

'Oh, I see.' Realization dawned. 'Like a party, you mean?'

'Well—'

'What do you think?' she asked, as Ryan came back with Joseph's bottle. 'Kev wants us all to go out for his birthday. Sounds good, doesn't it?'

She saw a look pass between Ryan and Kev.

'Are you sure I'm invited?' Ryan asked cautiously.

'Of course you are,' Finn said as Kev opened his mouth. 'The more the merrier, eh, Kev?'

'Er, yeah. Why not?'

'Sounds great. I haven't had a night out in ages. How about you, Gina?' she said as Gina appeared with Joseph in her arms. 'You'd like to come clubbing with us on Thursday night, wouldn't you?'

'Me? In a nightclub?' Gina's eyes widened in dismay. 'I don't know, I'd have to ask Stephen—'

'Gina, it's a club, not an orgy.' Finn rolled her eyes and turned back to Kev. 'We'd all love to come.'

'Great. I'll – um – see you.'

'He didn't seem very enthusiastic,' she commented as they watched him lope across the yard a few minutes later. 'I think he's gone off the idea. What?' She looked around at Ryan and Gina who were trying not to smile. 'Have I missed something?'

'You've got no idea, have you?' Ryan shook his head. 'I think the poor lad was trying to ask you out.'

'What? But he's only about twelve.'

'He's got a crush on you, Finn. He's probably spent days trying to pluck up the courage to ask you, and you've gone and invited us.' He grinned at Gina. 'But don't worry, we'll make our excuses so the two of you can be alone,' he teased.

'Don't you dare! You've got to come with me.' She looked from Ryan to Gina. 'Don't leave me alone with him, please.'

'We'll see,' Ryan said. 'We might have to check our diaries, won't we, Gina?'

A familiar depression settled over her as she drove home. She and her father were still barely speaking. They were both too proud and stubborn to make the first move, but Finn really missed their jokes and banter. And she hated the frosty atmosphere that hung over the house now.

And she wasn't the only one. As they all sat down for another silent dinner, Orla slammed down their plates and said, 'Right, that's it. I've had enough of this. I'm taking my dinner in the sitting room while you two sort yourselves out. And if you haven't got over this silly argument by the time *Corrie*'s finished, I'm packing my bags and going home. Understood?'

They sat in stunned silence for a moment or two after the door slammed behind her. Then Joe said, 'I suppose we'd better do as we're told.'

'I suppose so.' She stared down at her plate. 'You first.'

Joe was quiet for a while. Then he said, 'I still don't hold with the idea of you being in the business.'

'I know that. But it's all I've ever wanted to do, ever since I was a kid. Ever since I used to watch you working,' she added.

'So it's my fault, is it?' Joe grumbled. 'I don't know why you like it so much. It's no fun being out in all weathers, or coming home with your back aching.'

'I don't mind it.'

'But it's not what I wanted for you.'

'I know you would have preferred me to have a safe, boring office job. But that's just not me, Dad.'

'Aye, you always did like to be different.' He glanced at her, then looked away again. 'But I'm grateful to you for keeping the business afloat with everything that's been going on.'

It was the closest thing to an apology she would ever get from her father. 'That's OK. I've enjoyed it.'

'Ryan's told me what a good job you've been doing.'

'I had a good teacher, didn't I?'

They looked at each other. The briefest of glances, but it spoke volumes.

'I take it you two have sorted yourselves out?' Orla put her head around the door a few minutes later, as they were laughing about Marcus Stephenson's latest flight of fancy on his dream home.

'I reckon so,' Joe shrugged.

Finn knew her father would never approve of what she did, but at least now he understood.

'Here we are again,' Stephen said as the electronic gates swung open and they turned up the sweeping drive that led to Lytton Grange. 'Welcome to Southfork.'

He always said it, every time they came to her parents' house. Not to her father's face, of course, but he never failed to sneer at the tennis courts, the pavilion that housed the heated swimming pool and hot tub, or the spreading terrace with neatly trimmed shrubs. 'Very *Dallas*,' he would say. 'And your dad's JR Ewing.'

His parents were strictly old money, only there wasn't too much of it left and their rambling old house was distinctly in need of repair and more efficient central heating. Whenever they went to visit, Gina lay shivering under the chilly blankets and wonder how Stephen could possibly think it was superior to her parents' comfortable, warm home.

'Stephen, please.' Gina shot a look at Vicky, sitting in the back seat playing with her mobile phone. She'd come home for the February half-term holiday.

They were on their way to Sunday lunch with the rest of her family. Gina knew she should be grateful that she'd been invited back into the fold since her father sacked her. But family get-togethers were always an ordeal, and, just to make things even worse, Stephen was in a foul mood. He'd been sulking ever since she'd told him about her planned night out.

'You, in a nightclub?' Anyone would think she'd told him she was off to try her hand at a spot of lap-dancing. 'But why?'

'Why not? It's a night out.' And she got precious few of them, apart from the times she had to accompany Stephen to some dreadful political function or other.

'I'd hardly imagine it was your kind of thing.'

It wasn't, of course. She'd planned to make some excuse nearer the time, because the idea of spending the evening with Finn Delaney was hardly her idea of a good time. But now that Stephen was so against it she was determined to go.

'You never know, it might be fun.' Gina caught her daughter's eye in the rear-view mirror and winked. Vicky smiled back half-heartedly. She'd been quiet ever since they left Heath Manor. Gina wondered if she had something on her mind.

She glanced across at Stephen. 'You won't say anything about my job, will you?'

'Why not?'

'I just don't want them to know, that's all. I don't think my father would be happy about me working for a competitor.'

'They're hardly that. From what you've told me, Delaneys sound like pretty small fish compared to Tates.'

'Let's just say there's some bad blood between them.'

'Really?' Stephen looked interested. 'How intriguing. Tell me more.'

'I'll tell you later. We're here.' Gina changed the subject as they drew up outside the house.

The housekeeper let them in. Inside, a vast, sunny atrium reached up to the sky, flooding the ground floor with light. In front of them was a sweeping, Hollywood-style staircase designed for making an entrance. At the top it branched left and right, leading to a galleried landing that looked down over the marble-tiled hall. It was all decorated in restful, minimalist tones.

Her mother came out to greet them, looking stylish in a cream shift dress with a pale-gold pashmina draped around her shoulders.

'Rose, you're looking as ravishing as ever.' Stephen immediately switched on the smooth charm, leaning forward to kiss his mother-in-law's cheek. 'And what is that gorgeous scent you're wearing?'

'Do you like it?' Rose smiled flirtatiously at him. 'I didn't think men noticed things like that.'

Gina felt slightly sick as she watched the two of them. Ten minutes ago in the car Stephen had been bitching about giving up his day off to traipse all this way to pay court to her wretched family, and now anyone would think he wanted to have an affair with her mother. She glanced at Vicky, who was pulling a similarly nauseated face.

'Vicky, darling.' Rose finally dragged herself away to notice her grand-daughter and hugged her briefly. 'And Gina.' She bestowed an air kiss somewhere above her daughter's left ear.

'Is everyone here?' Gina looked beyond her mother's shoulder into the room. They were her family, yet she always found the idea of confronting them all rather daunting.

'James isn't. Your father's quite put out about it. He was supposed to be here early for a meeting. I suppose it's that girl's fault.'

'Is Molly coming?' Gina brightened.

'Unfortunately, yes. We thought it was about time she met the family properly, since James seems so determined to go on seeing her.'

Gina felt sorry for Molly. She wondered if she knew what she was letting herself in for.

They were all having pre-lunch drinks in the drawing room, a starkly elegant room decorated in soothing beige and cream tones, with modern furniture and long sofas. Windows at either end filled the room with light. Her father was standing with his back to the fireplace, dominating the room. Neil and Nicole sat on one of the sofas, Nicole looking stunning as usual in a striking white trouser suit that showed off her long legs and contrasted with her lustrous dark hair.

Her father looked up as Gina entered the room. She smiled hopefully but his gaze slid straight past her to Vicky.

'Vicky, sweetheart! Welcome home.' He swept his grand-daughter into his arms for a hug. Gina noticed how Nicole watched them jealously. Probably trying to work out if Max was going to leave his fortune to his grandchild, she decided.

'Still no sign of James?' Max looked over Vicky's head towards his wife. She shook her head. Gina caught her father's taut expression and felt sorry for her brother. James would be in trouble for keeping them waiting.

They arrived ten minutes later, just as Max had lost patience and insisted they should go into lunch without them. Molly's children were with them, an adorable little boy and girl who clung to their mother and seemed completely overawed by their surroundings.

'Sorry we're late,' Molly said. 'The dog ate Ben's X-Box and I had to take him to the vet's. The dog, that is, not Ben.'

Gina laughed, then quickly shut up when she saw everyone's frosty faces. Molly's smile faltered, too.

James took her arm protectively. 'These are Molly's children,' he said. 'This is Ben, who's six. And Abi's four. Say hello, kids,' he prompted them.

Abi hid her face in her mother's leg. Ben just went on staring.

'Now we've got the introductions out of the way, perhaps we could eat?' Max strode past them. Gina caught Molly's apprehensive expression and smiled encouragingly, as they all followed him into the dining room.

The meal was a very strained, formal affair. Molly tried hard to control her children and make them behave, but Gina could see it was a struggle for her. Ben took one look at the elaborate crown of lamb in front of him and declared he wanted sausages, while Abi climbed into Molly's lap, sucked her thumb noisily and gazed at Max in pure terror.

Poor Molly hardly managed to eat anything because she was so worried about keeping an eye on their table manners. Gina's heart went out to her. She'd probably expected this to be a friendly family occasion and instead she'd found herself in the middle of something as grand as a state banquet.

James seemed equally strained. He looked torn between agony for his girlfriend and the disapproval of his family, and wasn't sure which way to turn.

'Thank God that's over,' he whispered to Gina, as they drank their coffee after the meal. 'Look at the way they're treating her. They're like a pack of hyenas.'

'Then do something. Stand up for her.'

'What can I do?' Like the rest of them, he was terrified of offending his father.

Gina took charge. 'Vicky, why don't you take Abi and Ben outside and show them the garden?' she said. Vicky immediately got up. She looked relieved to be allowed to escape.

'But be careful you don't break anything,' Rose called after them, as Vicky left the room, a small child hanging on to each hand.

'Thanks,' Molly whispered. 'I wasn't sure how much longer I could make them behave. They're not always this monstrous.'

'They don't seem monstrous at all. Just children,' said Gina.

She glanced at her mother. Rose wouldn't know how normal children behaved. When they were growing up, the only time she ever saw them was during the school holidays. And then she had a nanny to make sure they were washed and fed before she headed off to some party or function with their father.

'I wouldn't have brought them with me but James insisted,' Molly went on. 'He thought it was time we all met the family. I just hope I haven't made things difficult for him.'

'Why should you do that?'

'Oh, you know. Somehow I don't think I'm the kind of girl they were hoping he'd bring home. A single mum with two wild kids!'

Gina looked at her friendly, freckled face. A single mum with two kids who also happened to be very nice, she thought. If only her snobbish family could look past the initial appearances they might see that.

'So are you divorced?' she asked.

Molly shook her head. 'Widowed.'

'But you must have been so young?'

'I was twenty-five when Barry died two years ago.'

Gina felt a rush of sympathy for her. 'How awful. Was it very sudden?'

'Pretty much. He was diagnosed with cancer and three months later he was dead. Not really long enough to get used to the idea.' She put down her coffee cup. 'I was so busy nursing him I didn't have time to think about the future, until I suddenly realized I was on my own with two young kids. And a string of debts.' She looked rueful. 'Barry was a wonderful guy and a great father, but he wasn't the most reliable of men. He didn't believe in insurance, or pensions, or anything like that. I suppose he didn't know he was going to die before he was thirty.' She twirled her spoon in her cup. 'Just before he died he remortgaged the house to set up a business. I didn't know anything about it until they came to take our home away for not keeping up the payments.' She spoke so matter-of-factly, Gina couldn't believe she could be so calm.

'Oh my God, what did you do?'

'What could I do? I had two kids to look after. I couldn't let myself sink into depression. I had to pick myself up, dust myself off and start earning a living. Luckily I could still remember all my old word-processing skills from college, otherwise I would have been sunk.'

Gina gazed at her admiringly. But at the same time Molly's story struck a painful chord. Molly had been at rock-bottom, but she'd refused to give in to depression and self-pity. She'd dragged herself back up again for the sake of her children. Unlike Gina, who'd tried to take the easy way out.

'Anyway, I don't want to drone on about myself all the time.' Molly brightened. 'James tells me you're married to an MP? I'm sure I've seen your husband on the telly.'

'I expect so.' Stephen never missed an excuse to get his face in the media.

'That must be a very exciting, glamorous life.'

'Why?' Gina stared at her blankly.

'Don't you get to travel a lot, meet all kinds of important people?'

'Stephen does. Mostly I just stay at home.' She couldn't believe how dull that made her sound. No wonder Stephen was bored with her.

'Have you ever thought about moving to London with him?'

'We talked about it, but decided it would be better if I stayed up here. We needed a house close to the constituency, and I wanted to be here for Vicky. I know she's at boarding school but I wouldn't have felt happy being so far away from her.'

Molly gazed out of the window. Vicky was playing on the lawn with Ben and Abi, chasing them as they squealed and ran away. 'She's a lovely girl. She's not Stephen's daughter, is she?'

'No, but he thinks of her as his own.'

'Do you ever hear from her real father?'

'Stephen is her real father as far as I'm concerned. The other one gave up any right to be called that when he walked out on me.'

'Yes, of course. I'm sorry.' Molly paused, then said, 'So you've never wondered why he didn't get back in touch?'

'I suppose he thought he'd had a lucky escape.' Gina fiddled with her napkin. She wondered why Molly was staring at her so intently. 'How does James get on with your children?' she asked, changing the subject.

'Oh, he's brilliant with them. And they adore him.' Molly smiled. 'He's promised to take them to Disneyland Paris for Ben's birthday next month.'

'Really?' Somehow Gina couldn't imagine her big brother in a theme park with Mickey Mouse. He really must be smitten, she decided. And she didn't blame him, either. Molly was a truly special girl.

As usual, the rest of the conversation around the table was all business. Max talked to his sons about the development in Paradise Road, and how sales on Windmill Meadows were going.

Then he said a name that made her blood run cold.

Stephen heard it, too. 'Did you say Delaneys?'

Max nodded. 'Do you know them?'

Gina held her breath. Please don't say anything, she begged silently.

Stephen sent her a taunting look across the table. 'The name seems familiar. Can't quite remember where from, though.'

'Pity,' Max said. 'We could have done with some dirt on them.'

'Maybe you should ask your daughter?' Stephen murmured.

Thankfully they were interrupted by Vicky, who burst in red-faced. 'Come quickly,' she panted. 'Ben's in the pond, and I can't get him out. He says he's fishing.'

'Oh lord.' Molly shot to her feet.

'If he's touched my koi carp—!' Max growled, following her.

By the time Ben had been dried off and the traumatized fish had been returned to their pond, Molly wisely decided it was time they were leaving. Max hardly bothered to say goodbye, and although Rose was her usual gracious self, not wanting to allow her perfect manners to slip for a moment, she was clearly irritated.

Molly looked unhappy and defeated as she bundled her children into their coats.

'Can we come back?' Ben asked.

'I'm not sure about that, darling.' If this was a test to see if she was good enough for the Tate family, she must have realized she'd failed it miserably.

James watched her, his face wretched. Gina willed him to step in, but he stayed obstinately silent. Until she'd almost reached the door when he suddenly said, 'Wait. I'll come with you.'

Rose looked surprised. 'Didn't your father have something he wanted to discuss with you?'

'I'm sure it can wait.'

'You know he doesn't like waiting.'

'You should stay,' Molly said. 'You don't have to come with me.'

James looked from her to his mother. 'I want to,' he said firmly.

Gina cheered silently as they drove off. At least James had finally had the guts to stand up for himself.

And she wasn't the only one who was pleased. 'He's really done it now,' Nicole whispered gleefully. 'Did you see Max's face during lunch? I think the golden boy's halo has slipped. There's no way he's going to make vice-chairman now.'

Gina turned on her in disgust. 'Is that all you think about? Power?'

Nicole's brows arched. 'Sweetie, what else is there?'

Chapter 20

'I don't believe it. When are these people going to give up?'

Gina looked up. 'Sorry?'

'It's another offer from the Tates' land agents.' Finn stared at the letter in her hands. 'What part of "we're not interested" don't they understand?' She screwed it up and tossed it into the bin.

She was glad her father hadn't seen it; he was doing so well in his recovery, the last thing she wanted was for him to suffer a setback.

'Maybe you should just sell it to them?' Gina said.

'What?'

'You've said yourself all the stress isn't good for your father. Why don't you sell it and save all the trouble?'

Why don't you mind your own business? Finn thought. What the hell did Gina know about it? 'Because they don't want to buy it, they want to steal it. This offer is far lower than we paid for it. My dad would be ruined if he took it.'

She didn't want to admit to herself how true that was. Things weren't going too well for them. At least they still had a steady stream of jobs coming in, but they didn't have much of a financial cushion to protect them if anything else went wrong.

'Maybe your dad paid too much for it in the first place? It can't be worth very much without planning permission, can it? Perhaps all Tates are offering is a fair market price?'

'There's nothing fair about that bunch of sharks! And the only reason we didn't get planning permission is because Max Tate leaned on his buddies at the council and made sure it didn't happen. You can bet as soon as he's got his hands on the land there won't be any problem with building on it.'

'You don't know that.' Gina stared down at her keyboard.

'Oh, I do. Max Tate is a crook.'

'Or just a good businessman.'

'Are you saying my father isn't?'

'I'm not saying anything. But just because things aren't going well for you, there's no need to start getting paranoid.'

'Paranoid?' Finn hit back. 'Listen, I worked for Tates once. I saw a man nearly killed because they compromised on safety. And they made sure the whole thing was covered up. They tried to offer me money to keep my mouth shut. And then when I didn't they trashed my van and put a brick through my window.'

'Perhaps that had more to do with your own family than the Tates?' Gina said.

'And what's that supposed to mean?'

'Your brother must know some dodgy people, surely? Isn't that why he got arrested?'

Finn could feel her temper rising. 'He was set up.'

'They all say that, don't they?'

'In this case it happens to be true. He was set up to teach him a lesson because he refused to torch a house. And do you know who asked him to do it? Your friends the Tates!'

Gina turned pale. 'That can't be true.'

'Well, it just so happens he was asked to burn a place in the very same street where Max Tate is busy buying up all the houses as they become empty – Paradise Road. And there's nothing like setting fire to someone's house to get them to move out, is there? From what I've heard, Max Tate isn't against bending the law to get what he wants.'

'So how come it's your brother on the run and not him?'

Finn stared at Gina, too furious to speak. How dare she sit there like butter wouldn't melt and stick up for the Tates. 'I don't know why you're defending them, anyway. They fired you.'

'Everything OK?' Ryan stuck his head around the door. His expression changed when he saw them squaring up to each other. 'What's going on?'

'Nothing.' Finn snatched up her tool bag. 'I'm going to work.'

'Have you two had a row?' Ryan asked Gina, after Finn had gone.

'It's impossible to have a row with someone who never listens, isn't it?' Gina glared out of the window.

'That's Finn,' Ryan agreed ruefully. 'Once she gets an idea in her head there's no talking to her. So what was it this time? No, let me guess. The Tates?' Gina nodded. 'You'll have to excuse her. She's a bit sensitive where they're concerned.'

She's not the only one, Gina thought. She knew she'd overstepped the mark, but she couldn't just sit there and listen to Finn Delaney calling her father a crook. 'I just think she might have got them wrong, that's all.'

'I'm sorry. I almost forgot you were one of them.'

'What?' She looked up sharply.

'You worked for Tates, didn't you?'

'Oh. Right. Yes, of course.' She could feel herself blushing.

'You must feel some loyalty towards them.'

'I owe them a lot.' She shuffled a pile of papers in front of her. 'Look, I don't know if I can handle this. It's obvious Finn and I aren't getting on. Do you think I should leave?'

'Are you kidding? This office would fall apart in five minutes flat if you weren't here.' Ryan perched on the edge of the desk. 'Don't worry about Finn. She loses her temper and it's all over in five minutes.'

Maybe, Gina thought. But she wasn't sure she could work with her any more. Especially if there were any more outbursts like today's.

She'd tried hard to keep a lid on her resentment towards her. She enjoyed her job and she got on well with Ryan. But Finn Delaney was another matter. She was arrogant, outspoken and seemed to have an opinion on everything. Especially the Tates. She knew her family was far from perfect but so was Finn's. At least neither of her brothers was wanted by the police.

Only because they had other people to do their dirty work for them, a small voice inside her head reminded her. The comment Finn had made about Paradise Road came into her mind, but she pushed it away. Her father would never do anything like that. He might be tough, but he wasn't a monster.

'So are you still coming out tonight?' Ryan interrupted her troubled thoughts.

'I'm not sure.' She wasn't particularly looking forward to it, anyway. 'Maybe it would be better if I wasn't there?'

'Because of Finn? Take no notice of her. Her bark's a lot worse than her bite, I assure you.'

'You obviously know her well.'

'We go back a long way. Her dad took me on as an apprentice when I was eighteen and she was a stroppy teenager.'

'I can't imagine her being any stroppier than she is now.'

'Believe me, she's mellowed a lot!' Ryan grinned. 'But deep down she's a good kid.'

Was there more to it than that? Gina wondered. She'd seen the way he looked at her. She didn't even know if Ryan was aware of it, but there was definitely something more than brotherly affection going on.

He frowned at her. 'Why are you smiling like that?'

'No reason.' She made up her mind not to say anything. It was none of her business. Besides, she thought Ryan could do a lot better for himself. She wouldn't wish Finn Delaney on her worst enemy.

Finn held the dress up against herself and frowned at her reflection. It had seemed fine when she'd grabbed it off the rail at French Connection. The jade-green print had caught her eye and the wrap style wasn't too skimpy or revealing. It even seemed to give her some of the curves that nature had failed to supply. But now she wasn't so sure. She'd fancied doing something different, being noticed for once instead of blending into the background in her jeans. But what if everyone laughed at her?

Lord, this was so hard. She was tempted to forget about dressing up, put on her safe black trousers and have done with it. She decided to ask Orla's advice.

'What do you think?' She did a half-hearted twirl in front of her, already self-conscious.

'You look gorgeous, love. That colour really suits you.'

'You don't think it's too much?'

'Absolutely not. You'll knock them dead. So is this for anyone's benefit in particular?' Orla asked archly.

'If you mean Ryan, no, it isn't.' Why did she keep going on about him? Finn had already made it clear there was nothing between them. 'I reckon if anyone's smitten with him, it's you.'

'I just think he's a nice young man, that's all.' Orla blushed. 'He's been so good since your father was taken ill.'

That was true. Not a day went by when Ryan didn't call or visit. And despite everything she'd said, Finn knew she couldn't have done without his help at the yard. He was a real tower of strength.

She also knew he'd had to make some sacrifices in his own business, giving up jobs so he could help her family.

But she was under no illusions about why he was doing it. It was for Joe's benefit, not hers. As he often told her, he owed her father a great deal.

'I know what you need. Some make-up,' Orla said.

'I've got my lipgloss and mascara in my bag. It's all I ever wear.'

'And very lovely you look, too. But I think you could be a bit more daring tonight, don't you? I'll get my make-up bag.'

Finn wasn't too sure as Orla brushed and blended, but she had to admit the finished result was pretty good. The smudgy green eyeshadow brought out the green and amber flecks in her brown eyes, her skin glowed and her lips glistened with peach gloss.

'You've done a great job, thanks.' She turned her head this way and that, examining her reflection from every angle.

'It wasn't difficult. You're a very pretty girl.'

'I don't know about that.' She'd never have thought she could look this good.

'You are. All you needed was someone to show you how to bring it out.'

Orla was right. All the time she should have been sharing make-up tips with her girlfriends and devouring fashion magazines, she'd been learning about bricklaying and joinery from her father, and hanging out with the lads on site.

'You should have been around years ago.' She smiled at Orla's reflection in the mirror.

Orla sighed. 'Believe me, my love, I wish I had been.'

She'd arranged to meet Ryan, Kev and Gina in the pub before they went on to the club. Kev perked up when she walked in.

'Wow, you look amazing.' He'd taken off his woolly hat, revealing gelled spikes of hair and another crop of acne on his forehead. 'Doesn't she look great, Ryan?'

'Great.' Ryan barely glanced up from his pint.

'You see, I do have legs,' she joked, showing them off.

'They're very nice, too.' Kev leaned over to admire them. Ryan ignored her.

Finn felt piqued. It wouldn't hurt him to look at her, would it? Maybe he only had eyes for Gina, she thought then. She was looking elegant as ever in an expensive-looking black dress than clung to her svelte curves. Her pregnancy was hardly showing at all. She barely looked at Finn, either, as she sat nursing an orange juice.

Some evening this was going to be, Finn thought as she headed for the bar with Kev to get another round in.

And she was right. The club was a dark, heaving sea of people, all bobbing up and down to the deafening beat of drum and bass. Every so often a laser searchlight would skim across the crowd, lighting up heads and shoulders and waving arms.

Finn decided within ten minutes that it wasn't her kind of place. The music was so loud it rattled her fillings, and she kept having to dodge to avoid people drunkenly lurching and weaving their way to the bar. Gina had turned comatose with boredom, the ultraviolet light streaking across her stiff smile, and Ryan seemed absorbed in keeping up a text conversation on his mobile.

'Wendy,' Kev shouted, his mouth so close to Finn's ears she caught a gust of beery breath. 'She's been texting him all day.'

She felt sorry for poor Kev. It was his birthday and no one seemed to want to celebrate with him. She ended up dragging him on to the dance floor just to cheer him up. But she regretted it instantly when Kev immediately put his arms around her and pressed his body against hers.

'You know, I really like you, Finn,' he yelled in her ear, his hands roaming up and down her spine, his hips grinding.

Finn smiled through gritted teeth, preparing to knee him in the groin if his hands strayed any lower, birthday or no birthday.

As soon as the song finished she shot off to the ladies, relieved to escape. She had the feeling that if it had gone on any longer Kev might have tried to kiss her. He was a nice boy, but she suppressed a shudder at the thought of that spotty face closing in on hers.

She was about to re-apply some of Auntie Orla's lipstick, then realized she'd left her bag back at their table with Gina while she was dancing. Instead she fluffed up her hair and went back outside.

Ryan was in the corridor, sending yet another text on his mobile.

'Another message to Wendy?' she said. 'You two can't bear to be apart, can you?'

'Never mind her.' He shoved the phone into his pocket. 'What are you playing at?'

'What do you mean?'

'Don't act innocent. You've been flirting with Kev all night.'

'I've been talking to him. No one else seemed to be making the effort,' she added pointedly.

'You were all over him on that dance floor. And that?' He pointed at her dress. 'Is that for his benefit, too?'

'What on earth do you mean?'

'He's just a lad, Finn. He doesn't need you encouraging him, leading him on.'

'I was just being friendly! Anyway, what's it got to do with you? Are you his mum, or something?'

'No, but I'm his mate. And I don't want you to get his hopes up. It's me who has to listen to him droning on and on about you all day.'

'Sorry if it's boring for you.'

'It isn't that.'

There was something about the way he said it that made Finn look at him. 'Then what is it?'

Ryan hesitated. 'It doesn't matter.' He made to move past her, but Finn grabbed his sleeve. The touch was like electricity, stopping them both in their tracks.

'What were you going to say?'

A gaggle of girls tottered past them, pushing them closer together. The warmth of his body against hers made it hard for her to breathe.

'Ryan?' She looked up into his face and suddenly she felt as if she was fourteen again, and in the grip of that overpowering infatuation she'd felt when he'd first walked in with Ciaran and her father – a tall, brooding young man who regarded the world with watchful eyes, taking everything in and giving nothing away.

'You don't know what it's like,' he said. 'Hearing him going on about you, when all the time—'

'Ryan!' They looked around. Wendy was coming up the corridor towards them, a glass of vodka in her hand, looking furious.

Finn heard Ryan's sigh. 'What are you doing here?'

'Looking for you.' She waved her drink at Finn. 'So is this why you've been avoiding me?'

'Can we talk about this later?'

'How can we talk about anything when you won't answer my calls?' Her voice rose hysterically. 'I want to know, Ryan. Is *she* the reason you dumped me?'

'Now hang on a minute—'

Wendy swung round to face her, teetering on her high heels. 'And you can shut up,' she snapped. 'You've been after him for ages, haven't you? Trying to worm your way between us.' She thrust her face closer to Finn's. Her lipgloss was smeared beyond the corners of her mouth. 'You're never going to get your claws into him.'

'I'll get my claws into you if you don't back off.' Finn put her hands up to protect herself, and Wendy staggered back.

'Did you see that? She pushed me. I could have you for assault.'

'Why don't you shut up and go home before you make an even

bigger fool of yourself?' Finn shrugged her off and turned away, just as Gina came rushing towards her. She had Finn's bag in one hand, her phone in the other.

'It's someone called Orla,' she said breathlessly, holding it out to her. 'She says they've found your brother.'

Chapter 21

'He's at the police station. I'll have to go,' she said, ending the call.

'I'll come with you,' Ryan said.

Finn looked at Wendy. 'You stay and sort her out. I'll go on my own. I can catch a cab.'

'I'll take you,' Gina offered.

Finn was about to refuse, then stopped herself. She was in such a state all she could think about was getting to her brother. 'Thanks,' she said.

But when they got to the station she wasn't allowed to see him. 'He's talking to the duty solicitor, then we've got to interview him,' the officer behind the desk said. 'It could be hours. You might as well go home and wait.'

'But what if he gets out and I'm not here?'

The police officer laughed. 'You think they'll let him out again after he did a runner?' He shook his head. 'They'll stick him on remand for sure. You might as well go home.'

'I'll stay here anyway, if it's all the same to you.'

The officer shrugged. 'I don't mind what you do. But I'm warning you, those chairs can get a bit hard after a few hours.'

She went to sit back down, just as Gina returned with two cups of coffee.

'I thought you might need this,' she said.

'Thanks.' Finn looked at Gina. She seemed so cool and out of place in her immaculate clothes, her make-up still perfect even under the harsh strip-lighting.

'Any news?'

'They won't let me see him.'

'Do you want me to give you a lift home?'

'Oh no, I'm staying.'

'But you just said—'

'I'm not leaving here until I make sure he's all right. However long it takes.'

She directed a long, level look at the officer behind the desk. If she pestered him often enough he was bound to relent eventually and try to help them. Either that or lock her in a cell, too. Then she noticed Gina's anxious look.

'It's OK, you don't have to stay with me.'

'I don't mind.'

The truth was Finn almost wished she would go home. She felt awkward sitting there in silence.

'Won't your husband be wondering where you are?'

'I doubt it,' Gina said shortly.

The silence between them stretched for a while longer.

Then Gina said, 'Will the rest of your family be coming soon?'

Finn shook her head. 'I've asked Orla not to tell my dad until I've sorted this out.'

'Surely he'd want to know?'

'I'll tell him later. I'm going to kill Ciaran when I get my hands on him.'

'Why are you here if you feel like that?'

'Because he's family.'

'But he's caused you so much trouble?'

'I know, but he's still my brother. And families stick together.' She looked at the officer behind the desk. 'I'm going to ask if I can see him yet.'

'But they've already said no.'

'Then I'll just have to make a nuisance of myself until they say yes, won't I?'

'Throw one of your tantrums, you mean?' Gina was tight-lipped. 'That'll get you a long way.'

Finn glared at her. 'Do you have any better ideas?'

'As a matter of fact, I have.' She handed Finn her coffee cup. 'Here, hold this.'

'Where are you going?'

'I won't be a minute.'

Finn watched, puzzled, as Gina went up to the counter and spoke quietly to the duty officer. She saw him look at Gina, then over at Finn, then back at Gina. Finally he nodded briefly and went off into the back room.

Gina returned. 'He's going to see what he can do,' she said. 'He thinks you might be able to see your brother for a couple of minutes before the police interview him.'

'Really?' Finn stared at her, shocked. 'How did you manage that?'

'I told him my husband was the local MP.'

Finn looked impressed. 'Blimey, that's a good one. How did you think that one up?'

'My husband *is* the local MP.'

'Really? You never told me that.'

'You never asked.'

Finn stared sidelong at Gina as she sat sipping her coffee. Come to think of it, they'd never really talked.

'Thanks,' she said.

'Anything's better than you making an exhibition of yourself and getting us both locked up.'

Before she could open her mouth to reply, the duty officer emerged and called her over.

'You've got five minutes,' he warned her sternly. 'And I'll be watching you.'

He was true to his word. Finn had strictly five minutes, but it was all she needed to find out that her brother was all right, if a little tired and dirty. He'd made it all the way down to Birmingham where he'd been sleeping rough or on friends' floors. He'd finally been picked up by the police after a 'misunderstanding' outside a pub.

By the time she came out Gina had gone and Ryan was waiting in her place.

'Where's Gina?' Finn asked.

'Gone home. I told her I'd stay with you. How's Ciaran?'

'A bit shaken up, but I think he's relieved it's all over. They're not planning to let him out though.'

'I'm not surprised.'

'How's Wendy?'

'I've taken her home.' Ryan glanced around uneasily. 'Can we get out of here? I hate these places.'

'OK. There's no point in staying now I've seen Ciaran. I might as well go home and let Dad and Orla know what's going on.'

'I'll give you a lift.'

They drove home in silence. Finn felt overwhelmingly sleepy, as if all the emotions of the day had finally caught up with her. She could feel her eyelids drooping in the warmth of the car.

Ryan was quiet, too. She glanced across at him. His gaze was fixed on the road ahead but from the set of his jaw and the way his hands gripped the wheel it was obvious his thoughts were somewhere else.

She closed her eyes and let her mind drift back to that moment in the club earlier on. What had he been about to say to her? She'd never found out. But it felt as if that moment had changed everything. Suddenly he'd stopped being Ryan, her father's apprentice, her brother's friend, and become an attractive man.

It was madness, of course, she told herself. There was no way it would ever work between them. She wasn't Ryan's type, was she? Anyway, neither of them was much good at sustaining relationships. What if they did get together and it all went wrong? Then she would have lost him as a friend for ever. It would certainly make working together hellishly awkward.

What was she thinking? He hadn't even kissed her, and already she was breaking up with him in her mind.

What would kissing him be like? she wondered then. She tried to imagine it, the feel of his lips against hers, slow and soft at first, then gradually becoming more urgent . . .

'We're here.'

She opened her eyes, startled that they were parked outside her house when she'd been a million miles away, in the middle of a lovely dream.

'Looks like they're waiting for you.' Ryan nodded towards the house, where lights still blazed in every window.

'Do you want to come in?' she offered.

'Only if you need moral support.'

'No, I can handle that. I just thought you might like a coffee, or something?'

'You're inviting me in for a coffee?' Ryan frowned at her, puzzled. As well he might, she thought. She was behaving like an idiot, and for no apparent reason.

'You're right, it was a stupid idea.' She scrabbled for the door handle, suddenly embarrassed. 'I'll see you in the morning, OK?'

'No, wait. I'd like that.' He took a deep breath. 'Besides, we should talk – about what happened earlier.'

So she hadn't imagined it. 'You'd better come in, then.'

Her dad was surprisingly calm when he found out Ciaran was back in police custody. 'At least we know where he is now,' he said. 'That's a weight off my mind. I didn't like to think of him out there on his own.'

He looked as if he would have liked to settle down for a good old chat with Ryan, but Orla firmly and tactfully suggested he go to bed. Finn tried to ignore the knowing look Orla gave her as she followed him out of the room.

She put the coffees down in front of them and curled up on the sofa, her feet tucked underneath her. Ryan sat at the far end of the sofa, staring into the empty fireplace. Finn waited for him to make the first move, but he didn't.

'So what did you want to talk about?' she said.

'I don't really know where to start.'

This wasn't going to be easy, she decided. Ryan was never the most talkative of people. Getting him to open up and admit his feelings was like pulling teeth. 'What were you going to say to me earlier on in the club?'

'That's not important now.'

'It might be.' She hesitated. 'Because if you were going to tell me you liked me – you know, in that way?' She could feel herself blushing as she said it, 'I was going to say I think I like you, too. In that way.'

Silence opened up between them like a yawning chasm. She didn't dare look at Ryan, but she could feel him staring at her. Suddenly it began to dawn on her that she might have made a terrible, embarrassing mistake. 'Well, say something!' she begged.

'Wendy's pregnant,' he said. Another silence. He glanced at her. 'Now it's your turn to say something.'

All kinds of thoughts tumbled over each other in her brain. 'When did you find this out?' she managed to say at last.

'She told me after you'd gone. She's been texting me for days wanting to meet up, but I thought she was just pestering me again, looking for another excuse to nag me into going back to her. But it seems this time she was genuine.'

Finn looked down at the hem of her dress. A thread had come loose and was unravelling. 'What are you going to do about it?'

'What can I do?' He rubbed his hand across his brow. 'It's all a bloody mess.'

You're telling me, Finn thought, plucking furiously at the loose thread. 'She doesn't have to have it, does she?'

'That's what she wants.'

And you're going to stand by her. Finn knew that straight away. Whatever else he did, Ryan would never walk away from his responsibilities. She could have hit him for being so bloody honourable.

'So that's it, then,' she said flatly.

Ryan raised his gaze to meet hers. 'I'm sorry.'

'You don't have to apologize to me. I'm not the one who's pregnant.'

'You know what I mean. I never meant for any of this to happen. What you just said – about liking me—'

'Forget it.'

'But I just wanted you to know—'

'I said forget it!' Her cheeks burned with humiliation. She wished she'd never put herself on the line like that. 'As you said, it doesn't matter now, does it?'

Ryan stared down at his hands. 'I suppose not,' he admitted heavily.

★

'You did what? Christ, Gina, why did you have to drag my name into it?'

Stephen was still up when Gina came home just before eleven, Mark was with him. There were rumours that a May election was on the cards, and they were planning their campaign strategy. Papers were strewn all over the sitting-room floor.

'You're supposed to be their MP. I thought it was your job to help them?' she said.

'Not known felons, it isn't. I can just see the campaign slogan now – "Vote for Stephen Farrell, the Criminal's Friend." Bloody hell, Gina, I'd have thought even you would have more sense than that.'

'I wanted to help.'

'You weren't helping me much, were you? I suppose I can kiss goodbye to any chance of a ministerial post after this.' He ran his hand through his hair in exasperation. 'I don't know why you insist on working for these low-lives. I don't like it, and neither would your father.'

'He doesn't have to know about it.'

'Maybe someone should tell him?'

The colour drained from her face. 'You wouldn't?'

'Of course he wouldn't,' Mark put in swiftly. 'Would you, Steve?'

The two men stared at each other for moment. 'I suppose not,' Stephen said grudgingly. He stood up. 'I'm going to bed.'

'What about the campaign?'

'We can sort it out in the morning. I'm not in the mood now.' Shooting another furious look at Gina, he slammed out of the room.

'You mustn't mind him,' Mark said when he'd gone. 'He's under a lot of strain at the moment. He's terrified something's going to happen to make him lose his seat.'

'If he's that worried about scandal, maybe he should think about cleaning up his act,' Gina muttered.

'What do you mean?'

'Come on, Mark, I'm not stupid. I've worked out what's going on.'

'And what would that be?'

'I know about Stephen and Lucy.'

Mark's face paled. 'What about them?'

'Well, they practically live together. And when they're apart they're always phoning and texting each other.'

'They work very closely together.'

'I also know they went to Scotland together. I found the ticket he'd hidden in his luggage. Why would he bother to hide it if there was nothing going on?'

Mark reached for the wine bottle and refilled his drink. He poured one for Gina, too. 'I'm sure I'd know if he was having an affair with her.'

'And I'm sure you wouldn't tell me about it if he was. Would you?'

She looked at his carefully blank face. Dear Mark, always the soul of discretion. She knew where his loyalties were bound to lie. She only wished she had a friend like him, someone who'd stick up for her through anything. Not even her own family would do that. Then she thought about Finn, waiting in the police station for her brother, and suddenly felt very lonely. Would anyone ever wait for her like that?

The next thing she knew she was crying, and Mark had his arms around her.

'I'm sorry,' she sobbed. 'It's probably just my wretched hormones or something. I'll be all right in a minute.'

It felt so nice in Mark's warm, comforting arms that she wanted to stay there, safe and protected. Finally she forced herself to pull away.

'Better?' Mark reached up and brushed a damp strand of hair from her cheek. His face was only inches away from hers. Their eyes met and suddenly it seemed like the most natural thing in the world to lean forward for a kiss . . .

For a moment he seemed to respond. Then he pulled away sharply.

'Oh God, I'm so sorry.' Gina put her hand over her mouth.

'It's OK, forget it.'

'I don't know why I did that. Forgive me.'

'No, honestly, it's fine.' He smiled feebly. 'Maybe it's your hormones again?'

She knew he was being kind, but it didn't make her feel any better. She buried her face in her hands. 'You must think I'm completely awful.'

He pulled her hands away and held them in his. 'I think you're the sweetest woman I know. You're just a bit confused at the moment, that's all. This is a very emotional time for you.'

'Don't. Please don't make excuses for me.' Gina couldn't meet his eye. The nicer he was the more wretched she felt. 'I think you'd better go now.'

'You're probably right.'

She didn't move as he found his coat and prepared to leave.

'I hope you're not going to let this stand in the way of us being friends?' Mark said.

She tried, and failed, to smile. 'I reckon it might be best if we stayed out of each other's way for a while, don't you?'

'If that's what you want.' As he was leaving, he turned. 'If it's any consolation to you, I think you could do a lot better than an idiot like Stephen,' he said. 'And if he wasn't my best friend then I probably wouldn't have pulled away when I did.'

Chapter 22

'Gina?'

'Daddy?' She looked around guiltily, as if he could somehow see her sitting behind her desk in the Delaneys' office.

'Don't sound so surprised. Aren't I allowed to call my own daughter?'

'No. I mean, yes, of course.' But he never did, so why now? 'What can I do for you?'

'I wondered if you could come and see me? How about this lunchtime?'

Gina frowned. 'I suppose so. Why?'

'I'll tell you when you get here. Don't worry, it's nothing too serious. Be here about one, OK?'

She ended the call on her mobile, feeling suddenly depressed. She'd been fine until then. Ryan and Finn had gone to court for Ciaran's appearance before the magistrates and Gina had the office to herself. She'd pottered around, sorting through the morning's post and mentally planning the rest of the day. She was considering putting some of the accounts on computer. It would certainly make it easier to keep track, although she wasn't sure how Finn would feel about it. She swore every time she went near a keyboard.

The February sun was shining and she'd felt happy in her own little world. This scruffy office was her domain. As she gazed out of the window at the yard, littered with piles of bricks and ladders, she'd never felt more at home. And then her father had called and spoilt everything.

But why had he called? It wasn't serious, he'd said. But Max Tate wasn't in the habit of making social calls, especially not to his daughter.

Whatever it was, it had to be personal, or he would have got his secretary to call her. Perhaps it had something to do with her parents' wedding anniversary. Their thirty-fifth was coming up the following month and her mother had organized a party. Maybe he wanted Gina's advice on a suitable gift, or, more likely, he wanted her to buy it. She'd never known her father to worry about birthdays and anniversaries; the women in his life dealt with all that.

It felt strange, walking into the Tate offices again. The receptionist greeted her coolly and sent her straight upstairs, where her father and brothers had their offices. There was no sign of Neil or James, but Nicole was waiting in Max's outer office.

'What are you doing here?' she said when Gina walked in.

'I'm here to meet my father.'

'You'll wait a long time. He's been in a meeting with the accountant for hours. And I'm due to see him next.'

Gina sat down beside her, refusing to be put off by her sister-in-law's rudeness. It was odd how calm she felt. Usually her nerves would have been raging at the thought of being summoned to see her father. But a few weeks away had given her a lot more confidence. Now she wasn't so easily intimidated.

But that didn't stop her jumping when the door to Max's office opened and the accountant came out. 'About time,' Nicole muttered, and was about to walk in when he emerged.

'Ah, Gina. I'm glad you could come.' It was hard to tell who was more shocked, her or Nicole, when he crossed the room to greet her with a kiss. 'I thought it might be better if we talked over lunch. Janice's booked us a table at Luigi's.'

'Er – hello?' Nicole cut in. 'You and I have a meeting this lunchtime, don't you remember?'

'I'm afraid I'm going to have to cancel. I have something important to discuss with my daughter.' He turned to look at her. 'Family business, you understand?'

There was a moment's silence. Then Nicole said in a clipped voice, 'Fine. Let me know when you're free, won't you?'

'I'll get Janice to set up another meeting.'

Gina could hardly bear to look at Nicole as she swept past. She'd really hate being put in her place like that. Gina felt sorry for the rest of the Human Resources department; she had a feeling Nicole would be taking out her temper on them that afternoon.

By the time they arrived at the restaurant she was completely bemused. What was going on?

But in spite of her confusion, it still gave her a kick to see how all eyes turned to stare at them as they headed to their table. Her father's presence dominated the room, like a king holding court. The maître d' seemed to know him well, asking after him and his family. Gina was proud as Max introduced her as his daughter. She didn't know when she'd felt so special.

And her father was so attentive, too, asking about Stephen and Vicky. Even though he was being so charming, Gina found it difficult to make small-talk with him. Especially when he started asking about her new job.

'Oh, you know. It's just an office.' She shredded a bread roll, praying he wouldn't ask any more.

'What kind of office?'

'Just general, really. Admin, accounts, that kind of thing.'

'You're very vague, Gina. Is there something you're not telling me?' Before she could think up an answer, he said, 'I suppose it's none of my business. It's not as if you work for me any more.' He gazed at her across the table. 'As long as you're happy.'

'Yes, I am. Very.'

'Then maybe it was a good thing I fired you when I did.' His eyes twinkled. 'Otherwise you might have ended up like your brothers, living on the company payroll and waiting for me to die.'

'I'm sure they don't think like that,' Gina said, as the waiter bought their wine and poured some into a glass for her father to taste.

'Don't they? Sometimes I think they're a pair of jackals, Neil especially, watching my every move, waiting for me to show any weakness so they can move in for the kill. Although I can't blame them, it's the way I've brought them up.' He took a sip of the wine and nodded to the waiter. 'My heirs apparent.' He smiled. 'But the way things are going there might not be too much left to inherit.'

'Why? Is the business in trouble?'

'Nothing for you to worry about.' Max waved her question away. 'Let's not talk about it.'

The conversation was stilted as they ate their meal. Gina picked over her salad, wishing she could think of something interesting and worthwhile to say. Did everyone have this much trouble talking to their fathers? she wondered.

The conversation turned to the forthcoming anniversary party. Max already seemed bored by the whole event. 'Your mother's planning it all. I'm having nothing to do with it. No doubt she's got some extravaganza in mind. All I've got to do is pay for it all.' He sighed. 'I just hope it doesn't cost the earth.'

'You know Mummy. She has expensive tastes.'

'You're telling me.'

Gina noticed the troubled look that passed briefly across his face. It wasn't like her father to complain about her mother's spending, except in a long-suffering way as he wrote out another cheque. But this time it seemed different.

'Daddy, is something wrong?'

He stared across the table at her for a long time. 'I need to talk to you,' he said at last. 'It's about your trust fund.'

'What about it?'

Max looked down at his plate. For the first time she could remember, he seemed ill at ease. 'I know I set it up for you and Vicky, but the thing is, I might need access to it. Temporarily, at least. I'll pay it all back, with interest.'

Gina was stunned. She didn't care about the money, but she'd never imagined in a million years her father would ask her for a loan. 'Are things that bad?'

'We're having a few temporary cash-flow problems,' Max admitted, his voice low.

'But why?'

His gaze was piercing and direct. 'I think you'd better ask your friends the Delaneys that one.'

She gasped, as if someone had thrown a bucket of icy water over her. 'How did you know?'

'Your husband telephoned me. I gather he doesn't approve of you working for them?'

Bloody Stephen. 'He promised he wouldn't say anything.'

'He's a politician, Gina. You should know what their promises are worth. So it's true, then? You're working for the Delaneys?'

She took a deep breath. 'Look, I know there have been some problems between you in the past, but I don't want to get involved. The fact is, I needed a job and I enjoy working there. And I'm not going to give it up,' she added, surprising herself with her defiance.

'Relax, I'm not asking you to. You're a grown woman, I can't tell you what to do.'

Gina eyed him uncertainly. 'You don't mind?'

'Of course I mind. But there isn't much I can do about it, is there?' He regarded her thoughtfully. 'I suppose you know she and her father are out to ruin me?'

'That's exactly what she says about you.'

'Why would I waste my time doing that?' He shook his head. 'All I want is what's rightfully mine.'

'The land?'

'Exactly. It should have been ours. We had an agreement with the owner. It was the only reason we went ahead and bought the plot behind it, on the understanding that we'd have first refusal on the land adjoining the road. Ours is useless without it.'

'But the Delaneys bought it fair and square.'

'I know that. We were both conned by the land-owner. He got greedy, thought he could push the price up. While I was trying to do a deal with him, he went and sold it to Joe Delaney. We were double-crossed.'

'So why didn't you take the landowner to court?'

'We could have done. But I thought it would be easier all round if we just explained the situation to the Delaneys and bought the land back. Except Mr Delaney decided he didn't want to sell.'

'Finn says you didn't offer a fair price.'

'The price was extremely fair, under the circumstances.' Max's voice rose. 'It's all he'd get for it on the open market. Especially with no planning consent.'

Gina was quiet for a moment. 'They think you fixed that so they'd get turned down.'

Max laughed. 'Who do they think I am, God?'

'You do know a few councillors.'

'Yes, I do. And I admit they've done me some favours in the past. But there's no way I could have that much influence.' He shook his head. 'Think about it. If I could affect decisions like that, why wouldn't I just get them to give me planning permission and forget about trying to get hold of Delaneys' land? I got turned down myself, remember?'

She hadn't thought of that. In that respect, Finn's claims didn't make sense at all.

'At the moment that land is useless to both of us,' Max went on. 'They'll never let Joe Delaney build houses on it, but they would let me use it to build an access road to my site. But it seems Delaneys have decided that if they can't use it, no one can. And unfortunately it's costing me money. I borrowed a huge amount from the bank to buy that land and I'm still having to make repayments on it even though we've got nothing to show for it. It's all cash down the drain.'

'But you can afford it, can't you?'

'At any other time, yes. If the rest of the business was doing well. But unfortunately we're having a few problems in other areas. The Windmill Meadows houses aren't moving as fast as we'd hoped, thanks to the slump in the market and your friend Finn's bad publicity.' He grimaced. 'Usually we would have weathered the storm, but the company's vulnerable . . .' He put down his knife and fork. 'Finn Delaney said she'd ruin me, and it looks like she couldn't have picked a better time.'

Gina sat back in her seat, stunned. 'Finn said that? When?'

'A couple of months back. Before Christmas.' Max regarded

her carefully. 'Are you sure you want to hear this? I don't want to put you in a difficult position.'

'I'm already in a difficult position, aren't I?' Gina pointed out.

'True. Like I said, it happened a couple of months ago. When Finn was working for us on the Windmill Meadows site. You knew she'd worked for us, I take it?' Gina nodded. 'From what I gather, she was a pretty good worker. But Finn thought she was too good. Better than a lot of the men who'd been working on site for years. Kept giving them orders, telling them what to do.'

I can believe that, Gina thought. 'So what happened?'

'She decided she wanted to be site manager, even though there were other people who were far more experienced than she was. When she got turned down, she started bleating about sex discrimination and how she'd been treated unfairly.'

'And was she?'

'Absolutely not. Like I said, there were far more experienced people who deserved the job more than she did. But she threatened us with all kinds of tribunals. She made a real nuisance of herself.'

'So what did you do?'

'I told her to get lost, obviously. And she told me I'd live to regret it. She swore she'd bring us down if she could. Two days later there was an accident on site. Some poor bloke fell off scaffolding and nearly broke his neck.'

'What did that have to do with Finn?'

'I really can't say.' Max regarded her steadily. 'But the health and safety people reckoned the scaffolding was unsafe because it had been tampered with.'

Gina gasped. She didn't like Finn much, but she couldn't imagine her deliberately putting someone's life in danger.

'Oh, I don't suppose she knew anyone would be using it,' Max went on. 'I think she just planned to make some trouble. And mud sticks, as you saw when she turned up at the Windmill Meadows opening. Since then she's been doing a lot of whispering against us, claiming all kinds of things. People are beginning to ask questions.'

Gina remembered how Finn had bitched about the Tates, blaming them for everything.

'Usually we could ride out a bit of bad publicity,' Max said. 'But, as I said, we've taken a few too many risks lately, and it's beginning to tell.' He saw Gina's worried face and smiled wearily. 'Hopefully things will pick up. Once we buy that last house on Paradise Road we can start developing and then maybe the cash will start rolling in again.'

Paradise Road. Gina remembered what Finn had said about her brother being asked to torch a house there. 'Why has it come up for sale?'

'I've no idea.' Max shrugged. 'The old couple have just decided they wanted to sell up at last. They're getting on a bit. I expect they want a nice quiet bungalow somewhere.'

So, that was another of Finn's lies. And she'd almost believed it.

'So you see why I need the money from your trust fund?' Max said. 'It is just a temporary measure, until the cash-flow picks up.'

'Of course,' Gina agreed. 'Send me the papers and I'll sign them. I just wish I could do more to help.'

An ominous silence followed her words. Max stared at her intently. 'Do you really mean that?'

'Yes, of course. Why?'

There was another silence. 'Maybe there is something you can do,' her father said slowly.

Gina felt suddenly wary. 'What?'

'Help me get even with Delaneys.'

How did she know this had been coming? Ever since she realized her father knew about her working for them, she'd felt it hanging over her head. 'What did you have in mind?' she asked, toying with her coffee spoon.

'You have access to their estimates, don't you?'

'Ye-es.'

'What if you were to tell us what they were quoting for jobs? We could go in and undercut them. It wouldn't have to be for long,' he added quickly, seeing Gina's face fall. 'But if we put the squeeze on them it might convince them to start liquidizing their assets. Then we could buy the land.'

'At a fair price?' Gina asked.

'Of course.' But there was a glint in her father's eye that made her think his idea of a fair price wouldn't be the same as Finn's. But then Finn *had* set out to ruin her father, she reminded herself.

'But they're only small jobs,' she protested. 'Way too small for you.'

'Don't you believe it,' Max said. 'The way things are at the moment I'd gladly put up an old lady's back fence myself if it meant a few more quid in the bank.'

'I had no idea.'

'No reason why you should. Luckily I've managed to keep most of our trouble to myself – even James and Neil don't know the full extent of it. But it's possible some of our properties might have to go. Including Lytton Grange.'

Gina was appalled. She'd never imagined things were so bad they might lose their family home. She could imagine what a blow that would be to her father. Lytton Grange represented everything he'd achieved in his life.

The waiter arrived with the bill, and she caught a glance of the total. 'Why are you spending so much in a place like this, if things are so bad?'

'If I didn't, people would start to sense something was wrong.' He dropped his credit card on to the silver plate. 'Let me tell you a little story. When I first started out in this business I didn't have a penny to my name. But I needed people to take me seriously and the bank to lend me large amounts of money. So, do you know what I did? I went to the tailors and bought myself the best suit I could find. I had to starve myself to do it but I knew I had to have it. And it worked. No one treated me like a snotty street urchin with no money to his name. They treated me with respect, and they fell over themselves to lend me money.' He pointed his finger at her, his face intent. 'It's all about impressions in this business. If you act like you're a millionaire, people will treat you like one, even if you don't have two halfpennies to rub together. But if you give the impression you're down on your luck, they'll be on you like wolves. And I've been torn apart too often in my life to let it happen again.' He caught her worried expression and smiled. 'I know I shouldn't be telling you all this,' he said. 'I've always tried to shield my family from the harsh realities of life. Especially you and your mother. I never wanted you to worry about anything. But I'm afraid you're the only one I can depend on now.' He reached across the table and patted her hand. 'This isn't easy for me to admit, but I'm relying on you, Gina.'

Gina looked down at his big hand covering hers. She felt torn in two. Flattered that her father had confided in her, she wanted desperately to help him. But at the same time . . .

'I'm sorry, I can't,' she said regretfully. 'I'll help you in any other way I possibly can – you can have *all* my trust fund money. But don't ask me to do something that wouldn't be right.'

She caught the thwarted look that flashed across his face and braced herself, waiting for the storm to rain down on her. But he just smiled.

'I somehow thought you'd say that,' he admitted ruefully. 'I don't know where you get those moral scruples from, though. Must be your mother's side of the family.'

'You – don't mind?'

'Well, obviously I'd rather you'd agreed to help me. But if you won't do it, I'll just have to deal with the problem some other way. I hope you understand I had to try. When I found out you were working for the Delaneys it seemed too good to be true. Almost as if fate was throwing me a lifeline . . .' He looked wistful. 'But life's kicked me in the teeth before and I've survived. I'm sure I'll be able to do it again.'

'I know you will,' Gina said, feeling horribly guilty.

'Oh, I'm not worried about me.' Max shrugged. 'I'm a survivor. I might even relish the challenge of going back and starting again. But it's your mother I'm worried about. She's always been used to the best in life, being pampered. I don't how she'd cope if we lost everything.'

Gina privately wondered if a harsh dose of reality wouldn't be good for her mother, but said nothing. It hurt her to see her father so low, and to know she could have done something to help.

'I'm so sorry,' was all she could say.

She felt wretched all the way back to the office. Maybe she

should have done as her father asked. After all, if Finn had done all the things he'd said, she deserved her comeuppance. But at the same time she knew two wrongs didn't make a right. And it wouldn't just be Finn Delaney who suffered, it would be her father Joe, too. And possibly Ryan. Gina knew that he'd given up a lot of his own work to help the Delaneys, and she liked him too much to see him lose out.

Back at the restaurant, Max slipped a £50 tip into the waiter's hand and ordered another brandy. As an afterthought, he asked for a cigar to go with it. He deserved one, after the blinding performance he'd put on that afternoon.

He thought about his daughter's distraught face as she'd left the restaurant. Poor Gina; he'd almost felt like crying himself. Trust her to be troubled by a conscience. She didn't have the killer instinct of her brothers, though James seemed to have gone a bit soft lately, since he'd hooked up with that scruffy girl.

But it had been worth it in the end, he decided, all the time he'd spent softening Gina up. She might have said no, but he knew his daughter better than she thought. Conscience or no conscience, it was only a matter of time before she came round to his way of thinking.

Finn and Ryan were in the office when she got back.

'Where have you been?' Finn turned on her the moment she walked in. She'd been going through the in-tray, scattering all Gina's carefully arranged papers.

Gina's resentment resurfaced. 'I had to go out. Why? Were you looking for something?'

'The company cheque book. I usually keep it in this drawer.' She upended another pile of papers on to the desk.

'I've locked it in the safe. I didn't think it was a good idea leaving it lying around. I'll get it for you, shall I?' She gritted her teeth, determined not to let Finn's bad mood wind her up.

'I wish you'd told me.' Finn watched Gina fiddling with the combination. 'Sometimes I wonder who's running this wretched company.'

'You're welcome,' Gina said, as Finn left the office, letting the door bang shut behind her.

'I'm sorry about that,' Ryan said.

'It's not you who should be apologizing.' Gina looked out of the window to where Finn was marching across the yard, then back to all the paperwork she'd left tipped out on her desk.

'You'll have to forgive her. She's had a rough morning. They've remanded Ciaran in custody.'

I'm not surprised, Gina thought. Did she seriously expect the magistrate to let him out so he could run away again? 'That doesn't give her the right to act like a spoilt child.' She hadn't realized she'd said it aloud until she saw the surprised look on Ryan's face.

'You're probably right,' he agreed. 'But there's another reason she's in a bad mood. I think she's angry with me.'

'Why? What have you done?'

Ryan gazed at the door. 'Let's just say I've let her down.'

After Ryan had gone, Gina set about picking up the papers Finn had scattered over her desk. As she picked up the first pile, she spotted the latest batch of estimates lying in the in-tray. Finn must have put them there that morning for her to type up.

She stared at them for a moment. Then she remembered the way Finn had spoken to her. Why should she deserve Gina's loyalty?

But her family did. They'd supported her through some bad times in her life. Now it was about time she paid them back.

She remembered something Finn had said, when they were sitting in the police station: *Families stick together.* Perhaps it was about time she started sticking with hers.

She took a deep breath, picked up the phone and dialled the number before she changed her mind.

'Hello? May I speak to my father please?'

Chapter 23

Orla was going home. Finn sat on the bed and watched her pack. 'We'll miss you,' she said. In the few weeks she'd been staying with them, she'd almost become part of the family.

'Miss having me under your feet, you mean.' Orla wedged her shoes into a corner of the suitcase. 'I've already stayed far longer than I meant to. I'll bet you'll be glad to have the place to yourself.'

'Are you serious? I don't know how I would have coped without you. I've loved having you here. And so has Dad.'

'Do you think so?' Orla's face brightened for a moment, then grew serious again. 'Well, I reckon you can both do well enough without me now,' she said briskly. 'Your father's almost back on his feet again, and you're busy with the business—'

'I wish,' Finn said. 'We're hardly busy at all these days.'

She'd never known it so slow. Usually there would be a steady stream of work for the month ahead. But even though she'd been out quoting for jobs for the past three weeks, for the first time she could remember, there was nothing booked in the diary.

'I daresay it will pick up soon,' she said, seeing Orla's worried expression. She would only tell her father, and Finn didn't want the bad news to get back to him just yet. She hoped the situation might have improved before he asked to see the books again.

Orla sent her a sideways look. 'Maybe your friend Ryan could put some work your way?'

'I doubt it. And he's not my friend either,' she added. They'd barely spoken since that awful night when he'd told her Wendy was pregnant.

'Oh dear, I'm sorry to hear that. Have you two had a row?'

'You could say that.' She was still bitterly angry with him for ending up in such a mess. Angry and disappointed.

'You should make it up with him before someone else snaps him up,' Orla said.

'It's a bit late for that.' Finn thought about confiding in her about Wendy, then changed her mind. 'Who says I want him, anyway?' She'd already decided that it was better to forget about Ryan completely.

'I do. And I'm old enough and wise enough to know what I'm talking about, believe me. I've got eyes in my head, I can see the way you look at him. If he's what you want you should grab him while you've got the chance. Don't make the same mistakes I did.'

Finn was intrigued. 'What mistakes?'

'Let's just say I let my chance slip through my fingers.' Orla began stuffing clothes into her case, her head down.

'Was this before or after you married Uncle Donal?'

'Long before. When I was still a teenager.' She looked up and saw Finn's face. 'And no, I'm not going to tell you about it.'

'Go on. You can't start a story like that and not finish it.' She crossed her legs and hugged her knees, settling down for a good yarn. 'So does he still live in Killmane, this old flame of yours?'

'Oh no, he moved on a long time ago.'

'Do you ever see him?'

'Sometimes.'

'And is the old spark still there?'

'That's none of your business.' Orla glared at Finn, her arms full of folded jumpers. Then she sighed and plonked herself down on the bed. 'Look, it's no big deal. I fell in love with this boy when I was very young and very stupid. Only, like you, I was too proud to do anything about it. I had my suspicions that he liked me, but there was no way I was going to make the first move and risk making a fool of myself.'

Too late for me, Finn thought. She'd already revealed far too much of how she felt. 'So what happened?'

'He married my best friend.'

'But I thought Mum was—' She stopped dead. 'You mean you were in love with my dad?'

'Shh! Not so loud.' Orla darted a look over her shoulder towards the door. 'Like I said, it was a long time ago.'

'Did my mum know?'

'I think so, but there was never any bitterness between us. We both knew I'd had my chance and I'd let it pass. It was only fair she should get him. Anyway, it all worked out for the best.' She smiled bravely. 'They loved each other very much and they were wonderfully happy together.'

Finn wondered if she'd been so happy with her own choice of husband. Or had she married Donal O'Brien on the rebound?

'It was just a teenage crush, nothing more.' Orla stood up to continue packing. 'I daresay your father doesn't even remember it.'

'But you do?'

'Of course. You never forget your first love, do you?'

'And do you still love him?'

'Joe's a good friend.'

'But do you love him?'

Orla looked wistful. 'Why do you think I have to go back to Killmane?' she said.

She and Ryan were working together the following day. He was helping her finish the roof of the Stephensons' extension.

'Don't reach over so far,' he called up as she stood on tiptoe on the top rung of the ladder and leaned over to tap the lead flashing in place. 'Come down and let me move the ladder.'

'There's no need.' She took another nail out of her tool belt and positioned it carefully. 'I'll just finish this next piece—'

'Finn, you're over-stretching. Come down now or I'll come up and get you.'

She leaned over to prove her point, lost her footing and almost toppled off. She heard Ryan's sharp intake of breath from below, and managed to steady herself.

'*Now* will you do as you're told?'

'I'm fine,' she insisted as she climbed down the ladder.

Although she was still shaking so much so that she missed the last two rungs and would have fallen if Ryan hadn't caught her. 'I know what I'm doing.' But as she'd come down she'd twisted her hand. She tried to move her fingers experimentally, wincing as a sharp pain shot up her arm.

'What's the matter? Have you hurt your hand? Let's have a look at it.'

'I'm fine.' She snatched it away. 'Stop fussing.'

They went back to work, this time with Ryan up the ladder. Finn watched him from below, taking the chance to study him. It was a warm March day and he'd taken off his flannel workshirt to reveal a white T-shirt. She admired the way the fabric stretched across his broad shoulders and found herself idly wondering what he'd look like without it.

This was no good, she told herself. She shouldn't keep day-dreaming about what might have been. She'd missed her chance, just like Orla.

They worked in near silence for the rest of the morning. It wasn't until they were heading home in the van that Ryan struck up a conversation. 'I've been thinking,' he said. 'I've got a load of shop renovations to do. They're pretty big jobs and I could use some help. Would you like to do them?'

Finn eyed him sceptically. It wasn't like Ryan to take on a job he couldn't handle. 'We don't need hand-outs, Ryan.'

'I'm not offering any. You need work and I need help. I can't see a problem.'

'I'll think about it.'

'You do that.' He smiled slightly. But his face clouded again when they pulled into the Delaney yard and saw the yellow Citroën parked there. Finn recognized it immediately.

'What a surprise, your stalker's here. Can't let you out of her sight for a minute, can she?'

Ryan climbed out of the van. Wendy came across the yard towards them.

'Hello, sweetheart.' She reached up and planted a kiss on his cheek, leaving an imprint of cerise lipgloss. 'All ready to go shopping?'

'I said I'd meet you in town.'

'I couldn't wait, could I? I'm so excited.' She beamed at Finn. 'Ryan and I are going shopping for something special.'

'A ball and chain?'

'An engagement ring, actually.' Wendy threaded her arm through Ryan's. 'Didn't he tell you? We're getting married.'

Finn's stomach plummeted. She stared at Ryan. 'Congratulations,' she managed to say. Then she turned and headed across the yard.

Behind her, she heard Ryan telling a protesting Wendy to wait in the car. He caught up with her in the timber shed.

'Finn, wait.'

'Nice of you to let me know.' She hated her voice for sounding so thick with emotion.

'I tried to tell you, but—'

'But what? You were too much of a coward?'

'I didn't want it to be true.' His eyes flickered, full of emotion. Finn steeled herself against the impulse to take him in her arms.

'Go back to your fiancée, Ryan.' She looked over his shoulder to where Wendy was leaning against the side of the car, tapping her foot. 'She's waiting for you.'

Gina watched them from the window with a wrench of guilt. She felt as if she was in the middle of a situation she couldn't control.

In some ways, she'd never been happier. After agreeing to help her father, suddenly her status in the family had risen. Her mother called and asked her to go shopping, her brothers – even Neil – were more than civil. And her father treated her like a princess. For the first time in her life she felt as if she really belonged in the Tate family.

And yet she hadn't felt so wretched in years.

Her life might have got better, but it meant other people being miserable, and she couldn't stand that. It went against her nature to hurt anyone, especially people who trusted her.

She looked around the office. She'd even stopped enjoying her job. It didn't feel like her sanctuary any more. Her family had invaded her space and now it was all spoiled. Thank God it was over for another day. The stress of smiling and acting as if everything was fine when she was double-crossing them had been like a physical pain inside her all day.

She stood up and reached over for her bag when she realized something was wrong. She stopped dead, her hand instinctively over her stomach.

She looked out of the window. Ryan and Wendy had gone, but Finn was still unloading the van in the yard.

She hammered on the glass with the flat of her hand, yelling. For a moment Finn carried on, back and forth across the yard; Gina realized the radio was blaring out and Finn couldn't hear her. Frantically, she wrenched at the window lock, throwing it open.

'Finn,' she called out. 'Please, help me. I think I'm losing my baby!'

'What do you mean, Mr Farrell's still busy? His wife's in hospital, for Christ's sake! Never mind his wretched diary – you tell him to get his backside straight up here!'

Finn hung up, still fuming. How dare that high-handed bitch speak to her like that? 'Mr Farrell's busy' indeed! She'd already phoned four times, and the snotty cow still refused to put her through. And all the time his wife was losing their baby. What the hell was he doing that was more important than being with her?

She stuffed her phone back into her bag and hurried back into the private hospital. The plush reception area and corridors looked more like a posh hotel.

The last couple of hours had been a nightmare. After hearing Gina cry out, she'd rushed to the office to find her in a panic. Somehow she'd managed to bundle her into the car and get her to hospital. But by then it was too late.

She'd felt so inadequate as she'd held Gina in her arms and stroked her hair while she sobbed her heart out. The most she could do was try to be practical. She talked to the nurses, made sure Gina had everything she needed. And she called her husband repeatedly.

Every time she had to go back into Gina's private room and tell her she hadn't managed to reach him, she saw the light fade a bit more from her eyes.

Thank heavens they'd given her something to help her sleep, so she was woozy by the time Finn went outside to call for the fourth time. But she opened her eyes when she slipped back into the room to check on her.

'Any luck?' she whispered. Her face was as white as the pillow. Her room, like the rest of the hospital, was all low lighting, warm peach walls and Scandinavian designer furniture.

'He's – um – on his way.'

'Liar.' Gina managed a faint smile.

Finn blushed. 'Sorry, I did try.'

'I know. It doesn't matter now, anyway.' She looked away. A cluster of tears gathered in the corner of her eye and rolled on to the pillow. 'I'm sorry,' she said. 'I'm sure the last thing you need is me blubbing away in front of you.'

'No, it's fine, honestly. But are you sure there's no one else I can phone? What about your mum?'

Gina shook her head. 'She's at a health spa.'

'But surely she'd want to be here?'

'I don't think she'd be much help.'

Finn was surprised. All her life, she'd imagined what it would be like to have a mother. She'd always thought every girl was close to her mum. 'There's no one else you'd like me to call? No friends, or anything?'

Gina shook her head. 'Not really. But you don't have to stay. I'll be OK.'

'I'm not going anywhere. Look,' she said as Gina was about to protest, 'you stayed with me at the police station when I needed you. The least I can do is be here for you.' She only wished she could do more. 'Now, is there anything you want?'

'There is something.'

'What's that?'

Gina gave her a watery smile. 'Stop being so nice to me. If you keep being kind I might start crying again.'

'So you'd rather I was my usual bitchy self?'

'It would make a change from everyone whispering around me.'

Then she started to cry anyway. Finn moved to the side of the bed to hug her. Her body was all bones and angles under her hospital gown.

'Come on, don't get upset.' As soon as she said it she realized how stupid it sounded. Of course the poor woman was going to be upset. She'd just lost her baby, for heaven's sake. How was she supposed to feel? 'Here, have a tissue.' She pulled one from the box beside the bed and stuffed it into Gina's hand.

'Thanks.' Gina shakily rubbed her eyes, her tears subsiding. 'I'm so sorry,' she said again. 'You must think I'm pathetic.'

'I think you're being very brave.' Her husband was the pathetic one, Finn thought. 'Are you absolutely sure I can't get you anything?'

'No, really, you've been very kind already.'

'But I haven't done anything.'

'You've been here, and that's what matters. I appreciate it.'

'Maybe I should try your husband again?' Finn suggested.

'Don't worry, he'll be here. I don't suppose he'll be in any hurry, though.'

'But it was his child, too!'

'I don't think Stephen sees it like that. He never wanted this baby,' she explained. 'I thought he'd get used to the idea, just as I had. But he didn't. He wanted me to have an abortion.' She sniffed back the tears. 'Looks like he saved himself some money, doesn't it?'

Finn had no idea what to say to that. Except maybe 'what a bastard', and somehow that didn't seem appropriate.

Gina must have noticed her appalled expression. 'I'm sorry, I shouldn't be telling you all this. I expect you've got enough problems of your own.'

She did, but somehow a failing business and a doomed love didn't seem important compared to Gina's tragic loss.

Gina stifled a yawn with the back of her hand. 'I'd quite like to sleep for a while, if you don't mind?'

'Of course.' Finn stood up. 'I'll pop back in the morning and see how you're getting on.'

'You don't have to,' Gina said.

'I want to.' And to her surprise, Finn realized she meant it.

★

Gina went to sleep, and dreamed about her baby. She was holding him in her arms, a little boy, all wrapped up in a blue knitted shawl. She was smiling down into his little face, and he was staring up at her with intense, unfocused eyes, the way Vicky used to when she was a baby.

But then her father came along and dragged him out of her arms. Gina tried to scream, but no sound came out. She couldn't follow him because her feet were rooted to the spot. All she could do was stand there, her mouth contorted in a silent scream, as he walked away with her baby.

She woke with a start. Stephen was sitting at her bedside. The table next to her was laden with flowers.

'How are you feeling?' he asked.

She pushed herself up against her pillows. 'How long have you been here?'

'Not long. I got here as soon as I got your message.'

'Where were you? Your mobile was switched off.'

'Yes, well, they don't approve of phones going off during debates in the House.'

'I thought you were in a meeting?'

'I was. And then I went straight into a debate.'

She could see from the way he avoided her eye that he was lying. But she was too exhausted and unhappy to care any more.

'So it's all over, then?' he said.

'The baby's gone, if that's what you mean.' And if you say it's probably all for the best so help me I'll kill you, she added silently.

'When did it happen?'

'This afternoon. I'd been having niggling pains all day but I was just leaving work when I started bleeding. I was frightened.' She hoped he might comfort her, but he didn't. 'Luckily Finn was around, so she brought me in.'

'Ah, so that was her? I was told some strange woman had been screeching down the phone every ten minutes.'

'She's been very good. She stayed with me.' When you should have been here, she thought. Stephen must have seen the accusation in her eyes because he looked away guiltily.

'I'm sorry,' he said.

'Are you? Let's face it, you never really wanted this baby, did you?'

Stephen looked taken aback. 'That's not true. OK, perhaps it took me a while to get used to the idea, but I was looking forward to being a father. Really,' he insisted as Gina looked sceptical. 'Did they say what caused it?' She shook her head. 'So they didn't think there was anything physical you might have done?'

'What makes you say that?'

'I just wondered, that's all. Sometimes certain things can bring it on. Like stress, for instance. Or a change of lifestyle.'

'What are you getting at?'

'I thought perhaps this new job of yours might have had something to do with it. After all, you have been working longer hours lately.'

If she hadn't felt so weak she might have hit him. How dare he try to make it seem that losing her baby was all her fault! As if she wasn't feeling bad enough. He was supposed to be reassuring her, trying to make her feel better. But instead he was heaping blame on her, making her feel she was in the wrong for losing a baby he'd never wanted in the first place. If anything had caused her stress it was him having an affair with another woman, she thought bitterly.

Just then the door opened a fraction and Mark stuck his head round. His face was almost hidden behind an enormous bouquet of gerberas.

'Sorry, am I interrupting?'

Yes, Gina wanted to scream. Just clear off and leave us alone for five minutes. Instead she forced a smile and said, 'Are those for me? How lovely.'

'I know they're hardly appropriate, but I didn't know what else to do.' As he put them by her bedside and swooped to kiss her cheek, Gina noticed his eyes were red-rimmed. He'd been crying. 'Oh Gina, I'm so sorry.'

Gina found herself hugging him, as another wave of misery swept over her. It should be Stephen holding her, she thought, not his friend. Stephen hadn't made any physical contact, not even reached out for her hand since he'd been here.

'You're a brave lady,' Mark said, releasing her. 'When Stephen first told me about this press conference I wasn't sure if it was a good idea. But if you really think you're up to it . . .'

'What press conference?'

Mark and Stephen exchanged glances. 'You haven't told her,' Mark said.

'I was just about to when you barged in,' Stephen snapped back.

'Told me what? What's going on?' She looked from one to the other.

'I've arranged for us to have a quick chat with the press,' Stephen said. 'I thought it might be a good idea to give them the whole story, just to get them off our backs. Don't worry, I'll be with you. And I'll answer anything difficult. You can let me do all the talking, if you like?'

'But you don't have to do it,' Mark put in quickly. 'If you feel it's too soon . . .'

'On the other hand, it might be better to get it over with,' Stephen added. 'You know what the press are like. They'll only go on snooping if we don't give them what they want. Don't look at me like that, it's not my fault I have a high profile, is it?' he added, as Gina and Mark stared at him.

'Stephen, your wife has just lost a baby. Your baby. If you seriously think she's in any state to be bullied into giving interviews—'

'Stephen's right,' Gina interrupted him. 'We should get it over with.'

'You see?' Stephen patted her hand. 'That's my girl.'

'And I expect the sympathy vote won't hurt your re-election chances, will it?'

Stephen looked at her blandly. 'The thought hadn't occurred to me.'

Chapter 24

She began to wish she hadn't agreed to the press conference by the time the ranks of journalists and photographers were ranged around her hospital bed.

Sitting there, wan under her make-up, listening to Stephen getting emotional over the lost child they'd 'already grown to love', made her feel sick. She could hardly believe what she was hearing. Was this heartbroken man really the same person who'd tried to bully her into an abortion a few weeks before?

At least the press were lapping it up. A couple of the female reporters were quite tearful as they made their notes. All Gina could do was keep her mouth closed. Luckily no one spoke to her; if she'd been asked a question she might not have been able to stop herself blurting out the truth.

She kept glancing at Mark. He stood at the window gazing out over the car park, unable to look at her. Even he seemed ashamed.

But as she listened to Stephen she tried to tell herself that maybe it wasn't just a sob story. Perhaps he'd had a change of heart and really did mean what he said. Surely even he couldn't be that cynical?

With that in mind, she hoped they might have some time together to talk honestly about their feelings. But after begging the journalists in a choked voice to 'respect their privacy' and allow them to 'grieve their loss' alone, Stephen astonished her by announcing that he was going back to London the following morning.

'But I thought you were staying.'

'Darling, I can't. There's a vote first thing tomorrow morning. The whips will have my bollocks if I'm not there.'

'Surely they wouldn't mind just this once?'

'You really don't know much about politics, do you?' He bobbed an affectionate kiss on the end of her nose. 'Anyway, Mark will keep an eye on you.'

'I don't want Mark. I want you.' She knew his return to London had nothing to do with any vote or the whips' office. He wanted to be with Lucy so much he didn't even care that his wife had just suffered a miscarriage. Perhaps she should be grateful he'd managed to tear himself away to come and visit her in the hospital, she thought bitterly, and tried not to let herself think he'd only done it for the photo opportunity.

She decided to discharge herself from the hospital that night. She had to talk to Stephen before he headed back to London.

But when the taxi pulled up, there was Mark's car parked outside the house. Didn't he ever go home? Gina wondered. She knew they were busy planning their election strategy, but she never got Stephen to herself these days.

But it wasn't the election they were discussing when she let herself in. There were raised voices coming from the kitchen. Gina put her bag down in the hall and crept closer to listen.

'I don't know how much longer I can go on doing this,' Mark was saying. 'You do realize you're making an utter fool of her, don't you?'

'It's never bothered you before.'

'Stephen, the poor woman's just lost a baby. Haven't you any compassion at all?'

'It's not my fault, is it?'

'Isn't it? I wouldn't be surprised if all the stress didn't have something to do with it. She knows, Stephen. She's even asked me about it.'

'And what did you tell her?'

'What do you think I told her?'

Stephen laughed. 'Dear old Mark, I knew I could depend on you.'

'Fuck off,' Mark growled back. 'Do you think I enjoy lying to her? I like Gina. I actually feel sorry for her, being married to a selfish bastard like you.'

'She hasn't done too badly out of it,' Stephen said in a low voice.

'Neither have you,' Mark pointed out.

'Of course I haven't. Why do you think I married her?'

She didn't want to hear any more. She stumbled back up the hall, opened the front door again and banged it shut.

A second later the kitchen door opened and Stephen looked out. 'Gina? Is that you? Darling, why aren't you still in hospital?'

'I wanted to come home.' She looked over his shoulder at Mark, 'Is that a problem?'

'Of course it isn't, as long as you're well enough. You should have told me, I would have picked you up.'

'I didn't want to put you to any trouble.'

'Darling, you're my wife. Of course it wouldn't be any trouble.' He hugged her. 'We were just about to have some supper. Can I get you anything?'

'No thanks. I think I'll go straight up to bed.'

'Good idea. It's been a long and traumatic day for you, hasn't it, sweetheart?'

But exhausted as she was, she knew she wouldn't sleep as she slipped between the sheets. Stephen's solicitous concern might have fooled her once, but not any more. Now she could see it for what it was, the professional charm of the politician. Had he ever really loved her?

The Farrells lived in an elegant Georgian townhouse overlooking the green space of Harrogate Stray. Finn felt intimidated just walking up to the front door. She had no idea Gina lived in such a grand place. But until last night she'd hardly known anything about her at all.

Gina looked pale when she opened the door. She was dressed in jeans and Finn could see the outline of her collarbone through her thin cotton sweater. 'Hello. I didn't expect to see you.'

'I said I'd visit, didn't I? I went to the hospital but they told me you'd discharged yourself last night. If you're not up to seeing anyone, I can always go—'

'No, no, come in.' Gina stood aside to let her enter.

'I've brought you these.' She handed over the bunch of flowers she'd bought from the corner shop. 'But it looks as if everyone has had the same idea.' She gazed ruefully at the beautiful blooms overflowing every vase. They all looked a lot classier than her humble arrangement.

'They're lovely, aren't they?' But Gina looked as if she needed a hug, not expensive bouquets. For a moment Finn was almost tempted to give her one, then decided against it.

'How are you feeling?' she asked.

'Much better, thank you.' She led the way down the hall, its pale-green walls hung with paintings. She didn't look any better. In fact, she looked worse than the day before. Her cheeks were sunken, and her eyes were dull in shadowed hollows. 'I was just about to make some coffee. Would you like one?'

'Thanks. As long as I'm not disturbing you?'

'Not at all. I could do with the company.'

Finn followed her into the kitchen. Like the rest of the house, it was as beautifully presented as a double-page spread in a homes magazine. Finn thought about their own kitchen, with pans piled in the sink, notes stuck to the fridge, the dresser stacked with bills and letters and flyers for takeaways that no one ever got round to throwing away. The mess infuriated her at times but she knew which she preferred.

'Isn't your husband here?'

'He had to go back to London first thing. There wasn't much point in him being here anyway. You know what men are like.'

Her hands shook as she fiddled with the espresso-maker. Finn wondered if it was important political business that had sent Stephen back to London, or if there was another reason. Whatever it was, Gina didn't look happy about it.

They took their coffee into what Gina called the family room. This seemed friendlier than the rest of the house, decorated in warm peach and coral, with big, relaxed sofas and a mantelpiece crowded with framed photographs. Light flooded in from the tall Georgian window that overlooked the sunny garden.

'This is my favourite room,' Gina said.

Finn examined the photos on the mantelpiece. A couple were of Gina, some of Stephen, but they were mostly pictures of a pretty child with dark-blonde hair and wide, solemn eyes just like her mother's. 'This has got to be your daughter. She looks so much like you.'

'Yes, that's Vicky.' Gina beamed with pride. She picked up a photo of Vicky on horseback, gazing out at the camera from under the peak of a riding cap, and dusted the frame with her sleeve. 'She's away at boarding school.' Her face fell. 'Oh Lord, I suppose I'll have to call her, let her know about the baby. She'll be devastated.' Her chin wobbled and her eyes filled with tears.

'Perhaps she should come home for a while? You should be together at a time like this.'

'Do you think so?' Gina said, then shook her head. 'No, that would be very selfish of me. This last year at school is very important, I shouldn't interfere with that.'

'She's not going to be able to concentrate much knowing what's just happened to you, is she?' Finn reasoned. 'She's your family. She'll want to be with you.'

'And I want to be with her.' Gina took one last regretful look at the photograph and put it back on the mantelpiece. 'But Stephen would be furious.'

'Stephen's not here, is he?'

They looked at each other for a moment. 'I'll ring the school,' Gina said.

Finn insisted on going with her, as Gina didn't look as if she'd be up to the journey alone. She also insisted on driving, even though it meant travelling in their works van.

'We can always pick up my car on the way, if you'd prefer?' she offered.

'This is fine.' Gina didn't look as if she cared whether they went up to Whitby by horse and cart, as long as she saw her daughter. Some of the sparkle had already come back into her eyes. She'd changed into smarter trousers and put on some make-up, but she still looked dreadfully pale.

'So, how did you and Stephen meet?' Finn tried to make conversation when the crackly radio reception finally died.

'Through my family. Stephen worked for my father's lawyer. We were introduced and just sort of hit it off.'

'Love at first sight?'

'It was for me.' Her voice was tight. 'I'm not so sure about him.' She twisted her wedding ring around on her finger. 'Actually, I think he married me for my money.'

'What?' Finn was so shocked she nearly drove into the back of the car in front.

'Either that, or he thought my father's connections might be useful in his political career.' She sounded flat, matter-of-fact.

'What makes you say that?'

'I overheard him talking to someone last night. He more or less admitted it. But I suppose I've always known. Why else would he marry someone like me?'

Finn glanced across at her. 'Are you serious? You could have any man you wanted. I mean it,' she said, seeing Gina's sceptical expression. 'You're beautiful, intelligent—'

Gina laughed. 'That's very kind of you, but you don't know the full story. When I met Stephen I was in a bad way. I'd been very ill.' Her voice faltered. 'After Vicky was born, I just fell apart. I couldn't cope.'

'I'm not surprised. You must have been very young.'

'No, you don't understand. I *really* fell apart. I tried to kill myself. I wanted to go to sleep and never wake up. I felt everyone would be better off without me – Vicky, my family, everyone . . .'

Finn concentrated on her driving for a moment, not knowing how to react. 'What happened?'

'My family helped me through it. They took care of me and Vicky until I was back on my feet. I couldn't have managed without them.' She looked wretched. 'I can't believe how stupid and selfish I was.'

'How do you work that out?'

'First I got pregnant by a man who didn't care about me. Then I couldn't look after my baby properly. Then I tried to abandon her and take the easy way out. It was all my fault.'

'You're being too hard on yourself,' Finn said gently. 'You were young and you were ill. Look, I don't know much about bringing up babies, but I do know about postnatal depression. My brother's girlfriend had it after she gave birth. But the doctor put her on some medication and it soon set her straight. She's fine now.'

'My father reckons only weak people allow themselves to get depressed.'

Then your father, whoever he is, needs a good kick up the backside, Finn felt like saying. 'You can't help getting depressed any more than you can help catching a cold.'

Gina smiled, but she didn't look convinced. 'You need to take the next turning on the right,' she said, changing the subject. 'Then follow the Whitby road.'

Finn stole a glance at Gina, before following a Volvo up the sliproad. She felt incredibly sorry for her. For all her wealth and class, she seemed desperately lonely. Her husband was a selfish pig, and clearly even her family kept their distance when she needed them most.

And she did need them. She might seem serene and in control, but underneath she was unbelievably vulnerable. She should be with people who really cared about her, not left alone in that big old house.

She took a deep breath, then made a decision.

'I've had an idea,' she said. 'How would you and Vicky like to come and stay with us for a couple of days?'

Chapter 25

'Are you sure about this?' Gina asked as they bundled Vicky's small case into the back of the van.

'Of course I'm sure. Now stop asking, will you? Everything will be fine.' She grinned at Vicky, who stood gazing warily up at the cab of the van. 'Do you want to jump in? You can sit in the middle.'

Gina wished she had Finn's breezy confidence. It must be wonderful not to feel so apprehensive all the time, she thought.

It had certainly been useful having her around when they picked Vicky up. Vicky's form teacher had been difficult as usual, huffing and puffing over Gina wanting to take her daughter out of school at such short notice. But she'd met her match in Finn, who refused to be intimidated and simply ushered Vicky out to the van.

The van had caused another stir, of course. Miss Hedges had been almost apoplectic when she saw it. 'I hope that . . . *vehicle* has suitable restraints for three people?'

'Don't worry,' Finn had called back over her shoulder. 'If the worst comes to the worst we can always strap her to the roof!'

Vicky sat between them, eating her way through a bag of toffees Finn had found in the glove compartment. She'd been subdued when Gina first broke the bad news about the baby. But she seemed to take it all in her usual calm, unfussed way, listening to her mother and saying little. It was so hard to tell what was going on in her mind sometimes.

'It's very kind of you to invite us,' Gina said to Finn.

'You might not say that when you've met my dad – oi, you!' She leaned out of the window to shout to a designer jeep as it sped past. 'How much flaming road do you need? You're not driving a tank, you know!'

Gina looked at Vicky, who grinned wryly back at her.

When they got home, Finn led the way straight into the kitchen where Joe Delaney sat at the table trying to do the crossword in the local paper.

'This is Gina and Vicky.' Finn introduced them as she shrugged off her jacket. 'This is my dad, Joe.'

'So you're the one who's taken on the job of keeping my daughter in her place?' Joe's eyes twinkled. 'I don't envy you. I've been trying for years.'

'Oh, come on. You've always made it quite clear where my place is. In the kitchen,' Finn mimicked his Irish accent.

'You, in the kitchen? Please God, no.' Joe rolled his eyes. 'Talking of which, you do realize there's nothing for dinner?'

'Looks like it's fish and chips all round again, doesn't it?'

'Come back, Orla, all is forgiven,' he muttered under his breath.

'Don't fuss, I'm sure I can find something in the freezer.'

'Would you like me to help?' Gina offered.

Joe looked hopeful. 'Are you a good cook?'

'Dad! Gina, I couldn't ask you to do that. You're a guest.'

'I'd like to. I hardly ever get to cook for anyone but myself. And I'd feel better if I could contribute something.'

'Well—'

'Oh, for heavens' sake, Finnuala, let the girl make herself useful,' Joe interrupted impatiently. 'We've had nothing edible since Orla left.'

It was hardly a feast, just sausages and mash hastily thrown together with some frozen vegetables, but Gina enjoyed it more than anything she'd eaten in a long time.

She'd never had a family meal like it. The Tates' get-togethers were chilly, restrained affairs. Her mother had insisted on correct table manners even when they were small children, and they were firmly reprimanded for picking up the wrong fork or speaking with their mouths full. Any conversation tended to be about Tate business. And quite often the meal would be interrupted by her father disappearing to take a call from some far-flung corner of the Tate empire or his latest mistress, leaving her mother tight-lipped.

Stephen also insisted on good manners around the dinner table, and kept a close eye on Vicky when she came home from school. But the Delaneys were different. They laughed and joked and argued, and no one seemed to care that their elbows were on the table or that their fork was in the wrong hand. Gina watched her daughter giggling at Joe's comical comments and thought she didn't seem like the same child.

But at the same time she couldn't help feeling she didn't belong here. She didn't deserve to be here, to be welcomed. Not when she was doing so much harm to the family. She was helping her father to put these people out of business, and yet here she was, sitting around their table with them as if she was one of the family herself.

She pushed away her plate, her appetite gone.

'Are you all right?' Finn watched her anxiously. 'You've gone very pale.'

'I'm fine. But I think I should be getting home now.'

'Absolutely not,' Finn said. 'You're staying here tonight.'

'Finnuala's right,' Joe said. 'It's not a time to be on your own. You need your friends around you.'

Friends? Gina thought. You wouldn't say that if you knew who I really was.

'Besides,' Joe said, 'I promised I'd challenge Vicky to a game of draughts after tea. She reckons she can beat me.' He winked across the table at her.

Vicky gazed at her with pleading eyes. 'Please, Mum? I'd like to stay.'

'If you're sure we won't be in the way?' Even though she felt uncomfortable, she couldn't face going home to an empty house either.

After they'd cleared the plates away and Joe and Vicky were happily huddled over the draughts board, Gina and Finn sat and watched TV. She'd even forgotten what it was like to spend an evening like this. When Stephen came home, he refused to have the television on, claiming he heard enough news in Westminster, and that everything else was a waste of time. And watching *EastEnders* on her own was no fun.

'Ah, you beat me again.' Joe groaned, sitting back in his chair. 'You're too good for me, you are.'

'I told you!' Vicky beamed triumphantly.

Gina had been watching the game out of the corner of her eye and knew Joe had cheated outrageously to let her win. She couldn't imagine her father ever doing the same.

But she noticed the mood changed when Finn tried to talk to her father about work. She was trying to ask his advice on how she'd sorted out a roofing problem on the Stephensons' extension, but Joe held up his hand and said, 'Not now, Finnuala. I'll speak to Ryan about it in the morning.'

'But Ryan's not doing the job. I am.'

'All the same, I'll talk to Ryan about it. He should be supervising you.'

'I don't need supervising. I do know what I'm doing.'

Joe turned to Gina. 'You see what I have to put up with? She's been doing the job five minutes and already she knows everything.'

'I think I'm doing a pretty good job so far.'

'We'll see what kind of a job you're doing when you finally let me see those books.'

Gina caught Finn's look of defeat. She knew exactly why she wasn't showing Joe the books, and felt a pang of shame.

Later, she put Vicky to bed. Finn had made up the single bed in the spare room for her, and put an extra campbed in there for Gina.

'Are you sure you'll be comfortable enough?' she whispered, as she watched Gina tucking Vicky in. 'You could have my room if you wanted? I don't mind sleeping on the sofa.'

'No, really, we'll be fine. You've already been too kind.'

'That's what friends are for,' Finn shrugged.

She followed Finn downstairs. Joe had already gone up to bed.

They sat side by side on the sofa, watching a dire American cop show. Gina sensed Finn's thoughts were as far away as hers.

'When are you going to show your dad those books?' she finally asked.

'I don't know.'

'He's got to see them sometime.' She was hoping that if Finn showed them to him sooner rather than later, he'd realize how bad the situation was and sell the land quickly. Then maybe her father would leave them alone.

'I don't want him to see what a mess they're in,' Finn said gloomily. 'I was hoping things would get better first.'

Gina wished she could warn her that things would only get worse. Even more, she wished she didn't have to be the cause of her problems.

'This is really important to you, isn't it?'

'More important than anything,' Finn nodded. 'My whole life I've been trying to prove to my dad that I can do something if only he'd give me the chance. But now I've had the chance and I've blown it. It looks like he was right not to trust me, doesn't it?'

Gina went back to staring unseeingly at the screen. They weren't so different after all, she reflected. They both wanted to impress their fathers. Unfortunately, pleasing her father meant that Finn had to disappoint hers.

By the following morning, Finn was cheerful again. They drove into work, having left Vicky with Joe, although it was difficult to tell who was supposed to be looking after whom.

'Are you sure you're OK to come in today?' she asked. 'If you want some time off—'

'No, really. I'd rather keep myself busy.' Gina didn't want to be alone with her conscience at the moment. 'I'll stay for a couple of hours to sort things out, then I'll pick Vicky up and spend the rest of the day with her.'

'Fine. But if you feel you want to go home before that, just do it. We can manage.'

'Thanks.' Gina stared out of the window. Why did she have to be so understanding? It was hard enough when she was being a cow, but now . . .

'Oh, great.' Finn pulled up at the yard. 'That's all we need. Love's young dream.'

Ryan was in front of them, getting out of his pick-up. Wendy was with him. They watched him help her down from the passenger seat.

'Pathetic,' Finn muttered in disgust. 'As if she can't get out by herself. Is she made of glass, or something?'

As Wendy reached up for a kiss, Finn leaned on the horn, making them both jump.

'When you're quite finished?' she mouthed through the windscreen as they looked around sharply. 'Thank you *so* much.' They moved out of the way, and she put the van into gear and swerved past them.

'Sickening,' Finn said under her breath. But Gina noticed she didn't take her eyes off them in the rear-view mirror as she pulled into her parking space.

'They don't seem very suited,' she commented.

'They wouldn't even be together if she wasn't having his baby.' Finn shot a look at her. 'Sorry.'

'It's OK, you can't avoid saying the B word for ever. But it's no reason to stay together, is it? Just because she's pregnant he doesn't have to marry her.'

'He'll never walk out on her, he's too honourable. That's one of the things I—'

One of the things I love about him. Gina guessed what she was going to say even though she pressed her lips tightly together and wouldn't allow the words to escape.

Wendy sidled up to them as they got out of the van. Ryan had gone up into the office. 'Guess where I've been?'

'No idea.' Finn went round to the back of the van and unlocked the doors.

Wendy turned to Gina. 'I've been to the hospital. For another scan. Do you want to see?'

'No!' Finn moved to stop her but she was already waving the blurred black-and-white print under Gina's nose.

'Isn't it sweet? Look, you can see its little head and arms and everything.' Gina flinched, but Finn had already snatched it out of Wendy's hand.

'Are you thick or just insensitive?' she hissed. 'You do realize Gina's just had a miscarriage? The last thing she wants is you flapping your baby photos under her nose.'

'It's OK, really,' Gina said, trying to keep the peace.

'Sorry.' Wendy looked sulky. 'I didn't think.'

'What's going on?' Ryan joined them.

'Just your girlfriend being her usual caring self.' Finn thrust the scan photo back at Wendy and headed to the office with Gina. 'I'm sorry if she upset you,' she muttered.

'As she said, she didn't think.'

'She never thinks about anyone but herself.' Finn slammed her bag down on the table.

Gina sat down at her desk and leaned down to switch on the computer. 'How pregnant did you say she was?' she asked.

'No idea. About twelve weeks, I think. Why?'

'No reason.' Gina watched the welcome message flash across her screen. It was probably nothing. But from the brief glimpse she'd caught of it, the image on the scan looked more than a few weeks old.

Finn and Ryan went off on a job, and Gina settled down to work. Her calm mood lasted until she saw the scribbled estimates Finn had left on the desk a couple of days before. She picked one up, then put it down again quickly. She couldn't do it, she couldn't. Not after the Delaneys had been so kind to her.

She put the estimates aside and called up some correspondence on her computer instead. Then her mobile rang.

Her heart sank when she saw the name on the caller ID screen. Daddy.

'How are you feeling? I rang the house last night but there was no reply.'

'I spent the night at – a friend's.'

'Good idea. You shouldn't be alone at a time like this. Although you know you could always come home if you wanted?

Your mother's due back from the spa today. She'd love to take care of you.'

Gina allowed herself a smile. Her mother was too absorbed in preparing for next month's anniversary party to take care of anyone. 'I'll bear that in mind,' she promised.

'You do that. Just remember, if there's anything you need, anything at all, you only have to pick up the phone and ask. We're your family. We're always here for you.'

She put the phone down, then reached over and gingerly picked up the estimate from the in-tray. She stared down at the jumble of figures. If only Finn had continued to be vile to her, things would have been a lot easier. But she'd been so generous, like a real friend. She couldn't betray her trust. She couldn't let her down.

But she couldn't let her family down, either.

Chapter 26

Max and Rose Tate's thirty-fifth wedding anniversary party was like a who's who of the rich and powerful, Gina reflected as she stood on the sidelines, admiring the gathering. Her mother had excelled herself. Not a detail had been overlooked, not a glittering crystal glass or an extravagant arrangement of orchids and lilies was out of place. It was Rose Tate's moment of triumph.

She was almost glad Stephen had stayed in London, she thought as she looked around her. He would have mocked all this, the marquee in the garden, the string quartet playing softly on the lawn in the early spring evening, mingling with the murmur of the fountains.

And there, in the middle of it, were her parents. They still made a striking couple. Gina watched them chatting to their guests, her father looking so handsome in his smart suit – he refused to wear a dinner jacket, no matter how much her mother pleaded with him – and Rose perfect and glamorous as ever in a beautiful lace gown, her ash-blonde hair upswept.

She went off to get a drink and found James on his own, looking mournful.

'Where's Molly?' She'd been looking forward to seeing her.

'She couldn't come.'

There was something about the way he said it that made her suspicious. 'Is everything all right with you two?'

He hesitated. 'If you must know, I haven't seen much of her recently. We've decided to cool it a bit.'

'Why? You were getting on so well?'

'Turns out we weren't really suited after all.' James glanced at their parents, a trace of bitterness in his voice. Gina immediately guessed the truth.

'You mean *they* didn't like her?'

'It wasn't that.' James looked defensive. 'I told you, we weren't suited.'

'You seemed fine to me.'

James sipped his drink. 'All right, maybe they did put some pressure on me,' he admitted reluctantly.

'Why did you let them do that?'

'It's not that simple, is it? Anyway, they didn't make me give her up. Mum just wondered if I knew what I was getting into, that's all. We come from different worlds, don't we? It would never have worked out.'

'So you just let them dictate your love-life?'

'Why not? They dictated yours.'

'What do you mean?'

'It doesn't matter.' James downed the rest of his drink. 'Just don't lecture me, all right?'

They were interrupted by Nicole, lurching up to the drinks table, a glass of wine in her hand. 'Hello,' she greeted James. 'Where's your little girlfriend tonight?'

'Piss off.' James shot her a look of contempt and stalked off.

'Ooh, was it something I said?'

'He and Molly aren't together any more.'

'I can't say I'm surprised. The Tates have a way of getting rid of people they don't like.' She was slurring her words and her eyes glittered dangerously. It wasn't like Nicole to get drunk, Gina thought. She usually liked to stay sober so she could take everything in.

'What's that supposed to mean?'

'Oh, come on! I know you hero-worship him, but even you must know what a ruthless bastard your father is? He uses people and then ditches them when he's finished.' She helped herself to another drink.

Gina watched her anxiously. 'Don't you think you've had enough?'

'Oh, I've had enough all right. Believe me, I've had more than enough.'

Just then Max's voice boomed out from the other side of the marquee. 'If I could just have everyone's attention for a moment?' Everyone stopped talking and turned to look at him as he stood with Rose at his side. 'Now, as you all know, we're here today to celebrate thirty-five years of happy marriage.'

'Happy!' Nicole snorted into her glass.

'People often ask me what's the secret of a long and successful marriage—'

'Being deaf, dumb and blind in her case,' Nicole muttered, not too quietly. People close to them turned to look.

'—and I tell them it helps if you're married to the right person. I've been lucky in my life, as I'm sure many of you will agree,' he paused, looking modest and waiting for a ripple of appreciative laughter to die down, 'but I reckon the best deal I ever struck was when I got this wonderful woman to agree to marry me.'

'She didn't do too badly out of it either,' Nicole said aloud.

Max frowned. 'It's very kind of you to say so.'

'Everyone laughed again, the moment defused. But Max's benign smile couldn't hide the glacial look he shot Nicole.

Max went on to eulogize about his 'beautiful' wife, and how she'd given him so many years of 'wonderful' marriage. Then he urged everyone to raise their glasses in a toast.

Nicole downed her drink and reached for a refill. 'Christ, what a joke,' she said. She didn't bother to lower her voice. Now she was making Gina nervous; she seemed so wild, drunk and dangerous.

'Nicole, please.'

'Well, it is. Their marriage is a sham. Everyone knows your father's a philandering bastard and your mother only puts up with him because he keeps her rolling in diamonds. Don't tell me you really believe all that fairytale marriage crap? Let me tell you a few things about the Tates—'

Before she could say any more, Neil came storming over. 'What the hell are you playing at?' he hissed. 'You're upsetting my parents.'

'Ooh, can't have that, can we?' Nicole smiled drunkenly at him. 'Not on such a *special* day.'

'Come on,' he grabbed Nicole roughly by the elbow, 'I'm taking you outside for some fresh air.'

He was back ten minutes later.

'Is she all right?' Gina asked.

'She's fine. I've left her in the house to sleep it off.'

'It's not like Nicole to act like that.' Usually her sister-in-law was discreet enough to keep her bitchy thoughts to herself.

Two hours later, the guests began to leave. Rose stood in the garden, saying goodbye to them.

'Your father should be here,' she whispered to Gina. 'He told me he was making a call from his office. Go in to the house and ask him to hurry up, would you?'

Obediently Gina went. But as she approached her father's study along the wide galleried landing, the sound of raised voices coming from the other side of the door stopped her in her tracks.

'Don't be so melodramatic, it doesn't suit you,' her father was saying.

'I won't be cast aside like this. I won't!' Gina's blood ran cold as she heard Nicole's voice rising dramatically.

'Oh, spare me the wronged virgin routine! What did you expect? You knew the score when we started this. Or did you seriously think I was going to walk out of thirty-five years of marriage?'

'You don't love her.'

'You know nothing about it.'

'I know you can't love her if you sleep around so much. You can't be happy, can you?'

'So now you're an amateur psychologist, too? Did you think you could be the one to change me, is that it? That all I needed was the love of a good woman? And you thought that was you.' His voice was mocking.

'You're a heartless bastard.' Gina wondered if she should go in, but her legs were too paralysed to carry her forward.

'It takes one to know one. Oh, don't look at me like that,' Max said. 'We're the same, Nicole. Cut from the same cloth. We're both chancers, taking our opportunities where we can.'

'All the more reason why we should be together.' Nicole sounded pleading now.

'For God's sake! How many more times? Look, it was fun while it lasted. But then you got greedy. You wanted it all. And that was never going to happen. Now, if I were you, I'd be a good girl and go back to your husband while you've still got one.'

'You didn't say that six months ago when you got into my bed.'

'I didn't see you put up a fight. As I recall, you were almost boringly easy.'

'You bastard!' Gina jumped back from the door, hearing a scuffle. Nicole had given Max a ringing slap and, from the sound of it, he'd hit back. She heard a scream and the skid of a chair as Nicole fell into it.

'Do that again and I'll kill you,' her father said in a low voice.

'Gina?' She jumped at the sound of Neil's voice. He was coming along the landing towards her. 'Mum sent me to find out what's keeping you.'

Gina stood in front of the door. 'I'll – er – be down in a minute.'

'What's going on?'

'Nothing, I—'

But then Nicole's sobbing voice rose up like a ghost from the other side of the door. 'I hate you, Max Tate. I wish you'd just fucking drop dead!'

Gina moved to block her brother's way, but Neil pushed straight past her and opened the door of the study.

Inside the room, her father was standing by the window, staring out over the garden. Nicole was slumped in a chair, her make-up streaked from crying.

'What the hell's going on?' Neil demanded, looking from one to the other.

'Your wife's had far too much to drink. She's hysterical and I was trying to calm her down.'

Neil looked at Nicole. 'Is this true?'

She looked back at him, her eyes glittering with defiance.

'Actually, we were discussing our affair,' she said in a surprisingly sober voice. 'Did you know I'd been sleeping with your father, Neil?'

Neil stared at Max, who shrugged. 'I told you, she's drunk. I don't know what she's talking about.'

'Of course he doesn't,' Nicole laughed. 'He's got a very selective memory, haven't you, Max? I can give you dates and places, if you like, Neil. All the hotels where we were making love while you were out doing your precious daddy's dirty work for him.' She smiled maliciously at Max. 'We even did it here, once. While your mother was out playing bridge, wasn't it, Max?'

Gina couldn't take her eyes off Neil. He looked stunned and oddly vulnerable as he stared from one to the other.

'Oh, for God's sake!' Max looked annoyed. 'All right, so she made a pass at me a few times. I turned her down and this is what happens. Can't you see the silly bitch is making it all up? Who are you going to believe, her or me?'

For a long moment no one spoke. Neil's face went through all kinds of emotions – confusion, disbelief, sheer agony. Finally he said, 'Nicole, I think you'd better go.'

'Good idea,' Max said. 'Gina, take her home.'

'No way! You're not getting rid of me that easily!' Nicole turned pleadingly to Neil. 'You're not seriously going to believe him, are you? Christ, why would I make up something like that? Why would I deliberately screw up my marriage?' Neil didn't reply. 'Well, say something, for God's sake!'

'We'll talk about this later,' Neil said quietly.

'Let's not talk about it at all. I can see you've already decided who you're going to believe.' Nicole stood up. 'Well, if that's what you want to think, then I hope you can live with it. And I hope one day you find out what a treacherous bastard your father really is!'

She pushed past them all and headed out of the door. 'Go after her, Gina,' Max ordered. No one moved. 'I said go after her,' he repeated, so loudly it made her jump to attention. 'I want to talk to your brother.'

Gina hurried out of the room, wondering if she should leave

the two of them together. From the way they were sizing each other up like a pair of prize fighters, she was afraid they might end up killing each other.

But downstairs, she found an even more worrying fight going on, as Nicole confronted her mother in the empty kitchen. They made a startling contrast. Nicole looked smudged, drunk and out of control; Rose was perfectly poised, not a hair out of place, still in her beautiful evening dress.

'He doesn't love you,' Nicole was saying. 'He hasn't loved you for years. You don't turn him on. Why do you think he needs all those other women? You bore him, in bed and out of it. He told me.'

'But he'll never leave me,' Rose stated with quiet confidence. Gina almost admired her mother's icy dignity. She knew she couldn't have done it.

'Nicole, please.' She moved to take her sister-in-law's arm, but Nicole shook her off.

'How can you do it?' she demanded. 'How can you stay with him, when all he does is humiliate you? Don't you have any pride?'

Rose looked her slowly up and down. 'It seems to me you're the one with no pride. Did you really think you could take him away from me? I've seen off bigger threats than you, believe me. You're just an opportunistic little whore.'

'It takes one to know one.'

Rose slapped her, hard. Gina stepped between them, pushing Nicole backwards, propelling her towards the door before she could retaliate. 'Come on, let me take you home.'

'No, I want to wait for Neil. I need to talk to him.'

'I don't think he's going to want to talk to you tonight. Why don't you leave it until the morning?'

Nicole finally relented and allowed her to drive her back to their flat. On the way home, she slumped in the passenger seat and sobbed out the whole story.

'I love him!' She wiped her nose on her sleeve. 'We're so alike. We both came from nothing, you see. I understand him. Better than that bitch does.'

That bitch happens to be my mother, Gina thought. 'But you're married to Neil.'

'So?' Nicole looked at her. 'That didn't stop me being drawn to Max, right from when I first started working for him.' She slumped back in her seat. 'I just never thought it would happen between us. God, I tried often enough. But he was never interested and Neil was . . .'

'So you took the consolation prize?' Gina said in disgust, wondering why she didn't just throw open the passenger door and ditch her in the gutter where she belonged.

'Look, don't get me wrong, I'm very fond of Neil. We get on, we want the same things out of life. But Max was the one who really turned me on. He's an incredible man.'

Oh, please. But she kept silent and let Nicole drone on.

'We were great together,' she said. 'It was so exciting, and he made me feel so special. I know I should have felt guilty, but I didn't. It just felt so right, you know.'

'No,' Gina said. 'I don't know.'

'Well, it was. In the beginning, anyway. But then he started to lose interest. He stopped calling me, kept coming up with reasons why we couldn't meet. I felt like I'd been cast aside.'

And you wouldn't like that, would you? Gina thought. She remembered the day she'd arrived at her father's office, and how put out Nicole had been when Max had cancelled a meeting with her to take Gina to lunch. Was that reservation really meant for them? she wondered.

If so, he'd chosen the wrong woman to mess with. Nicole wasn't the kind to take rejection lightly.

'Anyway, it's all over now.' Nicole started crying again. It took all Gina's strength not to slap her. The only one Nicole felt sorry for was herself.

'Maybe you can sort it out with Neil.'

'I don't want Neil. And he won't want me. Not after this. Your father will see to that.'

'But surely if he loves you—'

Nicole laughed harshly. 'Love conquers all, is that it? Listen, it doesn't matter whether he loves me or not, he'll still take your father's side. He knows where his loyalties lie, just like the rest of you. The Tates will close ranks, as usual. They always fall in and do exactly what Daddy wants them to do.'

'That's not true.'

'Isn't it?' Nicole said. 'James has given up his girlfriend. You've betrayed your friends. And Neil will dump me. You're all the same.'

It was late when Gina got back to the house. Lytton Grange seemed empty and sad, the balloons deflating, the remains of the party littered everywhere. Her parents had gone to bed and Neil's car had disappeared. Gina wondered if he'd gone home to patch things up with Nicole. In spite of everything, she hoped they could at least talk.

The following morning she woke up late. By the time she'd showered, dressed and gone downstairs, the men were taking down the marquee and her mother was in the middle of supervising the clean-up operation.

'You're too late for breakfast,' Rose told her. 'The cleaners are in the kitchen.'

'It's OK, I'm not hungry.' Gina stared out on the lawn where the men were packing away the last of the marquee poles. 'Where's Dad?'

'In his study, of course. Where else would he be? You don't expect him to be helping here, do you?'

She wasn't sure if he'd be there at all. She'd half expected her mother to have given him his marching orders.

She hesitated, wondering what to say. 'Are you all right?' she said finally.

'Of course I'm not all right,' her mother replied. 'Have you seen what they've done to my shrubs, taking down that tent?'

'That's not what I meant. I was thinking about Nicole.'

Rose rubbed at a water mark on the rosewood cupboard with steely determination. 'What about her?'

'What are you going to do?'

'Do? I'm not going to *do* anything. If your father said nothing happened, then nothing happened.'

'But you can't just ignore it.'

'Can't I?' Rose turned on her. 'I've managed it all these years. How do you think we've stayed married for so long?'

'So you're just going to turn a blind eye, pretend it never happened?'

'Why not? Don't look at me in that sanctimonious way, Gina. Do you think I like being humiliated? Sometimes I hate your father for what he does, the way he treats me.'

'Then why do you stay with him?'

'Because that's the life I've chosen.' She put down her cloth and straightened up to face her. 'Do you know the first time your father was unfaithful to me? When I was pregnant with your brother James. We'd only been married a matter of months, and he slept with someone else. My best friend, no less. I wanted to leave him then, but he begged me to stay. He promised it was over, that it would never happen again. And I loved him, so I gave him another chance. Except the next time I was pregnant, it happened again. And again. In the end he hardly went to the trouble of hiding it. He knew I wouldn't do anything about it.'

'Why didn't you leave?'

'Where could I go? I had two young children. I was trapped.'

'You could have still divorced him.'

'And end up living on the breadline?' Rose looked horrified. 'That's what it would have come to. Your father's a clever man, and so are the lawyers and accountants he has working for him. There's no way he would have let me walk out of this marriage a rich woman.'

'Maybe not. But you could have walked out a proud one.'

'What's pride got to do with it? Pride wouldn't keep us, would it? It wouldn't send you and your brothers to boarding school, or give us a home like this. Your father might not be perfect, but he's always looked after us. You'd be surprised what you can get used to when you don't have any choice.'

Gina looked at her mother, seeing her for the first time. She used to think Rose had courage, ignoring her husband's affairs to keep her family together. Now she realized she was a vain, shallow woman who'd sacrificed her pride for the sake of wealth and security. She'd chosen to be humiliated and live a life of luxury than to hold her head up and have nothing.

Then she remembered what Nicole said, about them closing ranks around her father. Max Tate was the centre of all their lives. They'd given up so much to please him – their love, their happiness, their self-respect.

And in her way, she was just as bad as her mother. She'd given in, too.

'You're wrong,' she said. 'You always have a choice. We all do.'

She went to see her father. It felt strange being in his office, the scene of so much trauma the previous night. But it was as if it had never happened. Max greeted her calmly, not in the least bit shamefaced about what she'd seen and heard. Gina began to wonder if she'd imagined the whole episode.

'What can I do for you?'

Gina took a deep breath. 'I've come to tell you, I'm not going to spy for you any more.'

'Can I ask why?'

'Because the Delaneys are good people and I don't want to see them suffer.'

'I see. And what about us?' Her father's voice was pleasant, but she sensed the iron beneath. 'Haven't we been good to you?'

'Yes, but—'

'Who took you in, looked after you when Vicky was born? Was it the Delaneys who took care of you after you tried to kill yourself?'

Gina winced. 'I know, and I'll always be grateful.'

'But not grateful enough to help us when we need you?'

She steeled herself. 'You can't ask me to do this. It's not fair. I'm sick of lying and pretending. The Delaneys are my friends.'

Max swung around in his chair to look out of the window, his fingers steepled in front of his face. 'I wonder if they'd still be your friends if they knew you'd tried to put them out of business?'

She wasn't surprised, she'd half expected him to say it, but she was still disappointed when he did.

'We'll find out, won't we?' she said. 'Because I'm going to tell them.'

Max swung back round to face her. 'And do you really think they'll forgive you when they know you're a Tate?' he said.

'That's a chance I'll have to take, isn't it?'

'You always were too honest for your own good, Gina.'

'That's the difference between you and me, isn't it?'

As she walked out of his study, she felt absurdly pleased with herself. She'd stood up to her father for once, and she'd won. And it hadn't been nearly as hard or traumatic as she'd thought. She'd expected her father to put pressure on her, to force her into doing what he wanted. But he'd hardly seemed to care.

She only hoped Ryan and Finn would be as understanding when she told them the truth.

Chapter 27

Finn hated the remand centre. She hated the bleak beige walls, the high narrow windows, the smell of stale sweat and cleaning fluid. Most of all she hated seeing her brother trying to put on a brave face even though he was clearly terrified.

Ciaran had lost more weight since she'd last seen him, and there were purple shadows like bruises under his eyes.

'It's not so bad in here,' he said cheerfully. 'At least the food's better than Mel's cooking. And I don't have to listen to you nagging, either!'

Finn looked at his big, clumsy hands resting on the table between them. His knuckles were grazed and scabbed. 'Have they said anything about your court case?'

'It won't be for another two months, my brief reckons.'

'Will you be able to cope in here that long?'

'Looks like I'll have to, won't I?' He glanced around. 'Do we have to talk about this place? I'd rather know what's going on outside.'

'Where do I start? Dad's doing OK, although he seems a bit lonely.'

'He's been on his own for years. You'd think he'd be used to it by now.'

'I know.' She didn't say anything to Ciaran, but she suspected her father was missing Orla. Not that he'd ever admit it.

'So what's going on with Ryan and Wendy?' Ciaran asked. 'Is it true she's not pregnant after all?'

Finn looked up sharply. 'Who told you that?'

'Mel says she saw her in town on Saturday, on a hen night. She reckons she's never seen a pregnant woman knock back vodka shots like that.'

'Ryan hasn't said anything about it.' Not that she and Ryan ever talked about Wendy, or much else for that matter. Finn found they could work alongside each other as long as they never discussed anything remotely personal. It was mostly self-conscious silence these days. 'As far as I know she's still pregnant.'

'If she ever was.'

'What's that supposed to mean?'

'Well, I never really bought that whole baby story anyway. Mel knows Wendy's sister and reckons Wendy tried a stunt like this a few years back. Some boyfriend dumped her, and the next thing he knows, she's telling everyone she's expecting and trying to shame him into marrying her.'

'So what happened?'

'She got rumbled, I s'pose. The wedding didn't happen, anyway.'

Finn thought for a moment. 'Does Ryan know about this?'

'I tried telling him, but he won't listen. You know what he's like. Mr Bloody Noble, always doing the right thing. That's how he ended up in a place like this.'

'I don't get you,' Finn said.

Ciaran rubbed at a graze on the back of his hand and looked reluctant. 'I shouldn't say anything. Ryan asked me never to tell anyone, not even Dad.'

'You've got to tell me now. You can't just leave it like that.'

He hesitated a moment. 'All right, then. But don't let on I've said anything, OK?' Finn nodded. 'Ryan didn't do that hit and run when he was a kid. His brother did.'

'Tony?' She'd met Ryan's younger brother once. He was a serious, bespectacled young man in a suit who looked as if he'd never had so much as a library fine in his life.

'He went off the rails when he was a teenager, got in with a bad crowd. One night he got high and went joyriding in a mate's car. He was behind the wheel when they hit that old man. Ryan knew he wouldn't last five minutes in a place like this. Or if he did, he'd come out ten times worse. So he took the blame and told everyone he was driving, on the understanding that Tony straightened his life out.'

'Which he did.'

'Oh, yeah. He's dead respectable now. Got a good job in computers, apparently.'

And Ryan's got a criminal record. Finn remembered what a hard time he'd had when he came out of jail, how no one would give him a chance. Especially her.

'I think you've got it wrong about Wendy, though,' she said. 'I've seen the scan photo.'

'Maybe she's on the level this time,' Ciaran shrugged. 'All I'm saying is Ryan should watch himself. That Wendy's a real predator.' He leaned towards her. 'I don't suppose you could buy me a couple of packets of cigs from the machine before you go, could you?'

Gina jumped when Finn walked into the office that evening on the way home, although Finn knew she'd seen her pulling up in the yard. She'd been in a strange mood for the past couple of days.

'Any news?' Finn asked, picking up that morning's post.

'We've had a couple of calls about jobs. I've written them on the pad.'

Finn picked up the pad and looked at the numbers. 'Did they say what they were?'

'A broken guttering and a new garage, I think. Listen Finn, I need to talk to you about something—'

'I need to talk to you, too.' Finn put down the pad. 'Do you think Wendy might be lying about being pregnant?'

Gina frowned. 'What makes you say that?'

'Just something my brother said. He reckons she's done it before. And Mel spotted her out drinking on Saturday night.'

'Lots of women drink during pregnancy. Listen, Finn—'

'Yes, but they don't end up falling down drunk, do they? Do you think I should say anything to Ryan about it?'

'I don't know. Perhaps. Finn, this is really important. I want—'

'Maybe I should just stay well out of it.' It was probably just wishful thinking on her part, anyway. 'Anyway, there was that scan photo, wasn't there? She couldn't fake that.'

'No, but she could borrow someone else's.'

'Do you think so?'

'If she was desperate enough, I suppose. Finn—'

'Later?' Finn was already backing out of the door. 'I need to talk to Ryan. Do you know where he is?'

'He took the day off, I think. Listen, I've been putting this off for days—'

'Then another couple of hours won't hurt, will it? Why don't you call me tonight? We can have a nice chat, then.'

'But—'

Call me, OK?'

All the way to Ryan's place, she told herself she was doing the right thing. If Ryan's fiancée was trying to trap him into marriage, he had a right to know, didn't he? She'd want to be warned if it was her. She was only doing what any concerned friend would do.

Who are you kidding? a voice in her head said.

The last time she'd seen Ryan's house, just after he'd bought it, it was a dilapidated, unloved 1950s semi with peeling paintwork and an overgrown front garden. 'A DIY enthusiast's dream', as the estate agents' blurb described it.

Nearly two years later, she hardly recognized the place. The doors and windows had all been replaced, the brickwork re-pointed and there was a new roof. The weed-filled garden had been transformed into a tidy lawn with a newly laid block drive-way. She was relieved to see Wendy's car wasn't there.

Lights were on in the downstairs bay window as Finn pulled up. She hesitated for second, then got out and headed up the path.

Ryan threw open the door, a roller in his hand. His jeans and T-shirt were spattered with paint.

'I need to talk to you,' she said.

'Come in.' He stood aside to let her enter. The hallway was littered with ladders and cans of paint, the walls half-stripped of faded flowery paper. 'Sorry about the mess, I wasn't expecting visitors.'

He led the way into the sitting room, which was bare apart from a stepladder in the middle of the room. Dust sheets covered the bare wooden floor. It smelled of fresh paint.

Ryan wiped his hands on a cloth. 'So, what can I do for you?'

'It's about Wendy.'

'What about her?'

'I think she might be taking you for a ride.'

His brow furrowed as he listened to what she had to say. 'Are you serious?' he said flatly, when she'd finished.

'I just wanted to know if you were sure she was pregnant.' Finn suddenly felt very foolish.

'Of course I'm sure. Do you honestly think I'd be in this mess if I wasn't?'

He looked so utterly wretched, Finn had to fight the urge to put her arms around him. 'You're right,' she said. 'I'm sorry, I shouldn't have come.'

'No, I'm glad you did.' He ran his hand through his tangled curls. He had a streak of paint on his jaw, Finn noticed. 'But don't you think I've gone through all this in my head a million times? Trying to work out some way around it, wishing it could all be different?'

'Maybe it could,' Finn said. 'You don't have to marry her, do you? You could still be a father without that.'

'And what kind of father would I be?' He shook his head. 'I want this baby to have a name, Finn. My name. I don't want it growing up thinking I wasn't there, or that I didn't care. My dad walked out on us and I know what it feels like. I'm not going to do the same to my child.'

There was such a quiet determination in his voice that she knew she couldn't argue with him. But she felt she had to try. 'You always have to do the right thing, don't you? Just like you did with your brother.'

Ryan frowned. 'Who told you about that?' Realization dawned and he sighed. 'Ciaran, I suppose? He never knew when to keep his mouth shut.'

'I wish you'd told me.'

'What was the point? It's all in the past, forgotten.' But from the shadowed look in his eyes Finn wondered if he would ever forget it. His experiences had clearly left deep scars.

'Why did you do it?'

'I needed to protect my brother. He was just a frightened kid when it happened, he didn't even know what he was doing. Going to jail would have ruined his life before it had even begun.'

'What about your life?'

'I could deal with it. Tony couldn't. But then, when I came out and found no one wanted to know me, that was tough. I couldn't get a job, I'd lost all my friends. I was just the boy who'd nearly killed an old man.' Ryan picked at a paint stain on his faded jeans. 'There were times that I wished I had let Tony take the blame. Then maybe everyone wouldn't have hated me so much.'

'Including me?' Finn said, remembering the hard time she'd given him when he first came to work for her father.

'Especially you.' Their eyes met. 'I detested my brother sometimes. He had his whole life ahead of him, could go where he pleased, do whatever he liked. But because of him, I knew I could never be good enough in your eyes.'

A lump of emotion blocked her throat. 'You should have told me the truth.'

'You probably wouldn't have believed me. Anyway, I still had a criminal record. I couldn't be the man I wanted to be for you.'

She looked around at the walls, half bare plaster, half painted in white. 'And there was me, thinking you never even noticed me,' she smiled. 'You and Ciaran used to watch all the other girls go by and make comments about them.'

'And you used to go mad and call us sexist.'

'Only because I was jealous,' she admitted. When she wasn't trying to be a boy for her father's sake, she'd been praying to St Jude the patron saint of lost causes for a cleavage to match her best friend Jenny MacGregor's.

'Oh, I noticed you, all right. But I wouldn't dare admit it. Half the time I wouldn't dare say a word to you in case you bit my head off.' He looked around the room. 'When I first bought this place, I even had this stupid fantasy that one day you might live here with me.'

'And now you'll be living here with your wife and baby.' Finn saw him wince, but she didn't care. She was hurting, too. 'Look, I'd better go.'

'Stay, please. I don't want you to go. I could show you the rest of the house, if you like?'

'That would be great, wouldn't it?' Her bitterness spilled out but she couldn't stop it. 'You can show me which room's going to be the nursery. Are you painting it pink or blue, by the way?'

'Finn, don't.'

'Or better still, why don't you show me your bedroom where you'll be sleeping with—'

He crossed the room in a second, stopping her mouth with a kiss that shocked her with its unexpectedness. His mouth was soft, warm and very insistent, sending erotic shockwaves through her. For a second she responded, then she pushed him away.

'No. This isn't fair.'

'You're right. None of this is fair. But that doesn't stop me wanting you.'

'You can't have us both.'

'Not just for one night?' His dark eyes pleaded with her. 'I'm sick of doing the right thing. Just for once I'd like to know what it's like to be truly happy myself.' His arms gripped her. 'She's going to have me for the rest of my life, whether I want it or not. But tonight I want you. Is that too much to ask?'

No, it wasn't too much to ask. It was all she wanted, too. 'I can't.' She pulled away from him. 'It would never be right.'

If he'd argued with her, if he'd said another word or even just looked at her, she would have given in. But instead he looked defeated. 'Maybe,' he said gruffly. 'We'll never know, will we?'

She left, and he didn't try to stop her. Finn reached her car and looked back. The sitting room was empty, Ryan hadn't gone back to his painting. She could see his blurred shape still outlined behind the frosted glass panel of the front door. She waited, but he didn't move.

She wanted him so much. She felt that if she walked away from him now she would be walking away from him for ever. She would never ever know what it was like to touch him, to hold him, even if it was just once . . .

Ryan must have had the same thought because, as she ran back up the drive and reached the door, he came flying out. She fell into his arms and they stumbled backwards into the hall, Ryan kicking the door closed behind them as he pressed her against the wall, hoisting her up so her face was level with his, her legs wrapped around his hips, his body against hers, their mouths fused together.

It was a conversation without words, a silent communication through lips, tongues, hands. They moved with the same urgent desperation, as if they shared the same instincts, both knowing what the other wanted. Ryan lowered Finn back on to her feet, his hands moving up to unbutton her shirt while she fumbled with the thick leather of his belt. Finn closed her eyes, blanking out everything but the sensation that was lancing through her. She couldn't allow herself to slow down or to think, because then she would realize how wrong it was. It would all be over, the moment lost.

Then their mouths parted, just for a second, and she saw the same look of shocked apprehension in Ryan's eyes that she was feeling herself. But it was too late to turn back, and the next second they were kissing hungrily again.

She would happily have made love there and then among the paint cans and scattered fragments of wallpaper. Anything to prolong the moment. But Ryan was insistent.

'No,' he said, taking her hand and leading her upstairs. 'You belong in my bed. It's where I've always imagined you.'

His room was cool and white, the bed covered by an expanse of cream linen. Now it was slower, less urgent, as they carefully undressed each other. Finn took her time touching, kissing, smelling his bare skin, exploring the hard play of his muscles as he moved. She knew this would be the only time and wanted to memorize every inch of him, to savour every sensation. This wasn't just sex; it was saying goodbye.

It was still dark when she crept away in the small hours of the morning. For a long time, she had watched him sleeping beside her, studying the curl of his dark lashes and the strong lines of his face. His mouth looked so inviting, she could hardly stop herself wanting to kiss him, to wake him up so she could feel herself in his arms again. More than anything she wanted to stay, to know what it was like to wake up with him in the morning.

But she knew she couldn't. Ryan had said she belonged in his bed, but she didn't. It was another woman's territory, and suddenly it felt all wrong for her to be there.

Everything had changed, and nothing had changed. He would never be hers, yet she wanted him more than ever. Last night hadn't solved anything, it just made her yearning harder to bear.

She got to the yard at the same time as Ryan the following morning. She groaned when she saw his pick-up pull in behind hers. She'd been hoping to collect her stuff and get away to another job before he arrived.

He wasn't smiling as he greeted her. 'What happened to you this morning?'

'There didn't seem to be much point in staying.'

She turned to walk away but he followed her. 'We have to talk.'

'There's nothing to say. Last night doesn't change anything.'

'It changes everything!' He moved around to stand in front of her. 'I love you.'

'But you're marrying Wendy.'

'I don't have to. I've been thinking about what you said, and you're right. Maybe we can find a way to sort this out—'

'It wouldn't work and we both know it. Do you honestly think Wendy will let you be a father to that baby if you don't marry her? She'll be vindictive, she'll keep you from your child. You wouldn't be able to live with the guilt, and neither could I. It would destroy us in the end, wouldn't it?'

She longed for him to argue, tell her she was wrong. But his bleak look told her everything she needed to know.

'So, it's best if we just forget last night ever happened.'

'And am I supposed to forget how I feel about you?'

But she wasn't listening. She was distracted by the Portakabin door banging open in the breeze.

'Who unlocked the office?' She looked around. 'Gina's car isn't here, so it can't be her. I hope no one's broken in.'

She headed for the office but Ryan stopped her. 'Let me go first. Just in case.'

Finn followed him up the stairs. The office seemed untouched. It hadn't been vandalized and the computers were still there.

'Doesn't look as if anything's missing,' Ryan said.

'We'd better check the files, make sure nothing's – what are you looking at?' She turned to Ryan, who was standing at Gina's desk, staring down at a piece of paper in his hand.

He gave it to her. 'I think you'd better see this.'

Chapter 28

It was a clipping from a magazine. A society wedding, complete with horse and flower-laden carriage, and endless small bridesmaids decked out in pink tulle. Finn recognized the bride immediately. There was no mistaking Gina, even though she didn't exactly look the picture of a radiant bride; her smile was strained and her eyes were apprehensive under her pearl-trimmed tiara. Beside her, Stephen Farrell MP beamed at the camera as if it were another political photo opportunity.

And on the other side were her proud parents.

'TATE GIRL WEDS' was the headline.

'It can't be,' she murmured.

'And they've left something else.' Ryan handed her another piece of paper. It was a photocopied estimate on Tate headed paper for a job she remembered quoting for.

Suddenly, horribly, it all started to add up. 'She's been spying on us.'

'Why would she do that?'

'Because she's a Tate.' Finn's disbelief was quickly replaced by anger. How could she not have known? How could she have trusted her? Gina had betrayed them. And to think she'd looked on her as a friend!

'What are you going to do?' Ryan asked.

'Confront her, of course.'

'Maybe I should talk to her?'

'No chance.' Finn looked down at the photo of the nervously smiling bride. 'This is between Gina and me.'

*

Finn was ready for her when she arrived twenty minutes later. Ryan was out in the yard, loading up the van. Finn had asked him to leave them alone.

Gina was surprised to see her. 'Oh, hello, I didn't expect you to be in so early.'

Finn forced herself to be pleasant, trying to smile as she replied neutrally, 'I had something I needed to deal with first.'

'Anything I can help you with?'

'I don't think so, somehow.'

She waited, facing the window, as Gina went to her desk, took off her jacket and hung it on the back of her chair. In the reflection from the window, she saw her pick up the clipping, her smile disappearing.

'It was waiting for me when I got in this morning,' Finn said. 'Makes interesting reading, don't you think?'

'I was going to tell you,' Gina said flatly. 'That's what I wanted to talk to you about yesterday. I tried calling you last night—'

'Why should I believe you, after what you've done?' Finn could feel her anger rising, and fought to control it. Ryan had made her promise she would stay calm before he agreed to leave her alone. 'That's why you took this job, isn't it? To help your father put us out of business?'

'No! I didn't want to do it. I told him I wanted to stop. That must be why he did this. To punish me.'

'We're the ones being punished. We *trusted* you. *I* trusted you. I thought you were a friend.'

'I was. I am.'

'Friends don't stab each other in the back!' Her anger was heating up inside her; she couldn't stop it. 'You knew how much this meant to me, how hard I was working.'

Gina sat down at the desk, her face buried in her hands. But her tears did nothing to melt Finn's anger. 'That's why I told him I had to stop. I couldn't do it to you anymore.'

'So why did you do it in the first place?'

Finn swung round as Ryan asked the question she'd been about to put herself. She hadn't heard him come in behind her. He must have heard their raised voices and decided to step in.

Gina looked up at him, relieved to have someone who might listen to her. 'I thought my family were in trouble,' she said. 'My father told me you were the ones plotting against *him*. He said you were trying to bring him down. He told me I was the only one who could help them.'

'Oh dear, was Daddy down to his last million?'

'I really thought he needed me,' Gina told her, 'and that this was something I could do – to repay him.' She looked up. 'You don't know how persuasive he can be. You can't say no to him.'

'So what?' Finn snapped. 'Am I supposed to feel sorry for you now? Poor little rich girl can't say no to her big bad daddy? You saw what we were going through. You knew how much it meant to me to keep the business going for my father.'

'Helping my father meant a lot to me, too.'

'Don't try to justify yourself to me. You make me sick!'

She made a move towards her, but Ryan caught her and held her back. 'I think you'd better go,' he told Gina.

'But—'

'You heard him. Get out of my sight!'

Gina moved slowly to pick up her bag and unhook her jacket from the back of the chair. As she reached the door she turned to look back at Finn.

'You know, we're not so different after all,' she said. 'I only did it because I wanted my father to accept me, to think I was worth something for once. I thought you of all people would understand that.'

'You didn't give her much of a chance,' Ryan said, when she'd gone.

'You were the one who told her to go.'

'Only because I thought you were going to hit her.'

'She deserved it. Anyway, why *should* I give her a chance? She didn't give us one.'

'She tried to explain.'

'She was just making excuses!' Finn didn't want to hear them.

She was already sick to her stomach of Gina, acting so nice and caring when all the time she'd been out to stitch them up. And she'd fallen for it. That was what made Finn most angry. She'd let her guard down and trusted her. She wouldn't make that mistake again.

'She was right, though. You two are alike.'

'Oh, yeah. I'm dressed head to toe in Gucci, too.'

'Maybe not that way. But you've both spent your whole lives trying to live up to your fathers' expectations.'

'Except I wouldn't lie and cheat and do anyone else down to get what I wanted.'

'Are you sure about that? If saving your family meant making the Tates suffer, what would you do?'

'That's different. The Tates deserve to suffer.'

'And she thought your family did.'

'She was wrong.'

'I think she knows that now.'

Finn glared at him, outraged. 'Whose side are you on, anyway?'

'I'm just trying to understand why she did it,' Ryan reasoned. 'Look at it from her point of view. It can't have been easy, growing up in a family like that.'

'Yeah, all that wealth and privilege must have been a living hell.'

'You know what I mean. Living with that monster of a father, and those brothers. I bet she's been made to feel worthless over the years.'

Finn was silent. She knew what that was like. Her father might not be as ruthless as Max Tate, but she'd still grown up feeling ignored.

'Maybe she can buy herself a new Porsche to cheer herself up,' she said. 'I don't care, anyway, as long as she stays away from me.'

'You don't mean that.'

'Who says?'

'I do. You're not that hard, whatever you like to think.' He sent her a long look.

'When it comes to the Tates, I am.' She looked away from him, resisting his gaze. 'I'm telling you, Gina Farrell's had all the chances she's going to have from me. It'll be a cold day in hell before I speak to that bitch again!'

★

Gina stood in the supermarket, staring at the racks of bottles on the shelves and wondering which one to buy. She was so miserable; all she wanted to do was go home and get plastered. She grabbed a few bottles at random, put them in her basket and was heading for the check-out when she heard a familiar voice on the other side of the bread aisle.

'Ben, put that down. If you don't put it down now, you're not having the Spiderman cake. I mean it. Abi? Oh Lord, where's your sister disappeared to now? *Abi*!'

Gina turned sharply in the other direction, too embarrassed to meet Molly when she was looking and feeling such a wreck. But five minutes later they collided by the frozen foods.

'Gina. Hi, how are you?' Molly looked tired and harassed, pushing a trolley with Abi standing up in it like a Roman charioteer.

'Fine. And you?'

'Oh, you know. Knackered. We're buying stuff for Ben's birthday party. I know I should be baking it all from scratch, but I'm such a rubbish mother I can never find the time,' she confided in a low voice. She glanced at the bottles in Gina's basket. 'It looks like we're not the only ones having a party?'

Gina was about to make up some lame excuse then she realized she was too tired to keep up any more pretences. 'Actually, I've just been fired, I've lost my baby, my best friend, and I'm pretty certain my husband is having an affair. So, basically, I was hoping to drown my sorrows.'

Molly stared at her, taken aback. 'Blimey, no wonder you need so many bottles,' she said. 'And there was me tearing my hair out because it was a teacher training day. Tell you what, why don't we forget about the shopping, I'll park these two little monsters in the crêche and we can have a drink together? It's got to be better than drinking alone.'

They ended up in an empty wine bar in the precinct. It was too early for the lunchtime crowd, and the young waitress looked askance at the two women working their way steadily through a bottle of Cabernet Sauvignon at eleven in the morning.

'She thinks we're a couple of alcoholics!' Molly giggled, staring back at her. 'So come on, tell your Auntie Molly everything.'

Gina poured out all her troubles about Stephen, and the baby, and losing her job.

'It's not really the job, it's more losing a friend,' she said. 'I let Finn down badly.'

'It sounds to me like you didn't have much choice.'

'I could have stood up to my father, said no right from the start.'

'When does anyone ever stand up to your father? Your brother certainly doesn't,' she muttered into her glass.

Gina saw her bitter expression. 'I was sorry to hear about you and James.'

'I bet you were the only one in your family who was.' Molly refilled her glass. 'Have you seen him lately?'

'Only at my parents' anniversary party.'

'How was he?'

'Fed-up, like you.' Gina smiled. 'He misses you, you know.'

'He knows where to find me, if he wants me,' Molly said stiffly. 'But he won't call.'

'Why do you say that?'

'Because I know the kind of hold Max Tate has over all of you. Even if we did try to make a go of it, I'd always have to come second to the rest of the family. And I don't think I could do that, even for James.'

'I don't blame you.'

'I shouldn't have got involved with him in the first place.' Molly ran her finger up her glass, collecting moisture on the tip of her finger. 'I should have known it wouldn't work out and I'd end up getting hurt. Your parents have a way of weeding out anyone they don't like, don't they?'

'Oh, I don't know. Nicole managed to get through.'

'Nicole is different. She's got drive and ambition, and your father likes that.'

It suddenly occurred to Gina that Molly hadn't heard how spectacularly Nicole had blotted her copybook. She wondered if she should tell her, but Molly seemed happier to go on talking about James.

'He was a different person when he was with me. He was kind and loving and funny. And he adored the kids. It was almost as if he wasn't a Tate any more. Do you know what I mean?' Gina nodded. She'd caught a glimpse of James when he was with Molly; he'd seemed much nicer.

'You were good for him,' she agreed.

'Well, it doesn't matter now, anyway,' Molly said bracingly. 'I expect Rose has already got some nice, suitable girl lined up for him. Someone who knows the right labels to wear and which wine to have with what, and who'll never step out of line and embarrass the family.'

'James would never let that happen.'

'Why should he be any different to the rest of you?'

As soon as she'd said it, Molly clamped her lips shut, as if she'd said something she shouldn't. She glanced at her watch. 'Is that the time? I'd better pick the kids up before they think I've abandoned them completely.' She reached for her bag but Gina stopped her.

'What did you mean just then?'

'You mustn't take any notice of me,' Molly gabbled. 'I've probably had a bit too much to drink. I don't know what I'm talking about when I've had a couple.'

'You know exactly what you're talking about. And you're not leaving until you've told me everything.'

Molly put her bag back on the table defeatedly. 'It's just something James told me once. He said your parents fixed you up with Stephen.'

'That's right, they did. He was working for my father's lawyers and we happened to meet.'

'*Happened* to meet?' Molly's brows rose questioningly. 'Are you sure about that?'

'Well . . .' Gina thought about it. It was true, her mother had been very keen for them to get together. She was always inviting him along to events or dragging Gina to places where he happened to be.

'He was hand-picked for you.' Molly read her thoughts. 'An ambitious young lawyer from a good family with a promising political career ahead of him. He must have seemed perfect.'

'What if he was?' Just because she could see now that it wasn't entirely an accident, that didn't make it a crime. 'They were probably just looking out for me, making sure I didn't pick another loser like Tom . . .' She caught the sideways look Molly gave her. 'What?'

'Nothing.' Molly put down her glass and started guiltily to her feet. 'Now I really must go. If I have another glass I'll be done for being drunk in charge of a shopping trolley.'

'Molly! Did James say anything to you about Tom?'

Molly hesitated, chewing her lip. Then she said, 'Do you know what happened to him?'

'Not really. All I know is he suddenly got this big research grant and took off.'

'And didn't that ever strike you as a bit convenient?'

'What do you mean?' She stopped abruptly. 'Oh my God.' She stared at Molly. 'That can't be true. Are you trying to say my father paid Tom off?'

Molly shrugged. 'Like I said, your parents have a way of weeding out anyone unsuitable.'

Gina tried calling her mother after Molly had gone, but the housekeeper said she'd gone shopping with a friend. She hesitated, then called her father's office. She needed some answers.

What Molly had told her made her rethink everything she'd ever believed about herself. If it was true, then her parents had changed the course of her whole life, as casually as a pawn in one of her father's chess games.

'I'm sorry, he's out,' Max's secretary said.

'Have you any idea where he is? It's urgent and his mobile's switched off.'

'I think he said something about going to the Paradise Road site. He's due back here for a meeting in an hour, if that helps?'

Gina found Paradise Road on the map and drove straight there. But she got stuck in a traffic snarl-up on the ring road and by the time she arrived there was no sign of her father's car. She banged the steering wheel in frustration. Damn, he must have gone back for his meeting. She'd probably driven straight past him heading in the opposite direction.

She was about to turn the car round and head back when she spotted the estate agent's board on a house right in the middle of the boarded-up terrace. She parked her car and got out to take a closer look.

'For Sale by Auction' it said. Gina frowned. This must be the house she'd heard her father and brothers talking about, the one he'd been so desperate to get his hands on and the one Finn's brother had been asked to burn down.

'Are you one of them?'

She looked up. An old man stood on the doorstep, frail in a threadbare cardigan and slippers, his arms folded across his chest. 'Because if you are, you can clear off!'

'I'm sorry?'

'I've told him, and I'll tell you the same. I'll leave this place when I'm ready, and I'll sell to whoever I like. And no amount of threats from your boss is going to get rid of me.' He hobbled down the steps towards her, picking his way through the broken bottles and takeaway wrappers that littered the small front garden. 'I'm not selling my house to that crook Tate. Not after what he's done to me and my poor Viv.'

'What exactly has he done, Mr—?'

'What hasn't he done? All these years living here with not a bit of trouble and suddenly we're hounded out. Teenagers turning up all hours of the day and night in their stolen cars, throwing stones, breaking down doors, painting all kinds of vile things on the walls.'

'Why didn't you go to the police?'

'We did, but what could they do about it? These weren't local kids messing about. They were real thugs, hooligans brought in to cause trouble by that Mr Tate.' He shoved a smashed plant pot out of the way with the toe of his slipper. A clod of earth and the remains of a few withered daffodils lay beside it. 'It broke my Viv's heart. Seeing what they did to our lovely home. And all the stress, wondering when they were going to come and terrorize us again. He killed her, as sure as if he'd held a gun to her head.'

'I'm so sorry,' Gina whispered.

'Are you? Seems to me you lot have got exactly what you wanted. My Viv's dead and now I'm selling up. I daresay Tate will get this place in the end and bulldoze this street to the ground to build his rabbit hutches, but at least I can make him sweat a bit.' He pointed to the sign above her head. 'I'm auctioning it, see? And it would just make my day if someone else bought it from under his nose.'

'Guess who's here?' Joe said.

'Auntie Orla!' Finn looked up from the TV, where she'd been mindlessly watching a documentary about glaciers. 'What are you doing back?'

'I asked her to come. I've been at a bit of a loose end with you working all hours. And Orla's contract has finished at the hospital, so . . .'

'So I offered to help keep him out of mischief,' Orla finished for him.

'That's great.' Finn looked from one to the other. Neither of them could stop smiling.

It was good to see her dad looking happy again. He didn't complain, but she had the feeling those few weeks with Orla had made him realize the companionship he'd been missing for so many years. And as for Orla, Finn only had to look at her to see she'd never got over her feelings for Joe Delaney, the boy she knew back in Killmane.

Half an hour later, they were still catching up with all their news over a cup of tea when the doorbell rang.

'Aren't we the popular ones tonight?' Joe shuffled off to answer it. A moment later he returned. 'It's someone for you, Finnuala.'

She was half expecting Ryan. Instead Gina stood there, huddled in a long black coat, her hands in the pockets, looking every inch the tragic heroine.

'What do *you* want?'

'To talk.'

'Would you like a cup of tea?' Orla asked.

'She's not staying,' Finn said.

Orla and Joe looked at each other. 'We'll take our tea in the kitchen,' Joe said, and they both beat a diplomatic retreat.

Finn turned back to stare at the TV. 'I've got nothing to say to you.'

'Fine. In that case, you can just listen.' Gina sat down in the armchair opposite. 'How would you like a chance to get even with my father?'

Finn pointed the remote control at the screen. 'Is this another trick? Because if it is I'm not falling for it.'

'I'm serious. I've thought of a way to get back at my father, *and* get planning permission for your land.'

'Yeah, right. First you try to put us out of business, then you come round here offering to do the same to your own family. Don't waste your breath.' She turned up the volume on the TV. Gina didn't move. Finn looked back at her. 'Why are you still here?'

'Because I want you to hear me out. Look, I don't like my dad any more than you do at the moment.'

'Sorry, but after the way you've behaved I find that hard to believe.'

'You can believe what you like, but it's true. We've both lost out to him.'

'Oh yes? And what have you lost, exactly?'

Gina looked down at her hands. 'A good friend.'

Finn was touched, but steeled herself.

'My father always gets his own way, even if it means trampling over other people,' Gina went on. 'I always knew he was ruthless, but I've never realized how ruthless he is until now. And not just because of what he did to you. He uses people.'

'Tell me something I don't know.'

'I can tell you how we can stop him getting his own way. Just for once.'

Finn kept her gaze focused on the screen. 'I'm listening.'

'You know about Paradise Road? The last house comes up for auction in two weeks.'

She stopped, waiting for Finn's reaction.

'Go on,' she said.

'I thought we could beat him at the auction and buy it. What do you think?'

'It sounds like a brilliant idea. A real masterstroke. Except for one thing.'

'What's that?'

'I don't have any money. If you recall, our business is on its last legs, thanks to you.'

Gina blushed. 'I haven't forgotten that. I have some money, in my trust fund. It's not exactly millions, but it should be enough.'

'Why would you want to use that?'

'I want to make it up to you. For what I did.'

Finn saw the openness in her eyes and almost felt sorry for her. 'So what would we get out of it? Are you planning to give us half a house?'

Gina shook her head. 'Oh no, I'll sell the house to my father. Eventually. But first I'll make sure he talks to his councillor friends so you get your planning permission. We could use it as a sort of bargaining tool.'

'You'd do that for us?'

'I told you, I want to make it up to you.'

There it was again, that look. Finn felt herself melting. Ryan was right, she thought ruefully. She wasn't nearly as hard as she liked to think. Unfortunately.

'But your dad's a millionaire. No matter how much money you've got or how high you bid, he can still outbid you. And he will, if he wants this house so much.'

'That's just it. He can't,' Gina said. 'He might be rich on paper but he doesn't have many liquid assets, especially at the moment. Most of Tates' money is tied up in other deals. And he owes a hell of a lot to the bank, too. He won't want to borrow any more.'

'How do you know all this?'

'He told me. That's why I agreed to – do what I did.' She looked away.

'And has it occurred to you he might have been lying?'

'Oh yes. I know he exaggerated most of it. But some of it's true. I know, because I checked.' She looked shamefaced. 'I still have my password from when I worked in the finance department. I accessed his personal banking records, and the company accounts.'

Finn was so admiring she almost forgot she was supposed to be angry. Then she remembered.

'Why should I trust you?'

'There's absolutely no reason,' Gina admitted. 'I probably wouldn't trust me either, if I were you. But what have you got to lose? It's not as if I'm asking you to put up any money. I'm the one taking the risk.'

'And what if I say no?'

'Then I'll do it anyway. I want to teach my father a lesson. I just thought you might like to get something out of it, too.' She looked at Finn. 'What do you think?'

Finn hesitated for a moment. The clock ticked on the mantelpiece, measuring out the seconds of silence. 'I think I need to hear some more about this plan,' she said finally.

'And if we get this house, we could keep it until we get planning permission for our land,' Finn explained. 'Clever, isn't it?'

'It's completely ridiculous,' Ryan said.

'All right, it probably won't work. But if nothing else it'll be fun to go to the auction and watch Max Tate's face when we push the price up and make him pay over the odds.'

'Maybe,' he admitted grudgingly.

Finn frowned at him. He'd been in a strange mood all day. Maybe them working together was getting to him as much as it was getting to her. They'd both learned to cope by pretending nothing had ever happened between them. But it was difficult when every look and accidental touch between them was charged with emotion.

'So will you come to the auction with us?' she asked.

'When is it?'

'Two weeks' time. The twenty-third.'

His face clouded. 'I can't,' he said.

'Oh, come on. It'll be fun.'

'I'm doing something that day.'

'So cancel it. What could be more important than seeing the smile wiped off Max Tate's face?'

Ryan met her gaze steadily. 'That's the day I'm getting married.'

Chapter 29

'I'm sorry, Gina, but there's nothing I can do. You signed the papers, didn't you?'

Gina sat in her solicitor's office, staring at him across the desk. 'But I didn't mean to sign my trust fund over permanently. It was only meant to be for a few weeks.'

'Nevertheless, you passed control to your father and that control hasn't been rescinded.'

Gina looked down at the papers in her hands. Her signature stared back at her. She remembered the day she'd signed them, how happy she'd been, thinking she was doing something to help her father. She hadn't realized just how much she'd be helping him.

'Perhaps you should talk to Mr Tate about this?' her solicitor suggested gently, seeing the shock on her face.

'Oh, I'll be talking to him, all right.'

She drove straight to the Tate offices. But when she breezily showed her pass to the security staff, they stepped in front of her.

'Sorry, Mrs Farrell, we can't let you in.'

'What?'

'Your pass has been made void.'

Other people were stopping to gawp at the scene. 'There must be some mistake. Let me speak to my father.'

The security guards exchanged embarrassed looks. 'It was your father who gave the order,' one of them said.

Gina looked around. People were staring openly, enjoying the spectacle.

'We're going to have to ask you to leave.'

'I'm not going anywhere. Not until I've spoken to my father.'

'What the hell's going on here?' The small crowd that had gathered moved aside as James cut through them.

'They won't let me in.' Gina was relieved to see one almost friendly face.

'Why on earth not?'

The security guards looked at each other again, 'She – um – doesn't work here any more,' the one who'd spoken before mumbled.

'So what? She's still Max Tate's daughter.'

'Apparently it was him who told them not to let me in.' She felt close to tears at being so publicly cold-shouldered.

James turned to the security guards. 'Let her in. I'll vouch for her.'

'But Mr Tate said—'

'My father can take it up with me if he has a problem.' He took Gina by the arm and steered her firmly towards the lifts.

'Thanks,' Gina said. But as soon as they were away from the gawping crowd his tone changed.

'I only did it because I couldn't stand to see you making a fool of yourself,' he said. 'Jesus, Gina, don't you think you've embarrassed this family enough?'

'Thanks for your support.'

'I got you in here, didn't I? And I expect our father will have something to say to me about it later.' The lift doors opened and they went inside. As they closed again, she caught a glimpse of Neil striding past on his way out.

She turned to James. 'Is Neil still here?'

'Where else would he be?'

'And Nicole?'

'Gone.'

'I can't believe it,' Gina said. 'After everything Dad did to him—'

'Probably forgotten by now,' James said. 'We all toe the line in the end, don't we?'

Gina guessed he was thinking about Molly.

The lift doors opened and they stepped out. Suddenly Gina felt very alone, and quite afraid. 'Will you come with me?'

James shook his head. 'This is where you and I part company.' He made it sound very final. 'And if you know what's good for you, you'll get straight back in that lift and go home. Don't take him on, Gina. You'll only lose.'

Gina squared her shoulders. 'I'm not running away.'

'In that case, you're on your own.'

She walked into her father's office. Max was sitting at the low table, studying a chess-board. Gina felt a familiar wave of panic when she saw it. It reminded her of all the games he'd forced them to play when they were children. There was no pleasure in the game, only in the winning. And their father had to win; his fierce, competitive streak wouldn't allow him to do anything else. Not that there was ever any danger of him losing, because he was a brilliant player. But it wasn't enough for him just to defeat them. He would go through the game step by step, pointing out their every wrong move.

'You have to learn from your mistakes,' he'd say to them. They were never allowed to make the same bad move twice.

He looked up, smiling. 'You found your way in, then? Would you like a game?'

'No thanks. I hate chess.'

'You always were a very poor player. Far too emotional. You gave away your game plan every time.' He reached across and moved a pawn across the board. 'So, what can I do for you?'

'I want control of my trust fund again.'

'So you can use it to buy my house on Paradise Road?'

Gina couldn't mask her shock. 'How did you know?'

Max shifted a black bishop, knocking a white pawn off the board. 'I make a point of knowing my opponent's next move. Several moves ahead, in fact. It's what makes me an unbeatable player.'

And an insufferable winner, Gina thought. The truth began to dawn on her. 'Is that why you made me sign it over? In case I used it against you?'

'I wasn't sure what you would do with it. But it did occur to me, yes.' He moved a white rook out of the way. 'Check, I think.' He looked up at her. 'I hear your friends have forgiven you. Or are you still trying to buy your way back into their affections? You do know that's the only reason they're interested in you, don't you? For your money? Or rather my money.'

'That's not true.'

'Isn't it? I reckon Finn will drop you like a hot brick when she finds out you don't have a penny to your name. You won't be useful to her any more.' He shook his head. 'When are you going to learn, Gina? Friends are no use to you. They let you down. The only people you can rely on are your family.'

Gina did her best to ignore him. 'I'll get the money from somewhere else.'

'Where are you going to get money from? Everything you've ever had has come from me.'

'I wouldn't take your blood money any more! 'Gina spat back at him. 'I know where it comes from and it makes me feel sick. You get it from terrorizing people out of their houses when they don't do as they're told.'

'It didn't make you feel sick when I was spending it on you. That blood money, as you call it, paid for your ponies and your posh school. It kept you in designer clothes and bought you a house. Christ, it even bought you a man!'

'And it helped get rid of Tom.'

She waited for him to deny it, but he didn't. 'He was no good to you,' he dismissed. 'Actually, he could hardly wait to get away.' He leaned forward, his voice low. 'He used you, Gina, just like everyone uses you. And you let them do it.'

'You're a monster,' Gina said, almost wonderingly. How could she have gone on adoring him for so long? She'd always known he was no angel, but she'd never realized what a selfish, controlling, amoral man he really was.

Max looked at her consideringly. 'You know, I'm beginning to worry about you.'

'Me?'

'This behaviour. It's so out of character. If you ask me, you haven't been yourself for a long time.'

'I'm fine.'

'Are you? I wonder. Perhaps it's all getting too much for you, what with losing the baby and everything. It was bound to take its toll on the strongest person. And you've never been strong, have you? Are you sure you're not getting ill again?'

'I'm not ill.'

'You didn't think you were ill the last time. Until you woke up in hospital after having your stomach pumped.' Gina flinched. 'Actually, your mother and I are very concerned about you. And Vicky.'

An alarm bell rang in her head. 'What's Vicky got to do with this?'

'You remember how sick you were, how you couldn't take care of her? We wouldn't want that to happen again, would we?'

There was no mistaking the threat in his voice. 'That was different. Vicky was just a baby.'

'And now she's old enough to know what's going on. How do you think she'd feel, watching you go downhill?'

Gina stared at him in panic. What was he saying? Was she losing it again? She didn't think she was, but perhaps he was right and everyone noticed it except her. Self-doubt began to creep back in, taking away some of her newly found confidence.

'Your mother and I were wondering if it might be better if Vicky came to stay with us during the holidays? Just until you get back on your feet.'

'Vicky's staying with me.'

'But if you're ill—'

'Stephen will take care of her.'

'Stephen's just as worried about you as the rest of us. Especially as he's away in London so often and can't give you the support you need. I spoke to him last night, actually. He agrees that it might be better if Vicky came to stay with us.'

Gina stared at him. So he'd even got her own husband conspiring against her. 'And how much did that cost you? Thirty pieces of silver?'

'He's worried, Gina. We all are. We wouldn't want you to get so bad you hurt yourself again. Or Vicky.'

'I'd never hurt Vicky.'

'How do you know that? How do you know what you're capable of doing, when you're ill?'

'Stop saying I'm ill!' She picked up the nearest thing to hand – a heavy glass ashtray – and flung it at the wall. It shattered with a noisy crash.

The door flew open and his secretary rushed in.

'It's OK, Janice. Just an accident,' Max said calmly. 'I'll sort it out later.' As the door closed he turned to Gina. 'And you say you couldn't hurt your daughter?'

Gina forced herself to calm down. 'I won't let you take her. She's the only thing in the world that means anything to me.'

'I know, darling. All the more reason for us not to let any harm come to her, isn't it?' His voice was soft and persuasive. 'We've only got your best interests at heart. Yours and Vicky's. Although perhaps your mother and I might be more reassured if you could promise us that this strange, unbalanced behaviour wouldn't go on?'

There it was, his unspoken threat: do as you're told or I'll take your daughter away. Her father knew how to hurt her in the worst way possible. The only way.

James's words drifted across her mind: *we all toe the line in the end.*

'The choice is yours.' Max reached across and moved the white queen into place. 'Checkmate, I think.'

The worst thing was having to break the news to Finn. Gina had expected her to fly off the handle in her usual way, but she didn't. She'd listened quietly as Gina explained about her father taking her trust fund. She'd even seemed sympathetic, which was the hardest thing of all for Gina to take.

'At least you tried,' she'd said. 'Thank you.'

She'd offered Gina her old job back. Gina had refused, but she hadn't told Finn she'd already taken up her father's offer of going back to work for him.

As if to punish her even further, he'd put her to work on the reception desk. All day she had to face the humiliation of her former colleagues coming and going, knowing they were all looking at her, laughing at her. She hated it, but there was nothing she could do. She knew if she didn't do as she was told, her father would take Vicky away from her. And she had no doubt he'd do it. He knew a lot of people, he could make things happen. His power used to make her feel safe and protected. Now it just made her feel very afraid.

The one bright spot on the horizon was Vicky coming home for the Easter holidays. Gina's heart leapt when she saw her running down the steps from the school, bumping bags and tennis rackets and hockey sticks behind her, her green blazer flapping.

'Can we visit Finn and Joe again?' she asked as she got into the car.

'I don't think so, darling. Now's not really a good time.'

'But Joe said he'd teach me to play backgammon. Please, Mummy? Just ask them, please?'

'I can't. I don't work there any more.'

Vicky's face fell. 'Did you get the sack?'

'Of course not.'

'But I thought you liked working there?'

'I did. But Grandad needed me to work for him again, so I've got a new job now.' She forced a smile.

'But you were happy in your old job. Why couldn't you stay there?'

'It's complicated.'

'Why?'

'Let's drop it, OK?'

Vicky looked reproachfully at her but said nothing.

After a few more miles the sullen silence began to get to her. 'So what else would you like to do this holidays?' Vicky shifted her shoulders in an eloquent shrug. 'We could go away for a few days, how about that?'

A sidelong glance told her Vicky was tempted. 'Where?' she said out of the side of her mouth.

'I don't know. Northumbria, maybe, to see Granny and Grandad.'

'Granny and Grandad don't live in Northumbria.'

'I meant Granny and Grandad Farrell.'

'They're Stephen's parents. That doesn't make them related to me.'

Gina looked at her, shocked. 'I'm sure they'd be very hurt to hear you say that.'

'Don't care.' Vicky folded her arms across her chest.

Gina didn't speak for a moment as she overtook a line of lorries proceeding up the slow lane. 'So where would you like to go on holiday?' she tried again.

'Barbados. Or the Bahamas. Or Cuba. That's meant to be really cool.'

'I don't suppose Stephen will be able to get enough time off to go to Cuba.'

'He doesn't have to come, does he? We always have a better time when he's not there anyway.'

'What have you got against Stephen all of a sudden?'

'He's all right.' Vicky stared out of the window. 'I just don't like the way he makes you so unhappy.'

'Who says he makes me unhappy?'

'He does. Anyone can see it. You're always miserable and frightened when he's around. He's a bully.'

Gina was mortified. She hadn't realized her misery was so transparent. 'I know he can be difficult, but that's just his way. Underneath it all he's a kind, decent man. And he's been very good to us. Besides, all married couples have their difficult times.'

'In that case I'm never getting married,' Vicky stated firmly, staring straight ahead of her.

'You can't say that. You might fall in love, and—'

'You don't love Stephen. You only stay with him because you're frightened of being on your own.'

Gina was so shocked she almost lost control of the car. She saw the way Vicky was looking at her and realized it was exactly the way she looked at her own mother. As someone weak, who put up with all kinds of misery rather than tough it out on her own. She despised her mother for staying with her father even though he humiliated her, yet she did exactly the same.

And if she wasn't careful, Vicky would do it, too. She might be defiant now, but she could go on to repeat exactly the same pattern in her own adult life. The last thing she wanted for her daughter was to get trapped in a loveless marriage because she was too spineless to find a way out.

When they got home, Stephen's car was parked outside.

Vicky groaned. 'You didn't tell me *he* was going to be here?'

'I didn't know myself.' He was supposed to be in London. Or on his way to New York for a fact-finding trip. She couldn't keep up with his plans these days.

She got out of the car and handed Vicky the door key while she unpacked her bags from the boot.

'It's locked,' Vicky called back to her from the top step. 'Someone's put the chain on the door.'

'Well, ring the doorbell.' Then Gina saw the sitting-room curtains twitch and Stephen's face appeared briefly. What was he playing at?

She hauled the bags up to the front door just as it opened a fraction. 'Get inside, quickly,' Stephen hissed. 'And lock it behind you.'

Everywhere was in darkness. All the curtains had been closed, throwing the house into shadow. Gina left the bags in the hall and went into the sitting room to open them, but Stephen stopped her. 'Don't touch those! I don't want them poking their camera lenses in here.'

Stephen looked a wreck. His shirt and trousers were rumpled, and he smelled strongly of cigarettes, even though he was supposed to have given up smoking months ago.

Suddenly she felt apprehensive. 'Vicky, why don't you take your bags upstairs?' she said lightly, trying not to betray her feelings to her daughter, who stood in the doorway.

She listened to her footsteps disappearing up the stairs, then turned back to Stephen. 'What is it? What's going on?'

'Something awful's happened. I really need your help.'

Chapter 30

The phone rang, shattering the silence.

'Don't answer that!' Stephen shouted, as Gina reached for it. 'It might be them.'

He moved to the window and edged the curtain aside to look out. 'They'll be here any moment. I swear a couple of the bastards followed me up the motorway.' He glanced back at her. 'We've got to act fast, before they get to us.'

He seemed so scared, Gina felt a cold thread of apprehension down her spine. 'Who are they, Stephen?'

'The press, of course.'

'Why? What have you done?'

He let the curtain drop. 'I've been lying to you,' he said bluntly. 'I have been having an affair.'

She'd known all along, but it was still a body blow to hear him admit it. 'I take it it's Lucy?' He nodded. 'How long has it been going on?'

'I don't know – a few months, maybe. Anyway, that's not important. The important thing is how we're going to deal with it.'

'We?' She looked at him blankly.

'You've got to stick by me, tell them it's all a pack of lies. Present a united front and all that. I've been thinking about it all the way up here, and here's what I think we should do . . .'

Gina listened, dazed, as he outlined a plan of action. He hadn't come up here to ask for her forgiveness, or even to try to soften the blow before the press turned up. He'd come because he wanted her to lie about it and pretend their marriage was still perfect. Could this really be happening?

'. . . And I thought maybe we could pose for a few photographs. You, me and Vicky. I wonder if I've got time to ring Mark?' he mused.

'Why? Do you want him in the photo, too? Just one big happy family?'

'This is no time to be flippant, Gina.'

'I'm sorry, I'm just finding it very hard to take you seriously. Do you really expect me to play the dutiful, doting wife after you've just told me you're sleeping with someone else?'

'Why not? That's why I married you.'

A car drew up outside and he darted to the window. 'Thank God, it's only next door's nanny.' He looked at his watch. 'I'm amazed they're not here yet, actually.'

'Maybe you're not as important as you think.' Gina said. 'Perhaps there's something more interesting going on in the world than your sordid love-life?'

'I doubt it.' She'd never quite realized how pompous he could be until that moment. 'The Sunday tabloids love this kind of thing. They'll crucify me.'

'You deserve it.'

He turned on her. 'This is my career we're talking about.'

'No, Stephen, we're talking about our marriage. If we ever had one. Why did you marry me, by the way? Was it for the money, or my father's connections? Or did you just fancy yourself as the poster boy for the party of family values?'

'Oh, for God's sake. This is no time to discuss our marital problems. The press will be here any minute.'

She sat back and crossed her arms. 'Then you'll just have to stall them until I get an answer, won't you?'

'All right,' Stephen let the curtain drop and turned to face her. 'You really want to know why I married you? I needed a wife and you needed a husband. It's as simple as that. OK?'

'No, I needed someone I could share my life with, and you needed a trophy wife to host your dinner parties. We were hardly compatible, were we?'

'Blame your parents for that. They practically forced me to marry you.' Stephen must have seen her expression change and realized he was getting nowhere fast. 'Not that I've ever regretted it,' he added hastily. 'Of course I adore you. And Vicky.'

'So much that you couldn't wait to jump into bed with another woman?'

'You don't know how lonely life gets in London,' Stephen sounded wheedling now, full of self-pity. 'All those long hours in the debating chamber, then going home to an empty flat night after night. No wonder so many MPs end up having affairs. Practically everyone's at it. Anyway, you should be more understanding,' he accused. 'Your father's done it enough times, but your mother always seems to cope. Why can't you be like her?'

That touched a nerve. 'Because I don't want to be married to a man like my father.'

The phone rang again. Stephen twitched visibly. 'Don't answer it.'

'I've got to pick it up sometime. I can't just let it ring and ring, can I?'

'Not until we've sorted out what we're going to do.'

'I don't know about you, but I'm going to take Vicky away for a few days. If the press are going to be camped on the doorstep I don't want to put her through that.' She stood up to go.

'What about me?'

'You'll have to look after yourself, won't you? You'll be good at that, you've had enough practice.'

She headed for the door, but Stephen blocked her way, 'Gina, you can't do this to me. This could be the end of my career.'

'Aren't you being rather melodramatic? Like you said, if they sacked every MP who'd had an affair, the House of Commons would probably be empty.'

'I'm not talking about that, although it could seriously scupper any chance of a ministerial job. I'm talking about here, in this constituency. You know how small-minded they can be. They're only interested in people who are straight, married and middle class. I'm meant to be the family values candidate. I could be de-selected.'

'Maybe you should be, since you're obviously not what they want.'

'You can't be serious!' He was sweating now. She could see beads of perspiration forming on his upper lip. 'OK, you've had your fun. What do you want me to do? Come on, I'm serious.' He grabbed her hand. 'I know I've screwed up, but we can make it right, I promise. We'll find a local school for Vicky. We'll try for another baby. I'll try harder to be a proper husband and father, I swear. Just do this for me and we can be a family again. You can have anything you want.'

Once she would have been overjoyed to hear him say those words. Now she only heard the emptiness behind them. She thought of how Vicky had looked at her in the car when she'd accused her of being too scared to live without Stephen. It was the same way she looked at herself in the mirror.

The phone rang again. Gina glanced at it, then back at Stephen.

'Anything?' she said.

I must be mad, Finn thought.

She didn't even know why she'd come to the auction, since she had no money and very little hope of getting what she'd come for.

Her father and Orla had made themselves comfortable in the front row, flicking through the catalogue with great interest. It was the two of them who'd insisted they should all be there, once Finn had told them everything.

'I could buy it,' Orla said.

'You?'

'Why not? Your Uncle Donal didn't exactly leave me penniless. And I've got some savings put by. It's not as if I've got much else to spend them on.'

'But this house could cost a fortune. Especially if Max Tate is that determined to get his hands on it.'

'Then I could sell my house in Killmane. I should think it's worth a fair amount.'

'Yes, but where would you live?'

She saw the look that passed between Orla and her father, and immediately knew the answer to that one.

'I've been meaning to talk to you about that.' Joe shuffled his feet like an embarrassed teenager. 'Orla and I have been talking about the possibility of her coming over here permanently.'

'But only if you approve,' Orla added quickly.

'You're going to live together?'

'It's not like that,' her father said. 'It's all platonic and respectable, isn't it, Orla?'

But seeing them together now, laughing over a shared joke, Finn wondered how long it would be before they realized they were head over heels in love.

Seeing them made her think about Ryan. She'd tried not to let him creep into her mind today. She'd stopped looking at her watch, but she could still feel the time of his wedding getting nearer. She wondered if he was feeling as wretched about it as she was. She went over to see her dad and Orla, determined to take her mind off it.

'All set?' Joe asked. 'What time's kick-off?'

'Any time now. Paradise Road is one of the first so we shouldn't have to wait too long.' She looked from one to the other. 'You do realize we probably won't get it? Even with Orla's money we barely make the guide price. The house is sure to go over that.'

Joe patted her on the hand. 'Don't look on the black side all the time, Finnuala. Haven't you ever heard of the luck of the Irish?'

'Oh, I've heard of it. I just haven't seen much of it lately.'

Unable to stand the tense atmosphere in the auction room, Finn decided to grab a quick coffee. She was queuing up at the refreshments kiosk when Neil Tate sauntered up.

'Finn! What a pleasant surprise. No need to ask what you're doing here. I take it you're after Paradise Road?'

'That would be telling, wouldn't it?'

'You're wasting your time, you know. That house is as good as ours.'

'What makes you so sure? Don't tell me, the auctioneer's a friend of your father's?'

'Money talks, Finn. You should know that. And you don't have a lot of it.'

'From what I've heard, neither does your father. A little bird told me Tates are having a few cash-flow problems?'

'That's not true.'

'Really? Maybe your father doesn't tell you everything. But I'm guessing he's given you an upper limit for bidding on this place?' She saw Neil's eyes flicker. So Gina was right. That gave her a bit of hope.

'We're not prepared to pay silly money, if that's what you mean.' Neil's confidence reasserted itself. 'Anyway, whatever we've got it's bound to be more than you.' He examined his fingernails casually. 'By the way, my sister sends her love. She's working for my father again, did you know? I think that's why she changed her mind about helping you. She finally came back to the winning side.'

Finn said nothing, but inside she was burning with anger. Gina had betrayed her *again*. And to think Finn had felt sorry for her and offered her her job back!

Just then Orla appeared at her shoulder. 'Finnuala, my love, Joe says we're to go in now if we don't want to miss anything.'

'So you see, you've lost out all round,' Neil said. 'You might as well just accept your losses and go home before you make a complete fool of yourself.'

'She's not going anywhere.'

Ryan stood behind them. He was wearing a suit, but his tie was stuffed in his pocket and the top buttons of his shirt were undone.

'Now why don't you get lost? We're not outside a courtroom now and, if I remember rightly, I owe you a pasting.'

'I don't respond to threats,' Neil said, backing off.

'Then why are you running away?' Finn asked.

'I don't need to get into a brawl with you. We're going to win, anyway.'

Ryan shook his head as they watched him walk off. 'I don't know what you ever saw in him.'

'Me neither. But what are you doing here? I thought you were getting married?'

'I was. But I kept thinking about you being here on your own, and I couldn't go through with it.' He reached for her hand. 'I called Wendy this morning.'

'I bet she wasn't happy about that?'

'She'll get over it. We can get married another day. Today you need me.'

Emotion rose in her throat, choking her. 'I don't know what to say. Thank you.'

Just at that moment everyone began moving towards the doors of the auction room.

'Looks like the fun's about to start.' Ryan squeezed her hand. 'Shall we go inside?'

'I need the loo,' Orla complained. 'The excitement's getting to me.'

'You'll have to wait. Paradise Road is up next.' Finn glanced at Neil. He was standing at the back of the room with his brother James. Neil waved insolently at her. James nudged him, frowning.

'Now let me handle this,' Joe ordered Orla, as the auctioneer announced Paradise Road.

'Why should you have all the fun?' she protested.

'Because I know what I'm doing.'

'Oh, and I don't, I suppose? I'm just the little woman.'

'Will you two please concentrate?' Finn hissed.

And so it began. As things got more and more tense, there was a nasty moment when her father got over-excited and bid twice, pushing the price up against himself.

Orla raised her eyes to heaven. 'Men!' she mouthed.

Finn glanced over at Neil. He was grinning all over his stupid face as his brother calmly continued to outbid them all. Then Neil's phone rang, and everyone turned to frown at him as he edged along the row and ducked outside to take the call.

Just as Finn had feared, Orla was soon outbid. 'Surely we could get some more cash somehow?' she whispered. 'Maybe I could sell my car?'

Finn shook her head. 'It's all over.' And the Tates had won. She risked a glance over her shoulder. Neil was still outside, taking his call. At least he wasn't there to witness their defeat.

'Any advance?' The auctioneer scanned the room, his gavel poised. 'Going once, going twice . . .'

A voice rang out from the back. Everyone looked round. Finn was stunned to see Gina standing there.

'Oh, look,' Joe said. 'Isn't that your friend, Finnuala?'

'What's she doing here?' Ryan and Finn looked at each other.

James looked just as surprised to see his sister. Finn saw him frown at Gina. She smiled back. James raised his hand to put in another bid. Quietly Gina topped it again. All heads turned back to James, who lifted his hand again. His eyes were fixed on his sister. It was electrifying.

'It's good here, isn't it?' Orla said. 'Better than the telly.'

It was like a tennis match, the bids bobbing between them, the price rising higher and higher. Then Gina put in another bid. The auctioneer turned to James. 'It's with you, sir?'

James hesitated. Finn caught the look that passed between them. It was a strange look, one that seemed to speak far more than words. Then James smiled, and slowly shook his head.

The auctioneer's hammer came down just as Neil walked back into the room. Finn watched him go over to James, and saw the smug smile die on his face as his brother whispered something and pointed over at Gina.

'Excuse me, I have to find out what's going on.' She pushed her way along the row and reached Gina at the same time as Neil and James.

Neil was incandescent with rage. 'What the fuck do you think you're doing?' Flecks of spittle flew from his lips. 'Have you gone completely fucking mental? What did you bid against us for, you stupid bitch?'

Gina didn't flinch. 'I wanted the house.'

'Why, you silly cow?'

'Why not?' She caught Finn's eye and smiled slightly. 'Now, if you'll excuse me, I need to pay a ten per cent cheque at the cash desk.'

She walked off, leaving them all staring in her wake.

'Oh dear,' said Finn.

Neil pulled out his phone. 'I'm ringing Dad.' While he was

dialling he said to James. 'And you can explain how you managed to lose that house.'

'I couldn't help it. We were outbid.'

'At that price? You know we could have gone higher.'

'It wasn't worth it.' But Finn knew there was more to it than that. She'd seen James's face at the moment of bidding. He'd deliberately held back.

Ryan joined her. 'What's going on?'

'I have no idea.'

Gina was coming back from the cash desk. She looked different somehow, serene and confident.

'What are you doing?' Finn asked.

'Why do people keep asking me that? Isn't it obvious? We're at an auction, and I'm buying a house. There's no great mystery.' Then in an undertone she added, 'Sorry I couldn't stick to our original plan. I've only just got the money together.'

'So how did you get it?'

'It was a sort of – divorce settlement.' Gina smiled mysteriously. 'Stephen was quite generous, actually. Once we'd reached an understanding.'

'You're getting divorced?'

'Not until after the election.'

Just then Neil appeared, his face like thunder. 'Dad wants to see you right away.'

'Mustn't keep him waiting then, must we?' Gina turned to Finn. 'Why don't you come, too? I think you might find it entertaining.'

Outside the auction room Wendy was waiting for them. Finn's heart sank when she saw her standing by the door, arms folded, looking furious. She'd almost forgotten about her in all the excitement.

From the look on his face, it seemed Ryan had, too. 'I'd better talk to her. I've got a lot of explaining to do.'

'So has she,' Gina said. As Ryan walked away she called after him, 'Why don't you get her to explain where she got her scan photo?'

Ryan turned back to her. 'Meaning?'

'Ask her, I'm sure she can tell you.' As he walked away she said to Finn, 'I think you were right. The baby in that photo was far more developed than Wendy's pregnancy should be. I reckon she borrowed it from someone else.'

'So she might not be pregnant?'

'Either that or she's about to give birth next week. And from the look of those jeans she's wearing, I very much doubt that. That photo troubled me for ages after I saw it,' she said. 'But I might not have even noticed if I hadn't just had a scan myself.'

Finn rubbed her brow. 'This is all getting far too weird for me. What the hell is going on?'

Gina smiled. 'All will be explained.' She looked at Neil, who was holding the door of his black Saab open for her. 'I'll take mine, if you don't mind? I have the feeling I might need to make a quick getaway after this.'

Max wasn't as calm as the last time Gina had seen him. He sat behind his desk, but she could see the suppressed rage on his face and the tension in his clenched fists. A game of chess was half finished on the table.

'What's she doing here?' he demanded, seeing Finn. 'Get her out. This is family business.'

'That's where you're wrong,' Gina said. 'This is *my* business, and my house. And I say she stays.'

Her father said nothing. Gina sat down on the opposite side of the desk facing him. 'So let's talk.'

'What have you got to say?'

Usually she would have been terrified of his icy anger, but she was surprised at how comparatively calm she felt. 'I'm prepared to let you have the house in Paradise Road. But first I want you to agree to my terms.'

'Which are?'

'I want Joe Delaney to get his planning permission.'

'You know I can't guarantee that. I don't have any control over council decisions.'

'Then you'd better find a way, or there's no deal.' Gina was glad no one could see her heart trying to hammer its way out of her chest. 'Actually, I've checked and there's a planning committee meeting in two weeks, so that shouldn't be a problem. Perhaps you could talk to one of your contacts and get it added as an emergency item?'

Max's mouth hardened into a line. 'I'll see what I can do.'

'I know you'll do your best. And maybe you'd also like to throw in your piece of land, as compensation?'

She heard Finn's indrawn breath behind her.

'Now just a minute —' Max began.

'Surely it's only fair? The land is useless to you, anyway. And you must admit you've caused the Delaney family a lot of stress, one way and another?'

Max glared at her. 'Is that it?'

'Almost. We still have to negotiate a price for the house.'

'You'll get what you paid for it.'

'I don't think you're really in any position to call the shots, do you, Daddy? After all, you want that house pretty badly from what I can gather. What do they call it? Market something?'

'Forces,' Finn put in helpfully. She seemed to be enjoying the moment almost as much as Gina.

'That's right. Market forces. Supply and demand, and all that.' Gina beamed at her father. 'Don't worry, I'm not going to be greedy. Twenty-five per cent over what I paid for it should be a good enough profit.'

'Twenty-five!'

'Or should I make it thirty? Or fifty? You know how hopeless I am with numbers.'

'I don't have to put up with this.' Max sat back. 'Forget it, the deal's off.'

'Fine. So I'll just keep the house and you can forget all about your luxury development.'

'I could still get my hands on it if I wanted.' There was no mistaking the threat in his voice.

'I wouldn't even think about trying to intimidate me,' Gina said calmly. 'Not in front of witnesses. Besides, if you or your thugs so much as set foot over that threshold without my permission, I'll get Finn's brother to tell everyone how Neil's friends tried to get him to commit arson. And I'm sure old Mr Palmer will be only too happy to back him up. After all, you did make his life a misery for the past two years.'

He was defeated. She could see it in his face. She could hardly believe she'd done it.

'You'll get your money,' he growled.

'I'd like it now, if you don't mind?'

Without taking his eyes off her, he reached into the drawer and pulled out a cheque book. He wrote the cheque and handed it to Neil, who passed it to her.

'Thank you.' She studied it carefully. 'As soon as this is cleared, I'll get my solicitor to draw up the necessary transfer deeds.'

'What's the matter?' Max said. 'Don't you trust me?'

Gina smiled. 'What do you think?' She reached over and moved a piece across the chessboard, toppling the king. 'Checkmate, I believe,' she said.

Chapter 31

'Why don't you move in?'

Finn rolled over to look at Ryan, lying next to her. Even after all these weeks, she still couldn't get used to waking up next to him. 'Do you mean it?'

'Why not? You're practically living here, anyway. And let's face it, you're getting a bit too old still to be living with your dad.'

'Cheek!' Finn pulled out a pillow and hit him with it. But she had to admit, he had a point. Ever since Orla had moved in, she'd started to feel slightly surplus to requirements. It wasn't that she was jealous – she loved to see her father so happy – but she could tell they needed some space.

But should she move in with Ryan? 'We haven't been seeing each other that long,' she pointed out.

'We've been seeing each other for twelve years.'

'You know what I mean. What if it turns out to be a mistake?'

He propped himself up on his elbow and looked down at her. 'Does it feel like a mistake to you?'

'No.' It felt like the most natural thing in the world. Her only regret was that she'd wasted so much time.

She shuddered to think how she'd almost lost him to Wendy. If Gina and Ciaran hadn't put those doubts in her head, perhaps Ryan would have gone ahead and married her. As it was, he'd confronted her at the auction. Wendy had crumbled and admitted that her pregnancy had all been a lie to trap him.

She'd given them both a hard time for a while, but finally she'd stopped bothering him when she realized that he and Finn were together.

But it all seemed too perfect to be true. 'I'd be a nightmare to live with,' she protested. 'I leave my clothes lying all over the place, I'm useless at housework and cooking—'

'If I wanted a housekeeper I'd advertise for one. Anyway, the fantastic sex makes up for everything else.' He leaned over and kissed her bare shoulder.

'Don't,' Finn said. 'I'm trying to make a big decision about my future here.'

'Then let me help you make up your mind,' Ryan said, pushing her back against the pillows.

Gina and Vicky were the only members of the Tate family at James and Molly's wedding. They got married very quietly, in the local register office. It was a long way from her own big white wedding, which had been more for show than anything else, she realized now. Her brother and his bride both looked so happy, Gina knew they couldn't have been more joyful if they'd had the full three-ring Tate circus.

Afterwards they went to eat in a local pub. The mild April weather had given way to murky grey, and rain lashed the windows. 'I hope this isn't an omen,' Molly said, gazing out.

'Let's face it, things couldn't be much worse,' James said. 'I'm a social outcast without a job, living on my wife's earnings.'

'Welcome to the club,' Gina said. 'At this rate there'll be more of us outside the Tate clan than in it.'

'Of course, I blame you,' James went on. 'If you hadn't turned up at that auction I might never have decided to rebel. I still can't believe you had the guts to do it.'

'Neither can I,' Gina admitted ruefully. She still trembled to think about it.

'I'm glad you did.' James leaned over to kiss Molly. 'It was seeing you there that made me realize I didn't have to toe the Tate line any more. I thought, if my spineless kid sister can do it, so can I.'

'Thanks a lot!'

'You know what I mean.' James grinned. 'And it made me realize I didn't want to end up as Dad's puppet like Neil.'

'Poor Neil,' Gina said, and was surprised to find that she meant it. He might be a bastard, but he was still her brother. 'I wonder what will happen to him?'

'He'll take over the family firm like he's always wanted,' James said, a trace of bitterness in his voice. 'And then I expect Mum will pick out a nice new wife for him. One that meets with her seal of approval.'

'And hopefully one that Dad can keep his hands off,' Gina added.

Molly looked anxious. 'You've given up so much for me,' she said. 'Are you sure about all this?'

'Darling, I couldn't be happier. I'd rather be in my shoes than Neil's any day. Besides, I don't know if there's going to be much left of the company by the time Neil gets his hands on it. I've seen the latest financial reports, and Tates have made some big losses. All those unfavourable press stories haven't helped.'

'Dad will bounce back, he always does,' Gina said.

Molly went off to look after the children, who had swapped their cute wedding outfits for jeans and were itching to go to the indoor play area. Vicky went with them 'to help', although Gina suspected she wanted a sneaky go in the ball pond.

James watched them go. 'My family,' he said. 'To think how close I came to losing them. I can't believe she took me back.'

'She loves you,' Gina said.

James looked pleased, and a little nonplussed, 'She does, doesn't she?' He turned back to Gina. 'What about you? What are you going to do now?'

'I've no idea,' Gina admitted. 'But I do know I'm not sending Vicky away to school any more. Once she's finished at Heath Lodge, that's it. She'll be going to a local school, wherever we end up.'

'You're thinking of moving?'

'Stephen and I are selling the house. I've never liked it much, anyway. And he agrees it's too big for one person. I expect he'll stay in London once it's sold.'

'So you're definitely getting a divorce?'

'Definitely.' Despite the glowing interview that had just appeared in the *Daily Mail* about their idyllic family life and scotching any rumours that he might have been having an affair. The hypocrisy of singing Stephen's praises as a wonderful family man and father had almost killed her, but that was part of the deal they'd struck. Along with her promise that she wouldn't file for divorce until he was safely re-elected.

She would leave Stephen to deal with the fall-out from the press over that one. No doubt he'd find a way to blame her, but she didn't care. At least she'd be free.

It was a heady feeling. She thought she and Vicky might go travelling together that summer. Maybe they'd even get as far as Cuba – Vicky would love that. And there was bound to be enough cash left over for a decent holiday, even after she'd paid for the memorial bench to Viv Palmer.

She'd already arranged with the council for it to be sited on the corner of Paradise Road, looking down the street where Viv had lived for most of her married life. Her father would have to look at it every time he visited his luxury flats. She hoped it might prick what little conscience he had left, but she doubted it. Anyway, the bench would be there as a permanent reminder, and there wasn't a damn thing he could do about it.

'So is there anyone else on the horizon?' James asked.

Gina smiled enigmatically. 'That would be telling, wouldn't it?' The truth was, she wasn't sure. Mark had called her when he'd heard about her break-up with Stephen, and he'd been round for dinner a couple of times, just as friends. She knew he was keen to take their relationship further once she and Stephen had officially separated, but Gina was determined that if she got involved with anyone again, it would be on her terms.

'That divorce pay-out came in handy,' James interrupted her thoughts. 'I had no idea Stephen was that well-off.'

'He isn't,' Gina said.

'Then how come he gave you all that money to buy the house?'

'He didn't. He only gave me enough to pay the ten per cent deposit. And then it was touch and go. Lucky you stopped bidding when you did – another few thousand and I couldn't have matched you.'

James marvelled. 'But you realize you were legally liable to pay the balance within twenty-eight days? How were you going to manage that with no cash?'

'I just hoped Dad would come up with the money before then.'

'Talk about brinkmanship! You've got some nerve,' he said admiringly. 'Dad would be proud of you.'

'I bloody well hope not,' Gina said.

It was the day of Ciaran's trial. As they all filed out of the courtroom, Ciaran looked pale and apprehensive, as if he couldn't quite believe it was all over. He'd been given a short sentence, but because of the time he'd spent on remand he'd been released straight away.

'But next time you might not get away so lightly,' Joe warned him, as they stood in the April sunshine.

'Don't worry, Pa, I'm not going back in there. I've seen enough of prison life to know I don't want any more. From now on, I'm sticking to the straight and narrow.'

Finn and her father exchanged knowing looks. She wondered how long his good intentions would last.

He invited them to the pub, but Finn refused. She was happy Ciaran was free but somehow she didn't feel like celebrating.

'What about you, Dad?' Ciaran asked.

'I'll follow you later, son.' He waited until Ciaran had gone off with Mel and the baby, then turned to Finn. 'What's bothering you, Finnuala? You've had a face as long as a fiddle since we left that courtroom. You weren't hoping your brother would get locked up, were you?'

'Of course not,' Finn said quickly. But deep down she knew Ciaran's release would mean the end of something for her. 'I suppose now that Ciaran's home he'll be coming to work back at the yard?'

'Well, he does have to have a trade,' Joe admitted. 'If he doesn't do something useful he'll go straight back downhill.'

'I know.'

'And there's only enough work for two at the yard.'

'I know that, too. It's just—'

'Just what?'

'Nothing.' There was no point in asking him if she could stay on. She'd only been there under sufferance, anyway. Now Ciaran was back there was no reason for her to stay. 'I'll go to the yard and pick up my tools.'

'You don't have to do it straight away.'

'I want to.' The sooner she got it over with, the better.

'Then I'll come with you,' Joe said.

When they got there, Finn saw Ryan's blue pick-up. 'What's he doing here?'

'See for yourself.'

She got out of the van and walked to the yard gates. 'What the . . .'

'It was supposed to be a surprise, but you insisted on coming here,' Joe said, catching up with her.

'But what does it mean?'

'You can read, can't you?'

'Yes, but I don't understand.'

'I'd like you to join the firm. If you want to. I'm planning to take more of a back seat in the business now Orla and I . . .' He looked embarrassed. He still couldn't bring himself to admit that he'd found love again at his age. 'Now we're together,' he finished. 'I want to relax and enjoy the next few years. So I'll need to leave the business in the hands of someone I can trust. Although make no mistake, I'll be keeping my eye on you,' he added sternly.

'But what about Ciaran?'

'We had a chat about it, and we both agreed the building trade was never going to suit him. It was like trying to fit a square peg into a round hole. Apparently he's learned all kinds of new skills in that remand centre that he'd like to try out. Cooking, would you believe?' Joe looked disgusted.

Finn shook her head in mock disapproval. 'Everyone knows the kitchen is no place for a man,' she said.

Joe looked at her severely. 'Any lip from you, young lady, and I might be tempted to change my mind again.'

'So what made you change it this time?'

'I saw how hard you'd worked while I was ill. And you're a very good builder. You must get that from me.' Then, before Finn could argue, he went on, 'And your man Ryan made me see I was a stubborn old fool who couldn't see the nose on my face. There I was, looking for someone to follow in my footsteps when you were there waiting all the time. I just had this daft idea that I had to turn you into a lady so I wouldn't let your mother down. But looking at you now, I reckon she'd be as proud of you as I am.'

Finn bit her lip, worried she might cry in front of him. 'I didn't think you were proud of me at all. I thought you wished I'd been born a boy.'

'Only because I knew nothing about bringing up girls. I thought I was getting it all wrong, especially when you started taking an interest in bricks and cement-mixers. So I panicked and tried to push you the other way, when all I needed to do was let you be.' He nodded at Ryan. 'Besides, I reckon *he's* glad you're not a lad.'

'Dad!'

'It's all right, Finnuala, I know you're old enough to have a boyfriend. God knows, you're old enough to have a husband and two kids by now, although that's probably too much to hope for?' he added.

'Maybe one day.'

She went closer, still looking up at the sign above the gates, afraid to take her eyes away in case it turned out to be a mirage and disappeared. Ryan came down the ladder and greeted her with a kiss. 'What do you think?'

She squinted at it. 'It's wonky. Are you sure you used a spirit level?'

'Bloody cheek.'

'You do realize this makes us rivals?' Finn said.

'Oh God, that's all I need.' He put his arm around her, pulling her into the solid warmth of his body as they both looked up at the sign. 'It looks pretty good, doesn't it?'

She stared at the words painted in big white letters above her: 'Delaney and Daughter'.

'It really does,' she said.